THE DUKE
OF ANDELOT

A SCHOOL OF GALLANTRY NOVEL

DELILAH MARVELLE

DELILAH MARVELLE PRODUCTIONS

Portland, Oregon

Delilah Marvelle Productions, LLC
Delilah@DelilahMarvelle.com
Portland, Oregon
www.DelilahMarvelle.com

Publisher's Note: This is a work of fiction. Names, characters, places, and incidents are a product of the author's crazy imagination. Locales and public names are sometimes used for atmospheric purposes. Any resemblance to actual people, living or dead, or to businesses, companies, events, institutions, or locales is completely coincidental.

Book Layout ©2015 BookDesignTemplates.com

The Duke of Andelot/Delilah Marvelle -- 1st ed.
ISBN-10: 1-939912-05-9
ISBN-13: 978-1-939912-05-3

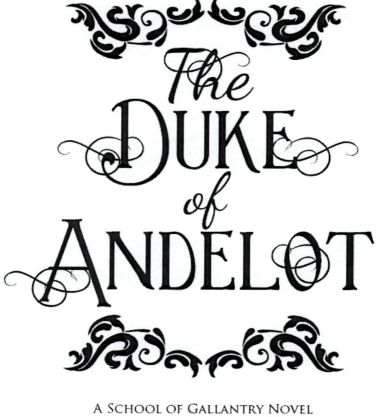

The Duke of Andelot

A School of Gallantry Novel

DELILAH MARVELLE

PART ONE

EVERY RISE HAS A FALL

LESSON ONE

If it is salvation you seek, gentlemen,

you might consider leaping out of a window.

Or off a bridge. Whatever you prefer.

-The School of Gallantry

The Andelot Estate - Paris, France
August 13, 1792 – Early evening

érard Antoine Tolbert, the last remaining heir to the great duché of Andelot, quietly unhinged the iron latch and folded out the oversized windows that faced the manicured gardens below. A warm summer breeze feathered his face and drifted into his bedchamber, fluttering the brocaded curtains that had once decorated his grandfather's deathbed.

While most aristocratic young men might consider the reuse of deathbed curtains morbid, he prided himself on being vigilantly practical and rummaged through trunks in the attic on a regular basis to see if there was anything he could use. Aside from the fact that his father had always preferred to spoil his older brothers and leave him to be more creative with his finances, too many

1

people in France were starving and it was Gérard's way of kneeling to their struggles.

He *used to* give well over a thousand *livres* to charity every month. He *used to* deliver crates of food to almshouses every Friday and would even dress in plain bourgeoisie clothing to ensure the people he helped did not feel so self-conscious about how little they had. But what had his compassion and generosity earned him?

Two dead brothers and a revolution.

His bewigged, over-powdered, lace-flouncing older siblings had been travelling in an unmarked coach in an idiotic attempt to leave the country (without him *or* their father), when they were ambushed by fifteen men. Certain factions from the Legislative Assembly anticipated their escape.

And so, on the side of a road near the border of Austria, his brothers had their genitals removed by blade, were repeatedly shot, roped and hanged by a group of revolutionaries determined to annihilate every last lineage connected to the throne. Marceau and Julien were only twenty-three and twenty-four and hadn't even been given the chance to become the men they should have been.

Unlike his brothers, who had a reputation for spitting on too many people, Gérard had countless friends amongst the lower classes due to all the charity work he had always been involved in. They warned him of any rumblings, but he knew after tonight, he was going to need a hell of a lot more than friends.

Setting the leather satchel against the window, which he had packed with food and frayed clothing that would allow him to blend into the countryside, he attached a primed pistol to his leather belt, along with a flask of brandy. He surveyed the dim lanterns illuminating the winding gravel path that led to a massive stone fountain.

A servant lingered with his horse by the iron gate.

Tying back his shoulder length hair with a blood-red ribbon he wore in honor of his brothers and countless aristocrats before them, Gérard buttoned his burgundy velvet coat and sat on the ledge of the window, propping one knee-high leather boot on the floor and the other on the sill. Pressing his back against the wood frame to balance himself, he peered down toward the shadow-covered hedge beneath the third story window.

He tossed the satchel out the window, letting it land with a rustling thud into the large hedge below. Leaning farther out, he gauged the distance, ready to—

The door rattled. "*Mon héritier?*" the duc called out in a concern, gruff tone. "I heard the window open. Is everything all right?"

Gérard froze. Gripping the window sill, he glanced back at the locked door that was outlined by candlelight. If he feigned sleep, the man would most likely get a footman to unhinge and take off the door. "Everything is fine. The night is warm and I needed some air, is all. Good night."

The door rattled again. "Gérard, why is this latched?"

Rot it. "Might we discuss this in the morning, *Monseigneur?*" he called out from the open window he was still propped on. "I need to sleep." Gérard feigned an exhausted yawn that was loud enough to echo throughout the room and even stretched for good measure, his muscled arm sweeping toward the open window. "I over-practiced my fencing today."

That tone hardened. "I know you better than you think, *mon héritier*. Both of your boots are hanging out of the window."

Gérard flopped his arm back to his side. Only *one* boot was hanging out the window. "I left you a missive in the library explaining when I would be back."

"So you were hoping I would find it in the morning after you were gone? Is that it?"

"I would have told you in person, but you have a tendency to get riled about everything I do and I prefer not to—"

"If you are so intent on destroying your life, why not go back to romancing your Madame Poulin? That certainly went well for you. Hell, you graced her entire family with more money than those *porcs* were worth. Even your brothers, God rest their souls, exhibited far more control around women than you ever did. At this point, I prefer you take up dice, for at least *there*, you have a chance at getting some of your money back. Unlike with your *Madame Poulin!*"

There was no such thing as forgiveness, was there? "I never see her anymore!" Gérard called back. "Not even when she comes to the door!"

His long done relationship with Madame Poulin was as complicated as it was vile. At eighteen, almost three years earlier, he had attended his first bourgeoisie soirée with a group of bourgeoisie friends who had dragged him to partake in the revelry of their own trades-people while introducing him to the sweetest part about life: bourgeoisie women.

Unlike pinch-faced, aristocratic young women his age who obediently waited in their mothers' parlors for a respectable match to save them from boredom, bourgeoisie girls jumped out of parlor windows and showed everyone in town how life was supposed to be lived.

He ended up hopelessly enamored by such a girl. A pretty brunette by the name of Mademoiselle Bellamy, the daughter of a tailor. Tired of being a gentleman, for it had kept him a virgin long enough in his aristocratic circle, he rolled on an expensive sheath he had bought to baptize their love, and serenaded her body at the most expensive hotel in Paris.

Given it was his first time (though clearly not hers), it was the most glorious moment of his life (that quickly turned into a goddamn nightmare). Mademoiselle Bellamy was actually Madame Poulin who was married *to* a tailor and had three children. Her husband demanded satisfaction and Gérard..accidentally shot the man's hand off.

The man lived, but..now had a stub.

Gérard's guilt had led him into making a substantial payment to the man that his father still roared about. Although Madame Poulin sometimes lingered outside his door, which he no longer opened, he did coolly incline his head to her on occasion when they passed each other on the street.

He was, after all, a gentleman. Sometimes. Well..no. Not anymore. He had learned to use women in the same way they used him.

Yanking out the flask from his leather belt, Gérard uncorked it and took a swig. "I find it exceedingly tasteless that you dare mock me after the tragedy that has befallen this family. Marceau and Julien are dead because of you."

"Me?" his father echoed.

"Yes. You. You bloody hanged them by their own silk stockings. You only ever spoiled them as children and made them believe they were untouchable during the greatest political crisis this country has ever seen. You—"

"*Open this door!*" the duc roared, vibrating the door with violent thuds that rattled the hinges. "How dare you speak to me as if I were one of these *bourgeoisie porcs*?! All that time you and your mother spent associating with the poor, encouraging them to demand rights, only made them rise up and choke us all! Your brother's deaths are on your hands, not mine!"

Struggling to remain calm, Gérard took another swig of brandy. He was done being a good son to a father who only ever thought the worst of him. He was also done mourning for his brothers. It wasn't as if they had ever been close anyway. Those two roosters had only ever reveled in having too much fun at his expense. Growing up, they regularly tied him to a tree on the farthest corner of their thousand acre estate and would leave him there for days, while feigning ignorance to everyone as to his whereabouts, even in a thunderstorm.

His brothers and his father had prepared him for what life was really like: disappointing.

Corking his flask, Gérard tucked it away into his coat. "I have to go. Unlike you, I cannot pretend the world is not burning."

There was a thud against the door, as if the duc was using his own head to try to understand him. "Cease pretending we have any control over what is happening anymore. They have sealed all borders and are confiscating anything I try to send to your mother's family in England."

"I am well aware of that." Scanning the shadows beyond his open window, Gérard shifted his jaw. "Our situation is dire, *Monseigneur*. Fortunately, the power of our money still commands whatever we want. Though who knows for how much longer. I suggest you start burying whatever gold you can."

His father's gruff voice cracked. "I have faith Austria will take back the country given their daughter is being held hostage along with *Sa Majesté*. This revolt has no teeth. None. It is all but pitchforks and hay."

Pitchforks and hay did not kill his brothers. These radicals in power were serious. The height of that seriousness further peaked barely a few weeks earlier, when he received a scrawled cryptic message, bearing the words, '*Remember the tears you once spilled on my desk? Gather everything from it and part with it not. If I succeed, I will attempt to send further word.*'

Gérard had *no* idea what the letter was referring to or who it was from. So he burned it in case someone was trying to get him or his father into trouble.

It wasn't until the recent capture and arrest of his godfather, *Sa Majesté*, who had tried to escape the country with the queen and their two children, that Gérard realized who had written it.

The King of France himself.

Though it was a memory long forgotten, Gérard had, indeed, spilled tears on a desk. Long ago, whilst visiting Versailles with his father, he had been inconsolable over the death of his dog, Alfonse. So he laid on the floor with his tear-streaked cheek mashed against the marble of the corridor, openly sobbing. His father only roared at him without pity for laying on the palace floor like a peasant.

His godfather proved more compassionate. The king ushered everyone away and knelt beside Gérard, promising a special day if he could set aside his tears. *Sa Majesté* then tapped his lips, led him down a maze of countless corridors to a hidden narrow set of stairs and into what looked like an ordinary sitting room.

After draping shut windows and turning the key in the door, his godfather winked and revealed a secret only bestowed from a dying king to his own son since sixteen hundred and eighty-two. Reaching beneath the hearth of the fireplace, he removed a narrow panel with a quick tug and turned a series of knobs that sounded like bolts being unlocked. His godfather then removed *another* panel beside the hearth revealed a hidden half-door cleverly between simple molding. Pushing it open, they entered a quiet, windowless room where they spent half the day writing poetry on a desk and talking about how special dogs really were.

Not even his father had taken the time to dry his tears like that.

And now, Gérard was being asked to dry the tears of his king.

Which he damn well would.

Dropping his booted foot from the ledge to the floor with a thud, Gérard pushed himself away from the open window. "Was there any word about the burial arrangements for Marceau and Julien? We should have heard something by now."

The duc was quiet for a moment. "Yes. I received a letter about it less than an hour ago. I would have knocked on your door sooner but I thought you were sleeping. The *gendarmerie nationale* rejected our plea to bury them. Their remains will be held indefinitely as evidence."

Tears burned Gérard's eyes. Christ. This revolution was a genocide. A genocide that was not giving the living a chance to pray or the dead their right to be buried.

But he'd be damned if *Sa Majesté* was next. *Damned!*

Gérard sniffed hard.

Stripping off his coat, he whipped it onto the four poster bed and trudged over to the paneled door. Turning the key, he unlatched the bolt and yanked open the door. He stepped out into the candlelit corridor toward his father. "If I do not return in fourteen days, it means I am dead."

The old duc ceased pacing and swung toward him, curling grey hair falling into blue eyes. Lines etched into that aged, regal face, deepened. "What do you mean? Where are you going?"

"I was asked to do something for *Sa Majesté*, whom as you well know, was taken into custody for fleeing. I genuinely fear what will be done to him. If members of the Assembly had no reservations about executing my brothers on the side of a road, I can only imagine what awaits our king. It is my hope what he is asking me to do will help him."

The duc swung away and set trembling hands onto his head. "*Merde a la puissance treize.*" His father swung back to him. Those fierce blue eyes hardened to lethal, revealing the unbridled man Gérard knew all too well. "You have lost your mind thinking you can take on an army of men."

"I am not taking them on alone. I started working with several other aristocrats to try to get people out of this country. It will take time, but I have faith with all our resources, we can help each other."

His father choked. "Are you— What they did to your brothers is nothing compared to what they will do to you! You cannot—"

"I am trying to do something outside of smashing furniture against walls like you do on the hour."

The duc gritted his teeth and backhanded Gérard's head. "Enough of that tongue! Not even your brothers would have dared use words against me."

Gérard adjusted the ribbon in his tied dark hair which had loosened from the stinging blow. As many as a few months ago, he would have permitted it. But now? He was done playing by everyone else's rules. He was only playing by his own.

He shoved his father's away, making the man stumble. "There. I am no longer the perfect son. Now what?"

Those eyes widened. "How dare you—"

"No." Gérard leveled the man with a hard stare, angling in close. "You, along with the rest of this godforsaken world, seem to think because I used to frequent almshouses every Friday that I am some sort of sop. I am no longer the spare you can slap around but the heir. Remember that. Touch me again and I will show you what this charitable son of yours can do."

The duc paused. "I smell brandy. Are you drunk?"

Gérard puffed out an exasperated breath. "No. I reserve all drunkenness when I am about to retire for the night. And as you can see, I am not retiring. I have a three hour ride ahead of me."

Those features stilled. "You told me you were done drinking."

"In the face of what is happening to the world, brandy is hardly a problem."

The duc pointed. "You are still waist-high with these people. Waist high! These *bourgeoisie* simpletons you have been carousing with since youth have taught you to not only drink but defy your own father!"

"You know nothing about my life or why I do anything." Gérard held out a gloved hand, trying to be civil. "Give me your blessing should I not return."

The old man glared. "No. You are all that remains of this name and I will be damned if I let you walk out that door." The duc stripped off his coat and tossed it. He wagged both hands, sending the lace cuffs on his sleeves swaying. "'Tis obvious you need me to knock that head back into place. Come at me. We will settle this the way your friends on the streets do."

Hell. When old marble fell, it shattered into a million pieces. While shouts had always defined their relationship since his mother's death, Gérard knew if he ever tried to swing at the man, he would do more than hurt the son of a bitch. He would kill him.

"Cease being ridiculous. Given your age, I would only hurt you." Gérard rolled his eyes. "How you ever won my mother's hand and heart whilst she lived is beyond my comprehension."

The duc's hardened features wavered.

The memory of his mother was the only softness his father clung to. And sadly, even that was fading. It was all fading. "Little remains of our family, *Monseigneur*. My godfather needs me and if I have to put up fists to leave this house, I will. Because if I cannot be a hero to the one man who inspired me to be more, what good am I? What purpose have I? I would become like you. Bloody useless."

There was a moment of silence.

Gérard swallowed, sensing he had stabbed the man a bit too deep. "Forgive me."

Averting his gaze, the duc shrugged. "No. You are quite right. I am useless. I cannot even protect my one remaining son from himself. I gave you all too much freedom." Grabbing up his evening coat, he tugged it on. "Go serve our king. If you are not back in fourteen days, I will assume you are dead. And although we never get along, I wish to assure you, I will still mourn for you." Stalking down the corridor, the duc disappeared into his room and slammed the door.

Gérard sagged against the nearest wall.

Him die? Nay. Unlike his brothers, he always planned everything right down to the splinter and never went into anything blind. Or drunk. Yanking out the flask from his pocket, he uncorked it and numbly took one last swallow of brandy to keep his hands from shaking. No more brandy until he was at Château de Versailles.

LESSON TWO

If you are so unhappy about your life,

why not do something about it? I did.

-The School of Gallantry

Nine days later - Late morning
On the farthest outskirts of Paris, France

Chirping birds scattered into the nearby forest, breaking the silence as several large crows scavenged the dew softened fields.

It was eerily quiet. A bit *too* quiet. Even for the countryside.

Thérèse Angelique Clavette peered through the low hanging branches of the orchard she had taken refuge in the night before and strained to listen for anyone coming down the dirt path.

The pulsing silence was interrupted only on occasion by gathering crows and the buzzing of flies and bees. Strangely, no one had been on the road or in the fields since her journey commenced days earlier.

The revolution had certainly changed the world.

With so much equality being heralded across the land, no one wanted to work anymore.

The vast orchard surrounding her hinted that farmers had decided to move on to other things. Rusting scythes lay abandoned amongst piles of gathered hay and poorly nailed ladders had been left propped against various apple trees next to wooden buckets gathering debris and insects.

She hoped to have been in Paris by now, but without a single cart on the road to get her there, she had been forced to walk the entire way.

She *knew* she should have bought those ugly leather ankle boots, but had naïvely wanted to go to Paris in style. She had therefore opted to trade her best bonnet for a pair of satin slippers from the only fashionable woman in her village: the inn-keeper's wife.

The pretty, indigo slippers had been difficult to resist. They were stitched with beautiful, delicate patterns of yellow flowers and had wooden heels that were absolutely fabulous. Only.. they were too tight given they were meant to be worn with silk stockings, not thick, knitted ones. As such, Thérèse had been forced to walk without said slippers for almost two days, proving to her that being vain was no different than being stupid.

Grudgingly folding the blanket she had slept on, Thérèse set it into her travelling basket and leaned over the grass to spit out remnants of the chalk she had used to brush her teeth. She held up a small cracked mirror and used the wool sleeve of her gown to rub away the gritty residue. Each white tooth squeaked in glorious cleanliness.

She tucked away the mirror, convinced her teeth alone were going to make her famous.

Ready for the long day ahead, Thérèse adjusted her straw bonnet back into place and dragged in a regal breath, hefting up the wicker basket full of neatly folded clothing and apples she had picked from the abandoned orchard. Pushing her blonde braid over her slim shoulder, she trudged through the high grass in thick wool stockings. Her patched skirts and faded blue petticoats dragged behind her as her shoeless feet crunched their way out onto the dirt path of the small forest.

She hoped she was going the right way. She honestly didn't know anymore.

Shaking out her skirts to rid the fabric of any hay, she marched onward, thankful the ground wasn't muddy and that the sky still held onto sunshine. Despite being lost, she was rather proud of herself. She was about to become something no woman in her village had ever dared to be: independent.

Due to all the attention she received from countless men who kept fawning over her to the point of leaving coins and flowers on the windowsill of their cottage, her parents panicked and decided a quick marriage was the only option.

Of course, the moment her availability had been announced during a barn gathering, chaos of the worst sort ensued. Men, both young and old, from in and around Giverny, started competing for her to the point of smothering common sense.

Despite being the daughter of a butcher, she had always been popular due to men thinking she was attractive. And she was. She had dealt with it her whole life.

Ever since she came into her sizable breasts at the age of fourteen, men would stop her on the side of the road and eagerly offer her a cage full of chickens in return for a kiss. As if a chicken were worth that much. Others would insist she help herself to a barrel of oats in return for a peek at her calves and stockings. One bastard became so obsessed, he followed her almost every day to the market, insisting she take his goat well-known for producing the best milk in France. In return for her mouth on his cock. Not the rooster in his coop, but the one in his trousers.

One by one these fools pushed whatever they owned at her in an effort to flip up her skirts. And one by one she denied them. Because she wanted far more than mere chickens and goats.

She wanted a dashing man capable of seducing her soul.

Mind you, it *was* mildly entertaining getting so much attention from men. After all, with ten siblings, she barely got any at home. But she quickly realized the attention was lusty and self-serving. These men thought she would somehow fulfill their salacious fantasies that would make their cocks and their lives perfect. And whilst, yes, she was prettier than most, she was anything but perfect. She had horrible habits that included using her acting skills to get what she wanted, biting her nails and falling asleep in her corset. Not that they cared. All they wanted was a prized cow with big udders.

Genuinely concerned about the direction of her life, she secretly wrote to her favorite cousin Rémy, who lived in Paris, asking if there was a place for her in the theatre he managed. It was a controversial theatre well-known for comedy and showcasing actresses in knee-high skirts and colorful stockings.

She was desperate.

While she would have preferred a more prestigious theatre to perform in, she knew an aspiring actress could only command so much. Fortunately, Rémy was thrilled and insisted she come to Paris at once, promising her a leading role and a room of her own. He believed in her talent and understood her woes. He himself had escaped the village of Giverny at sixteen, almost fifteen years to the day, refusing to become the blacksmith his father wanted him to be. She was determined to follow in the glory of her cousin's steps and become famous.

Only.. her parents engaged her to the pastor's eldest son, Didier Dubois. They claimed she needed a respectable man to tame her ungovernable nature and forced her to sit with him during supper. He was thirty years older and treated her as if she was his daughter, constantly commenting that her ankle length skirts were not long enough.

She *begged* her parents to end the engagement. It resulted in her getting slapped and being told she was ungrateful. Imagine that. *Her. Ungrateful.* She, who was practically raising her ten younger brothers for her parents who kept having children because of their unbridled lust for each other. She, who was doing all of the sewing and the cooking and the cleaning and helping in the butcher shop to the point of only sleeping four hours most nights. It made her realize she only had one choice.

She was going to wear knee-high skirts and colorful stockings.

So she kissed the foreheads of her brothers, one by one, and promised to send them all money if they told her parents she was off to the market and would be at a friend's house for the day. They eagerly pushed her out the door and pinched her arm for luck so she might become rich *and* famous.

Under the fading sunlight that then led to countless stars, she disappeared, determined to be more than a wife or a headstone everyone in the village would come to forget when the letters in the stone faded.

Those stars had turned to a greying sky going on its second day.

Adjusting the basket against her hip, Thérèse marched onward.

The sooner she got to Paris, the sooner life could begin. She didn't mind showing off her legs to a whistling crowd. It was better than cleaning up after eleven males, breaking up fights, or using a cleaver to chop the heads off innocent chickens who had been merrily clucking a few minutes earlier.

It was all about perspective. And she had plenty of it.

Halfway down the forest path, a pebble wedged itself into the stocking between her toes. Thérèse puffed out an exasperated breath, but kept walking, determined not to stop. Another pebble nudged its way into her *other* stocking and pinched her heel.

How could something so small be *so* annoying?

She jerked to a halt, setting the basket down. Removing each stocking with gritted teeth, she shook out the pebbles, flinging them toward the forest around her.

At this pace, she would never get to Paris.

She kept following road signs claiming the city was somewhere ahead only to find it never was. She sensed she was officially lost. Bundling her stockings together, she tucked them into the far corner of her basket and plucked up by the basket by the wicker handle.

Crows cawed from the trees above as the sun briefly disappeared behind a looming dark cloud. Those blue skies weren't so blue anymore. Lifting her gaze to the swaying high branches of green trees, she hastened her step, avoiding cart grooves.

Thunder sounded in the far distance.

She groaned, knowing she was about to get soaked.

A growing gust of wind whipped at her ballooning skirts and flapped the wide rim of her bonnet. Leaves from the ground rose up in a flurry and scattered. It was as if the weather had decided to throw a tantrum merely because she wanted a new life. How rude.

Determined not to be intimidated by the darkening morning and forest, Thérèse marched onward and occupied herself by singing. When she eventually got bored of that, she started to openly practice the lines her cousin scribed for her to memorize. *"Is it possible for a mere commoner, like myself, to attain a measure of good cheer in a world dominated by—"* The wind picked up in ferocity, fluttering her bonnet upward. She squeaked and grabbed at her bonnet to keep it in place.

The ground beneath her bare feet trembled.

She paused, glancing down. It was as if the devil were approaching.

LESSON THREE

There are certain people who will change the way you breathe. Are you ready to meet them?

-The School of Gallantry

Thérèse frantically veered to the side of the forest path to ensure she wasn't trampled by whoever was approaching. Glancing back, she came to an astounded halt.

Heavens. The devil *was* approaching.

A broad-shouldered gentleman in a dark green riding coat rode toward her on a black stallion at a furious gallop, kicking up dead leaves and dirt through the forest path. The curved rim of his black felt hat had been pulled forward over a black velvet mask that barely revealed the end of a nose and the lower half of a square jaw that had clearly not been shaven in days.

It was a highwayman.

Not that she was in the least bit concerned. She had a paring knife and nothing of worth for him to take (aside from..her virginity). Annoyingly, she was lost and hadn't seen a person in two days. Better a highwayman than being stranded out in the country long enough for her parents to find her. Which they would. They had a horse and a cart and she did not.

Thérèse faced him and waved a bare hand in the hopes of slowing his pace. "*Monsieur! Monsieur!*" she yelled. "Is this the right way to Paris? *Do you know?*"

Upon seeing her, his eyes widened from behind his mask. Gloved hands jerked back the reins hard. Pressing leather boots into the sides of his black stallion, he brought the galloping horse to a skidding trot before coming to a full halt beside her on the narrow path.

It was obvious by the sleek, brushed sides of the horse that its owner had the financial means to coddle it. The masked gentleman on its saddle, however, wore a very frayed, outdated, double-breasted waistcoat with tarnished brass buttons that appeared to have been given far less attention than the horse.

His long black hair was tied back with a blood-red ribbon that glared against the color of his worn velvet coat. The cravat knotted around his throat had a fading sheen that hinted it was made out of linen fabricated twenty years ago. Huh.

She offered him a quick smile. "'Tis certainly a fine day to be robbing people, *Monsieur Highwayman.*" She hoped he had a sense of humor. Most highwaymen did. Or at least the ones who had passed through her village. "I regret to announce I have no money, for which I apologize, but feel free to check my basket."

He rolled his eyes, then untied and removed the mask. "I am no highwayman, *mademoiselle.*" Adjusting the felt hat back into place on his dark head, he tucked the mask into his pocket with gloved fingers, revealing the face of a young man who couldn't have been more than a few dashes over twenty.

She gaped. Unfashionable, frayed clothing aside, he was beautiful. Square jaw. Defined cheekbones. Full lips. Even a dent in his chin. He was *also* well-muscled and very rugged. He was everything a woman could ever want from a man in the hopes of producing the perfect child.

He was indeed no highwayman. He would not have removed his mask if he were.

Unless he planned to kill her.

Noting there were *five* rosewood pistols, a sizable sheathed dagger and a sword attached to the leather saddle of his horse, she paused. The weapons were too expensive to belong to a mere highwayman with outdated clothing.

This one was cleverly hiding his wealth.

Well, now. Maybe she could get some money out of this divine creature.

Lifting her gaze to his, she counterfeited a smile, intent on showcasing that she was fully capable of charming men out of whatever she wanted. Only a real actress could convince a man of *anything*. "I wish you a very grand morning, *monsieur*." She regally curtsied and ensured her voice remained breathy and sultry. "I thank you for stopping and wish to extend my vast appreciation knowing you appear to be a very busy man. I am on my way to Paris and require assistance regarding the direction I should take. Do you know the way?"

His rugged face tightened as he searched her face. Penetrating bright blue eyes met her gaze for a pulsing moment. "Mayhap," he offered in a deep, ragged tone.

She blinked. Mayhap? "Do you or do you not? Because I need to get to Paris."

He continued to stare.

She stared back. Apparently the sultry voice was working a bit too well. His brain was not functioning. "Should I be concerned, *monsieur*? Did you hit your head on a branch whilst coming into the forest? Because you appear quite dazed."

He set his shoulders, his rapier gaze now passing over her gown. "Not at all. I simply was not expecting to see anyone. Few know of these paths."

She eyed him. "You know of it."

His eyes became flat and unreadable. "Might I ask why you are walking alone in this forest?" His French was upper crust, well-educated and immaculate. "The closest village outside of Paris is a few hours away. Either you are stupid or you seem to think I am."

Her brows went up. She knew these well-to-do *fils de basts* were known for being overly righteous, but she didn't expect them to live up to their reputation. "Be careful with those insults, *monsieur*. Back in my village, I can skin a pig in less than thirty minutes. My father is a butcher, and I will warn you, he taught me everything I know. So refrain from annoying me. I have a paring knife."

A tremor touched his lips as if he were fighting an amusement he didn't wish to feel. "I have been duly warned." He skimmed her appearance, including her bare feet and hesitated, lingering on the exposed skin above her breasts her knitted scarf didn't cover. His jaw tightened. "The tops of your breasts are on full display. Is that intentional?"

Her eyes widened, realizing he had a direct view down her sizable cleavage given he was up on a horse. "Of course not. How dare you look." She rearranged her fichu over her décolletage and patted it into place, tucking it into her bodice. "It slipped," she tossed back. "The wind is a bit strong. Or did you not notice given how fast you were going?"

He puffed out a breath. Leaning back in the leather saddle enough to showcase his broad chest, he adjusted the reins in his large gloved hands. "Seeing you have no shoes, *mademoiselle*, and that the weather is about to turn dire, I suggest you make haste and go home."

She snorted. "Home is the last place I wish to be." Rather pleased with herself for seizing her own independence, she cradled the basket against her corseted waist, knowing a little advertisement was in order. "My cousin is graciously giving me an opportunity to be part of an upcoming performance he thinks will change all of Paris. I am to be his leading actress in a controversial script he wrote called...*The Delights of Life*. I will be performing on stage this Friday at *Spetacle des Variétés Amusantes*. Would you like to hear a few lines and maybe consider coming to a performance? Tickets will be selling for three *sols* a piece. Quite the bargain."

His gaze snapped to hers.

Without giving him a chance to decline, she breathlessly announced to her audience of one, "*Is it possible for a mere commoner, like myself, to attain a measure of good cheer in a world dominated by men, politics, wealth, murder, intrigue and greed? Most certainly! Under the new Republic, one must simply know how to make these aristocrats in power crawl.*" She slapped her derriere and gripped it. "*And crawl you shall, o lords of this ravaged land. For I am your new harlot better known as the queen!'*

He stared.

She grinned. "You ought to see my rendition of Calderón. I make death look real." She curtsied and regally held out an open palm with the roll of her bare hand. "Might you offer an aspiring actress a few *sols* for her journey into stardom? It would be greatly appreciated."

He lowered his chin. "I only give money to those in need."

The cheeky bastard. "I *am* in need. I left the house without a single *sol*."

"And how is that my problem?"

She dropped her hand to her side in exasperation. "I was hoping for a sliver of generosity. What else will you have me do? I sing. I dance. I *also* do a variety of impersonations. The only thing I will *not* do is bare my breasts or offer up sexual favors. However, if you insist, you may kiss my hand. But not with an open mouth or your tongue. I had a man once lick my hand and I swear I can still feel it."

An inexplicable look of withdrawal came over his face. "You and I are clearly at an impasse."

She pointed. "You really ought to work on that comedy routine. You are far too serious in nature."

He leaned back against his saddle, still staring her down. "What the hell is this? A forest and a show? Are you lost?"

She puffed out a breath. "I dare not say it, but I could be. I have been walking for over two days now following signs that appear to be misplaced. I am *trying* to get to Paris." She held up her basket and brightly offered, "I have apples. Might I barter a few in exchange for directions? Or maybe even a ride?" Still smiling, she enthusiastically patted the sleek, soft neck of his horse with one hand, while still holding the basket up. "He is so magnificent. I can barely breathe in his presence."

He edged his hand away from where she had been patting the horse. "Are you referring to me or the horse?"

She rolled her eyes. "And I thought I was conceited. Not to insult you or your glorious steed, but I intend to own something far more exotic once I rise into the glory of fame I deserve."

He said nothing.

"I intend to own a zebra," she added conversationally. "'Tis an African white horse with black stripes. I was fortunate enough to glimpse a sketch of one in an old gazette I was wrapping meat in. No one ever sees those pulling a carriage on the street. Which got me thinking about publicity. Every actress ought to have a definable persona that will separate her from the masses. And a zebra will do that and more. I can imagine it already. A black lacquered carriage whose interior is lined with red velvet being drawn by not one, not two, not three..but *four* zebras! Everyone would elbow each other and line the street just to watch me wave. And if I put my full name on the side of that carriage, they would even follow me straight to the theatre. Brilliant, *non?*"

His aloofness showed on his face. "I have a conscience, *ma biche,* so permit me to give you some advice." Ignoring the basket she still held up, he rigidly leaned down toward her from within the saddle and rumbled out, "Go home. Paris does not need another penniless country girl trying to get famous. You will only end up whoring yourself out of desperation once you realize the stage pays nothing. Is that what you want? Because that is what awaits you. Acting, whoring, the pox, blaming everyone for your demise, followed by a quick death. *If* you are fortunate enough to die quick, that is."

He was clearly not an optimist.

She gave him a withering look, lowering her basket. "I have much bigger plans and I can assure you, they do not include whoring myself to a man. If I wanted to do that, I could have easily stayed in Giverny. And whilst, yes, I often barter with men for whatever I need, my stage career comes first. I intend to be the next Mademoiselle Raucourt."

"I certainly hope not. That woman is a whore. And not a very nice one at that."

She glared. "How dare you insult the greatest actress in all of France?"

He lifted a brow. "How the hell do you think she became great?"

She gasped. "I am *not* about to listen to your vile gossip. I happen to like her. Ambition amongst females should be trumpeted not slapped." Swinging away, she adjusted the heavy basket, wishing she hadn't picked so many apples and trudged onward. "I will find my own way to Paris, *merci*. *Whore myself, indeed.* I have yet to find a man worthy of it. All you apes ever think about is food, wine and *poom-poom*."

He paused from adjusting his felt hat. "What the devil are you talking about?"

Why did no one ever get it? "*Sex*. It sounds exactly what it looks like. *Poom-poom*."

A cough escaped him. "Are you saying you have done such things?"

She rolled her eyes. "No. I have ten brothers under the age of eighteen. The eldest of them, at seventeen, is already engaged to one of the girls in the village due to his inability to control the stick between his now hairy legs. I caught Benoit with his bare arse in the air, grunting like the pig that he is. Not a pretty sight. Whilst my parents? Those two lusty rabbits have made their bed squeak so much over the years, there are visible grooves in the wood floor that will soon take them and the entire bed to China."

A laugh, low and deep and well-amused, escaped him. "I uh..thank you. I needed that. I have not laughed in..a long time." He slowly trotted his horse after her and eyed her, amusement lighting his eyes. "I wish to be of assistance, my dear. Whatever you need, it is yours. How can I help?"

Oh, now he cared. She eyed him in exasperation. "Service I can do without. What I need is money. I hear Paris is expensive."

"Unfortunately, yes. It is. You would never survive it."

She sighed. "How much would you be willing to give to a girl for free?"

Half-smiling, his voice turned to velvet. "If you answer a few questions about yourself, given you have sparked my interest, I promise to be incredibly generous."

"How generous is generous?"

"Enough to make you faint."

She quirked a brow. "You are quite the lawyer. So be it. Ask whatever questions you have. Do, however, keep them civil. No gown or corset sizes."

His mouth lifted. "What is it with the bare feet? Where are your shoes? Do you not own any?"

She was getting paid for this? Life was sometimes too easy to warrant breathing. "Of course I have shoes. You see?" She gestured toward the satin slippers peering out of the basket. "Shoes."

"How kind of you to let your basket wear them."

He was beginning to annoy her. "My basket is wearing them because I happen to prefer dirty feet over blisters. So leave off."

"I was teasing."

"Were you also teasing about Mademoiselle Raucourt when you insulted her? I met her once outside a theatre she performed in when I visited my cousin in Paris years ago. She was very gracious and even tossed coins to those less fortunate."

He paused. "Appearances can be deceiving. Two summers ago, Mademoiselle Raucourt seduced and broke a good man I once knew. He was a struggling carpenter who committed suicide over her by drinking an entire bottle of some concoction he bought at the apothecary. And the worst of it? She did not even bother to attend his funeral. In my opinion, you women are heartless."

She winced. Apparently, her idol was quite the cold tart. Eck. "How awful."

"It was. For him, anyway."

This one was quite the philosopher.

He continued trotting his horse alongside her. "So how old are you?"

What she did for money. She gave him a pointed look despite him being up on his horse. "My mother tells me I have been forty since the age of five, which puts me at about..oh..fifty-eight- years-old."

He thrust out his unshaven jaw and lifted his gaze to the heavens as if asking for patience.

She smirked, weighing those rugged features in between her own steps. My, my. She never thought a man was capable of being so well-muscled and physically perfect. And yet this one was.

Whilst he very much looked like a man, he also looked a touch young. Definitely not in his thirties. "I am eighteen," she offered, sensing she had teased him long enough. "How old are you?"

He snapped his gaze back to her. "I am one and twenty." He trotted the horse even closer. "Which makes me your elder."

Was he bragging?

There was a heightened strain to his tone. "Where are you from?"

"Giverny."

"And you walked?"

"Yes."

"Giverny is over twenty *pied du roi* in distance."

"I know. Believe me, I know. My feet keep reminding me of the distance."

His brows came together. "What are you doing out here alone? Who are your parents? What are their names?"

She sighed and kept walking. "At this rate, forget paying me. Because I have to get to Paris or my cousin might very well give my lead to another. And then where will I be? The theatrical debuts in three days. *Three.* Which means..I have to be in Paris by tomorrow nightfall *at the latest.* I have knee-high skirts to be fitted into."

"Knee-high skirts?" He shifted in his saddle and let out a whistle between straight teeth. "You certainly are ambitious. I foresee great things for you in the back of some man's carriage."

She put up a hand. "I have officially ceased listening to anything you are saying. If I choose to show off my legs, at whatever price I set, that is my business, not yours."

Dismounting with the swing of his long leg, he landed with a heavy thud onto the ground behind her. "You and those legs became my business the moment you stopped me." He stalked after her and snapped out a gloved hand. "Give me your basket. You and I are going to talk."

She turned and lifted an astounded brow. "Have we not been talking?"

"Only superficially." Still holding out his hand, he wagged the tips of his fingers. "Give me your basket. I want see what you have in it."

She scrambled back, swinging her basket away. "'Tis none of your business what I have in it. Off with you!"

He lowered his gloved hand, the tails of his coat whipping around his muscled frame.

Drops of rain spattered her face. "I believe you owe me money." She presented a hand. "I expect to faint the moment those coins touch my hand."

His features and tone hardened. "You are wandering a forest alone without any shoes, are asking me for money and look like you have been sleeping in hay for days. What sort of trouble are you in? Are you on your own? Or did someone hire you to intercept me?"

She pulled in her chin. "Intercept you? What are you— If you must know, my parents engaged me to a horrid man twice my age and I had no choice but to leave. Unfortunately, I got lost and here I am."

His gaze slid to her breasts for a moment, causing him to scratch at his chin. He met her eyes. "Are you wanting to travel with me?"

The perusal of her breasts aside, she was beginning to wonder if she should trust him. She gripped the basket. "That depends on who you really are. I assume given your casual approach to visually molesting my breasts, coupled with your impeccable use of language and expensive firearms, you must be a merchant of some sort."

"No. I am not *bourgeoisie*. I am well above it."

Well above it? There was nothing above *bourgeoisie*. Nothing except for...

Her eyes widened. "Are you saying you are of the elite?"

"Yes."

"As in a real *aristocrat*?"

He widened his stance. "Yes. As in a real *aristocrat*."

Not good. His kind didn't like her kind anymore than her kind liked his kind. "That would certainly explain the sour demeanor, the weapons, the mask and an attempt to wear outdated clothing. Are you in hiding?"

"No. I am merely travelling back from an...engagement."

"That required a mask?"

He swiped at his mouth in agitation. "You are clearly on to me. So what happens next? What should we do about each other?"

Thérèse hesitated. Either he was not used to making friends or he was not used to people at all. "You appear to be under duress, and while I completely understand, there is no need to take that duress and fling it at me. I share your distrust. This revolution went to muck the moment they started killing people. The things I have been hearing are enough to turn the stomach of even the devil. Did you know the Legislative Assembly oversaw the execution of two aristocratic young men barely a breath over twenty? And they were brothers, no less. It was all maliciously done on the side of a road as opposed to a court-room, which is how things ought to be done. Even worse, these poor aristos had more than their toes sliced off. They were shot and hanged like animals merely because they tried to quietly leave the country. Did you hear of it?"

He blinked rapidly, as if unable to comprehend what she was saying, and glanced away. "Yes." Dropping his hand to his side, his tone darkened. "For a country girl, you appear to be incredibly well-informed on what is happening. Why is that?"

She sighed. "My cousin Rémy is a bit of gossip. He lives in Paris and has been writing about the chaos since it started back in '89. He even joined in a few of the riots."

His expression grew tight with strain. "And knowing this, you still wish to go into Paris and perform for him? Knowing he is contributing to the mount-ing chaos?"

Thérèse shrugged. "Better my cousin than what my parents have planned for me. Rémy is a good man and anything but violent. He only joined in on a few of the riots to show support and petition change. The theatre he manages was getting so heavily taxed by the Lord Mayor, he almost had to shut it down. The aristocracy owns countless theatrical venues of a similar nature and were never taxed. These wealthy bastards think they can—" Remembering who she was talking to, she cringed. "Forgive me. I was raised in a very opinionated and vocal household. There were thirteen of us and we never held anything back."

Hooking his thumbs against the pockets of his trousers, he bit out, "I can see that. Unfortunately, you are part of the growing problem in this country. All tongue but no mind."

"I beg your pardon?"

He narrowed his gaze. "You swallow propaganda merely because you hear it or because it was written. Be it about a zebra or anything else, those gazettes and pamphlets are paid for and printed by people with a specific agenda. Remember that." His tone hardened. "And while you insult my way of life by calling me a bastard, your gazettes and pamphlets are pushing the masses to violence in the name of overtaking what little remains of this country. Aristocrats are not the problem anymore. You people are."

No wonder the country was going to hell. If a man of privilege refused to acknowledge the struggles happening outside his golden gates, it would seem this revolution was just getting started.

In truth, she wasn't a *staunch* believer in the revolution. The idea of eliminating *Sa Majesté* was pointless. What would it change? Nothing. Because men in power equated to men in power. And said power would simply go on to yet another self-righteous prick who would only use the government like the devil paging through the bible looking for new words to tear out.

But she understood why people were demanding change.

They were out of hope. Much like she was.

Knowing it was best to leave, for she was getting a bit *too* riled about their conversation, she edged back. "I suggest you aristos stop blaming the pamphlets and do something about the taxes and the food prices. Maybe *then*, your kind would be more respected. For without the respect of the people, what keeps us in place? *Nothing*. Propaganda is only ever allowed to fester when there is nothing left for the people to believe in. *That* may be why I am prancing off to Paris to be an actress. Because I have *nothing* left to believe in."

He said nothing.

Thérèse offered him a theatrical bow. "Thank you for wasting my time. I bid you a very good day and ask that you stop following me." She swung away and started walking again. Only faster.

She almost hit her head against her own basket, unable to believe she had just delivered a political lashing to an aristocratic man who had five rosewood pistols, a dagger and a sword.

LESSON FOUR

Nothing is ever as it seems.

-The School of Gallantry

Not only did the blighter not pay her the money he promised, he continued to follow her.

As if it were his right!

"Maybe I ought to take you back to Giverny and marry you off," he called. "That would certainly keep you out of trouble."

Her heart skidded. She had told him where she was from. Which meant—

Thérèse broke out into a run, cradling her wicker basket against herself to keep everything within it from bouncing out.

Determined booted feet thudded after her. "Why the hell are you running?!" he yelled.

"*Because I am not going back to Giverny! So you might as well start shooting with every pistol you have!*" Her parents, who were as stubborn as she, would lock her in a room until she married Didier. And then she would find herself covered in his facial powder every single night for life. For life!

Her heart pounded as she ran even faster. An apple bounced out. She frantically tried to catch it, but it rolled off to the side.

"*Mademoiselle,* cease—" Rounding her with astounding speed, he blocked her path with his broad frame by skidding in before her. He grabbed her closest arm, yanking her to a halt that made them both stumble. "For mercy's sake, *arrêtez!*"

Thérèse jerked to a halt in exasperation and winced, knowing he wasn't going to let her pass. She swallowed, her chest still heaving from the sprint she had attempted. She tore herself away from his grasp.

There was only one thing left to do. Take to the stage. Like she always did.

Forcing tears to streak her eyes in a well-practiced attempt to save herself, she choked out, "Please, *Monseigneur.* I..I beg of you not to insist." She focused on ensuring her voice quivered just enough to sound real. "I am well aware of your superiority and apologize for my overly passionate words, but I cannot go back to Giverny and marry a man I do not love. It would ruin more than my heart. Is that what you seek to do? *To take what remains of my insignificant life and fling me into perpetual misery?* Would you be that cruel?" She would have let her lip tremble, but decided it would have been a bit much.

His commanding blue eyes grew all the more amused. As did his husky voice. "You are an incredibly good actress. Do you toy with men like this all the time?"

She cringed. It was the first time she failed to produce the effect she wanted. "No. Not *all* the time."

He assessed her, his amusement fading. "Do you really have a cousin in Paris?"

She daintily swiped at what remained of the tears she had theatrically produced. "Yes, of course, I have a cousin. Just because I am an actress does not mean whatever comes out of my mouth is a lie."

His brows came together. "I am astounded he would let you walk to Paris alone. Women of all classes are being assaulted on the streets given there are no *maréchaussées* to oversee the chaos. Some of these revolutionaries are merrily raping women on the street in the name of 'freedom'. Do you know that?"

She swallowed. No. She didn't. But she wasn't surprised. Men were like that. Self-serving.

He searched her face. "Your level of intelligence is astoundingly unusual for the daughter of a mere butcher. I cannot help but be skeptical as to who you really are."

Thérèse blinked through the last of her fake tears. It was so strange, but this close, those steel blue eyes of his had become more than a color. They were fiercely passionate, soulful and heart-wrenchingly beautiful.

Those eyes didn't seem to trust her anymore than she trusted him.

She heaved out a sigh, ready to call it a truce. "Unusual though it is, I was actually sent to a seminary in Paris for three years. It was paid for by a very generous and wealthy patron my mother used to be a governess to. I thought my parents had lost the last of their *bourgeoisie* minds trying to overeducate me, only to discover I was an investment. They dragged me back to Giverny and forced me to teach everything I learned at the seminary to every single one of my ten unruly brothers. I taught the same bloody lesson plan for so many years, I am fully convinced I have been to Russia eighteen times."

"Russia?"

Sensing he still wasn't believing it, she added, "Yes. Russia. 'Tis an aspiration of mine to visit Saint Petersburg one of these days. They call it the city of giants given how massive the boulevards and buildings are. Apparently, these Russians are so hardened by the snow and life they chew glass for dinner."

He smirked. "I doubt they chew glass for dinner. But then what do I know? I have never been." Rubbing a hand against his jaw, he turned and strode back toward the horse. Unsheathing the single dagger attached to the saddle of the horse, he gripped it.

Her heart popped as she scrambled back. "What are you doing?"

He glanced at her. "You are not the only actor in our midst."

With that, he detached the brass buttons on his coat with the tip of his dagger, letting the buttons fall onto the dirt path one by one. He kicked them away and detached the remaining buttons on his waistcoat, as well, before sweeping the dagger back into its leather sheath on the saddle.

Thunder cracked again, startling her. The cooling wind, that whispered summer was almost at an end, gusted through the trees and flapped her skirts, causing them to balloon upward. She gasped, scrambling to keep her gown from exposing her lack of undergarments.

He eyed her and smirked. Removing his coat with a shrug, he revealed a yellowing linen shirt and well-fitted waistcoat. Pausing before her and the basket that separated them, he held out his coat. "Here. Put it on. It will keep your gown from lifting."

She was officially impressed. "You, *monsieur*, would be the first to try to keep my skirt from lifting."

"I did not say I was doing it willingly, dearest."

She gave him a withering look. "I take it you offer your coat to every woman you meet?"

He lifted a brow. "I used to let beautiful women take far, far more than my coat." He leveled her with a stare. "But I have learned not to trust them to take off with my heart."

She blinked. "Are you flirting with me?"

"Whatever gave you that idea?" He tossed the coat at her, startling her. "Take it." He stepped back. "The wind appears to be strong enough to push this weather through. So hopefully, it will not rain."

She scrambled into his coat before her gown decided to put on another show. The thick fabric was heavy and smooth, weighing her shoulders with an impressive expanse that draped down well past her knees.

Adjusting it over herself to keep it from falling, she paused, realizing the fabric had a melting scent of expensive cologne. It smelled like freshly hewn amberwood and spice and was so achingly divine, she wanted to do nothing but sniff, nuzzle and cuddle it.

She refrained. "Thank you for the coat."

He said nothing. He simply removed his felt hat, causing strands of longer black hair to fall into his eyes. Brushing it back into his queue, he whipped the hat into the forest, well beyond the trees. Lifting his unshaven chin, he casually undid his cravat and flicked it aside. Stripping off his waistcoat that fully exposed his linen shirt, he hurled it.

She tightened her hold on his coat. "What are you doing?"

"I try never to be seen in the same clothing for long. I changed out of my last ensemble over an hour ago by a lake. After I went for a swim."

She gaped. "Is there a warrant for your arrest?"

"I have no doubt there will be." Holding her gaze, he set a gloved hand to his chest. "The name is Gérard. We will keep it to that until I have established what our relationship will be. I am still deciding."

Still deciding? "Do tell the jury my name is Thérèse."

He lingered. "*Thérèse.*" He intently searched her face, dragging in a slow breath. "You certainly were blessed. Everything about you is...your face is—" He still lingered, searching her features.

She edged back. "Leave my face out of this."

He lifted a dark brow. "What? Did I say anything?"

"You did not have to. I get it all the time. If you ever wonder why I wish to take to the stage, it is because my life *is* a stage. There is no difference. You men lose your minds around me. And whilst I appreciate the never ending parade of adoration, it does get to be annoying."

He hesitated as if intrigued. "Are you saying men crawl for you?"

He had no idea. Men were the bane of her existence.

She had always wanted to be known for her intelligence and quick wit that had been rightfully earned whilst raising ten very rambunctious brothers, but how was a woman to become more than a face in a world obsessed with beauty?

She considered herself rather pathetic.

For she had no friends outside of her family. She never had.

All the girls in the village always snubbed her, snickering that she thought too much of herself. Which wasn't true. They simply didn't like the attention she always received. They blamed her for the fact that the boy of their dreams ignored them. Little did they know the boy of their dreams wasn't even worth an oyster pie.

She set her chin. "They do more than crawl. Giverny and its men about exhausted me."

"Is that so?" He rolled his tongue against the inside of his cheek. "If you are so tired of the attention, my dear, then why take to the stage? It will only make it worse. Actresses are the epitome of every man's dream."

She kept her chin set. "True. But at least I will get paid for it."

"Money only ever shrouds other problems, you know." He glanced judiciously around the forest, as if preoccupied by too many thoughts. The wind flapped the billowing sleeves of his linen shirt, outlining his broad physique and hinting at the impressive definition of taut muscle beneath.

Thérèse tried not to stare, but every time the wind shifted his linen shirt against his muscled arms and chest, it gave her more to admire. She pinched her lips in an effort not to dash up to him and tap each pectoral to see if it was real.

He eyed her and veered his gaze upward, searching the sky through the branches of the trees. "Fortunately, the weather does not appear to be getting worse. In fact, I am quite certain of it." He pointed at the sky with a gloved finger and stared up at it with contempt. "I command you not to rain. I need to get to Paris without my gunpowder getting wet. Do you hear me?"

This aristocrat was talking to the rain. *To the rain.* As if he had power over it.

No wonder these people were getting stoned.

She peered up at the sky through the leaves and branches above and paused. Large patches of blue sky pushed out from between the dark clouds. Her lips parted. "Did you just command the weather into cooperation?"

He smugly adjusted his linen shirt. "I do it all the time. Whatever I want, I get. No matter what it is. The universe is quite used to it. You should get used to it, too." His wry tone indicated he was attempting humor.

She tossed his coat back at him, grabbing up the basket. "It must be nice being able to control the universe."

Gérard effortlessly snatched hold of his coat in midair and stared. "I am not in control of it yet. But I damn well hope to be."

She rolled her eyes. "Let me know when you are."

He still stared. "Are you really a virgin? Or are you pretending to be?"

The prickling of heat overtook her cheeks. She *never* blushed around men. After all, she was the one in control of how they behaved around her. It was an art she had perfected since she had grown into her breasts. "You are being downright crude. I refuse to answer that."

He pointed. "So you *are* a virgin."

She glared. "What are you? The *virgin* magistrate?"

"Pardon me for saying it, but I am a touch confused as to how *worldly* you appear to be for a virgin." He eyed her basket, as if attempting to assess its contents. "You certainly travel lightly." He lingered on the apples crowding it. "But well."

Averting his gaze, he shrugged on his coat.

That was certainly him asking for an apple. She paused. There were two leather satchels attached to his saddle. One appeared to be stuffed with stacks of parchment that peered out beneath a tightly fastened flap. The other was well-packed with clothing and several frayed wool blankets that had traces of hay as if he had been sleeping in the fields.

He wasn't hiding his wealth. He had *no* wealth.

Which would explain why he still hadn't paid her.

She sighed. Plucking up an apple out of her basket, she held it out. "Here. Go on."

His gaze veered to the apple. "Pardon?"

She closed the distance between them and held it out. "You practically invited yourself into eating it. Take it. They are a bit tart, but still surprisingly good."

He widened his stance. "I thank you, dearest, but no. Those are yours."

"Oh, cease with your high and mighty business already. I can see the hay clinging to your blanket. You were sleeping in a field just like me. Which means you are not as well-heeled as you tout yourself to be and are probably hungry. *Here.* The apples were free and came out of the orchard I was passing through earlier. You would hardly be imposing. Go on."

He hesitated but still did not take it.

She sighed. Wedging herself closer, she was about to shove it into his hand, but noted his gloves were crusted with dry mud.

So she did the one thing she could. The one thing she always did for her brothers. She brought out her paring knife and balancing the basket on the crook of her elbow, sliced off a piece of the fruit. Tucking the small knife away, she leaned in and daintily reaching up, set it against his lips, wiggling it. "Eat, *Gérard*. Consider it payment for my ride into Paris."

He met her gaze for a long moment, his broad chest visibly rising and falling. "Thank you." Bending his dark head, he opened his full lips and ever so slowly dragged the sliced apple into his mouth. He leaned in more to take the whole thing into his mouth.

His teeth and hot tongue grazed the tips of her fingers.

Her pulse roared as her skin tingled from the unexpected contact. She jerked her hand away. Taking several steps back, she swiped her wet fingers against her skirt, trying to rid herself of the tingling she *still* felt. "You almost ate my finger."

The muscles in his jaw showcased each methodical chew as he continued to heatedly hold her gaze. "It was in the way." His blue eyes now held a spark of some indefinable emotion. One full of so many secrets he wasn't telling.

Swallowing, he said in a low, husky tone, "Bring the apple back over. I would like more."

He wasn't looking to eat apples anymore. She tried to remain calm and held out the apple, keeping her distance. "Here. Take the whole thing."

"I would but my gloves are a bit dirty." He held them up.

It appeared the bite of an apple had turned this one into a full-fledged rake. "Then I suggest you remove your gloves."

He lowered his hands and flexed them, flaking mud off the leather. "Do you think it wise to ask me to remove more clothing?"

She eyed him. Something in his demeanor had changed. And she didn't understand why. "No more slices for you. You are making a game of this."

Brushing off the remaining dirt from his gloves, he slowly closed the distance between them. "Maybe I am." He edged in until they were almost nose to nose. The scent of amberwood, spice and leather tinged the air. "Are you too scared to play along? I thought you were a butcher's daughter capable of cleaving your way through anything."

He was too close and was beginning to play the sort of games she was used to. The ones where men tried to sidle up close and touch her.

Scrambling back, her bare ankle rolled against a large branch lying on the path behind her. She winced, stumbled and gasped as the basket tipped and fell to the ground, thudding apples and the items within everywhere.

He jumped and grabbed her waist hard to keep her from following the basket to the ground. Jerking her upward and toward himself to steady her, his rigid body and expression stilled.

Pausing, he eyed her lips.

She could feel the pulse of his large hands on her waist as he edged his mouth down and closer to hers. The heat of his apple-sweetened breath fanned her lips.

He hovered, but did nothing.

She stiffly clung to him, her heart pounding as the intensity of his blue eyes dug into her, hinting that he wanted far, far more than mere lips. It made her stomach flip.

She had only ever kissed a man once. A year earlier a young royal soldier who was off to fight against the riots had jogged out of line from the regiment and begged her for a kiss on the side of the road. She only did it because she doubted he would ever get another.

She swallowed and waited for those lips to take hers.

He released her and stepped back, his expression unreadable.

She staggered between breaths. Was she losing her ability to charm? Any other man would have kissed more than her mouth by now.

He widened his stance, surveying her with annoyed superiority. "Why did you not kiss me? I gave you plenty of time."

She gasped, regaining what little common sense she had left. The blighter! He had been waiting for her to—

The horse perked and quickly hoofed its way between them to the nearest apple, swiping it up with its large, yellow teeth. With the shake of its head, it chewed obnoxiously, spraying juice as it headed for another apple and another and another, fully intending on eating them all.

She gasped again and waved a hand toward the horse. "Tell him to stop eating my apples!"

"Oh, come now," he drawled. "Has he not earned it? This here chap is taking you to Paris."

She set her hands on her hips. "He could be gracious enough to leave me *one*. Now call him off. I have not eaten anything all morning."

The horse stepped onto her cracked mirror, shattering it.

She gasped again as it dragged her gown along the path to find another apple.

A throaty laugh escaped Gérard. "Pardon his manners. He takes after me."

She swung toward him, a shaky breath escaping her. "Your horse is destroying what little I own, and you find that amusing?"

His amusement faded. He stared at her, his eyes penetrating the distance between them. "Forgive him and forgive me."

Something about him unnerved her, yet lured her. It was as if he were a higher being struggling to be human. Averting her gaze, she straightened her basket and gathered what few items she could. The ones that hadn't been mangled, that was.

She scrambled for her leather-bound book.

He knelt beside her on the dirt path. "Leave it be. I will do it."

"No, I—" She paused noting the expensive wool of his beige breeches had stretched and tightened against the taut, bulking muscle pushing beneath them. It was as if his entire body were made of steel. The flap of his trouser appeared to be well-filled, too.

She cringed at noticing.

Picking up the book, he turned it over to glance at the golden lettering and paused. His gaze veered to hers in astonishment. "Do you speak English?"

"No. Of course not. I am as French as champagne."

He lowered his chin. "Then why do you have a book written in English?"

Puckering her lips in annoyance, she took it from his hand and tucked it into her basket where it belonged. The last thing she wanted or needed was for him or any man knowing that, at heart, she was a weakling of a stupid romantic. Because she knew full well men took advantage of women with stars in their eyes. "Because one day," she tossed out, "I plan to read it."

A travelling British couple who had spent an entire day cooing at each other in English over a meal at the inn had left it. While she had tried to run it after them, their coach had already departed, and they never came back to claim it. The way the two had gloried in one another made her hold onto the book and believe she might one day have such a thing. She imagined it held the secret to their entire marriage. "Its mystery holds a certain power over me," she confessed. "When I have enough money, I intend to hire a British tutor so I can read every last sentence."

"Is that so?" He tilted his dark head, his eyes brightening. "I speak English, you know. Fluently. My mother was British. I still have family in London, actually."

Her heart popped. Dearest God. They were *meant* to meet!

She shoved the book back at him, still on her knees, and frantically opened it to the first page, her hands almost trembling in excitement. "You have no idea how long I have waited to meet someone who can speak English." She pointed at the book. "Might you translate a few words? Can you tell me if it is a romantic novel? One with a happy ending?"

He searched her face.

She tapped at the page. "Cease being a man and read it."

He took the book from her hands, still kneeling on the ground beside her, and glanced at the golden letters on the front leather binding of the book. "*Candide: or The Optimist* by Voltaire." He edged it open. "Tis actually a translation. I read this in French some time ago. It was quite good. I enjoyed it."

"Did you? What was it about?"

He flipped to another page, where an array of words started the first line of the book. He silently read, his brows coming together.

Thérèse leaned in, peering down at the page and then up at him. She waited.

He continued reading intently in concentrated silence. Time passed. He rapidly blinked, then turned the page and read on.

She elbowed him. "If you keep at it, you will read the whole book twice. What does it say?"

He slapped the book shut and shoved it into her basket. "Allow me to sum up the story. It is all too much like real life. Candide's love for Cunégonde propels him to abandon paradise, he commits murders in her name, avoids execution and when they can at long last be together, he no longer wants her." He gave her a pointed look.

Thérèse swallowed. After waiting *years* to learn about its contents, it appeared the happy couple had been carrying a foray of mockery.

She veered her gaze away, grabbing up a dirt streaked gown and her cousin's letter that held the address she was supposed to travel to. "So much for marital secrets," she grouched. "And yet again, another male writer rips apart the glory of love and happy endings in a book. What do you men have against love and happy endings anyway?"

He lifted his gaze to hers, an arrested expression settling onto his rugged features. His square jaw tensed visibly. "Nothing. We simply recognize that they can be dangerous to a man. It gives him too much hope, and some men need more than hope. They need a full guarantee."

She swallowed. That was certainly a confession she did not expect.

His brow creased. "So this is, in fact, real. You really are heading to Paris to be an actress."

She blinked. "Yes, of course. What— Was there any doubt?"

"A part of me was worried you had been hired by the *gendarmerie nationale*."

The..oh. *Oh!* "No. I..no, no, no. I..no. I would never work for men like that. Not given all the murders and the butchering they do. I am nothing more than an aspiring actress trying to get to Paris." She poked at each cheek to emphasize how real she was. "See? Nothing nefarious here."

He intently searched her face, his masculine mouth softening. "Your appearance into my life is unprecedented." His steel blue eyes smoldered as if he were *finally* introducing her to who he really was. "Do you know how many times I kept thinking I was going to die? And how every person that crossed my path only brought me closer to death? Do you know what that does to your mind?"

Her throat ached.

He hesitated and leaned in, searching her face. "Kiss me."

And she thought *she* was overly forward in nature.

She leaned far back and awkwardly patted his unshaven cheek none too lightly, more than forgiving him given his mind did not appear to be in the right place. "If I were madly in love with you, I would most certainly let kisses and far more happen. But given we just met..you know..a girl has to have standards."

The wind scattered some of his hair against his forehead. He placed an apple and a folded, muddy gown into her basket. He said nothing.

His self-effacing silence pinched her given his earlier words of others wanting him dead. "Are you all right?"

He lifted his gaze to hers.

The pulsing disquiet in those striking eyes punched her. It was as if he were recovering from seeing something no man should have seen. She leaned toward him. "What is it?"

He only held her gaze.

Good Lord. What had this man been through?

Leaving the basket on the ground, she stood and brushed off her skirts. She hesitated and held out her hand. "Come. Get up off the ground." She scanned the split apples whose inner pieces were mashed into the ground and rolled her eyes. "Leave the rest of the apples. Sadly, they are too damaged."

He jumped onto his booted feet, startling her. Grabbing her outstretched hand, he kissed it with warm lips and then yanked her rigidly close, squeezing her hard.

She froze, her cheek mashed against that hard, muscled chest and linen. The scent of his cologne pierced her astounded breath. Her pulse roared. "The hand was meant to help you up, you know. Not..this."

He only tightened his hold and rubbed her shoulders. "Let a man be happy knowing he is alive *and* in the presence of a beautiful woman who is going to change his life. Or rather, *my* life. I have plans for us, *ma biche*. Plans."

She didn't know whether to be flattered or worried.

Glancing at his horse, he let out a quick whistle through his upper teeth and gestured toward the smashed apples. "Have at it," he prodded. "You have earned it more than I, my friend."

The horse eagerly moved forward, dipped his head toward the pieces and slopped each piece off the dirt road with oversized lips.

Thérèse tried not to get comfortable in those muscled arms that continued to boldly hold and rub her as if she were his to rub and hold. Especially after his talk of plans. She wanted to be an actress first, mistress last. Or at least second. But definitely not first.

She edged herself out of Gérard's firm grip after a few leaning tugs. "Might you..?"

His large fingers finally, though barely, released her hand.

Stepping back, she puffed out an exasperated breath. His intensity still pulsed against her skin, and his cologne had practically rubbed itself into more than her pores. Watching the horse noisily chew, she tried to lighten the mood. "Look at that. Country dining at its finest."

"*Thérèse.*" That low voice broke with huskiness. "Come here."

Unadulterated and uncensored need reverberated from that deep voice beside her.

Veering her astounded gaze to his, she sensed he wanted her back in his arms.

She swallowed.

Slipping his hand into the leather purse attached to the belt of his waist, he dug out everything in it. He held out a sizable stash of two-Louis gold coins, displaying well over twenty in the palm of his glove. "I believe I owe you money."

Her eyes widened. Holy— Those coins had to be worth about a thousand *livres*. A thousand! Heavens, those coins could have easily sustained her entire family of thirteen *and* a few neighbors in Giverny for a whole year.

So much for him being poor.

She eyed him. "I get to keep all of it?"

He edged it further out. "This is just the beginning." His expression stilled. "I need you to be completely and utterly devoted to me and only me. In return, whatever you desire, I will ensure you get."

Every inch of her skin turned to fire. He was asking her to be his mistress.

Whilst a part of her wanted to be offended enough to smack him so hard all of his dead ancestors would feel it whether they were in heaven or hell, she sensed whatever this man had been through warranted this idiocy *and* her leniency.

She stepped back, ensuring her tone was firm. "I understand my forward nature might have led you to believe you could make an offer of my person, but I am not that sort of woman."

His steel blue eyes held hers. "Us being lovers is only a breath of what I want. I need you for something more."

Her breath hitched, and she found herself extremely conscious that unlike other men, this one wanted to control far more than her body. He wanted control over her mind. As if he didn't trust her mind.

He tossed the coins he was still holding into her basket, announcing they were in agreement.

She eyed him in riled exasperation. "No. No, no, no. What are you— Take it back! I am not— Even for a full thousand, I am not kissing you."

He stared. "Then we will do everything else."

Thunder cracked again, startling her as much as his words.

A downpour of cold rain rustled its way through the trees, soaking her. Feeling water trickling down her hair, forehead, nose and cheeks, she glowered up at him. "I thought you had a talk with the rain."

He dragged back wet strands of dark hair from his eyes. "Maybe the rain and I made arrangements to ensure you stayed." Slowly removing his coat again, he draped it over her head and leaned in, adjusting it onto her with a firm tug. His gaze dropped to her lips. "Do you trust me?"

She peered up at him, trying to throttle the fluttering in her stomach knowing he was looking at her lips and using the rain and his coat as an excuse to kiss her. "No. Not really."

"Thérèse." He searched her face. "I do not trust easily myself. But if we could make this work, if we do this right, I foresee us doing great things for the world."

She swallowed. "What sort of things?"

Dragging in a ragged breath, he edged in closer, his body pressing into her.

Her pulse pounded.

He brushed his masculine lips across her forehead, grazing the warmth of his own lips against the moisture of the rain that had cooled her skin.

She swayed, unable to even resist.

His chest rose and fell unevenly. Slowly removing his gloves, he tucked them into her basket, revealing calloused hands that clearly did not belong to an aristocrat but a man who dug himself into real work. Holding her gaze with rising intensity, he cupped her face, pressing his large fingers into her skin with silent urgency.

She almost dropped the basket, but her trembling hand managed to hold on to the wicker handle. Her breaths mingled against his while the rain continued to gently fall around them.

It was like a dream. Unreal.

He dragged his hands down her throat to her bodice. Lowering his gaze, he tugged the bodice down just above her nipples, exposing the upper full rounds of her breasts.

She stilled in disbelief of what she was letting him do.

He bent his dark head and kissed each top, lingering with the heat of his lips. He dragged his lips from one to the other.

Her skin felt so hot, she wanted it to rain harder. Her head lulled back in complete submission as the cool, misting rain overwhelmed her heated senses.

The tip of his rigid hot tongue traced the dip between both breasts. His hands dragged her skirts and petticoats up just enough to let the heat of his bare hand touch the skin of her thigh.

Her chest heaved as she leveled her head, waiting for that hand to drift toward her inner thigh.

He hesitated, making no attempt to hide that he was now watching her. Holding her gaze, he released her skirt and slid her bodice back up, his large fingers grazing her breasts beneath the fabric of her gown. "As you can see," he breathed out, "lust is as equally powerful as any love. Did you give in to me, *ma biche*, because you loved me? No. But it certainly felt like it, did it not?"

Their eyes locked as their breathing came in unison.

Her throat tightened. For the first time in her life, she had no words. None. He had erased them with but a touch and pointed out something she was too stunned to admit. That he was right. She had indeed allowed lust to choke out everything she thought she had wanted out of a man. She had let him touch her and tongue her breasts even though she did not..love him.

Stepping back, he smoothed the flap of his breeches that displayed a thick erection beneath. "Pardon the uh..display." He turned and guided his horse off the road.

Thérèse staggered.

Removing the blanket from his saddle, he tucked it beneath his arm and wove into the canopy of low hanging branches. He bent far forward, to fit beneath the thick, green foliage, and laid out the blanket.

Falling onto it with a breath, he leaned back on both elbows, crossing his boots at the ankles and held her gaze. "Are you coming?"

An explosive current zipped through her, making her knees wobble. This one was a smooth lover of women. So smooth silk poured right out of his nostrils. "Uh..no. I..no. We should try to head to Paris. It may rain all day."

"I cannot afford to get my satchel drenched." He patted the space beside him, his gaze never once leaving hers. "Come. I want you here."

"No. I prefer getting wet."

"You already are." Setting both hands behind his head, he stretched fully on-to his back, broadening his frame and stared up at the canopy of leaves above him. "Come, *ma biche*. I want to talk to you. I have a proposition."

Oh, yes. Like *that* was reassuring given they were alone in the forest.

Thérèse glanced down the narrow path of trees, both before her and be-hind. There wasn't even a field or an opening in sight. She would be running blindly into a thicket. In bare feet.

Thunder rolled. The rain now came down harder through the branches above the path, soaking her and the coat she held over her head. She winced against the onslaught of heavy drops that angled in past the coat. Her cold feet now miserably stood in a large puddle of what would soon be a large river of mud. She groaned.

It was as if this aristocrat had indeed conspired with the weather.

God had to be a man. There was no other explanation for the amount of torture the Lord put a good woman through. She paused and eyed *Monsieur Aristocrate*. "Tell the rain to stop."

Smoothing a large hand over the curve of his unshaven jaw, he flicked his gaze to her gown. "Why would I do that? In a few moments, I will be blessed to see everything beneath the fabric." He hesitated. "Cease being stubborn and come here."

She sighed. There was no sense in being stupid.

Better to be seduced by a gorgeous half-god than end up dead from pneu-monia.

Cradling her basket, while keeping his heavy coat in place over her head, she frantically hurried toward him, dodging branches. Rounding his booted feet, she settled herself next to him beneath the thick canopy that was surpris-ingly cozy. She set her basket aside, just off the blanket, shook out her wool stockings and hitched up her skirts to her knees and yanked on a stocking.

He leaned toward her on a propped elbow, his gaze skimming her legs.

She paused. "Did I invite you to look?"

He shifted his jaw, still perusing her legs. He reached out and dragged a finger down her exposed calf.

She almost fainted against the unexpected caress, her thighs and knees instinctively pressing together. Heart pounding, she smacked his hand. "What are you doing?" she rasped.

He lifted his gaze to hers, tilting his dark head. "I know you felt it. You closed your thighs."

Her breath hitched. Dearest God. She was going to end up pregnant by the end of this night. "I felt nothing. Absolutely *nothing*."

She finished yanking up her other stocking and folded her skirts back over her legs in an effort to save herself. She bundled her skirts around herself tighter. "Despite what I allowed you to do earlier, I suggest you not get any ideas."

He searched her face.

Thérèse pinched her lips together and stared out into the forest, listening to the rain rustling through. She had encouraged this overly amorous libertine by letting him yank her bodice down in the middle of a forest and lick her almost to the nipples. Not even days out of Giverny and she was already a strumpet.

He shifted closer and peered up at her.

She ignored him and shifted away, fully aware she was already on the edge of the blanket.

Leaning in, he scraped his lower teeth against the sleeve of her slightly damp gown.

Her body trembled from heightened awareness. She pressed her knees together to ensure they didn't fall open.

He nudged her with his chin. Twice.

Lord save her, he was acting like an animal seeking attention. "I am not doing this."

"Why not?" He reached over her and gripping her waist, hoisted her up and toward him. "We are beyond attracted to each other, and you know it." Setting her onto his lap, he intently held her gaze and wrapped each of her legs around his waist, forcing the heat of his large body against her own. "You and I met in this forest for a reason. Ask me what that reason is. Go on. Ask me."

His nearness and the intensity of those steel blue eyes and that rugged face made her so weak she almost just wanted to flop. "I..fate?"

He shook his head from side to side. "No. Not even fate could have devised something as perfect as this." Still holding her gaze, he dragged her skirts up higher. "If you help me, o darling actress of mine, I will help you. Say yes to me in what I want, and I will give you everything you ever wanted out of life. *Everything.*"

Thérèse grabbed hold of his muscled shoulders hard, torn between wanting to stop him and wanting him to continue so she could thoroughly explore this fabulous whole idea of 'everything'. She was no fool. There was no such thing as getting everything in life, but this was fairly darn close to it.

He was gorgeous. And..*gorgeous.*

Deny it though she may, *this* was her definition of the ultimate fantasy. He was rich, muscled, beautiful, and he desperately wanted her. Not in that *oh-look-at-what-I-can-do* sort of way. But rather in a *you-will-never-forget-me-for-life* sort of way.

Maybe, just maybe, she was about to become a strumpet.

Tilting her head, she walked the tips of her fingers across his solid chest, trying to appear in control of what appeared to be a most promising situation. "Define everything."

He sensually rubbed her thighs as his full mouth drew near. "You can have zebras and velvet-lined carriages along with whatever you want or need. And if you want your own theatre with your name on it, with a script written for you and only you, I can make it happen by quietly tossing a few thousand at the right people. *Théâtre Française* is the most prestigious venue in all of France. I know half the people there, and they owe me more favors than I know what to do with. Give me a month, and you will be famous in three."

She searched his face in between half-breaths. He was damned serious. *Théâtre Française* was every actor's dream. It was the same stage that made Mademoiselle Raucourt famous. It was where the best of *bourgeoisie*, and now the new Republic, congregated, and would make her a *real* actor. Not a variety show. Her legs would *never* be on display. Only her talents.

She would have a chance to prove to the world she was more than a face and a pair of legs. "You could make that happen?" she rasped in disbelief. "You could actually get me onto the stage of *Théâtre Française?*"

He nodded. "Oh, yes."

Holy God. "What if I wanted my cousin to manage *Théâtre Française?* Is that at all possible? Because I cannot abandon him. He and I are very close and—"

"Consider it done. He will be the new manager. He will, however, have to prove to the owner of the theatre that he can maintain the position."

She dragged in an uneven breath. This was almost too good to be true. Even for just sex. "So, in return, what do you want?"

His large fingers skimmed her thighs. "A bit of sex and.. a bit of gossip."

Why was it she was more worried about the gossip part? "Define.. *gossip.*"

His hands rounded her breasts. "We will discuss it later," he murmured. "Simply know that if the gossip part does not appeal to you, you are under no obligation and I will gladly pay you an additional five thousand to go our separate ways. Because serenading you, even once, would be more than enough for this man."

Six thousand alone was going to change her life, and that did not include the zebras or getting on stage. Shifting against his lap, she smoothed her hands against his broad shoulders in an effort to remain calm. "How do I know you will keep any of your promises? I barely know you."

He dragged in a breath, staring at her mouth. "If you are not famous in three months, I give you permission to take any one of my pistols and shoot me dead."

She stared him down, wishing to assure him she was damn serious. "I *will* shoot you dead if you take advantage of me."

His mouth quirked. "I would like that."

She swallowed.

"So are we doing this?" He nestled her hips closer against his. "Am I allowed to make love to you, and give you the rest of my proposition later?"

Her lips parted in one last effort to deny him, but the intensity of those gorgeous eyes kept her from having any power. She was about to sell her soul to this blue-eyed devil for a chance at grabbing everything she wanted. "I..suppose."

Gérard searched her face. "You suppose?" He dragged her skirts down and covered her thighs. "Woman, it is either yes or no. *Suppose* indicates a probability but not a guarantee."

She blinked. He had covered her thighs as if the sex didn't matter. Which meant whatever he really wanted, was of far greater importance to him. It intrigued her. Because what on earth was more important to a man than sex? Something whispered to her that this man deserved a chance. He deserved a yes.

At least once.

At worst, she *would* shoot him. "Before I say yes to any of this," she warned, "here are my rules. A mere, simple two. You will *never* lie to me about anything and I cannot and will not get pregnant." Not after raising all ten of her brothers. She was done with that. Done. She needed a bit of freedom. At least five years' worth. At least. "I do not want any children. Not a single one. And I most certainly do not plan on getting married any time soon. The stage comes first. Which means you will withdraw every time. Every. Single. Time. Do you understand me?"

His eyes mockingly brightened. "Are you certain? Can you not imagine how beautiful our children would be given how gorgeous we both are?"

She poked his nose. "I am quite serious."

He lifted his chin and nipped at her pointed finger with his warm lips. "I will never lie to you. *Ever.* That is not who I am. And I promise to withdraw every time. I am not ready to have children anymore than you are. Now is there anything else you require? Are there any other rules?"

She paused in an attempt to think of more. A career, money, a good-looking man and no children. What more was there to want out of life? "No."

"Are you certain?"

"Quite."

"Do we have an alliance?" He dragged his tongue across her still pointed finger.

She hazily watched his tongue, her finger unable to stay still. "Yes."

"No regrets?"

She lowered her hand and swallowed. "Regrets only come after promises are broken."

"Well said and I agree." He searched her face. Gently tugging down her bodice, he exposed her breasts and slid his hands all over them. Dipping his head toward her, his hot mouth licked and circled and sucked on each nipple.

She swayed. Dearest Lord. *This* was the best yes of her life. No wonder women became strumpets. It was amazing. Money and fame for..*this?* Money and fame to feel..*amazing?*

Why was this considered a sin?

Gently grabbing her hands, he pushed them beneath the wide opening of his linen shirt. "Touch me. Show me you want this."

The smooth warmth of his skin ridged over bunched, hard muscle made her want to gape, groan and fall into him. Lowering her gaze to his chiseled chest, she slid her hands up and down, reveling in every inch of it.

Birds chirped. Rain rustled leaves. Everything in that moment felt like a dream.

It was too perfect to be real.

"You are so beautiful," he murmured against her breasts. "I can barely breathe."

For the first time in her life she was grateful the good Lord had blessed her enough for a man like this to notice. "I cannot believe you and this is real," she murmured back, running her fingers up his throat, face and hair. He was so divine, she would have gladly done all of this for free.

He slipped his hand between her exposed open thighs, sliding a large finger slowly, slowly against her slit. He rubbed her wetness and nub while sucking on her breast.

She choked, gripping his broad shoulders hard. Pulsing sensations gripped her body and breath, rippling through her relentlessly with a rising need that made her feel animalistic and savage.

Watching her face, he alternated between rubbing and flicking her nub.

She swayed in an effort to stay up and on his lap. It felt so good. Too good.

He slid the tip of his large finger into her wet opening, teasing his way in and out, in and out. "In this moment, we are madly in love with each other. Believe it."

In that moment, she did. She really, really did. Lust, love. It blurred and became the same.

"Do you love me?" he whispered, searching her face.

"I..." He wanted her to *lie?* "We just met."

"Pretend."

Oh. "I do."

He rubbed her nub harder. "You are an actress, Thérèse. Make me believe it."

Even an actress would have trouble focusing in between all the rubbing that made her pulse roar and her core tighten. "I..."

He flicked her nub. "Do you love me?"

"Yes," she gushed, pushing against his hand. Even she wanted to believe it in that moment given how he was making her feel.

"Now tell me how incredible I am." His finger stilled, no longer moving. "Tell me that even if I had nothing and could not get you on that stage, you would still let me do this to you."

Her breaths came in uneven takes. "I would do this even if you..had nothing," she choked out, no longer thinking.

His nostrils flared. He pushed his finger in deep to his upper knuckle.

A sharp pinch made her stiffen against him and gasp, but he quickly rubbed and flicked her nub harder, distracting her from the reality that he tore her hymen with his finger.

He increased the pace, slipping in one finger, two fingers, then three fingers deep into her opening as his thumb circled her nub.

Her mind, her breath, her body was no longer hers. It was his. All his. And he knew it. She instinctively rolled against his hand, giving into what her body wanted.

Reaching up, he possessively gripped her head and pressed her forehead against his own, forcing her to look down at what he was doing to her.

Thérèse watched in disbelief as his fingers pumped her over and over. She gasped, quivering against the building sensations seizing her. Her thighs quivered as her core grew tighter and tighter and..tighter. Her breaths grew so uneven, her throat started closing.

She cried out in disbelief, letting herself drown in the glory of pleasure.

Removing his finger, he quickly unfastened the buttons on his breeches. Releasing the thick length of his cock, he positioned it and edged his way half in.

They both gasped.

Holding her gaze, he slowly, slowly pushed up further into her stretching wetness, his ragged breaths mingling with her own in the silence of the forest that still rustled with rain. "I will refrain from moving until you tell me to," he said in a low, terse tone.

That overly thick fullness made her inner thighs ache beyond bearing in an effort to hold him so deep. His hard length seemed to pulse within her, making her all too aware he was in complete control of whether she survived or not.

His fingers dug harder into the back of her head and gripped her braid, tilting and edging her head down toward him. He captured her mouth and rolled his hot tongue against hers.

She melted and found herself so oblivious and mesmerized, she almost forgot to kiss him. Because it was the closest thing to perfection she had ever experienced.

Releasing her mouth, Gérard smeared his lips down the length of her throat.

Uneven breaths escaped her. "You can try to move."

Securing her legs better around his waist, he rigidly stroked his cock into her. He increased the pace of his hips, pushing his cock progressively deeper and deeper. Curving his entire mouth to her shoulder, he buried his head into is curve.

The progressive, urgent pace of his large cock within her tightness made her realize the discomfort was becoming too great to take anymore pleasure. He was stroking into her too deep and too hard.

Razor sharp, raw pain made her flinch. "Gérard. No more. I—"

He rolled them and set her onto her back. Holding her gaze in between breaths that made his broad chest visibly rise and fall, he set both hands against her head. Smoothing her hair and sides of her face with large trembling hands, he whispered, "Do you want me to stop?"

The urgency and need in that voice and in those eyes, along with those hands that attempted to soothe away her discomfort, made her relent. "No," she choked out.

"Are you certain?"

She nodded.

He captured her lips and rolled his hips into her, dipping the full length of his cock in and out. He rolled faster. Gripping her body tight as he kissed her, he pounded into her full force, feverishly thudding her into the ground and blanket.

She gasped against the searing pain and shoved at his bunched shoulders that were making it impossible for her to breathe.

He stilled, his uneven harsh breaths filling the space between them. "Forgive me." He pulled out, his chest heaving and raised himself over her exposed breasts. Straddling her, he gathered the well-glistened root of his rigid cock and holding it with one hand, dragged his other hand from root to tip and back again. "Hold your breasts together."

She did exactly what he wanted.

Towering above her, he jerked his erection, his gaze riveted to her breasts. He breathed out, "*Thérèse*," and ejaculated the warmth of his seed onto her breasts, startling her.

At least the man had said *her* name. Not someone else's.

Groaning, he spilled out more, making her gape in disbelief that he had no shame.

He swayed above her, and then stilled. In between heavy breaths, he lowered himself and used the edge of the wool blanket to wipe the seed off her breasts. He captured her gaze.

She swallowed, knowing this officially made them lovers. She covered herself.

He rolled off and buttoned his breeches. Propping himself on an elbow beside her, he leaned in close. He traced a finger across her arm. "Are you all right?"

If that voice had not softened with genuine concern, she would have smacked him. For it had hurt a touch more than she wanted it to. A remaining tear from her earlier pain spilled over the rim of her eye and trailed down her cheek.

His brows flickered. "Thérèse." He cupped her chin and nudged it toward himself. A breath escaped him as his thumb slid her tear away.

She sniffed.

He dragged in a breath and slowly let it out. He was quiet for a long moment. "Thank you for making love to me." He leaned in and softly kissed her head. Once. Twice. Thrice.

She melted against those words and with each and every kiss. Did all men thank women for making love to their bodies? It was nice. She nestled her head against his chest and pressed herself tighter against him, reveling in his warmth.

He smoothed her hair. "Are you comfortable?" he murmured.

She nodded against him. "Yes. Are you?"

"Yes. Very. You make me forget we just met."

She shifted, loosening her hold.

His hands dragged hers back up and over his shoulders. "Keep your arms around me for a bit longer. I like it." He kissed her head.

She bit back a smile. The promise of great fortune and fame aside, she had to admit she liked this one.

LESSON FIVE

Yearning often blooms in that moment when we realize we are not living to our fullest potential.

-The School of Gallantry

Nightfall

Although the rain had finally stopped, the roads were too dark to travel on, because there was no moon light peering through the thick, cloud-ridden sky. So they stayed in the forest and talked about everything but nothing in particular.

It was going to be a long night.

Gérard quietly watched the fire he managed to start by flint despite the wet branches. He had strategically burned whatever blank parchments of paper he could find from within the large stacks of documents he swiped out of his godfather's desk that had remained untouched within the secret room of the palace back at Versailles.

The vandalism and missing furniture, shattered chandeliers and slashed portraits that had once graced Versailles' pristine façade had been shocking. Gérard had grown up running through those corridors whenever he and his family had been invited to stay. He'd been fortunate. Except for some vagabonds looking for a place to sleep, no one was there. Walking through that echoing silence of a marble palace that might never see another king made him realize he was running out of time. And hope.

But he had found his hope. And it was brilliant.

Glancing toward Thérèse who had grown quiet, he dug into his leather satchel, which he had earlier set on the blanket they sat on. That lone tear of hers that had trickled down her face shortly after they made love, made him achingly realize he never wanted to see another tear roll from that eye again.

He carefully nudged past the stack of documents and, pushing aside several empty silver flasks, he removed his very last flask that was still full of brandy. He closed the satchel to ensure the documents remained hidden.

Uncorking the flask, he hesitated and held it out toward her. "Here." He softened his tone in the hopes of winning back her attention. "Have some."

She shook her braided blonde head, setting her chin primly on the bent knees of her arranged skirts. She stared at the fire, her flawless pale skin glowing against the flickering light. Her sultry, heavy-lidded azure eyes gave the illusion she was trying to seduce the flame.

She was so beautiful. It almost hurt looking at her.

Gérard took a swig of brandy, savoring the stinging warmth of its spicy oak flavor.

When they first met, he had weighed the possibility she had been hired to lure him and take the papers. But an array of wavering, niggling, unabating doubts led him into realizing the gendarmerie nationale would not have hired a woman to seduce him who was clearly against doing the job.

So what did he do? He lost what little was left of his rational mind.

He had been too damn aroused by her presence to pretend he wanted anything else but sex. For he knew if death was going to take him for the papers he held, he was going out in style. With her. Now. Here. For hell only knew what awaited him in Paris.

"Did you always want to be an actress?" he asked.

Her eyes flicked over to him. "Yes."

Prior to his bold advance of proving to her sex didn't require love, she had been incredibly chatty. Overly chatty. And now? She barely offered complete sentences.

He blamed himself. He had a tendency to dig his teeth in deep and quick when it came to a particular woman he wanted. And she had sparked far, far more than his body. She had sparked his mind and soul into believing in the power of women again. Within the first hour of meeting her, he had quickly fit this Thérèse into the 'soul on fire' category.

And together, they were going to take over Paris and slit the throat of the Republic.

He leaned toward her and corked the brandy, knowing he had to focus on her and not drinking. He set the flask beside him. "So what made you want to be an actress?"

She returned her gaze to the fire, her slim finger absently tracing the hem covering her feet. "Why did you want me to tell you that I loved you? Knowing it was a lie?"

He scrubbed his face in exasperation. Him and his misguided fantasies. "I just like feeling I belong to someone. Women have a tendency to flock to me for all the wrong reasons, and I wanted to pretend I found the right one."

Her lips parted. "I see." Averting her gaze, she chewed on a nail. She kept chewing.

"Are you hungry?" he softly chided.

She gave him a withering look, dropping her hand. "No, I— You baffle me."

His chest tightened. "How so?"

"With your talk of wanting to be with someone, why settle for a mistress? Why not marry?"

He shifted, sensing she was probably probing for what chances she had. Like women always did. "Marriage is not for me, dearest. It would complicate my life."

She snorted. "How does marriage complicate a man's life? It really only complicates a woman's life. She becomes his property, bears his children and is his life-long servant to all his needs."

"Not true." Tapping at his chest, he humbly confessed, "If I were to marry, I would become the servant. Which is why I will never do it."

She squinted. "What do you mean?"

He lifted a brow. "What is this? Are you hoping to be my wife? What happened to all that talk of men being disgusting, wanting nothing but food, wine and poom-poom?"

She eyed him, her pale cheeks flushing. "I hardly find you disgusting."

Uh-oh. This one had just elevated him above the male population. Which meant she would expect him to leap higher than his boots would allow. He swiped at his mouth. "I ask that you not place such lofty expectations on me. I disappoint enough people in my life." Or what was left of them.

They were quiet for a moment.

She searched his face.

He reveled in those sultry eyes that didn't look real. As fiery and stubborn as she was, he was surprised he had been able to seduce her. Either he was that damn good or she was that damn naughty. "You are the most beautiful woman I have ever met. Ever."

She pinched her lips in an attempt to hide a smile. "Do you always flatter women after you seduce them?"

"Only if they are worthy of it." He tilted his head. "You never answered my question. Why did you want to be an actress? Hm? When did that start?"

She set her chin on her hand. "When I visited my cousin in Paris at the age of twelve. He let me sing for a crowd opening night. My parents about boxed his ears bloody when they heard of it, but it was the most glorious moment of my life. When my boots touched the apron of that stage, I knew it was what I was destined for. I, with but a song, was in command of more than their eyes. I was in command of their minds and their hearts. I was able to make them believe I was more than the mere daughter of a butcher. That I was, in fact, born a queen."

He knew she was perfect for what he planned.

She was the stronghold he had been looking for who defined everything bourgeoisie.

With her on the stage of Théâtre Française, the epicenter of all life and gossip in Paris, she would have access to all sorts of people. Bourgeoisie and Legislative Assembly members alike. And if he was having trouble breathing around her, he could only imagine what this siren could do if they formed an alliance. Men always put their cocks first.

He was proof of it.

Grabbing up his flask, he uncorked it. He took another swig of brandy and draped an arm over his bent knee. "Allow me to get to the point of what I really want from you."

"You mean sex was merely you getting started?" She smirked. "Do go on. Make me an offer."

He held her gaze, taking another swig of his brandy. "I will give you everything you want, from dirt to sky, and in return, you will do what I tell you."

"Which is what?"

"I need someone who will not betray me. And I am asking you to be that person. I am about to entrust my very breath to you and am asking that you entrust your breath to me."

She eyed him. "Mighty words given we are not married."

"Mighty, indeed. Everyone in my circle still seems to think that what is happening across France is temporary. That once the king has been completely removed from power, the country will settle back into a state of peace and calm. I, on the other hand, have proof that something far bigger is happening. Something that will change France as we know it. Given who I am, the people who usually confide in me, tell me nothing. Whilst certain people of the *bourgeoisie* and lower classes revere me, they fear the new Republic too much. I therefore need someone they can relate to. Someone who will be able to inform me of what is happening on and off the stage, so to speak. Someone like you."

She stared. "Are you asking me to spy for you?"

He met her gaze. "Yes. Judging by your wit alone, I am utterly convinced you are more than a pretty face. Prove it. I am asking you to help me put an end to some of the bloodshed. My brothers were actually the two aristocrats you spoke of who were butchered on the side of a road. Marceau and Julien are not even being given a burial because the Legislative Assembly commanded the *gendarmerie nationale* to hold their remains as evidence. Which means their bones will remain locked in a back room until they decide to throw those bones into an underground pell-mell bone repository better known as *Tombelssoire.*"

Her eyes widened. Clasping a pale hand to her mouth, she held it in place before choking out through her fingers, "Gérard, how can they do that?"

He shrugged. "The people of France gave this new government permission to do whatever it needs to. By eliminating our existence, there will be no opposition."

She chewed on her lip.

"And things are about to get worse. The Legislative Assembly is about to become a single-chamber assembly of power held by a select group of men. Whilst titles have already been done away with, I have heard rumblings that these particular deputies plan to altogether abolish royalty from France. Which means I and every aristocrat in the land will cease to exist by the mere stroke of a quill."

Gérard rubbed at his chin in a riled effort to remain calm. "There are over a thousand royalists being held in Parisian prisons that have yet to stand trial. And based on the closing of the borders, I firmly believe a mass genocide of the aristocracy is planned. Which means they will find a way to kill us all, including the king whom I mean to save. *Sa Majesté* is like a father to me and has been for many, many years."

Her features stilled. "And you think a mere actress is going to stop all of this from happening?"

He rolled his eyes. "No. All I need is information. I have a group of young aristocrats I am working with. We started assisting each other in trying to unearth information about what is happening to this country and to us."

"I see." She leaned toward him. "So if I help you, our earlier agreement stands? You will put me on stage and pay for everything, yes?"

So much for thinking she cared about anything else but the offer. He thought *maybe* there was more to this woman after she had enchantingly insisted on feeding him the apple he had been too proud to ask for. It was obvious, however, she fed all of the men apples in return for what she wanted: money. He was astounded she had actually been a virgin. But then again, she was *bourgeoisie*. Her priorities were typical of her kind. Money and fame.

Gérard tried to keep his tone polite. "Yes. If you help me, our earlier agreement stands."

She fiddled with her fingers, glancing up at the branches above them, then held out a hand. "I will spy for you."

A breath escaped him. He grabbed her hand and squeezed it hard, willing her to accept that there was no going back. "Are you certain?"

"How difficult can it be to prod men for information I want?"

He released her hand, leveling her with a stare. "Whilst I admire your never-ending confidence, try not to be overly presumptuous. This can and will get dangerous."

"Women know a bit more about danger than men ever will. Have you ever thought you were going to get raped merely because you walked past a man at the wrong hour?"

Very good point. Swiveling toward the edge of the blanket they sat on, he withdrew the rosewood pistol he had set beside his leather satchel. Holding it by the barrel, he held out the handle toward her. "I want you to keep this with you at all times. Take it."

She wrinkled her nose. "Absolutely not. Pistols make my skin crawl."

He wagged it at her. "If you plan on living in Paris, I suggest you get comfortable with the idea of holding a weapon. Take it. I will show you to load it and prime it tomorrow morning. Practicing with it every day is important."

She leaned back. "If you insist on giving me a weapon, give me a cleaver. Cleavers can be as equally effective and require no other skill other than swinging. The less I have to think about, the better off I will be." She paused. "I can also use it to make dinner."

There was no doubt she was the epitome of the sort of woman he needed to get this job done. "I will ensure you get that cleaver." He casually flipped the pistol and set it aside. "A weapon is only a precaution. In truth, our association will not require much. All I want is information pertaining to any plans that involve the aristocracy, and in particular, anything related to the king. Which means once we get you into *Théâtre Française* all you have to do is flutter those pretty eyes and get the men to talk politics."

"Will I have to do it in private?" she echoed. "As in my *boudoir?*"

Sensing her discomfort, he skimmed his hand across her thigh. "No. There will be no compromising of yourself. They are not allowed to touch you or be alone with you. Always ensure you are with others in the name of your safety. Because I am not one to tolerate anyone coming in on what is mine. Which you now are given this association."

She eyed his hand and her thigh and adjusted her braid, smoothing it against her shoulder. "Staking your claim, are you?"

He captured her gaze. "I only make love to a woman I am interested in keeping."

She continued to smooth her braid against her shoulder. "Are you suggesting you are capable of offering more than sex to a woman?"

"Of course I am." He tapped her thigh. "I am not like other men, Thérèse. I never play games. What you see is exactly what you get. While the sex was incredible, there is more to me than that and I wish to assure you, I will be devoted to you for however long we can make this last."

She squinted playfully. "Does this mean I now own your soul?"

"Prove yourself, and I will ensure you get it right along with anything else you want."

She sat up. "I was teasing."

"I was not."

She was quiet for a moment. "So what happens next?"

Gérard spaced his words out so she damn well understood what needed to happen. "The moment we get to Paris, what we share here in the forest ends. Private meetings will be rare. There are far too many eyes watching. Which means, whenever we are in public, I become nothing more than a besotted admirer you will have no choice but to scorn. And I am quite serious about that."

He stared her down. "If you hint, even for a breath, to anyone that we mean anything to each other, not only will no one trust you, but it will be used against you *and* me. Try to remember your task throughout all of this is only to prod for political gossip. Which actresses are well-known for doing anyway, so it will hardly raise any brows. Anything you think might be of worth to me, you will pass along using hair ribbons as a method of communication. My mother, who was heavily involved in assisting others, used the same method to keep battered women away from their husbands."

She sat up, her brows going up. "Hair ribbons?"

"Yes. You will purchase and only ever wear three colors in your hair: blue, white and red. Like the cockade. It will make you incredibly popular. Little will anyone know that those same ribbons are going to be used to communicate with me. Every Friday at noon, you will step outside the theatre for three minutes, wearing whatever ribbon is required to pass on information. A red ribbon will indicate you have a lead. I will send a man I trust so you and he can go over all the details. A white ribbon will indicate you merely wish to see me." He lifted a brow. "It could be for sex or anything else you may need. I expect to see a lot of those in your hair."

She tsked.

"And then there is the blue ribbon." He grew serious again. "Never use it unless your life depends on it."

She lowered her chin. "This sounds ominous."

"It is. You will *only* ever use it in response to any danger you may be in. It is the only ribbon you will actually send, not wear. The moment I receive that blue ribbon, no matter the hour, I will be at your door looking to slit throats. So do not *ever* send me a blue ribbon. For it will only expose our association."

Observing him for a long moment, she asked softly, "Where would I send it?"

"Five Luxembourg. It will go directly to a very close friend of mine. That way, there will be no visible connections between you and me."

She glanced upward toward the overhang of the dark forest barely outlined and illuminated by the fire. "Red for leads, white for everything else, and blue only if I need a few throats slit in my honor. Number five at Luxembourg." She tapped her temple. "This is my ink and parchment." She leveled her eyes back to him and hesitated.

He lifted a brow. "What is it? I can see you thinking."

"What is your association with *Sa Majesté*? You mentioned he was like a father to you."

This was where the creek that separated them became the size of a cavern.

It was inevitable. She was going to find out the moment they got into Paris anyway.

Rolling his tongue on the inside of his mouth, he eventually offered, "*Sa Majesté* is my godfather. If he were to die without heirs, and the *duc d'Orléans* were to die, as well, my father would be the next in line as king. And I, by right, directly after him."

Her eyes widened. She searched his face, her pale face flushing to bright red. "You are *that* closely related to the king?" she echoed.

And there it was. She was no longer impressed by him or his looks but the title. Much like women had always been, even when his brothers had been alive and he was a damn spare. He *hated* sharing who he was. He *hated* tainting people's perception of him.

After all, he was no God. Nor had he ever tried to be, much to his father's dismay. He rather liked being human. It allowed him to be what he was: anything but perfect. His love for sex and brandy was too great to pretend otherwise.

He gallantly inclined his head. "The name is Gérard Antoine Tolbert, and I am the last remaining heir to the great *duché* of Andelot." Knowing she deserved the honor, he gestured toward her resting hand. "Might I have the pleasure of a full introduction, *mademoiselle*? You only ever gave me your first name."

She hesitated and slowly held out her hand, her slim wrist almost floppy. "I am..." She gaped. "I am Thérèse Angelique Clavette."

At least she was capable of saying her name.

Taking her hand, which seemed so charmingly small against his own, he leaned over it and kissed it. He lingered, brushing his lips against her soft skin and held her gaze. "Despite who I am, from this moment on, you and I are equals. I am not above you, and you are not above me. I am devoted to you and you are devoted to me."

She dragged back her hand and smoothed her skirts, eyeing him. "I take it you are *beyond* wealthy? Yes?"

He shifted his jaw, trying not to get annoyed knowing he had offered her equality and devotion and the first thing out of her mouth was money. This is *exactly* why he kept himself from ever loving any of these women, especially after Madame Poulin. Because it kept his standards low enough for him to walk right over them when he was done. "Oh, yes. Beyond. My father is worth ten million *livres*, and we own fourteen estates across France."

She choked. "Fourteen estates? And you *still* have ten million *livre* left over? That should be illegal."

Women. "Each estate produces almost half a million a year. It is pure mathematics. No laws broken, and we pay our tenants eight times more than most. Our generosity to our tenants has proven effective as they work twice as hard and have remained devoted to us and our name even during the turmoil that has overtaken France."

Her eyes skimmed him. Twice. "Forgive me, but I find it very difficult to believe you are worth ten million. Your appearance is— I do not mean to insult you, Gérard dear, for you are beyond gorgeous, but...why under heaven's name are you wearing such horrid, outdated clothing? Is this because you are incognito? Or is this what you *usually* wear?"

"Does it matter?"

"Of course it does. You are the son of a *duc*." She tugged at the sleeve of her frayed blue gown. "Do you think I *want* to wear this? I have better fashion sense than this. The trouble is my taste is beyond what I can afford. You should be so lucky."

Who knew taking one bite from this siren's apple would make him regret every minute of it?

"When we get to Paris," she added, "might I go shopping for clothes? You know...the expensive sort?"

Of course she would ask for clothes. Women always asked for clothes. He wagged the flask he held. "I will ensure whatever you want, you get."

Her heavy-lidded azure eyes brightened as her stunning and overly perfect pale features softened. "I like you. I like you well beyond what I should."

"I am glad to hear it." He lowered his gaze to that exposed, pale throat and imagined her softness all over him again. "Would you like diamonds for that throat?" He might as well show off. "I can arrange for that, too."

Her mouth opened. "A diamond necklace? As in a *real* one? Made out of diamonds?"

He smirked. "Yes. Last I knew diamond necklaces were made out diamonds."

Pertly scooting closer, she tapped his knee. "Can I have pearls, too? A long set that will drape itself to my waist? I rather like the idea of having over a thousand pearls on one string."

If he wasn't careful, she was going to run off with his father's ten million.

Taking another long swig from his flask, Gérard swallowed hard and tried not to look at those sizable breasts he had thoroughly enjoyed masturbating into earlier. "Why settle for one that falls to the waist? We can have your pearls trail the floor."

An excited giggle escaped her in between claps. "Who knew giving up my virginity would turn into *this*!"

Unbelievable. She was like a fairy-demon.

It was actually nice having a lover again.

Though it never did last.

They always disappointed him.

Eyeing Thérèse, he took another long swig, letting it sit in his mouth long enough for his tongue to bathe in it before swallowing. He could feel the haze of the brandy already overtaking him like an old friend. The one friend he knew would always be there.

He drank more. And more.

She lowered her chin. "You certainly are enjoying that flask."

It was one of the few things he *could* enjoy given everything he had been through. He tilted the drink toward her. "Do you want some?"

She leaned forward, primly taking the flask. "*Merci.*" She peered into it and sniffed its rim. "What is it?"

"Brandy. 'Tis fermented fruit mashed into liquid perfection I cannot do without. Of all the spirits in the cupboard of cupboards, that *there* is my definition of true refinement. It hits me faster and harder than the wine, rum, whiskey, gin or anything else. Those do nothing for me. A complete waste of time."

Both of her brows went up. "So are you a connoisseur or a drunk?"

How utterly charming. This one thought she was now his wife. "I am a drunk first and a connoisseur last. I drink about a decanter every night. Get used to it."

She sat up. "Are you being serious?" she echoed in riled concern.

"Yes. I started drinking shortly after my mother died. Even prior to her death, I was always partial to the taste of brandy. The sting wakes your soul."

She hesitated. "I am ever so sorry to hear about your mother."

His throat tightened. He shrugged, trying to pretend it didn't matter. "Her carriage was robbed. The driver was ignorant enough to try to fight the men, instead of letting them take the goddamn money. One of the men fired a pistol, and she got hit. The three men were hanged, but my father ended up beating that driver to near death for instigating the violence."

Gérard swallowed, refusing to linger on how his mother's limp, bleeding body had been carried into the house by his wailing father. "'Tis painfully wrong and morbid to see this world full of so many vile people living and breathing, doing nothing but wrong, whilst someone so good, who had done so much for the world, is no longer part of it." He swiped the flask from her hand and indulged in several swallows of liquor.

A small hand touched his and slipped between his fingers.

The unexpected affection made Gérard swallow. He dug his fingers into that hand, wanting to believe her concern was genuine and not..paid for.

He swallowed a mouthful of brandy, hissing out against the sting from swallowing too much. "By the age of fourteen, I was passing out in my room every night. It was not until the butler informed my father why all of the brandy kept going missing that he figured it out. He had it removed from the house, but I still find a way to get it." He shrugged.

She scooted closer, tightening her hold on his hand. "I doubt your mother would have approved of you hurting yourself like this."

Her overly honest observation pinched. "I know."

"Do you?"

He wondered if her concern had been paid for by the lifestyle he was now offering her. He couldn't tell. "I am addressing it." He took another swig.

Releasing his hand, she grabbed hold of the flask. "Addressing it means not drinking it." She pointed at him. "In my opinion, you ought to refrain from even carrying it if it holds this much power over you. What are you doing? You are more than this."

Was he? How did she know?

The haze was already crawling into his head and into his mind. It was nice not to think about anything anymore and to know he had finally found a way to choke out secrets from the Republic. He was exhausted. He was done feeling like every day was his last day and was tired of caring too much for a world that didn't give a damn at all. "I like getting drunk before I retire. It allows me to stop thinking about my life."

She drew the rim of the flask closer to her mouth, brows coming together, and dabbed her tongue against the rim several times. "'Tis overly strong. How can you even drink this on a regular basis?" She paused and dabbed her wet pink tongue on it again.

He stared at her, his body and mouth tingling. Why was his damn flask getting more tongue than he was? He felt bloody underappreciated.

He leaned in, swaying, and tried to kiss her.

A hand popped up between him and his tongue. "You, *Gérard,* are soused. You may kiss me in the morning when you return to reality."

"But I want to kiss you now," he slurred. "I paid for it."

She gave him a withering look. "How about I give you a slap in the face for free? Now leave off and lie down. You are no longer yourself."

Women were so damn predictable. They used every excuse not to have sex. He pushed at her hand and leaned back in exasperation. Diamonds and pearls sure as hell didn't seem to get a man far these days. "How about I get you that zebra then? So I can kiss you?'

She tsked. "If I accept a zebra from you, it means we are heavily involved." She held up the flask in a mock salute. "You may not remember this in the morning, aristo dear, but this is me agreeing to our alliance for however long you need me. May France arise to the level it genuinely deserves: money for everyone."

He blinked against the haze. "Money is for the devil. It makes you think you have everything when in fact you have nothing."

She lifted a blonde brow. "'Tis fairly obvious you need someone to keep you out of trouble. And I know how to keep men out of trouble. I have ten brothers. Now. The sooner we get rid of this brandy, the sooner you have nothing to drink. *Santé!*" Leaning toward the rim of the flask, she lowered her full lips to the edge of it and tilted it back. She kept tilting further back and back, clearly waiting for its contents to find a way out.

He pointed. "Do be...careful. It has a tendency to—"

It filled and spilled well outside of her mouth. She choked, sputtered and gagged, her features twisting as if she were incapable of untwisting it. She dropped the now empty flask and frantically waved at her now tear-streaked face with both hands, trying to be as dainty about it as possible. "Ggggggggg..." She shook her head, over-inflating her cheeks that were still stubbornly filled with the brandy she refused to swallow.

Gérard rumbled out a laugh. She was going to do more than entertain him. She was going to set his damn world on fire if he wasn't careful. He staggered toward her. "Come here." He leaned over and grabbed her face.

She stilled, gaping at him with still puffed cheeks.

He grinned sloppily, taking far too much pleasure in the moment she set up for him. Because he wanted to do more than kiss her. He wanted to make love to her all over again.

"Hold still." His chest tightened as he captured those pinched, soft lips with his mouth.

Gérard leaned all the way back onto the blanket, forcefully dragging her curvaceous body to lie on top of him. His hands dragged down to those large breasts he had gloried in earlier. He inwardly dissolved knowing he was *never* going to forget touching her. Something about her made him want to believe she wanted far more than his money.

He cupped those breasts, rubbing them. He squeezed them. Hard.

She gasped, the brandy in her lips spilling out into his mouth.

He leisurely swallowed what he knew would be the last of whatever brandy he would have until Paris and still holding her face hard, forced her mouth open against his. Tilting her head to one side to better suit him, he tongued her, taking full command of that velvet mouth that tasted of the very thing he loved: brandy.

She grabbed his face and feverishly kissed him back, her tongue moving faster and faster against his. She tugged at his shirt, stuffing her hands beneath to touch his chest.

Christ. *This* was more like it. *This* is what money bought a man. *This.*

Lost in her and what he wanted, he tongued her faster and harder, ready to show her that sex was only the beginning of what he would offer her if she remained true.

He rigidly rolled his hips into and against her thigh to soothe and rub his hard cock that desperately wanted her body again. The urge was too overwhelming.

He flipped her on her back and shoved her skirts up and past her waist. Frantically freeing his thick erection, he found her wet opening and rammed himself deep into that tightness.

She gasped. *"Gérard, for heaven's sake, I...slow down!"*

He glared. "Damn you, woman, I am not one for slow. Maybe you should keep up."

She glared back. "I will end this in two breaths if you do not do it my way."

Point well taken. "Allow me to give the queen her crown." He captured her mouth and slowly tongued her back into submissive silence.

Fighting the more aggressive side of his nature, he skimmed the curves of her body with his hands and in her honor, delivered very slow, very precise smooth pumps into her, letting that sweet tightness squeeze him. While the climax he desperately needed and wanted required pounding into her, he refrained. Barely.

She moaned and arched her hips up and up against him.

He stroked, keeping a rolling, easy pace to ensure she kept moaning.

Her hands jumped to his hair and gripped it hard. She cried out against his mouth, shuddering.

Gritting his teeth, he mindlessly thumped into her and then rammed himself deep into that tight womb in an effort to altogether keep himself from spilling. It was too late. He gasped and spilled his seed, allowing that glorious, glorious sensation of rapture to overtake him.

A hand smacked the side of his head hard, making him wince and roll off to the side.

"Christ, Thérèse, what are you—" Gérard didn't even bother to button his trousers. He heavily flopped his arms to his sides and stared up at the now starry night sky he could see swaying through the branches. "That was hardly necessary."

She sat up and thudded a fist against his chest.

"Stop—" He sat up and sloppily grabbed at her hands, trying to stop her. "What are you doing?"

She stilled, no longer meeting his gaze.

Dragging in a long breath, he tilted his head toward her. "What is it?"

With the flip of her braid, she glared.

"What?" he slurred. "Why are you glaring and hitting me? What did I do?"

"Do you need a list? *First*, you *pound* yourself into a virgin. A virgin. Twice now! As if getting pounded is every woman's fantasy. Second, you—"

His brows went up. "Are you telling me I am a bad lover?"

She pointed. "That is *exactly* what I am telling you."

He snorted. "You would be the first woman to complain."

"Maybe because you were paying them not to," she icily countered.

His breath burned. He sat further up, feeling more than his dignity being slapped and leveled her with a hard stare. "I have no trouble doing it the way *you* want. Go on. Educate me."

She glared. "Oh, I will educate you. I will open a school in your honor. Did no one tell you being rough with a woman during her first few times is likely to rip something?"

Christ. "Did something rip?" he echoed.

"No!"

"Then why the hell scare me like that? I thought I did!" There was no such thing as a perfect woman, was there? "Slow and gentle is for people who know nothing about passion. Without a few bruises, my dear, there are no mementos of what has been. And in my opinion, I *was* gentle. Incredibly so. I simply prefer things a bit rough. Always have. So I suggest you get used to it. Because that body of yours is going to get pounded."

She gasped. "The only thing about to get pounded is your head!" Gritting her teeth, she used her foot to shove him away. "Make room on the blanket knowing you will *never* touch this body again because you obviously know *nothing* about control. And do not *dare* think you can change my mind or your pistols will be put to use well before the Legislative Assembly can get to you."

He hissed out an exasperated breath at the very mention of the Legislative Assembly and grudgingly scooted over, still lying on his back. *Fils de salope.* He just lost fornication rights to the most beautiful woman he ever met.

She corked the flask, using her skirts to dry the silver, and tossed it onto the blanket beside him.

It was obvious she did not enjoy the sex. He puffed out a breath. "Did you not climax?"

She swung her torso toward him. "My climax is not the problem."

"Then what *is* the problem?" he demanded. "Because I cannot address whatever is plaguing you if you intend on—"

"You spilled seed into me!" A faint thread of hysteria overtook her voice. "So much of it, in fact, I think it will continue to run down my legs *for another hour*!"

He swallowed past the haze, gaping at her. Oh, shite. He did not even remember pulling out. Which meant he— Christ.

She glared. "You are a *blaireau*. A *blaireau*!"

A nauseating, sinking feeling seized him knowing he had broken her trust. Usually it was the women who broke their promises. "Thérèse, forgive me," he pressed, trying to better see her face. He wished he hadn't gotten so drunk. "That was..I did not spill intentionally. I..the brandy..I..."

She muttered something and chewed on a fingernail.

He tried to focus through the blur. "I give you permission to deliver as many blows as you need to. Go on. Make yourself..feel better."

Chewing on her nail, she said nothing.

He swallowed. "Thérèse. I have never gotten a woman pregnant." Of course, he hadn't spilled into a woman before. Ever. He never engaged them while drunk *or* without a sheath. What the hell was he doing?

He leaned in close, swaying. He squinted at her. Was she still chewing on her nails? "What are you— Cease doing that. 'Tis hardly becoming."

She held up her finger and then put it back into her mouth, chewing more enthusiastically.

He reached out and tapped her hand. "Enough. Are you a lady or a goat?"

She eyed her finger and pinched her lips.

Women. They always tried to control him when they could barely control themselves. If being a drunk was the worst he could be, he would take it over what most men were.

With his outstretched hand, Gérard grabbed up the flask she tossed, uncorked it and grudgingly tilted it upside down. She had spilled all of it. Christ. He tried corking it several times, but kept missing the rim. He kept trying.

She rolled her eyes, leaned in, swiped the flask and cork from his hands and popped the cork into the rim with the quick hit of her palm. "There." She thrust it back toward him.

Meeting her gaze, he took the flask back and smiled. "You see? You still like me."

She narrowed her gaze.

Maybe not. He sighed. Lifting his head from the blanket just enough to see what he was doing, he carefully tucked it into his leather satchel, closing it. He tucked the entire satchel beneath his heavy head, ensuring its safety through the sway of the world.

Eyeing the thick satchel he rested on, she said, "I saw all those papers earlier. What are you carrying?"

This one just got curious.

To ease some of the coiled tension not even sex and brandy could free him from, he shifted his neck enough to let it crack. He knew it was best she know nothing about the documents. Trust aside, it was for her own safety.

The documents, after all, chronicled disturbing secrets that were going to blow a few massive cannons through the heart of everything the new Republic stood for. That the revolution so many lower classes and *bourgeoisie* were so damn proud of, was being privately led and funded by the very root of its corruption: a fellow aristocrat, the *Duc* d'Orleans.

Gérard had met the man on a few occasions, given they were distant cousins. The sword-swinging, long wigged man had millions in coin to distribute, much like Gérard's family, and was so vile in his personal endeavor for power, he had repeatedly tried to seduce the queen of France. A queen who resisted each and every one of his overambitious advances.

Was it any wonder pamphlets started showing up all across France calling her a whore?

Some of the documents Gérard had in his satchel also detailed how the Bastille had been seized by a disgruntled, angry mob of a thousand who had strangely not all come out of the regular eight hundred thousand inhabitants of Paris. Most had been gathered and hired. The morning of the massacre, more than a dozen witnesses claimed groups of well-dressed men extravagantly tossed countless coins into the gathered crowd, shouting directions and instructions as to what was supposed to happen next.

And that didn't include the greatest lie of all.

The famine had been devised.

While, yes, weather had affected a good number of crops throughout the land, the main allocation of stocked grain had been more than sufficient to feed most of France. The staple of grain, which was usually held by the state itself, had gone missing. Various *assignats* in ledgers found by royal spies were able to determine that the monopoly of grain had been almost entirely bought up by the *Duc* d'Orleans who allocated most of it out of the country.

Conveniently...the man was next in line to be king.

It was a viciously brilliant way of assuming power. Creating a famine manipulated the greatest basic need humanity was willing to fight and die for: food.

After Gérard figured out how to talk to his godfather, he planned on getting the documents into Austria's hands before they were destroyed. For he had a feeling this new grab for power was going to try to erase the truth from the world. An entire generation was going to believe the next set of men in power were going to represent them.

He called horse shite on that.

In the meantime, the less his darling actress knew, the better off she would be. "If I were to tell you what was in this satchel, too many people would want you dead. Which is why you will never ask me about it again. It does not exist. Do you understand?"

Lowering her chin, she stared. "Which means you are in possession of something the Republic will destroy you for."

He smirked drunkenly, wagging a knowing finger. "Exactly. But I intend to destroy them all first. They will not write history. I will."

Her brows flickered and her features now softened with concern. "Do not put yourself in anymore danger than you already are. Wealthy though you may be, you are only one man."

That concern, so soft and genuine, made his chest unexpectedly tighten. He had almost forgotten what it was like to have someone care. He searched her face. "Do you really care? Or are you pretending to care because I am paying for it?"

She said nothing.

He tapped his chest, almost missing it. "Lie here."

She hesitated.

"Thérèse, cease being angry about something that cannot very well be changed. Now come here." Grabbing her waist hard, he yanked her down onto him and with a hand, set her head on his chest.

She stiffened.

He smoothed her hair in assurance, reveling in its silken and rain-softened strands that had yet to dry. "What will be, will be. I will care for you and the babe. I swear it."

Those shoulders and body relaxed. A soft breath escaped her. She tucked herself better against him, her hand circling his waist. "In the morning, when you are yourself again, we will talk," she whispered.

Swallowing hard, he stared up at the blur of stars that peered through the branches of the darkness and wondered if it was at all possible to hold onto her despite his vices.

If anything, he knew his money would make her stay. Either way, she had to. He had entrusted her with too much. Enough to destroy him.

She was bound to him whether she liked it or not.

LESSON SIX

What be this?

A glimpse of what will soon be?

Or a glimpse of what shall soon flee?

-The School of Gallantry

T he sound of a determined boot thudding hard into the ground made her snap open her eyes. Thérèse paused, realizing the dark wool of Gérard's blanket had been folded, tucked and wrapped around her. Her throat tightened, knowing he had done it.

She had agreed to be his own personal actress. And now? This son of a duke was intent on taking far, far more than her body. If she let him, he was going to reach past her breasts and into her chest and rip out her beating heart with one hand and merrily drink his brandy with the other.

Whilst she hadn't given into his original game of 'come-hither-and-play-spy-with-me-while- we-make-love' thinking she would end up finding a husband or love, she was not settling for getting pregnant by a drunk, either. The inn-keeper's wife had dealt with a husband just like it. Sweet, darling, devoted, overly generous, but one who staggered around and drank inventory, completely useless. Reliable only *half* the time.

Scrambling up, she averted her gaze from Gérard, who was still intently scattering last night's charred remains and burying it. She cringed against the soreness between her thighs and tried not to panic knowing he had spilled seed into her.

A child would bind her to this man for life.

Grudgingly removing her stockings, she bundled them and tossed them into her basket. She chalked her teeth in an effort to remove the taste of stale brandy from her mouth and spit out the grit into a pile of leaves.

There. Fresh breath. Now she could take him on without making either of them faint.

Shaking out and folding the blanket that had been wrapped around her, she marched over to him and held it out. "We are lovers no more. You are never touching me again. *Ever.*"

He paused from his endeavor of using leaves and debris to cover the char, his steel blue eyes capturing hers.

Their startling clarity assured her he was the man she first met. The brandy was gone.

He didn't take the blanket. He simply turned his tall, broad frame toward her and stepped in close. "Good morrow to you, too," he rumbled out.

Thérèse dragged in a breath, determined not to let those gorgeous eyes or that good-looking rugged face sway her. She wagged the blanket, pushing it into his chest. "Your drinking is a problem, Gérard. And I think you know that. The man I met yesterday morning was capable of being everything I could have ever wanted in a man. As for the man I met last night? It was like being at sea with a pirate who drank a barrel of rum and decided he wanted to have a baby."

Gérard leaned toward her. His voice softened. "Try to keep your voice civil, *mon ange.* My head hurts. I promise to make it up to you. When we get to Paris, whatever you want, I will ensure you get it."

She gasped. "Is that how you usually deal with women? You buy off their anger?"

He lingered.

God keep her from strangling him. "What you did last night was *irresponsible*. You are not allowed to touch me again." She held his gaze. "Because I need someone I can depend on all the time. Not half the time. Are we understood in this?"

His features darkened. "Are you saying we are done?"

"As lovers, yes. Our alliance, however, will stand. Because unlike you, I always keep my end of the bargain. I also need money and a career if I am ever to survive in a world you men continue to stupidly dominate. My only hope is that when I do have to send you that blue ribbon, you actually show up sober." She rattled the blanket at him, trying to keep her voice calm. "Now take your blanket. Because I am walking to Paris. The last thing I want or need is to ride on your lap for over an hour."

His expression stilled. "You belong to me now, Thérèse. Me. Because you said yes to me. Do you remember? You said yes. Not *suppose*. You said *yes*. And in saying yes to me, you are no longer allowed to say no."

Oh, this was going well. She had said yes to fornicating and now had no life.

She narrowed her gaze and hardened her tone. "I cannot and will not belong to a man who does not respect my body."

His brows went up. "Whatever are you— I respect your body."

She gave him a withering look. "Not when you are drunk."

He swiped his face with a hand. "If you are with child, I will take full responsibility."

She angled toward him. "Damn right you will. If I am with child, you had better believe, I am no longer playing mistress. You will marry me. You will take me straight to church and make the whole world stand up to see it. Why? So they can clap and call me duchess. Because my child, *Gérard,* will *not* be growing up scorned by society. Not when all of France is already going to hell."

His voice quieted. "Thérèse. I cannot marry you given who I am. Even if I set aside my own distaste for the sort of marriage society approves of, my father would never allow for it. And he..the man is not right in the head since my mother died. But I can and will provide for you. You and our babe will never want for anything. I promise."

Thérèse stared. "So you will only throw money at me and the child? And nothing else? Is that what you are saying? Despite the fact that you spilled yourself entirely into me *knowing* I had not wanted children at all?"

He said nothing.

Gritting her teeth, she jumped toward him and punched his arm. "*That* is what I think of you and your brandy. *That!*"

He lingered for a moment, then grabbed the blanket and tossed it into the forest. Muttering something, he stalked away, the long tails of his coat shifting against the movement of his body. Tightening the straps on the last of his belongings to the horse, he grabbed the saddle and swung himself up onto it.

Gathering the reins, he said in a low hard tone, "If you wish to walk to Paris, so be it. Simply know that I will follow you by horse while you walk. Regardless of whether we ever share a bed again matters not to me. What does matter is that I confided in you, and as such, you and I are bound for however long this revolution lasts. So get used to it. Get used to seeing my face. Because I am now yours. Brandy and all."

She had no one to blame but herself. She wanted to be wealthy and famous, and now she would have it all, *including* a baby but *no* husband.

May she never lust for another man again.

"We will address this again if the need arises." Whipping out the velvet mask from his pocket, he unfolded it, still holding her gaze. "*Sa Majesté* needs me. I am therefore depending on you to help me save him and his family. And because the people I love have a tendency to die, I have to ensure he lives even if it means *I* die. And that is the sort of devotion I offer you despite my being a drunk. How many men do you know would take on all of France to save the life of a man everyone despises? *How many?*"

Her chest tightened. Not a single one.

Tying on his mask, he adjusted it over his eyes and nose. "No one can know who is behind this mask. And I mean no one. I am entrusting you to protect my name when we ride into Paris and expect you to be the ever brilliant actress I hired and convince everyone I am nothing more than a highwayman who came to your rescue. Can you do that?"

"I suppose."

He glared. "What did I tell you about 'suppose'? Never and none of that. It is either yes or no. Which is it?"

This man was going to end more than her career. "*Yes*. You are now a highwayman."

"Thank you." He snapped out a rigid hand. "Now get up here, Thérèse. And do not test me. Because I am not leaving you to walk to Paris. Especially if you are pregnant with my child. I would sooner take you by force. And I will. Is that what you want?"

A breath escaped her. She could continue to parade her pride and walk to Paris for who knows how many hours or..she could be there in an hour with a masked drunk who was gruff, stubborn, animalistic, yet..darling.

Life was so unfair.

She grabbed up her basket. "There is no need for threats. I hardly wanted to walk."

"I am glad to hear it." He set his shoulders. "What street in Paris are we riding to? So I know what road to take."

"*Rue St. Antoine*. Number Twenty-two."

His brows shot up as he veered his gaze toward her. "Hell on earth. Are you— That is a spit-fall from the Bastille."

Well, well. He knew the city. And not just the wealthy sections. "Yes, I know. Apparently, it started bringing quite a bit of traffic past the theatre and is making my cousin incredibly popular. He calls it free advertising."

"Christ. I..." Gérard dismounted the horse, still muttering. "I will ensure I get you into *Théâtre Française* as soon as possible. Before you end up dead. Free advertising, indeed." Without asking for permission, he grabbed her corseted waist and effortlessly lifted her onto the saddle so she sat as a lady should. Hoisting himself up behind her, his large hands yanked her possessively against himself as he grabbed the reins and positioned them both into the saddle.

His unshaven chin brushed against her braided hair, causing her bonnet to tilt forward.

The heat and flex of hard muscles at her back made her pulse roar. It was like sitting against a rock at the bottom of a valley. She tightened her hold on the basket, feeling squeezed.

"Are you comfortable?" he rumbled out.

She tried to push back her bonnet with a hand, but his head kept pushing it forward. She leaned forward in exasperation. "Not really. We are sharing one saddle."

He tsked. "If only this mere steed were a zebra, you might appreciate its breadth." He cued the horse into moving.

"I find your humor sorely lacking this morning."

"I was not placed on this earth to entertain you, my dear."

"Oh, well, thank goodness for *that* or I would have died of boredom by now."

"Are you done nagging me?"

"Quite."

They trotted through the remaining forest and out into the open fields, the cool wind rushing at their faces. The sun brightened the expanse of the blue sky, pushing away the few remaining dark clouds that had disappeared toward the horizon.

He tightened his muscled hold around her, one arm resting dominantly beneath her breasts.

She swallowed, her breaths growing more and more uneven. He was holding his arm beneath her breasts. Was he doing it on purpose? Or was she being overly suspicious?

They kept riding, the pace of the horse remaining steady.

Pushing down on his arm so it wasn't quite so close her breasts, she eventually offered, "I appreciate the ride." It was the right thing to say.

"Are you still angry with me?"

"Yes."

"Be nice to me while you can. I may not be here tomorrow. Have you thought of that?"

She stared out at the dirt road before them, her body swaying against the quicker movements of the horse. Her throat tightened. How was it she already cared what happened to him? How was it— "What if I am with child?"

"Then you are. We cannot very well change that. Either way, I will not abandon my responsibilities."

Was he too blind not to see the horizon? "If we take on the Republic and anything goes wrong, the babe will have no father."

He seethed out a breath and trailed his hand farther beneath her breasts, better positioning her. "I do not plan on dying, *ma biche*. I have survived too much in life to die." His large fingers cupped one side of her breast.

She stilled. "Must you grope me?"

His head leaned in and down from behind her. "I am keeping you from falling off the horse. Would you rather I let go?" His lips brushed against her ear and cheek twice.

She almost fainted against the warmth of those full lips nudging in with the heat of his breath. Because it reminded her of what those lips were capable of. "Can you not lean in so close?"

He shifted sideways. "Would you prefer to straddle me from behind?"

"Straddling will not be necessary."

"Are you certain? You could..oh..hitch up your skirts and wrap your legs around me. And seeing you do not plan on giving me anymore *poom-poom*, I would like that."

She tried glaring back at him, but annoyingly, her bonnet kept bumping into his face and head. And she *still* couldn't see past the large straw rim to be able to glare at him.

Releasing the rein he was holding, he reached around her and yanked on the ribbon beneath her chin hard, tugging it loose.

She tried slapping his quick-moving hand away. "What are you—"

He grabbed her bonnet and whipped it aside, sending it fluttering behind them onto the road. "*There.* Now you can glare at me all you want."

"Did you just—" She turned her shoulder and head toward him. "I rather liked that bonnet. I—" She captured his gaze, realizing their faces were almost cheek to cheek. Her heart skid.

Why was it even her pulse betrayed her? What was it about this man that made her want to give him everything every time she looked at him?

His jaw tightened. His blue eyes through the slits of the velvet mask flicked past her features back to the road ahead of them. "What was it you were going to say? It seemed important."

She stiffly turned back. "It was not."

"Ah."

They rode in silence for a long time. So long, the dirt path turned into a cobbled one and sloped them down a small hill leading toward a massive sprawl of overcrowded buildings with smoking chimneys that stretched beyond sight in and around a river.

Paris. Her eyes widened. It looked nothing like the city she used to visit.

Random, billowing black plumes of burning buildings smeared and hazed the vast blue-grey sky, blocking any view of the valley beyond it.

"Are those fires from the riots?" she rasped in disbelief.

"Yes." He sighed. "New ones break out every few weeks depending on the mood these idiots are in. I keep writing to the Legislative Assembly about it, but they do nothing. They encourage it. Which tells you they care nothing about the people. Because they are putting everyone in danger. *Everyone.*"

A shaky breath escaped her. "France has lost the last of its mind thinking it can burn down Paris. After all, who under heaven is going to be able to *live* in that city once everything is burned? Maybe I ought to visit a few places before it all goes."

"I would," he muttered. "I plan to leave France once I oversee this mess. Because there will be nothing but ash left by the time they are done." He was quiet for a moment. "Maybe you and I could go to Russia together? You know..see those Russians chew glass? I could wrap you up in furs and take you through the snow of Saint Petersburg. We could even live there for a while. Would you like that?" The tips of his gloved fingers nudged away her braid from her shoulder, grazing her throat. He skimmed her shoulder.

A shiver rippled through her body straight down to her inner thighs.

This man was dangerous. He knew how to make her body and her soul tingle in too many places. He knew how to control her very breath.

She couldn't allow herself to love him. She couldn't. For she knew full well what happened to women who knelt to *real* passion. Her poor mother ended up with eleven children because of it. Something she swore she would never do. Even the idea of one child scared her.

She had *always* been ungovernable in nature. Having sex with a complete stranger was proof of that. But she certainly didn't need to push herself into the realm of insanity by falling in love with a man intent on putting out the fires of Paris with his bare hands.

She gently tapped his gloved hand. "I would rather you not do that."

His hand stilled against her arm. "I would be forever grateful, *ma biche,* if you could forgive me. I will refrain from ever drinking around you again."

Damn him for wanting to amble into *her* life with promises he wouldn't be able to keep. "It will take more than a promise. I have met men like you back in Giverny. There is not an hour you do not think about drinking your beloved brandy."

"True, but—" He nudged her. "I thought you wanted those diamonds and those pearls."

Of all the—

He shifted against her. "I was thinking."

"Should I be worried knowing that?"

He flicked a finger at her shoulder. "Cease being rude. I was thinking you and I ought to...well..get to know each other more. Outside of being lovers. If we become parents, after all, we *should* be on good terms for the sake of our child. Do you not think?"

Why did he have to be a drunk? He was too beautiful for that. "Perhaps I am not ready to get to know a man who has no desire of ever marrying me even if I do end up pregnant."

He sighed. "Thérèse. My father would never allow for it. His disdain for the lower classes aside, he and I barely get along. He forgives me nothing and holds everything against me. Everything."

A breath escaped her knowing he was not on good terms with his father. Whilst, yes, she had left her own family behind in less than good circumstance, they had all loved each other very much. She knew her parents would eventually forgive her. In a year or two or three. That was what people did when they sought to love each other.

They.. forgave each other.

She paused. He *wanted* her to love him and forgive him anything. And he *wanted* to do it in a most unconventional way: without any guarantees of her ever seeing matrimony.

He hesitated. "Honor me by giving me another chance, Thérèse. Please. The very thought of not ever being able to kiss you again is..."

She closed her eyes, determined not to be swayed. "I am not interested in ending up with a child after raising ten of them for my parents." She opened her eyes. "This is my time to finally embrace everything I want out of life and I will not expose my body to your drunken advances that are clearly unreliable."

He gripped her waist hard. "I will never engage you whilst drunk again. I swear it."

"Even if you could uphold such a promise, we are both overly passionate and such things are not bound to end well." Her throat tightened. "What if we become too attached to each other? What happens then? There is danger in us wanting each other too much. Especially given who you are. You are third cousin to the king!"

His voice darkened. "I hardly need to be reminded who I am."

A shaky breath escaped her. This was getting too complicated for them to even try to make it work. "I am giving you permission to engage other women."

He said nothing.

His silence poked her into asking the one thing that had bothered her all of last night. "How many others were there before me?"

He shifted in the saddle, adjusting her against himself. "Four."

"Were you in love with any of these women?"

"One." He was quiet for a long moment. "She was married. Her name was..Madame Poulin."

She blinked. "Did you know she was married?"

He dug his chin into her head. "No. I have a stupid tendency to let passion blur common sense."

A vivid flash of seeing his nude body and bunched muscles savagely pounding his hips into another woman made her want to smack him off the horse for making her jealous. She hated being made to feel as if she was fourteen.

Tightening her hold on her basket, she coolly offered, "Was she pretty?"

"Not as pretty as you," he breathed out against her ear.

She unwittingly tilted her ear into those lips that clearly sought to lure her. "I assume it ended badly."

"More than you will ever know." He heaved out a breath. "The whole thing was staged by her husband. She was coerced into making me believe our relationship was real. The whole moon and the stars sort of nonsense. After she and I fell into bed a few times, her husband made himself known and demanded half a million *livres* from my father."

Thérèse felt her throat tighten in disbelief.

His tone became ragged. "This mudsill of a tailor had the audacity to tell me if I did not pay it in full, he would publicly demand satisfaction. My father was anything but understanding. When I told Poulin to piss off, the man demanded satisfaction, and in an effort not to kill the *fils de salope*, I aimed at his leg. Only I shot off his hand. A hand he can no longer use to support his family. So he and the wife I thought I knew and loved, along with their three children, ended up in an almshouse because of me. So what did I do? I gave them ten thousand to ensure they lived well. And they do. Believe me, they still do. They have carriages and a house and go shopping for things they do not need and merrily live off my guilt going on a few years now. Just like they planned. And the best part? This tailor now stands on the street with a sign that says, '*The Duc of Andelot's son raped my wife and took my trade and my hand.*'"

Her heart skidded. She jerked her head toward him, her lips parting in disbelief.

He didn't meet her gaze. "He parades my shame, after he and his wife orchestrated it, openly spits on my name thinking I deserve nothing less. And *that* is the direction this country is going in. *That* is why this city is burning. Because some people would rather see everything burn than admit we are all equal in our sins. Long live your kind and the revolution."

Tears stung her eyes. "He is not my kind."

He shifted his jaw, still refusing to look at her.

She swallowed. Holding up a trembling hand, she gently touched the side of his masked face, wishing he was not wearing it. "I am ever so sorry that was done to you."

He shrugged. "I suppose I earned it."

"How can you say that?"

He said nothing.

Maybe this was why she came into his life. Brandy aside, he clearly lacked the faith in trying to save himself because he was too busy saving the world. "I appreciate you sharing that with me. I cannot imagine it was easy to say aloud."

He tugged her closer against himself, tightening his hold on her to the point of digging his fingers into her gown and the skin beneath. "Paris is ahead. I suggest you listen as I will not have a chance to repeat myself lest we risk someone overhearing it."

He gripped her braid and wagged its end. "I will take you straight to your cousin's theatre, after which we will no longer see very much of each other. My mask will come off and I will resume my regular way of life. In the next few days, a dark-eyed gentleman by the name of Serge Naudet will call on you. Only he will know of our association. So trust no one but him. Aside from delivering you money, Naudet will supply a weekly list of people you ought to talk to and will funnel whatever messages you and I have for each other. Do you remember the address where the blue ribbon is supposed to go to if you need me?"

This all became too real. "Yes. Five Luxembourg."

"Good." He released her braid. "As for us, the next time we see each other, we will no longer be allowed to be anything to each other but strangers in public, so I suppose you and I are lovers no more, much like you want. In truth, I hardly earned it and ask that you not forgive me. I have to learn to be more responsible."

Her throat tightened. Now she felt bad.

Dragging in a breath, Thérèse nestled herself against his broad, muscled frame trying not to revel in his warmth *too* much. It was so odd to think that she, a mere daughter of a third generation butcher, was riding into Paris on a steed in the arms of an aristocrat worth ten million.

This revolution was creating a form of equality even she had not been prepared to embrace.

LESSON SEVEN

Paris glitters with countless opportunities

anyone can touch. Touching those opportunities,

however, does involve a bit of misadventure.

-The School of Gallantry

The dense, angled cobbled streets were so overcrowded with people, the horse had to be guided off the actual road and through narrow pathways in between torched buildings and small courtyards strewn with shattered glass, bricks and charred pieces of furniture.

Men and women in bundled rags gathered before the small window of a dilapidated print shop where an unshaven man in a red cap bearing a tricolor cockade, stood on a wooden crate with a newly printed pamphlet. He shook it at those around him.

"Despite countless pleas from our own voices at the esteemed Assembly, our basic needs are *still* not being addressed!" he yelled. "It says here due to the continued shortage of food, all bread prices will remain the same. At fifteen *sous* a loaf. Fifteen! What, *I ask you,* are these loaves made of? *Sa Majesté's breeches*?! Or the queen's two tits?"

Laughter and disgruntled shouts echoed within the narrow space of the street.

Gérard shifted his jaw, chanting to himself that beating the blood out of a man for insulting his godparents was pointless. Because then these strutting turkeys would only cluck to each other about how *violent* aristocrats were toward them.

Which was why he trained his pride to ride by the jargon and never engage. He was not his father who always got into the faces of these people on the street.

He also wasn't alone.

In truth, he barely noticed the rumbling chaos the way he usually did. How could he? His hands were sweating beneath his gloves and his body felt as if it was being assaulted by fire. Even after everything that had been said between them, the woman still nestled against him as if they were back to being on good terms.

She was exhausting the hell out of him.

With her blonde head tucked against his chest and the warm softness of her voluptuous body folded into his arms, all he could think of was how the hell he was going to survive not making love to her body again.

Thérèse sat up against him, bumping his chin and pointed at the young man yelling about the bread prices. "Whatever is that idiot wearing?" she echoed. "He has *no* sense of fashion. Absolutely none. That red hat makes him look like a troll."

Gérard choked, grabbed her hand and lowered it against her thigh in reprimand. "Try not to get us into trouble."

She paused. "Am I not allowed to comment on what people wear? Pardon me for being a woman. I notice these things and most men have no fashion sense. At all."

He kept pushing the horse through the crowds. Everything coming out of her mouth was an adventure. More than he needed. "That cap signifies he is in support of the new Republic. Do not comment or try to engage them, because they are all like roaches. Where there is one, there is a hundred. And whilst I wish I could boast that my fighting skills are that of God, I cannot very well fight a hundred men on my own and in your honor. Do you understand?"

Concern edged into her voice. "They would try to fight us? Merely because I commented on his sense of fashion?"

Gérard tightened his jaw in an attempt to remind himself she was new to what was happening in Paris. "Any comment can be construed as you supporting *Sa Majesté*. So never comment on those caps. *Ever.* These bastards are bold. They forget they still have a king. Be he in prison or not, he still lives."

A boisterous group of young men sharing what appeared to be several large bottles of stolen champagne out of a crate, paused in unison. Some shifted against the brick wall they were propped against. The entire group stared at them.

Or rather.. they stared at Thérèse.

All fourteen of them.

Gérard instinctively tightened his arms around her and veered his horse to the other side of the street. He cued his horse into a quicker pace lest he start shooting their eyes out.

A few whistled as others nudged each other to keep looking.

One of the young men holding a bottle of champagne, stumbled forward, gaping up at them as he tried to keep up with their horse. "My heart will never be the same." He set a dirt-crusted hand on his narrow chest and scrambled forward, his scuff-whitened boots trying to keep up as he held up the bottle he held. "*Mademoiselle*, my heart tells me we have met before. In a dream, I dare say! And in that dream, I knelt before you and kissed your hand well over a dozen times after you promised to be mine. Marry me, so we may have a dozen children as beautiful as you!"

Gérard's lips parted. He didn't know what astounded him more. Seeing men act like buffoons after a mere glance at Thérèse or the fact it *bothered* him knowing other men were interested in *being* buffoons in her honor. Whilst, yes, she was *insanely* attractive, and he himself had trouble resisting, he thought she had been exaggerating about the men.

She wasn't even on stage yet. Shite. "Step away," he rumbled out in warning.

The young blond only kept running beside them at a sprint, glancing up at Thérèse. "What is your name, *mon amour?*" he called. "Assure me this outdated fop is not your husband or I will take a pistol to my head for it! He does not even appear to be capable of providing you shoes!"

Jésus. Gérard glared down at the man, trying to keep the horse at a respectable pace so they wouldn't fall off. "Being capable of providing her shoes is not my problem," he delivered through teeth. "So I suggest you keep sucking on that champagne and leave off. Leave off, or I will damn well jump off this horse and—"

Thérèse elbowed him hard. "There is no need, Gérard. Allow me." She leaned slightly toward the blond still running beside them and primly offered in a honeyed voice, "Come see me at the opening night of 'The Delights of Life' this Friday evening at *Spetacle des Variétés Amusantes* on *Rue St. Antoine.* It will be short-lived given I will be going on to a bigger stage, so bring all of your friends, and I promise to sing a song for you and only you." She scrunched her nose in an excessive form of flirtation and then blew him an ardent kiss with the pucker of lips.

Gérard sucked in an astounded breath at her tasteless attempt to advertise her cousin's theatre.

The youth stumbled and grabbed at the air as if she had actually thrown something. "I will be there with all of Paris, *mon amour!*" He turned back to his friends and jerking to a halt, guzzled more champagne that dribbled down his unshaven chin before throwing up an arm in mocking triumph. "*Long live the Republic and its beautiful women whom I adore!*"

Gérard shifted his jaw in a riled attempt not to get off the horse and use all five of his pistols to show what he thought of this new Republic. Barely a few weeks earlier, he had saved a young woman from being raped by a massive man who held her face to the ground shouting, '*Prove yourself to the Republic!*' He almost killed the son of a bitch. Given there were too many others watching, however, Gérard could only grudgingly rope the bastard to a lamp post after a few good kicks to the head and demanded no one untie him for a week. It won him an applause and even a few pats on the back, despite him being an aristo.

Of course, *this* champagne-guzzling dunce had been encouraged. By Thérèse, no less.

He half-shook her. "What the devil are you doing? If you think I am incapable of control, you just introduced yourself to rape with that one. Christ, you— That was tasteless and uncalled for. Are you telling me you always tweak your nose at every man in the name of making money?"

She glared. "Of course not. But what was I to do? Let you fight some halfling in my honor whilst thirteen others watched and would have joined in? I was protecting you, is all. How is that wrong?"

His pulse hitched. Why did he like knowing she had protected him? It had to mean she had a bit of regard for him. Maybe even more than a bit. "You do realize that idiot will expect to see you now."

She patted his forearm. "And he most certainly will. *After* he pays for it. I can afford to give him two minutes after the show and toss a song at him. It is what an actress does. After he gets his song, he gets escorted straight out of the building by burly men with knives Rémy hires to protect his talent. My cousin told me all about how they deal with unwanted admirers. So you need not worry."

She pushed her braid over her shoulder, smacking his face and glanced back at him, her large blue eyes brightening in earnest. "Advertising to the right people is the only way to ensure Rémy's success. And his success is my success. And my success is *your* success. I cannot very well gather the information you want by treating these men with disdain, can I?"

Everything about this woman made him want to grab her face and kiss her until neither of them knew the difference between heaven or hell. He wanted to rip her gown in half, leave bite marks on that skin and—

She still peered up at him from over her shoulder. "Why are you looking at me like that?"

His nostrils flared in an attempt not to do all the things he was thinking. "I am not looking at you at all."

She smirked, her eyes brightening. "Oh, yes you are." She set her chin. "Admit it. Without me, you are *nothing*."

It was obvious she was well aware of how much control she had over him and was glorying in it. Gérard jerked her against his body as tight as he could so they were both aware of what his body was capable of.

"Without me," he returned in a growling tone, "you are *also* nothing. I suggest you remember that when I drape diamonds and pearls on your neck."

Her chest rose and fell against his hand. "You are pinching my skin."

He swallowed and eased his grip. "Forgive me."

She puffed out a breath. "You almost popped both of my breasts out of my corset."

"I beg to differ. They do that on their own. I suggest buying yourself a larger corset with the money I give you."

She elbowed him hard.

He rolled his eyes and glanced out toward passing buildings.

A large wooden plaque with the words *Spetacle des Variétés Amusantes* made his brows go up and his lips part. He slowed his horse to a halt. The sign, boasting crudely painted but shapely female legs in red wool stockings, was affixed to the façade of the building with more nails than was needed. A long line of men – and *only* men – waited to purchase tickets.

A dark-haired gent selling the tickets, busily went from person to person, collecting coins in exchange for the papers he ripped. "Hold onto that there ticket, *citoyen*." He pointed to the single door painted red. "No entries today but nay do fear. Friday at seven will be the first of this showing, and not a single one of you will want to miss it! New talent this time. New talent. Come see the new face of the future Republic. With but a glance, she will steal what little you have of your heart!"

The man enthusiastically kept nodding and going down the line as others left with their tickets. He tapped his bright blue felt hat forward, displaying the tri-colored cockade pinned to it and flicked it with a bare finger. "If any of you gents need yourselves a cockade, I most certainly sell those, too. They are in a crate inside. Buy three, and this here ticket is free, free, free."

It was obvious the man was a peddler of all trades.

That bright blue hat was seriously mismatched against the man's foppish striped green and pink clothing. Clothing that was much too tight for his stocky frame. Everything bulged in all the wrong places in an attempt to free the rolls of fat beneath. Even the stretching flap on his trousers appeared to want to rip the buttons off.

"*Rémy!*" Thérèse called out, cupping the side of her mouth with a hand. "Look at this bit of *bourgeoisie* coming into town! I arrived on my own steed!" She set her shoulder and chin toward him to better display herself on the horse she sat on. "And I have this lusty highwayman to thank! He made love to me twice!"

Gérard choked as every burly man, including the ticket seller, known as her cousin, turned in unison to gape. "What are you—"

She elbowed him. "Play along."

"Right." Leaning back, he grudgingly slid off the horse and landed onto the cobbled street with a thud. He ensured his mask stayed in place by tugging at the binding and knot behind his head twice. Removing the satchel which held the documents, he bound it tightly around his shoulder and chest to ensure it was protected.

He wasn't in the forest anymore.

Without meeting her gaze, he tied the horse to the lamppost with the leather reins. Taking her basket, he set it onto the uneven pavement leading to the entrance of the small theatre and reached up for her waist. "Lean toward me, if you please."

She pertly leaned toward him to make the descent possible. "Like *so?*"

The tops of her round, large breasts pushed against the fabric of her décolletage, giving him an overly generous display that made him all too aware that if he willed it, they could be his. Every night. For the rest of his life.

His chest tightened. "You did that on purpose."

Her mouth quirked. "Enjoy the view while you can."

It was like she was putting on a far bigger show than he wanted.

Grabbing her, he lowered her and settled her bare feet onto the pavement, releasing her. He leaned in. "Try not to overexert yourself, dearest."

"You paid for it."

He shifted his jaw, wishing she would let him see past the tawdry actress she always seemed to play. "Is this who you really are? Is money all you aspire to acquire?"

Her ocean blue eyes softened and took on the persona of someone he had yet to meet. She leaned in close. "If money was all I aspired to acquire, I would have never kissed you."

He swiped at his mouth in an effort to keep calm. He could tell she meant it. Leaning in close, he whispered, "Be careful. Never allow yourself to be alone with any of these men. They will only want one thing from you."

"The same thing you did?"

He stared her down, his heart pounding. "I will ensure nothing happens to you. I will be watching over you even when you think I am not."

She searched his masked face, her features softening. "I appreciate that." She hesitated. "Despite what I said earlier—" A breath escaped her. "Maybe we can still make time for each other outside of all this smoke and fire business. We probably should get to know each other."

He angled toward her and almost grabbed her face and kissed her, sensing she was giving him another chance. She was.. forgiving him. "I would like that."

A few whistles from the man standing in line drifted toward them. "Show us that there talent, *citoyenesse*! Come now and lift that skirt and shake an ankle at us!"

Gérard rigidly swung toward the men who were rattling their tickets and legs toward her. His gloved hands fisted.

"*Refrain* and say nothing." She squeezed his arm hard. "Welcome to the elaborate farce known as my life. Men act like this around me even when there is no stage. And that, *mon grand*, is a sad truth I have long accepted." She patted his arm one last time. "Until we meet again..." She sashayed past and over to her cousin, abandoning the basket she left at his booted feet.

A breath escaped Gérard as he watched her shapely figure make its way toward the crowd of men. Her derriere swayed beneath the wool fabric of her skirts tauntingly matching the jiggle of her corseted breasts. He almost bit his hand in an attempt not to keep looking at it.

She spread her slim arms wide, greeting the long line of men as a beautiful melody, almost too lush and perfect to be real, suddenly breezed from her lips. "I have at last found *loooove*..and now that I have seen what it can *dooooo*..all I will ever ask..is that you *neveeeer* break *my heart*..in..*twooooo*."

Gérard couldn't breathe.

Everything about her was surreal. It made him want to believe in the beauty of everything again. A beauty he didn't think existed amongst the chaos of Paris and his life. And twisted though it was, he...well..he actually *wanted* her to be pregnant. Just so he could see her singing to their child at night, its small head peacefully cradled in the crook of her ivory arm.

He had never thought he would ever want that. Ever.

There was a moment of stunned silence, which Gérard shared in, followed by a roar of men hollering and clapping feverishly as they scrambled toward her.

He swallowed. This woman was going to make him kneel to far more than he was ready for. He could feel it. He could see it. He could taste it. She was full of so much mettle and warmth and wit, it was spilling onto the very pavement she walked on.

It made him want to worship and adore even her shadow.

Rémy jumped toward her with a playful half-squat and pointed. "Ah, now, *there she is!* The Republic's greatest talent and the *only* cousin I have who can shake more than a fist!" He grabbed her and folded his thick arms around her tightly, swaying her. He kissed the top of her head twice then grabbed her hand and quickly ushered her past the whistles, toward the door. "I say we give these animals time to regain themselves after *that* performance. I have cheese and wine on the table right off stage. Go greet the girls you will be working with inside."

Edging forward, Gérard mentally willed her to look at him before she went inside. To give him a whisper of hope that beyond their alliance there could be..more. More than the sex. More than what he had ever shared with any woman.

She excitedly chatted with Rémy, giggling about something and tapping his shoulder.

Not once did she look his way. Not even once. Resentment bit into him. It was as if they had never fallen asleep in each other's arms under the stars.

Opening the door wide, Rémy revealed a candlelit parlor unevenly draped with shoddy, smalt- colored fabric. Women garbed in floor-length robes peered out from where they lounged on chairs. Thérèse was ushered inside as men scrambled to look at her, bending far forward and whistling.

Gérard wanted to beat the pulp out of every last one of them.

Thérèse turned against the hands of her cousin and enthusiastically blew the men kisses as if she knew each and every one of them. "Friday night, I shall see you all!" She pertly kept at it, blowing more and more kisses to ensure no one felt left out.

Why did he feel like all of this was a very bad idea?

Something told him if he allowed her to enter the theatrical world, and play the dangerous game he was instructing her to play, this bright-eyed girl who literally gave him a slice of heaven in the silence of the forest would be taken from him. She would be swallowed by lies and lust-ridden admirers. He would never be able to compete with them, because it was obvious money was only a sliver of what this creature wanted.

She wanted to be esteemed and loved in the grandest manner possible. And she was using her beauty and talent to get it.

So what now?

Did he have her coo at men so he could save his godfather and help other aristocrats? Or should he yank her from the stage and find another way? But what other way? Even if he set aside his belief that marriage was nothing but a legal document, he was not the spare anymore. He was not able to marry into whatever social circle pleased him. Because equality did not break the foundation of what his father and his ancestors and lineage expected of him and the name. He was heir. And with his father's deeply rooted loathing of the lower classes and *bourgeoisie*, the man would never—

Merde. As always, Gérard would have to keep living one life for his father and the other for himself. He stalked over to her basket she had abandoned on the pavement and removed the additional leather satchel attached at his waist, opening the strings on it. He emptied all of his coins into it and covered it with her gown. Now she had well over two thousand. Not just the one. He quickly tied his satchel back on and carried it to the door she had entered.

Rémy swung toward him and put up a hand, his features becoming all too playful. "Whether you delivered her on a steed or not, *citoyen*, you and that mask still have to wait until Friday for the performance."

Well over a dozen faces now stared him down, collectively announcing they would see to it.

There was nothing in the world like Paris to make a rich man feel poor.

Gérard inclined his head. "I would never dare impose. I am merely delivering the basket she left behind. Am I allowed to see her one last time and return it to her?"

Rémy eyed the basket and puffed out a breath. "That girl will one day be the death of me. And the worst of it? She knows it." Tapping his blue felt hat back with a thumb, he yelled over his shoulder. "*Thérèse!* Your highwayman seems to think he can continue making love to you right in front of a crowd. Is there something I ought to know?"

Thérèse hurried out and settling herself beside her cousin, sighed and took the wicker basket. "Oh, dear." Those azure eyes mockingly met his. She tsked. "Will you look at this besotted fool? He thinks he stands a chance because he was kind enough to keep me from walking all the way to Paris."

Ouch. Why did this feel real?

She gave Gérard a look of pity before turning to her cousin. "As much as I would like you to toss him on his nose, Rémy, given he robs people for a living, that would be rude. And you and I both know being rude will never resolve anything. So give this unshaven, outdated gallant a free ticket in honor of us being related. 'Tis the polite thing to do."

Rémy's brow furrowed. "A free ticket?" He glanced at Gérard and then at her. "*Thérèse*. Setting aside that he robs people for a living, and can probably afford said ticket, this here is a business. Every time I give away a free ticket, I lose more than respect."

She leaned in and nuzzled her cousin's shaven oversized cheek with the tip of her nose. "If you give him a free ticket, I promise I will make you whatever you want for supper tonight. I know how much you love freshly made beef *bourguignon*."

Rémy paused, setting a large hand on his protruding belly. "Beef *bourguignon?*"

"Oh, yes," she cooed. "With carrots and potatoes. Like your mother always used to make. Remember how we used to eat straight out of the cauldron?"

Rémy hissed out a breath and grudgingly smoothed a hand over her braid. "You always did know me best in our family. And I always give into you because of it. One of these days, you will be the—"

"Death of you, I know, I know." She grinned. "What is a ticket to you or him anyway? If all the men in the theatre beat up on him or kill him due to his profession in life that will no longer be our problem but his. Right?"

Gérard's pulse roared in disbelief. Her acting was a little *too* good.

Rémy grudgingly held out a ticket toward him. "Here. In honor of what you did. Though I suggest you bring more than a pistol if you plan on making it through the entire show. We here do not approve of robbing anyone. Not even those that deserve it. The world is insane enough."

Everyone around him widened their stance as several men whispered to each other behind bare hands that had been visibly battered.

It was like receiving an admission to one's funeral. "*Merci, citoyen*." Taking the ticket, Gérard crushed it in his gloved hand, knowing the more distance he kept from Thérèse, the better off they would both be.

She averted her gaze and disappeared back inside.

A breath escaped him. He would miss the woman he met in the forest.

THE DUKE OF ANDELOT | 105

LESSON EIGHT

Love and lust, lust and love,

to find out which is why,

one must simply give into trust.

-The School of Gallantry

Fourteen days later – well past midnight
At a masked ball celebrating the instatement of the National Convention

Between the slits of her gold-painted mask, Thérèse did her best to navigate through the crowds of people gathered in the great hall. She angled her body to better squeeze through drunken men and women who staggered and laughed with crooked masks.

Someone swatted her derriere twice. "Is that padding or your bum?" a man slurred from behind. He gathered her skirts, trying to shove them up.

She gasped and swung toward the man who was fumbling to adjust his elephant mask in between grabbing her skirts. Stepping toward him, she whipped off his mask, to ensure she had better access to his bearded face and using her reticule, which she had purposefully weighted with a book of poetry, thwacked him upside the head.

He stumbled off to the side, falling into a bunch of men who shoved him to the floor and started laughing.

She set her chin and kept walking.

Being a spy was hard work.

Fortunately, she was done for the night.

Violins tried to play, but were drowned out by too many voices.

Despite hundreds of candles illuminating the uneven stone walls, there were still more shadows than light. And she had just lost her damn escort for the night. Where on earth had her cousin gone? He'd been right behind her barely a few minutes earlier.

Searching for his massive horse mask, she wandered about the great hall, moving past peacocks and giraffes and other countless misshapen animals. Her cousin was nowhere in sight.

Gathering her skirts, she whisked her way toward the alcoves and veered into the nearest corridor. She scanned the tables laden with fruit, cakes and bottles of wine and champagne, where crowds pushed to grab whatever they could. Several apples rolled toward her feet from the shoving chaos.

A tall gentleman wearing a patched grey velvet ensemble veered in and swiped up one of the apples at her feet. He bowed, turning his gloved hand in her direction to present the apple. His zebra mask leaned in closer. "An apple for a kiss, *mademoiselle?*" he rumbled.

She eyed him and was about to thwack that apple out of his hand with her reticule, when all too familiar masculine blue eyes met hers through the slits of the mask.

Her lips parted, realizing it was Gérard.

Her breath hitched in astonishment. He was breaking his own rules. "Are you— Whatever are you doing here?"

His full lips smirked beneath his zebra mask as he tossed the apple from one gloved hand to the other. "Ensuring my investment is paying off."

She grabbed his arm and hurried him toward the farthest curtained alcove, away from the crowds. Draping aside the frayed curtain to ensure no one was occupying the small space, she bustled them both inside and yanked the curtain shut behind them.

Gérard leaned against the wall opposite her, adjusting his velvet coat. "Naudet was busy tonight. So I came in his stead. I have an hour before I have to get back."

She pushed up her mask to better see him and smirked, realizing he was wearing a zebra mask. "My. I inspire you every day."

He pushed up his own mask, his blue eyes brightening and set his broad shoulders against the wall. "I thought maybe it would inspire you to ride me."

She snorted. "Unlikely. I am still waiting for my pearls."

"They are much closer than you think." He skimmed her coral gown, lingering on her breasts. "Any new gossip?"

Thérèse tapped at her face. "Up here."

His eyes captured hers. "You make it difficult for a man to focus. That gown is…" He let out a low whistle. "My money is being well spent."

Biting back a smile, she closed the distance between them and draped herself against him, causing him to drag in a breath. She smoothed her hands up his waistcoat, noting the buttons were made of tin. So clever, as always. No one would ever suspect him of having a single *sol*.

She flicked each tin button. "According to *Monsieur Moquin*, there will be another shift in power. Robespierre and a few others are trying to persuade the *Convention Nationale* to permit the creation of a committee that would basically be in full of command of guillotining anyone they deem a threat to the Republic."

He stilled, intently searching her face. "When are they going to establish it?"

Thérèse lifted her gaze to his. "There is no word on that yet. It is a relatively new idea. But from what the man was saying, the moment it is implemented, the guillotine in the square would be falling every two minutes."

He stared. "I have to ensure the right people in my circle know about it." He leaned in closer. "Did you learn anything else?"

"No," she grouched. "I spent the rest of the time listening to *Monsieur Moquin* talk about his cats. He has eight of them and renamed them all in honor of the revolution. They are now called Justice, Liberty, Equality, Rebellion, Fraternity, Vengeance, Morality and by far my favorite *Quietus*. Which means death. The poor things. They are being forced to bear the very name of chaos."

Gérard smirked, gently set her aside and yanked his mask back on. "Cover your face. We have been in here too long."

She yanked down her mask, adjusting it into place. So much for romance. It was back to being a spy. Not that she was wanting to engage him after he had so drunkenly—

He grabbed the sides of her masked face and captured her exposed mouth, forcing her lips apart with his tongue.

She staggered and returned his kiss by working her tongue against his, their masks catching on each other.

He shoved her into the wall, causing her to gasp. Kissing her harder, he finally broke away and stepped back. "I had to see if you would kiss me," he rasped.

Her eyes flew open, her pulse roaring. "I suppose you got your answer."

Adjusting his crooked mask, he smoothed his lace cravat. "I did." He cleared his throat, angling toward her. "Are you up for dancing with me? I have about a half hour. Honor me."

She bit her lip, which was still moist from the contact of his mouth, and traced her gloved fingers longingly against the wall behind her. It was so unexpected to know outside of the money she was getting and what they had left behind in the forest that he was trying to embrace more for them.

It seemed inevitable that they would never be able to stay away from each other. Fortunately, everyone here wore masks tonight. "I would like that."

He grinned and swept aside the curtain, gesturing toward the great hall beyond.

Gathering her skirts, she sashayed past. "I will meet you by the violins."

He mockingly inclined his head. "Get there before I do, *ma biche,* or there will be no pearls for you tonight." His muscled frame dodged past and disappeared into the crowd.

Someone was feeling playful tonight.

Gathering her skirts, she darted forward and through the crowd, yelling, "Actress in need of pearls coming through! Do make way!" Thankful she wasn't wearing a wig, for she knew it would have flopped off by now, she dodged left and right in her heels, determined to make it to the violins before he did.

The sound of the violins drew closer as she frantically pushed her way through more and more people. She stumbled to a halt.

He was already waiting with his hands in his pockets. "What took you so long?"

She groaned.

He tsked and held out a hand. "Not being able to admit defeat can be a serious problem." He wagged his gloved fingers. "Come to me."

She held out her hand. "How about you come to me?"

He captured her outstretched hand and yanked her close, his hand skimming across her back as he folded her within his arms. He pressed her tighter against himself, gripping her uplifted hand with one hand and setting his other hand on her corseted waist. "Thank you for being here tonight. I appreciate it."

"I wish I had been able to unearth more."

"We will. Be patient. We are doing everything right."

She glanced over the side of his broad shoulder.

Couples around them trotted at a full arm's length away, holding hands and abiding by the dance dictated by the violins.

Gérard continued to merely sway them from side to side, searching her eyes, as if he didn't care they were breaking dancing convention.

She grinned up at him, trying to see past the slits of her mask. "You seem different. More at ease. I like it."

He shrugged and turned her once, swaying them from side to side again. "I find it rather nice to have someone I can rely on. It is not something I am used to."

Why did she want to melt against him for admitting he needed her? "I wish we could see each other more."

He searched her face. "We are always together. You are always in my thoughts."

She tightened her hold on his hand and shoulder. "Am I?"

"Cease preening about it."

"When do I get my pearls?"

He shifted his jaw. "Forget the pearls. We are dancing right now." He rigidly pushed her backward with his upper and lower body as if to emphasize he was in control of what happened next. "I am beginning to believe I like you more than you like me. Am I wrong in that?"

"Are you insinuating we get married?"

"I doubt either of us is ready for that sort of commitment."

Her hand, which had been resting on the muscled bulk of his arm, skimmed toward his solid chest and his coat. "Then why talk about who likes who more?"

He shrugged and averted his gaze, still swaying them.

This man was so much more vulnerable than he wanted to let on. It squeezed her chest and her heart knowing it. She raised herself on her heeled toes and kissed the curve of his shaven jaw.

He lowered his chin to better see her past his mask. "What was that for?"

"I find vulnerability very attractive in a man."

He tightened his hold for a long moment, then released her. He leaned in. "How vulnerable do you need me to be? I can make it happen."

She bit back a laugh and shoved him.

He grinned, grabbed her hand back and tugged her across the floor to join in on the faster dancing, releasing her to allow for each of them to dance with the people around them.

Every now and then, in between the dancing, those incredible blue eyes would capture hers through the blur of music and her heart would flip at a speed even her feet couldn't keep up with. Something tauntingly whispered that she had found her dance partner for life.

He grabbed her hand again, his grin widening, and called out over the music, "Follow me out! Unfortunately, I have to go!" Releasing her hand, he effortlessly wove his way through the dancers and disappeared through the crowd.

She was going to lose sight of him and who knew when she would see him again. Frantically gathering her skirts, she hurried after him only to bump into one of the dancing masked gentlemen. "Pardon me. I have to—"

The gentleman jumped toward her and merrily grabbed her hand, dragging her back into the circle of dancing. He lifted his other hand in the air, leading them in time to the music. She stumbled and gaped, realizing that other arm appeared to be missing a hand at its laced cuff.

She choked. How many men in Paris had stubs? A few, she supposed, but how many of them would be here tonight enjoying the revelry of the revolution as much as this one appeared to be?

Why was it this revolution had to assault what she and Gérard shared? It more than irked her.

This society wanted to seize everything. Including what wasn't theirs.

Jumping toward him, she grabbed the gentleman hard by the lapels of his black, embroidered coat and jerked him to a halt. "Pray give your name, *monsieur*." She attempted to be polite. In case it turned out to be another man. "I wish to know."

He froze, his crow mask and its black feathers fluttering. "Begging your pardon, but I came with my wife."

She tightened her hold on that coat. "Only your name will result in the release of your coat."

He gritted his teeth and stiffly removed her hands from his coat. "I am *Monsieur* Poulin, a *bourgeoisie* tailor by trade. Does that answer your question?"

She knew it.

Stripping his mask, she tossed it to the other dancers surrounding them and stared the gentleman straight in those dark eyes that clearly had no soul. Angling toward him, she said loud enough for everyone on the dance floor to hear, "How it is you dare to celebrate our revolution as if you were one of us? You, *Monsieur Poulin*, are a disgrace to the *bourgeoisie* and all we represent. From my understanding, you whored your own wife to an aristocrat for ten thousand *livres* after asking for a half a million. No paltry sum."

People stopped dancing. Some turned toward them and stared. Others whispered and removed their masks to better see the man.

Oh, yes. Gossip was a dagger and this one had earned it.

Poulin's dark eyes widened. He glanced toward the floor to find his mask, edging back. Unable to find it, he glared. "The aristocrat you speak of, Madame, was nothing but a vile scoundrel who forcefully seduced and raped my wife. And when I bloody sought to defend her honor, *this* was done to me. *This!*" He shook the stub at her.

She narrowed her gaze, knowing full well her Gérard would never force himself on a woman. "You are a liar and not at all one of us. You sought to better your circumstance at the cost of another whilst letting your fellow *bourgeoisie* suffer. Why did you not offer a single *sol* of the ten thousand you swindled to help the revolution? Are you not in support of our cause?"

Various men now angled in, removing their masks, one by one.

A young man in a queue squinted and stepped past her toward Poulin. "I represent the new Convention we are openly celebrating tonight, monsieur. I was voted in three days ago and find this conversation might require closer attention." He wagged his gloved fingers, signaling a few other gentlemen to join in. "By law, if funds were taken from an aristocrat, it belongs to the Republic. As such, we wish to see all ledgers pertaining to your finances and will make an appointment to do so this week."

Poulin scrambled back.

A masked brunette scurried toward them and frantically grabbed at the arm of Monsieur Poulin. "Say nothing more," the woman begged. "Do not engage it!"

This went even better than planned. She was done here.

Inclining her head to all of them, Thérèse regally pushed back her skirts away from her feet and swept her way off the dance floor. A few months in prison for a man who had vilely swindled Gérard and whored his wife seemed exceedingly fair.

She paused, realizing Gérard was lingering on the edge of the dance floor a few feet away. A muscle quivered in his clenched jaw right beneath his half-mask.

She cringed knowing she had probably made a much bigger scene than his private affair warranted. It was the actress in her. She quickly walked past him but said nothing knowing it would be no different than announcing to everyone that the man behind the zebra mask was who she had sought to defend.

Hopefully he wasn't too upset. She had been overseeing his honor. Surely, he would—

Gérard weaved in from behind and grabbed her arm hard, now directing their pace faster toward the back entrance of the hall. His fingers dug into her arm tighter and tighter. "Remind me to never leave you alone for five minutes."

She winced and out of the side of her mouth offered, "Did I overdo it?"

He leaned in. "Everything you ever do is overdone. Now move. We have to go. Lest they damn well want your name on record. *Move.*"

She almost broke into a run.

He jerked her back hard, tightening his hold. "Fast but not that fast, dearest," he drawled. "Or you will draw attention."

Leading them out of the great hall and down the corridor faster, her slippered heels clicked rhythmically with his boots across the marble floor.

Fast but not too fast, she chanted to herself.

They soon headed out through a side entrance and into the night that was still warm from the heat of the day. A breath escaped her.

She glanced up at his towering frame, trying to keep up as they left the light and noise of the festivities behind and headed down a cobble stone path toward a long line of hackneys whose seats were lopsided from overuse. "Are you angry?"

"Let us not discuss this on the street." Lifting a gloved hand, Gérard let out a whistle through his teeth, causing one of the hired hackneys to stop a few feet past them. He hurried them forward, leaned forward and yanked open the side door leading to the hackney. "After you."

She scrambled up the iron step and in. Flopping herself onto the frayed seat, she pushed aside the debris of pamphlets left by the last person.

"Forty Rue Saint Martin!" Gérard called out before getting in and slamming the door behind his large frame.

She eyed him, realizing they were going back to her new flat. "My cousin is still back at—"

"He knows the city and will be more than fine." As the hackney pulled away, Gérard yanked all the patched curtains shut over each side of the window, only allowing a sliver of light to come in from the lantern hanging on the side of the window. "Move over."

"What are you—"

He wedged himself between her and the hackney wall of the window. His arm jumped around her. Leaning in, he stripped her mask and his, tossing them both onto the seat. Gripping her outer shoulder hard with one hand, he used his other hand to smooth her hair, his shadowed face hovering close. "Why did you do that?"

She swallowed and searched his face, those eyes barely visible in the shadows. The heat of his hands, his body and his mouth made it difficult for her to breathe. "He earned it."

His gloved fingers dragged its way across her cheek and then her throat. "I am not arguing with you in that. I know he earned it." He skimmed the tips of his fingers across the tops of her breasts. "What I am asking is *why* you did it?"

Half-breaths escaped her. "I have a very strong sense of justice."

He flicked her ear with a finger. "If you think I believe that, *ma biche,* you are delusional. Your sense of justice includes getting paid. And I did not pay you to do that." He leaned in closer and used the tip of his tongue to trace her lips. "Tell me why you did it. Say it."

She felt faint as she reveled in the feel of that hot tongue. She wasn't ready to admit to him or herself that she wanted him outside of their alliance. She angled her mouth toward that tongue, drawing it into her mouth.

He broke away. "Why did you do it?" he pressed.

She slipped her arms around his broad shoulders and draped her legs over his. She sighed. "Because I feel like everyone around us is against us. Their ideals are not ours."

He raked his fingers through her hair, tightening his hold on it. "Ours? Are you admitting we share in something more than mere attraction?"

Their conversation was getting serious. "I suppose I am."

He lingered. "Reach into the left side of my inner coat pocket."

She paused and slipped her hand past the warmth of that solid chest she could barely see and slid her hand into the pocket.

His chest rose and fell unevenly against her, but he didn't move.

Her fingers grazed what felt like bundled velvet. She grasped it and pulled out the heavy bundle. The sound of sifting pearls made her eyes widen.

"Anything you want, you get," he said in a husky tone. "As promised."

She clutched it to her chest in disbelief, knowing she was actually holding a set of pearls. Real pearls. Something her own mother could have never afforded. She searched his face. "Thank you. This is—" She pressed her lips to his mouth and lingered before saying against him, "I am a butcher girl no more. And I thank you for that."

He edged away. Taking up her mask, he set it against her face, tying the lace ribbon back into place. "There is no shame in being a butcher girl, you know."

She rolled her eyes. "There is if you are one. Chickens fear me. I always felt very conscious about that."

He tsked and tied his own mask on and lingered. He nudged her. "Open it."

She excitedly unraveled the strings holding the velvet fabric closed and pulled it apart. Pulling out the string of pearls by the tips of her fingers, she raised the entire length of her arm and hand toward the ceiling of the hackney. The string of glistening white pearls continued to unravel out of the small satchel well beyond what she could hold up. Her lips parted in disbelief as she wound the pearls around her hand several times in an attempt to get it all out. It kept rustling and rustling out like a never-ending parade.

The end finally swung out and swayed.

In awe, she draped the heavy pearls over her head, looping it several times around her throat, before letting the rest fall well past her waist. Holy God. She pressed a quaking hand against it, not even wanting to know how much it cost him. "Was it terribly expensive?"

He leaned over and yanked open each curtain to let in more light. "Yes. Terribly."

She frantically grabbed his face and kissed him. Once. Twice. Thrice. "You are the most amazing man I have ever met. Thank you!"

A gruff laugh escaped him. "Wait until you see the diamonds. They are being cut for you as we speak." He leaned in closer, until their noses and masks were touching. "I never had a woman defend my honor before."

The hackney came to a halt, causing their heads to bump.

They winced.

The driver called out, "Forty Rue Saint Martin!"

Gérard glanced toward the limestone building beyond the window. "How do you like your new living quarters? Is it acceptable?"

"I about fainted," she gushed. "I have a bed the size of a field all to myself. I keep rolling and rolling and never seem to be able to fall off. 'Tis marvelous. And there is so much beautiful furniture all over the place, I keep trying to sit on everything just so I can say I used it."

He smirked. "Good. If you need anything else, let Naudet know. In about another two weeks or so, you should be starting over at *Théâtre Française.* I am finalizing a few sizable payments to the owner." He kissed her gloved hand. "I am afraid I must bid you *adieu.*"

Life was so unfair. She searched his masked face. "When will I see you again?"

"Not for some time."

Her heart dropped. "Why not?"

"The less we associate, the less likely people will suspect anything."

She softened her voice. "Is that the only reason?"

He touched her cheek, skimming his fingers toward her throat. "If we go any faster, we might ruin this."

Leaning into that hand, she half-nodded. "Maybe you are right."

"Forty Rue Saint Martin!" the driver called in agitation, his boot hitting his seat. "Ey! Out and out already! Is someone going to pay me double for waiting?"

Gérard rolled his eyes. "I swear this revolution is making people rude." He rose and opened the door, jumping out. He extended a hand.

She stood and grabbed his hand, stepping out of the hackney. Her pearls rustled against her movements, reminding her that she was no longer a butcher girl from Giverny. She was an actress, spy extraordinaire *and* her lover was third cousin to the king.

Clutching the velvet satchel and her reticule, she reluctantly released that large, gloved hand. "Thank you for a lovely night. I really enjoyed dancing with you."

He inclined his head. "I will wait until you find your way inside."

She hesitated, knowing she had a whole flat to herself and no one in it. Maybe..? "Are you wanting to come upstairs?" she blurted, trying to be casual about it. "For tea or anything?"

Gérard set his shoulders, no longer meeting her gaze. "No. I have to go."

She sensed that whatever was happening between them was overwhelming him. It was so darling. One would think they hadn't even kissed. "I understand." Digging out the key from her reticule, she turned and hurried to her door. She paused, biting back a smile knowing it was *her* door. Not her father's or her mother's or her ten brothers'. Hers.

Unlatching the door, she pushed its weight open, stuffing the key back into her reticule and stepped inside, glancing back at him one last time. "Good night."

He inclined his head again. "You certainly made it such."

She smiled and put up a gloved hand.

Turning, he paid the hackney with a few coins, then adjusted his evening coat around himself and strode off into the darkness of the night, his mask still in place.

She leaned out, watching that tall, muscled figure stride down the pavement.

He paused and glanced back. "What?"

She blew him an ardent kiss and used her sultriest voice. "I wish you could stay. I need someone to help me out of my corset, you know."

He groaned and threw back his head. "None of that. I have to go. I have people waiting and things to do." He hissed out a breath, swung around and stalked away, disappearing around a corner.

She dreamily set her head against the frame of the doorway, her pearls rustling. She eased out a breath, sensing this was only the beginning of far more than an alliance.

LESSON NINE

Welcome to the show.

-The School of Gallantry

Three months later

Théâtre Française – evening

Thundering applause pulsed around her and mingled with the humming of voices drifting up to the rafters. It made Thérèse breathe in deep in an effort not to..vomit. She fought the rolling nausea that had gripped her all week. The scent of smoking candles that illuminated the expanse of the apron's stage, along with so many countless perfumed bodies that clung to the stagnant air, made her want to wretch.

Despite that, she did her best to enjoy the moment knowing there was nothing quite like being adored for more than what God slapped on one's face. Being able to prove her talent to all of Paris was more than she could have ever dreamed.

Her life had become amazing. Surreal. A dream.

Everything had bloomed into being perfect. Too perfect.

Thérèse scanned the clapping crowd who had risen to their feet in the large auditorium and continued to over-smile, regally sweeping her slim arms wide open to acknowledge that she was deeply touched by the unending applause that had lasted much longer than last night's performance.

Only one thing was missing in the glory of that moment: Gérard.

Her chest tightened at the thought of him.

She hadn't seen him since they parted three months earlier. It was wretched of him, regardless of whether the Republic or the world was watching. He could have attended a performance. While Naudet, damn him, had turned out to be a burly man with a squint who offered very few words that never went beyond, 'He is doing rather well' or 'There is no other message' or 'I know not' or 'May God piss on that.'

It was anything but helpful.

Curtseying regally to the crowd one last time, she turned and gathering her lace gown and silk petticoats, she swept off stage. The smile she'd held for her audience faded. She set a trembling hand to her stomacher. Something was not right, but she wasn't quite certain of it yet. Her menses was never regular and usually skipped two to four months at a time.

Which meant..she wouldn't know for certain for another month.

It was unnerving. She wasn't ready to have a baby. Not during a revolution.

"There she be, there she be!" Rémy strutted over to her like a rooster, his elbows out and dressed in his latest burgundy satin and velvet ensemble worth three hundred livre. The man always told everyone what his wardrobe cost given he was so proud of it. "By God, I do believe we made more today on the ticket sales than we have all week. It means I get to keep this here managing position and the clothing that goes with it."

Despite the rolling nausea, she smiled. It was easy enough to do. Rémy always made her smile. He was always so cheerful and happy. And now more than ever. "I still cannot believe this is happening to us. Giverny is no doubt pissing itself right along with Mama and Papa."

Rémy grinned, displaying crooked teeth that personified him and halted before her. "I knew having you in Paris would change the city." He nudged her. "How about you and I tell that incredible, overpaid chef of yours to make us some of that fancy food again? You know...with all those-those..meats and gra-

vy? Are you up for a late supper?" He patted his large belly. "Collecting money gives a man a big appetite."

She smirked and patted that oversized belly. "Then I say we feed that appetite so you can keep up with all the collecting. The moment you finish counting the rest of the money and organizing the bills, make your way over to my dressing room. I will ensure I stay late."

He grabbed her face and rattled it. "A personal blessing is what you are. I knew it ever since you could toddle." He jumped back and pointed at her in his usual half-squat position that showcased his excitement. "Try not to let your admirers keep you from our supper. I should be done no later than midnight."

"Midnight it is." She did a half-squat herself and pointed back. "I will see you and that big belly later."

Rémy smacked his belly and bustled off with the shake of his coat tails, nodding enthusiastically in greeting to everyone he passed. "Best night yet, I say," he yelled out. "I went ahead and left champagne in everyone's basket!"

She tsked. Rémy had a tendency to spoil them and always used his own money to do it.

Jacques and Léon now hurried toward her, their eyes brightening in rehearsed unison. One held out a crystal glass of gingered tea and the other held up a silver tray, which usually sat in her dressing room.

"You were glorious," Jacques announced with the pert wiggle of his powdered periwig. "That was the most incredible rendition of *Nina* I have seen from you yet."

"Quite so," Léon chimed in. "The audience kept you on stage twice as long. By the end of this week, we may have to set out a chair for you and *Nina* to sit on. I never laughed so hard."

She bit back an exasperated smile, knowing full well these two ambitious blighters were being paid to make her feel glorious. Much like everyone else. "I thank you both for *always* making me believe in my talent."

Removing her satin gloves, she deposited them onto the tray Léon held, along with the lightweight paste jewelry that was part of her costume. She slid a powdered handkerchief from the tray and dabbed at her throat, face and neck, nudging up the heavy black periwig that weighed on her head.

Barely a month on stage at *Théâtre Française,* and she felt like it had been a year. So much joy, yes, but..so much work. Her makeup and wardrobe alone took three hours.

A breath escaped her as she set the handkerchief back onto the tray. "Thank you, Léon."

Léon inclined his head and with the puff of his narrow chest, hurried away.

Turning to Jacques, Thérèse primly took her glass of gingered tea. Her chef had it made that very afternoon and had it delivered to the theatre just for her. She paused, realizing that she, Thérèse Angelique Clavette from Giverny, had a chef. And not just a chef, but also servants for each day of the week. Only they all stayed for the entire week, every single week.

Nausea aside, she was so in love with her new life she occasionally did a little wiggle.

When she wasn't rehearsing or on stage, she went shopping almost every day, and half the time, usually ended up dragging random people off the street who appeared to be in need of good cheer. She very much enjoyed seeing the faces of young and old women with frayed bonnets getting boxes and boxes of new ones. She also enjoyed merrily pushing mothers into toy shops with their children who had all been lingering outside and announcing to them that whatever they wanted was theirs. She *loved* playing the part of a wealthy godmother to everyone.

She took a dainty swig, reveling in the spicy taste of her tea. She took another dainty swig. And another. She paused and slowly felt the nausea washing itself away. Thank God. "Jacques, you have outdone yourself. Thank you for fetching this from my chef. It seems to be the only thing helping given how bilious my stomach feels."

Jacques paused. Clearing his throat, he leaned in and whispered from behind a gloved hand, "You did not hear it from me, but..all this drinking of gingered tea is creating quite a stir amongst the other actors given you usually drink red wine. They seem to think you are expecting the babe of one of your admirers. Are you?"

She cringed. So much for the actress knowing how to act whilst pregnant. Fortunately, Jacques and his brother Léon were two of the few people she did trust amongst the gossip-hungry trenches of the theatre.

Taking a dainty swig of her tea, she leaned in. "Unfortunately, I cannot refute it quite yet."

Those dark eyes searched her face and grew serious. "I will take a damn carriage wheel to his head for— The man should have taken precautions."

"Yes, well, I should have, too." She shouldn't have taken on Gérard knowing he was drunk.

Jacques squinted. "Who is this bastard? I will ensure he never walks straight again. Do I know him? Is he from the theatre? Or an admirer?"

Now *that* she sure as heaven was not saying. Not even to Jacques. Disapproval from the world aside, half-aristo babies were anything but welcome in this new society. "I have no idea who the father is," she tossed, playing her flippant, usual self. Better to be seen as a whore in complete control of the world than to be seen as virgin who had no control at all. "There have been so many. So, so many. I am downright exhausting myself merely thinking about it."

Jacques drew his lips in, taking on the very visible age of what he was: seventeen. "Why do you never give me a chance? I adore you. What will it take for us to—"

"You and I have had this discussion before. I like you too much for that."

He gave her a withering look. "Then I suggest you start hating me."

She let out a pert laugh, tapping his arm. "Cease. The last thing you need in your life is an actress who has no time for you. I would neglect you."

A look of anguish overtook his boyish features. "Am I really that unattractive?"

"Of course not."

"Then why do women avoid me? Not even the ones here at the theatre scrubbing floors want to look my way. For some reason you women only ever prefer the broody, moody, muscular types. Why?"

A laugh escaped her. "The moody, broody, muscular types attract most women, yes, but they cause far too many problems. Believe me. Never change anything about yourself. Gallantry, my dear friend, is *always* rewarded, and the moody, broody types only appeal to certain girls. Not all of them. That leaves you a sizable selection of women to choose from. You simply have to wait for the right girl."

He puffed out a breath, grudgingly looking off to the side. "What is the point? No girl is even willing to kiss me."

Men were so grouchy when it came to women. She sighed, leaned in and gently kissed his smoothly shaven cheek. "There. Now you can you say you are no longer a virgin. Go tell the boys."

His lips parted. He gaped. "You kissed me."

She patted his shoulder, still smirking. "I told you gallantry is rewarded. But that is where this ends. You and I are friends, and I will not repeat that. Now cease gaping and go. Go, go, go. I will see to it my cousin issues you and Léon an additional five *livres* a week. Given every seat has been accounted for every night since *Nina* took to the stage, you both earned it with all the hours you put in."

Jacques's brows went up. "Five more *livres* a week? Are you *certain* you are not madly in love with me? Maybe we could attend a musical together? Or...visit your flat?"

She rolled her eyes. "Cease being a flirt and remember to be outside my dressing room in twenty-five minutes to help me with the crowds. I have countless letters to write and plan to have supper with Rémy later tonight. The only person you may allow entrance is *Citoyen* de Sade. Everyone else, give them my apologies and turn them away."

Jacques hesitated. "Did you not see *Citoyen* de Sade yesterday?"

"Yes. But he forgot his gloves."

"No doubt strategic."

"Everything you men do around women is strategic."

"Then why entertain the bastard? Why—"

"Because he is part of the *convention nationale* and given the way some of these theatres are being shut down for content by the Republic, I cannot afford to agitate the wrong men and put us all out of business." She sighed and rubbed his shoulder. "I thank you for the tea. Now, go. I will speak to Rémy later tonight about you and your brother getting an additional five *livres* starting next week. Agreed?"

He hesitated, then grabbed her face with both hands and startled her with a sound kiss to her lips. "You, madame, are the reason why I breathe. Never forget it." He released her and lowered his voice. "Friends can turn into lovers, you know. It will happen." He slowly grinned and waggled his brows. "We already kissed twice." Still smugly grinning, he trotted backward, then turned and with the click of boots into the air, scurried off.

She tsked and called after him, "Do not make me hire a new apprentice!"

He turned and amorously set a hand to his heart. "One day, *ma poupée*, you and I will make passionate love under the stage lights for the world to see. One day!" He thudded his chest with an assured fist and darted off.

Gah, gah, gah. Even the ones she trusted turned against her and only ever wanted sex.

Taking another sip of tea, she sighed and sashayed toward her dressing room, which she knew she had better get to before the crowds descended in the next twenty minutes. Making her way through the bustle of actors in costumes, angling left and right, she turned into a private, narrow corridor leading to her dressing room.

She paused.

The long private corridor, which was usually well lit with more than sixteen candles, was barely lit with a single one by the door, blackening everything except for a sliver of the door itself. She couldn't see anything before or after it.

Something was not right. Jacques always ensured the candles were lit.

Not trusting it, she quickly set her glass down outside the corridor and hitched up her skirt, tugging out the small blade she always carried with her. Her admirers had a tendency to be a bit more amorous than she liked.

Angling the blade out, she cautiously made her way into the darkness toward the door.

Someone was hiding in the darkness. She could feel their presence.

Coming to a halt before the closed door that bore the gilded letters of *MADAME DE MAITENON*, she touched a hand to her stage name and called out in firm tone, "I have a blade. Leave, or by God, I will use it."

The shadow of a tall, male figure pushed away from the nearest wall, startling her.

Tightening her hold on the blade, she scrambled back, her heart pounding. "Do not *dare* come any closer or everything below your waist will get sliced into too many pieces for you to pick up!"

A gruff laugh reverberated in the narrow corridor. "Still the butcher's daughter, I see," a deep male voice rumbled out, stepping toward her from the shadows. "Despite all the finery, you are still the same girl I met in the forest."

She gasped and almost dropped the blade. She dragged in a disbelieving breath, her gaze veering up past an expensive ensemble of smoke grey and dark blue even the shadows could not hide.

Steel blue eyes and a rugged good-looking face with a square jaw she knew all too well made her almost drop the blade again. "Gérard," she breathed.

He eyed her. "I am pleased to know you still remember my name. Now put the blade away. God forbid you try to hug me."

A startled laugh escaped her. She frantically hitched up her skirt and scrambled to slide it back into the leather belt and sheath attached to her thigh. She peered up at him in between attaching it. "My. You look divine." She skimmed his outfit that showcased those broad, muscled shoulders and wide chest. "Bravo for finally wearing something worthy of you."

He shifted his jaw and held her gaze for a long moment in the sliver of light from the lone candle. "Is that all you have to say after three months?"

She puffed out an exasperated breath, letting her skirts drop and glanced down the empty, shadow-infested corridor. She knew it wouldn't remain empty long. They barely had twenty minutes.

Opening the door, she peered into the well-lit room of pale blue velvet, to ensure it was empty, then grabbed that muscled arm and shoved him into the room, slamming the door behind them. She latched the door, then turned and fell against it in an effort to keep her heart from popping out of her chest.

Calm. She had to remain calm. He didn't need to know she wanted to grab him and kiss him and molest him beyond measure for turning her life into a fairy-tale.

Potential pregnancy aside.

He adjusted the red ribbon in his dark hair, indicating she had overly mussed his appearance, and turned toward her, widening his stance with each boot. "Next time, ask me to come in. Because my queue barely survived that, and I have places to be and countless women to see."

Well, well. Someone wanted to look good and brag about his life.

Annoyingly, she felt a large pinch of jealousy. Was he really entertaining other women? And why did it bother her? It wasn't as if they were married, but the last time they had seen each other had given her hope for..more.

She stared him down, scraping her nails down the wooden surface of the door she leaned against. "It certainly took you long enough to make time for me. I wore several white ribbons in my hair over these past few weeks and yet you never once bothered to see me. You keep sending over Naudet who rarely speaks enough to make up for the disappointment."

Gérard searched her face and offered in a cool tone, "I am a very busy man and have little time for socializing with overambitious actresses."

She blinked, sensing he was anything but pleased. "Overambitious? What is this? Have I not been producing enough leads?"

"Quite the contrary. You have been keeping me busy and are performing well beyond my expectations. We have already used most of your leads to prevent thirteen arrests."

She lowered her chin. "Then what is it? Why are you upset?"

"Do you really expect me to say it?" Gérard scanned the dressing room surrounding them, momentarily pausing on an array of her satin corsets piled on a red velvet chaise lounge. A large pair of male leather gloves were still draped over one of the corsets. A muscle flicked in his square jaw. "I did not realize your hands had grown so large."

Heat flooded her cheeks, knowing full well what he was thinking. "They were left there last night. They belong to *Citoyen* de Sade." She lowered her voice. "He visited me yesterday after the performance and will be coming back to fetch them shortly. I am still getting to know him, but he is about to become a member of the Piques section that is part of the committee of the Convention. Unlike the rest of these men coming to my door, his elbow is about to rest on the very same bench with that of *Citoyen* Robespierre. This man will have the ability to give us the sort of information you seek pertaining to *Sa Majesté.*"

Setting both gloved hands behind his back and locking it in place, Gérard stared her down. "I already know about Sade. Naudet told me this morning."

"Impossible. I only met Sade last night and never told Naudet. In fact, I have not seen Naudet in almost a week."

"Do not seem overly surprised. I pay him several hundred a week to watch over you given you do not appear to watch over yourself. And just because you do not see him, *or me*, does not mean either of us are not watching. We are. Believe me, we are."

This man was certainly miffed about something. She lifted a brow. "I appreciate your concern but ask that you deliver it with less.. *bite*. I hardly deserve it. I am working my wig off here."

"Yes, I know. I can assure you, I appreciate that."

Sensing he was still agitated, she pressed, "Then what is it?"

He was quiet for a moment. "I came to..." He shoved his hands into his coat pockets. "I am waiting for you to say it."

She blinked. "Waiting for me to say what?"

Gérard crossed his arms over his chest, his eyes roaming over her gown and towering wig. "For one, you look nothing like yourself."

Was this about her appearance? "Are you daft? I am in costume and have more powder on my face than there ever was in the jar. I am *required* to look like this. Have you not been to any of the performances?"

"All of them. And you, madame, are an inspiration to watch." His nostrils flared. "But that is not what I meant or why I came to talk."

"Well then say it. Before your nose falls off from all that heavy breathing."

He drew in a ragged breath. "You appear to have gained some weight."

She gasped, knowing full well she *had* gained half a stone. Her new chef was making incredible food neither she or Rémy could resist. There was also the possibility she was pregnant. Neither of which she appreciated.

She glared. "So you came here to insult me?"

"No. You misunderstand." He continued to stare her down. "I am merely disappointed that you would not have tried to confide in me given all of the concoctions you have been drinking on the hour. 'Tis obvious you know something you have not deigned to pass on to Naudet. Because nothing you do ever goes on without my knowing it. *Nothing*. Let me be clear in that. When you breathe, I hear it from a mile. Now out with it. Are you pregnant or not?"

Ohhhh. Now she knew why he was here being all grouchy-grouchy. He was obviously stressed about it. Which made two of them.

She puffed out a breath in exasperation. "Whilst I have been battling a bit of nausea, it could be nerves. I am rather hoping it is. I am, after all, still getting used to stage life and its harried nature and therefore cannot be certain. I most likely will not know for another month or so."

His brows came together as he edged closer. "How the hell can you not be certain? It has been three months. *Three*. Did your mother not educate you about your menses?"

Barely five minutes in his presence and she wanted to smack him. "My menses is irregular. Sometimes it arrives in two months and sometimes it arrives in four. Which means, in another month, I most certainly *will* know. But not sooner. So do calm yourself and be thankful you are a man. Because my menses appears to be about as irrational as you."

He swiped his face. "Christ, this is— I have to wait another month? And then I have to wait *another* five months after that for the babe to come?"

She paused. One would think he wanted to be a father. It was.. *unexpected*. But then again, he had three months to think about it. She had rather come to accept it herself.

Still leaning against the door, she apprehensively dragged her velvet covered slipper across the floor, toward herself. "Are you actually hoping I am pregnant? Is that what you are announcing?"

He dropped his hand to his side but didn't meet her gaze. "I have certainly prepared myself for the possibility."

Her smile broadened. "Are you saying you missed me, *Monsieur Aristocrate?*"

He snapped his gaze to hers and glared, his chest now rising and falling more heavily. "Hardly. You, *Madame de Maitenon*, are having quite the adventure at my expense. And the best part? I am paying for it through the nostrils and the mouth. *Especially* given what people are saying about you. Whilst I normally do not listen to rumor, it is a touch difficult to ignore the *vast* amount of men across all of Paris who continue to boast that you have entertained each and every one of them in a carriage, in a bed, against a wall and in every park there is. Look at me and assure me they are all lying."

A bubble of a laugh escaped her given how serious he was. "You and these men are delusional. I ask of you, if I were *that* much of a whore, how would I ever find the time to go on stage?"

He still glared. "I can easily ignore what these men are saying given I wish to respect you, but what I *cannot* and *will not* ignore is what I saw with my own eyes barely a few moments earlier. Watching you serenade your rosy-cheeked Jacques whom you were whispering to so adoringly and kissing on the cheek *and* lips, mind you, certainly tells me these men are conveying half-truths. You are letting these men touch you. Admit it."

She glared. "What is this? We are not married or engaged. So I suggest you stop heaving about it."

He narrowed his gaze. "I made you. I made you into the success you are now vastly enjoying at my expense. Which means *you* and that body are *mine*. Regardless of a piece of paper."

Och. Male jealousy was such a vile, vile little creature. It scratched and bit and made even the most gallant of men turn into the animals they really were. A part of her wanted to return the favor by becoming an animal herself and scratching his eyes out. But given she no longer chewed on her nails because she only ever heard his deep voice of '*Are you a lady or a goat?*' she decided to be a lady. Not a goat.

She stayed pasted to the door lest she stray from being said goat. "Sometimes, Gérard, we see what we want to see as opposed to what actually is. Jacques is my friend. Nothing more."

"I see. So you let your male friends grab your face and kiss you on the mouth like that? Hm?"

"The boy was overly excited. He—"

"Oh, I bet he was. He was practically scratching his trousers off. I heard him." He wiggled his head and pitched his voice higher to mock Jacques. "'*One day, ma poupée, you and I will make passionate love under the stage lights for the world to see.*'"

A giggle escaped Thérèse. "That was actually quite good. You ought to take to the stage with me."

"Why are you not taking me seriously?"

She sighed. "Oh, come now. Are you actually jealous of someone who barely started shaving? The boy is seventeen. Hardly an age I would ever be interested in."

"You seem to forget you are eighteen."

"Not true. I am nineteen as of four days ago. I simply did not care to openly celebrate it. There was no time for it."

He paused. "You are now... nineteen?"

"Yes. I am."

Averting his gaze, he murmured, "I will send you something. Do you want more jewelry?"

She rolled her eyes. "How about none of this vile jealousy?"

He angled toward her. "Maybe I am a bit confused. Naudet tells me you two giggle and hook arms with each other all the time."

"I giggle and hook arms with all the actors and people here at the theatre. Does that also make me a lover of women, too? Because I love hooking my arms and giggling with women, as well."

He pulled in his chin. "Are you saying you wish to engage other women?"

This man was exhausting her. "No! No, I— Will you cease? Let us not add women to the list or we will be here all night. The only reason I kissed Jacques on the cheek is because none of the other girls like him. Not that you would understand, *Monsieur Aristocrate*, given your good looks and all your money."

He said nothing.

She sighed, trying to understand what was going on in his head. No doubt thoughts of his Madame Poulin who betrayed him. "If you must know, Gérard, I think about you all the time. How can I not? You have changed my entire life in the most glorious of ways. Look at me." She pushed away from the door, regally twirling her satin and lace gown. She gestured toward the dressing room around them. "Everything I could have ever wanted, I now have. And none of this would have been possible if you had not made it possible."

He adjusted his coat over his large frame, but his features remained stubbornly aloof. "You have everything but me, Madame. And if you do not care to prove your affection for me in the manner I deserve, you will *never* have me."

It was obvious he wanted her. And annoyingly, she wanted him, too. "Gérard, if you are interested in getting involved with me, I already laid out the rules. Rules you were not willing to follow. Setting aside the fact that I do like you very much, this level of jealousy is unacceptable. For even if we were involved again, I am only doing what is expected of me. I am associating with a long list of men you asked me to. I am also an actress. I am expected to socialize and most of my admirers are men."

He didn't meet her gaze. "Are you interested in anyone outside of me? Be honest."

It was obvious he needed assurance. She softened her voice. "No. There is no one. I am not Madame Poulin. I have a bit more in my head and in my heart. As I said before, you have no right to be angry. Especially given what you did to me. You broke my trust barely a day into making it."

He winced. "I know and I have been living with it for three months. *Three*. Try to understand, Thérèse, that I—" His gaze held hers. Striding toward her, he used his large frame to edge her back against the door. "Maybe I am trying not to hope for more. Maybe, just maybe, I want you so damn much, I am trying so damn hard not to let on that I want you at all. Because as you well know, my affection has been played with before. And given the game we are playing, I am having trouble deciphering between what is real and what is not."

Her heart skidded. He really did want her in the same way she wanted him. Even after three months of being left to think about it. "I would never play with your affection. That is not who I am. What we shared in the forest was..."

He quickly veered in close. "Was what?"

Her backside hit the door, her heart pounding. The scent of his expensive cologne, though spiced and alluring as it had once been, made her throat tighten. Her stomach churned with renewed nausea.

Oh, no. She swallowed against the excessive watering in her mouth. "Gérard, I..feel ill. I..."

He set his hands on each side of her, above her head and held her gaze, his chest rising and falling. His tone and his features softened. "What is it? More nausea?"

A shaky breath escaped her as she glanced up. She half-nodded. "Your cologne. I..."

He searched her face, his brows flickering. "My cologne? What about it?"

She gagged and projected all of the contents of her stomach, including the pea soup she had earlier eaten, all over the front of his clothing. Trying to keep the rest from rolling out, she choked. Her heavy periwig tipped toward him, all the pins holding it up falling one by one.

His eyes widened, his expensive ensemble covered in vomit as he grabbed at her black wig. Lifting it up and off her head, he frantically tossed it aside and far from them.

She gasped, trying not to move or use the sleeve of her gown to touch her wet mouth. "Oh my..*dieu*. I..I am ever so sorry." Her face burned knowing she had retched all over the one and only man she ever wanted to impress. She had never been more humiliated in her entire life. Chewing on one's nails was one thing, but *this?*

"Never mind me," he rasped. Jumping toward the side, he grabbed a vase of flowers from the nearest table and flung its contents onto the floor, sending water spraying everywhere. He jumped back and held it out toward her. "Here. Aim."

She gargled out an exasperated laugh, setting her mouth close to the opening of the vase. "Such..gallantry. I adore you for that alone. I—" She felt her chest tighten and her mouth water again. She heaved and sputtered out whatever tea and food was left over, filling the vase with a splatter.

Gérard winced and leaned slightly back, while still holding the vase in place.

She closed her eyes, letting the nausea fade and lifted her head from the opening of the vase. No longer caring, she used the entire white sleeve of her costume to wipe her mouth clean. She staggered over to the chaise lounge and flopped herself onto it. "It appears I am pregnant."

He glanced down at the vase and cringed.

A knock came to the door making her pop her head back up.

Countless male voices and yelling now filled the corridor outside.

"*Madame?*" Jacques called out. "*Citoyen* de Sade wishes to see you."

She groaned, wanting to hit her head against something hard. The night was almost over. That was all that mattered. "*Merci*, Jacques! I need a few minutes. I am not quite ready!" She sat up and pointed Gérard toward her dressing screen, mouthing, "*Hide yourself behind it!*"

Gérard bared his teeth in exasperation and skidded to a side table, setting the vase on it. He scrambled to the other side of the room, frantically removing his coat, gloves and waistcoat that were splattered with vomit and slid behind her dressing screen.

Staggering back up to her slippered heels, she undid the row of hooks on the front of her costume which was spattered. She yanked down the sleeves and pushed everything down and past her corset and waist. Stepping out of it, she gathered the gown and hurried it over to the basket the maid always collected at the end of the night.

Within moments, she unraveled her blonde hair from its bundled state, letting it cascade down her shoulders and waist and scrubbed her face clean of all the powder and rouge that covered her face, using the basin of water and soap. She kept scrubbing and scrubbing until her face felt raw. Finally dabbing her face clean, she glanced at herself in the mirror and was surprised to find she looked relatively decent for the amount she had spewed.

There was another knock to the door through all the noise. *"Madame?"* Jacques called out. "The crowd is pushing at *Citoyen* de Sade a bit more than this man needs!"

"Yes, yes! *Do allow me another moment!"* Grabbing the chalk, she brushed her teeth with it and spit several times into a tin cup. Yanking on her dressing robe, she tied it into place and then paused, realizing the room smelled like vomit. And there was no window to even open. Ack! She swiped up her perfume bottle and bustled around the room spraying everything, including the vase itself and behind the dressing screen where Gérard was.

He gagged and coughed.

She winced and obnoxiously coughed in an effort to cover his male sounding one. Leaning over the side of the dressing screen, she tapped her lips and whispered, "Stay quiet." She held out the perfume bottle for him to take.

He gave her a withering look but grudgingly took it.

She tweaked her nose at him in vast appreciation and then bustled over to the door. Regally setting her chin, she swept the door open, ready to entertain.

The corridor was now well-lit and over-crowded with men who pushed forward to see her.

"Madame de Maitenon!" a young man hollered, wagging his calling card. "I beg of you to honor me! I have attended every single one of your performances. Every one!"

Several others attempted to shove past with their calling cards and flowers.

Jacques and Léon scrambled to keep everyone back using stage swords *"Step away!* Step away lest we use force, gentlemen! There will be no more callers tonight! Only this one!"

An older gentleman, a touch over fifty with sharp, regal features and piercing dark eyes that were all the more pronounced against the snowy white of his powdered periwig set with side curls, swept off his black, tall crowned hat.

He grinned and set the hat against his chest. "*Citoyen* Donatien Alphonse François de Sade..yet again," he said in a deep silken tone above the shouts. "I left my gloves in your dressing room last night. Might I fetch them?"

She stepped aside. "*Mais oui.* Do come in."

"*Merci.*" He strode past with long legs encased in faded gold knee breeches and dulling white stockings. Halfway into the room, he called, "Might you close the door, Madame? All the noise is agitating me."

Amen. She closed the door and turned back toward him, arranging her robe about her feet. "I have only a few moments, for which I apologize. I have countless letters to write and over thirty-two invitations to respond to."

"I will do my best to keep this business brief." Citoyen de Sade leaned toward his gloves set on her corset and swiped them up. He tucked them into his coat pocket and casually seated himself on the red velvet chaise lounge. He crossed a leg over his other knee, the brass buckle on his scuffed black slipper gleaming in the candlelight from the quick movement.

So much for keeping his business brief. She sighed.

His dark eyes critically scanned the entire room twice before finally settling on her. He tilted his head. "I do not particularly care for blonde women, but your spirit reminds me of a character I have in mind for a book I am writing." He twirled his hat, eyeing her. "I hear incredibly scandalous things about you, madame. Are they at all true?"

"When one is as popular as I, *citoyen,*" she countered, "men begin to make up stories that allow them to feel important when I turn them away. Does that answer your question?"

"Yes. It does." The older gentleman set his felt hat beside him. Opening his coat, he removed a calling card from its inner pocket and held it out between gloved fingers. He continued to hold the card out.

Knowing full well he expected *her* to cross the room for it, she sighed and did exactly that. Pausing before him, she reached out to take it.

He jerked it back.

She straightened and gave him a pointed look.

He tapped the edge of the card against his lips. "Sit beside me, Madame. You and I have a few things to discuss."

Why were men so predictable? She turned and seated herself beside him, ensuring there was an arm's length between them. She set her hands on her thighs, just above where her blade was hidden beneath her robe and undergarments.

Sade kept tapping the card against his bottom lip, inspecting her. "The stench of vomit you so cleverly hoped to erase with your perfume still clings to the air. Are you not well?"

She inwardly cringed. Someone was overly observant. "I am much better, thank you. The meal I ate earlier tonight before going on stage did not sit well with me. Too much..pea soup."

"You poor creature. Pea soup ought to be banned." He turned his wrist toward her, presenting his card. "I am here to inform the *duc's* dashing blue-eyed heir who is 'hiding' behind the screen that I am on to you both and have been for about a week. I simply was not expecting your 'benefactor' to appear on the same night I planned to talk to you about it."

Her eyes widened. He knew!

Sade glanced toward the screen and lifted a grey brow. "I suggest you come out."

Gérard swept aside the screen, sending it clattering to the floor. He stared the man down from where he stood, perfume bottle still in hand. He widened his stance. "To what do I owe this honor, *Citoyen?*"

"The honor, I assure you, is all mine. The perfume bottle says it all." Sade smirked and wagged the card at Thérèse, signaling impatiently she had best take the card.

She groaned and tugged it from his fingers.

Sade continued to intently observe Gérard. "You may find this difficult to believe, but I admire what you are attempting to do. As such, if you help me, *mon grande*, I will help you. Why? Because I do not particularly care for the direction this new government is taking. Mass death is but the beginning of what these mouth-breathers have planned. Not a single church or even the word *God* will be allowed to stand by the time they are done. For God no longer exists in their eyes. God, after all, is the reason they all suffer. And whilst I myself am well known for being incredibly partial to allowing for freedoms most deem too demented to be allowed, the moment we allocate death to even God, it means *nothing* remains. Not even the glory of pain. Which..pardon the expression.. *pains* me."

Rising from the chaise, he angled his hat onto his frayed wigged head and announced in a low, low tone that dripped with malevolence, "I am and will always be at heart an aristocrat despite my having denounced my name and title of Marquis. The only reason any of these men trust me is because I have spent half my life in prison under *letters de cachet*, which as you know, is the royal decree of imprisoning a man without trial. Hardly fair. To them, I am a glorified martyr of the *ancien régime* and have set a good example of rising against its overall conventions. And whilst, yes, I am endlessly touched by their new endearing trust in me—" his tone turned lethal, "—I fucking despise every last one of them so much I would gladly rape and whip their women to death and do it all over again."

Thérèse swallowed and edged back against the chaise, sensing he meant it.

Sade eyed them both, his dark, playful eyes penetrating the space. "Allow me to get to the point of this visit. I will give you both whatever information you want, when you want it and how you want it. In return you will both help me write a book. Because I am struggling with trying to give it meaning. It lacks a certain.. *substance*."

Thérèse lowered her chin. Was he serious? "Are you referring to an actual book?"

Sade's full lips curved. "But, of course, *my puce*. I am first and foremost a writer. The more I observe, the more I am able to write. How do you think I survived prison?"

Gérard narrowed his gaze. "You are about to be elected into the same committee and section as Robespierre. How am I to trust you?"

Sade rolled his eyes. "Do toss aside being coy, my dear boy. Trust has nothing to do with this. Ask yourself *why* I did not already report you and your actress given you and she are busy shuffling people out of the country like coyotes herding sheep."

Gérard stared. "How the hell do you know? I have been impeccably—"

"Careful. Yes, I am well aware of that. But you and I share a mutual friend: Naudet." He tapped his lips with a forefinger. "Did you know that gruff, burly, quiet and dependable man of yours *loves* being sodomized and whipped so damn much, and so damn hard, he tells me everything? And I do mean.. *everything*."

Thérèse cringed and lifted a hand to the side of her face so she wouldn't have to look at Gérard. It was *always* the quiet ones.

Gérard hissed out a long breath. "So you and Naudet are—"

"Involved. Yes. Naudet is my whipping whore. Marvelous man. His oversized back can take a four-inch whip with nails embedded into it without even flinching. And he comes to me each and every week because I know how to make him flinch. I ask you not blame the oaf for what I know. Pleasure and pain have a tendency to tap into the brain a bit too much. I was asking him questions about his life during a session and it simply rolled out."

Gérard threw back his head and groaned.

With the self-satisfied smack of lips, Sade rounded them. "Given there is a clear issue of distrust between us, which I completely understand, allow me to toss a branch of my genuine offer of reliance by sharing a sliver of what I know and what I can share." He cracked his knuckles, one by one. "This has yet to be announced to the public, but the upcoming trial of *Sa Majesté* has been set and will take place this December third. A full thirty-three charges will be set against him."

Startled, Thérèse met Gérard's gaze.

Gérard quickly stalked toward the man. "Thirty-three charges? *For what?* How can there even be that many?! Christ, he— Are they mad?"

Sade inclined his head. "Oh, yes. They are, in fact, loons. Every last one of them. Why do you think they are about to put me on the committee?" He let out a self-pleasured, over-enthused laugh, rolling both hands as if listening to applause. "Of course, *Citoyen* Robespierre, bless his missing heart, is what I call the ultimate loon of a lawyer in the guise of death itself. Given all of the charges set against *Sa Majesté* it most certainly will result in deportation or death, and I know deportation is not an option. That would be too risky for the stability of our new government and allow uprisings this country does not need. Which means.. most votes will go toward overseeing *Sa Majesté's* head in a basket; so, whilst it is endearing for you to think you can save him, more than a few royalists have already tried, and they are all *dead, dead, dead.*

"You would need an army of about two hundred. Because forty guards are outside the king's doors and a hundred more are inside overseeing several iron doors. They have orders to butcher anyone who even walks down the corridor leading toward any of those doors. Which means.. *Sa Majesté* will stand trial and die."

Gérard closed his eyes and staggered.

Disbelief punched Thérèse. Oh, God. He was barely standing.

Scrambling to her feet, she hurried over to him and grabbed him, wrapping her arms around his waist in an attempt to keep him from falling. Tears stung her eyes knowing his godfather was the one person he wanted to save out of all of this. It was the sole reason why they had created their alliance.

Citoyen de Sade heaved out a soft breath. "You have my condolences." Setting his shoulders, he rounded the room, glancing at everything as he walked. He strode over to the vase, paused, peered into it and wrinkled his sharp nose. "Life is anything but pretty. It *reeks.*"

She smoothed her trembling hands across Gérard's linen shirt. "I am so sorry," she choked out. "I know what he means to you."

Gérard set her head against his chest and mashed her cheek against his broad chest. "The Assembly will not even let me see him. I tried." His voice was half-smothered. "I.. failed him."

She tightened her hold, knowing this strong man was breaking. "There must be a way for you to see him," she gently offered. "If only once."

Rounding them, Sade peered in. "Unfortunately no, madame. Too many attempts to rescue him have banned his right to visitors. However, he *would* be permitted a one-sentence missive. It would be reviewed by five men before being delivered into the king's hands. As long as the missive passes the approval of public safety and is free of any mischief, it would be delivered directly to the king. But that would only be allowed prior to the trial. Not during or after. So I suggest you do it soon. It would have to be written in the next week."

Gérard released Thérèse and scrubbed his face in a clear effort to rid himself of any emotion. He dropped his hands, revealing an anguished, tear-streaked face. He sniffed hard, turned away and half-nodded. "Better a one-sentence farewell than nothing at all."

"I will ensure it gets the extra nudge it needs." Sade inclined his wigged head. "Whilst I cannot assist in saving your godfather or his family, I can continue to share whatever information you require. Though I honestly cannot say for how much longer. There are several ongoing debates in the chamber right now about Robespierre, Danton and seven others forming a committee for public safety."

Sade turned toward them. "Which means *no one* in this country will be safe. Not even me. So I suggest we make use of each other whilst we still can. For whilst you, Madame de Maitenon, are not in any danger given your newfound popularity with the Republic and on stage, I am afraid your uh.. son of *duc* will eventually find his way to the guillotine given his father is so closely related to *Sa Majesté*. All but three days ago, Robespierre announced plans to take the *duc's* money, his lands, and apply all funds into the new government. And in order to do that, he will have to make an example of the *duc* by creating a long list of charges. They have yet to decide what those charges will be, but rest assured, these greedy little *chèvres* always come up with something. Your father's neck and your neck will be theirs. Count on it."

Overwhelmed and half-panicked, Thérèse grabbed Gérard's arm.

He dragged in uneven breaths. "I knew things were getting worse. I have seen the changes on the streets. My father and I recently dismissed our servants in an effort to keep them from harm." He hesitated. "How much time do I have before the charges are set? Do you know?"

Sade tsked, wagging a large forefinger. "I do believe I have already supplied you far more than you have supplied me. Are you ready to negotiate?"

Dread seized Thérèse sensing whatever this Sade wanted would not be good.

Gérard squeezed her hand and released her, fully turning to Sade. "What do you want?"

Those dark eyes brightened. Citoyen de Sade smoothed his lace cravat twice. "Not very much. A mere bit of..*inspiration*. A one-time affair. Hardly anything."

Gérard narrowed his gaze. "What do you want? Say it."

Sade grinned, his gaze skimming Gérard from queue to boot. "I was hoping to get a private showing of you and your actress...oh..how shall I say this politely? *Fucking*. I need a few sketches for my upcoming book, and I rather envision the both of you in it. Publication is set for this June."

Thérèse gasped.

Gérard stared at the man. "Allow me to respond to your offer, *citoyen*." Leaning toward her, Gérard drawled, "Pardon me, *ma biche*. You may want to close your eyes."

Gérard swept out a dagger attached to the inner leather belt of his waist hidden beneath his coat. Stalking over to Sade, he angled the large blade out. Jumping forward, he grabbed the man by the throat hard and whipped him toward the nearest wall, causing the entire room to shake as Sade's hat and periwig tumbled off to the side.

Thérèse flinched.

Citoyen de Sade burst into maniacal laughter despite the blade now resting dangerously against his throat. He gleefully tapped at the edge of the blade with a gloved hand. "Oh, yes, yes, yes. Do go and slit my throat in a theatre, no less. How *whimsical*! I can see all of the pamphleteers yelling it already, '*Marquis de Sade murdered for nothing!*'"

Sade's aged, sharp features almost twitched from continued amusement. Leaning far forward against the blade, he drawled, "Are you really *that* opposed to giving an artist something to write about? You mean to say you prefer death itself over supporting the arts? How demented are you?"

Gérard's hand visibly trembled as the dagger almost scraped that face.

Swallowing hard, Thérèse knew full well Gérard was thinking about doing it. And although a part of her wanted him to, she knew if it happened here in her dressing room, the entire committee would ensure they *both* die.

Pulse roaring, she scrambled toward Gérard and grabbed at his trembling wrist hard. "Gérard," she choked out. "You cannot do it. *You cannot!*"

Sade further extended his throat.

Gérard released Sade with a shove. "'Tis obvious your mother sucked animal cock for money, you—" Gritting his teeth, Gérard whipped the blade aside, sending it clattering against the farthest corner of the room. He slammed a full fist into the man's gut, causing Sade to gasp and fall into the wall.

Thérèse winced and genuinely hoped it hurt.

An exasperated grin overtook Sade's flickering features as he casually staggered up. He pointed at Gérard. "You, my fellow aristo friend, define a true hero. So angry and obscene toward the wicked. But...will it save you from the guillotine that now sits in the square? I dare say no. You need me in order to survive. And all you have to do is help me write a book."

She edged back, unable to decide if this man was deranged or wanted to be deranged.

"I need these sketches," Sade grouched. "You two are the epitome of what I see in my head. I promise it will be genuinely worthy of your approval."

Gérard swung away, raking his hand several times through his hair, while adjusting his queue. He stalked across the room. "This is— No. Absolutely not. *Especially* if she is with child. Are you— no."

Citoyen de Sade let out a breathy, half-disappointed sigh. Swiping up his periwig and hat, he set each on his head and wiggled it back into place. "I wish to assure you our session would have been done tastefully. I usually sit behind a viewing screen. It allows for more natural interactions. Whenever I sketch, you see, I cannot play. I think I am being perfectly reasonable and would only require *one* session. If you give me what I want, I will give you the secrets of the committee. Or...I can take your scheming to the committee. You decide."

Maybe she was used to men being mad or maybe the idea of death just didn't appeal to her. Either way, knowing that Sade was not going to be joining in on any of it and would be hidden behind a screen, sketching, made it more—

How difficult could it be? Sex was sex. She cleared her throat. "Gérard, dear?"

Gérard turned toward her, his gaze capturing hers.

She gave him a prim and pointed look. "All that matters is that we would have an ally on the committee. I can easily survive one session. And if I can, I know you can."

His shaven face flushed. "Setting aside that I do not *want* this maggot seeing us together in that way, I am *not* taking a whip to you. Do you think so little of me, Thérèse, that you would allow for any of this?"

She edged back. Apparently, she was far more sexually liberated than he was.

Citoyen de Sade cleared his throat. "I have no trouble counter-offering. All you had to do was ask. Given her pregnancy, which a vase full of pea soup has more than verified, I will grant leniency. I rather like the idea of giving this book a new perspective. Usually the women sustain most of the injuries. So she can whip and cane you instead. It matters not to me. There will be plenty of food and wine on hand, including whatever salve you need to ease your pain. Are we in agreement?"

Gérard choked.

Food and wine and salve and pain. How utterly fitting. It was the epitome of the revolution at its finest. And the fact that the committee was about to instate this man into the chambers of the new Republic said it all.

Sade drew in a well-satisfied breath. "So. Shall we plan for early next week? Say...Monday, early evening? I should be done sketching shortly after midnight, depending on how well things go." He smiled and leaned toward her. "Madame, you still have my card, yes?"

One would think they were making *soirée* arrangements. She tried not to let on that she was mildly amused, lest Gérard think *she* was deranged. "I am afraid this rests with Gérard. I am not the prude here. He is."

Gérard stared, betraying no emotion. "I am more than fine with it. Monday at seven."

She dropped her hands to her sides. Holy God. They were doing it?

Citoyen de Sade swept up her hand and bowed over it, kissing it once. "I foresee this publication being a success and promise to alter your features enough to hide your identities from the public." He thumbed toward the vase set on the side table. "You may want to put a few flowers into that. The stench is overtaking the room."

She gave him a withering look.

Striding up to Gérard, Sade snapped out a hand. "Until Monday, my beloved prude."

Gérard narrowed his gaze. "You are not touching me. Get out."

Sade smirked and adjusted his coat. "Long live the Republic, and adieu to you both." With that, he strutted to the door, whistling. Yanking open the door, he winked at Thérèse and slammed the door after himself.

Gérard swung toward her and glared. "You, *Thérèse*, are outrageous. Do you know that? *Outrageous.* You encouraged him!"

She gaped. "I did not! How did I encourage him? Are you saying I gave him the idea of turning us into the committee if we did not entertain his sexual delusions?"

He still glared. "You know full well what I mean. You clearly *want* that man watching us copulate like animals in a cage rattling shackles. And whilst I have no trouble with us using shackles and whips and whatever the hell you want, I am *not* doing it in front of an audience!"

He really was a prude. "Unlike you, I have no trouble letting an artist watch us do what we do best if it means we are not going to *die.* 'Tis a matter of priorities, Gérard. *Priorities.* What else would you have us do? He said he would go to the committee. And as deranged as he appears to be, I believe him! And so should you."

"I need brandy." He swiped at his mouth with a trembling hand. "I have not even had a finger of brandy in three goddamn weeks. *Three*! And now with my godfather going to trial and this..*I am losing the last of my rational mind!*"

Her brows rose. Heavens above. The darling! That certainly explained his agitation throughout this entire evening. He'd done away with the brandy.

Her heart squeezed, knowing full well he did it for her.

How could she not adore this man?

She quickly strode toward him, her robe rustling around her feet. Leaning in, she smoothed her hand across his shaven jaw.

He stiffened, capturing her gaze.

She softened her voice. "Did you set aside the brandy for me?"

A breath escaped him. "Yes. I was tired of being weak."

She kissed his jaw. "No man has ever fought to prove himself like this to me. I am in awe and so proud of you. Three weeks is something to celebrate."

His dark brows flickered. "Thérèse. We cannot reduce ourselves to the sort of corruption this man wants us to. We are better than this."

Bless his noble heart. She *knew* even if they never ended up together, she would spend the rest of her life dreaming about him and wanting him. Because he was the definition of the same thing that beat within her: passion. She dragged in a breath knowing it. "I agree that you and I are better than this. But being better does not make us invincible. We are all mortal. Even you, O dear son of a *duc*. You bleed like the rest of us."

He hesitated. "My mother used to say that right will always win out over wrong. And yet nothing but wrong seems to win." After a long moment, he lowered his hand, gently setting it to her stomach. "I vow to protect you both. No harm will come to either of you."

This man was trying to steal her heart *and* soul.

She ardently pressed his hand against her belly.

Drawing his hand back, he averted his gaze. He quickly rounded her and gathered his clothes from the floor behind the fallen dressing screen. He bundled them tight. "I have to go."

She swung toward him, her breath hitching. "Where are you going?"

"We are not reducing ourselves to the vile games of the Republic. I am done with this shite. I am going straight to my father."

"And then what?"

He stared her down. "We get the hell out of France, is what. Well before Monday ever has a chance to rise." He averted his gaze and choked out, "Though it breaks me, if I try to stay and save my godfather, we will all die. Which means you, my father and I have two days to plan an escape and less than three to carry it out."

Her throat tightened. Dearest God. He wanted her to leave France.

Setting aside how close she was to her cousin, her brothers and parents were still in Giverny. And though they had yet to respond to any of her letters or the money she had repeatedly sent, she owed them to stay. She *needed* to stay. After all, what if they *died* because of her? "Gérard. I-I cannot leave. My life is here."

Coming closer, he leaned in and whispered, "Given our alliance, they will kill you if you stay. Do you not understand that?"

She dragged in an uneven breath, knowing it. "They will also kill me if I try to flee. At least if I stay, I would not be putting my cousin or my family in harm's way. Because you and I both know if I flee, the Convention will go after them. And I would *never* toss them toward the direction of the guillotine given I was the one to make this decision. I was the one who agreed to help you and will therefore live by it or die by it. Whatever I deserve."

He leaned in and gripped her shoulders hard. "Cease talking nonsense. You and the babe are coming with me. I am *not* leaving either of you to die."

She swallowed back whatever panic threatened to overtake her. She slowly removed his hands from her shoulders, first the left, then the right. "You speak as if you can protect us from harm. You cannot guarantee my safety anymore than you can guarantee your own."

He angled toward her. "Upon all that I am, I hold something that will ensure no one touches us. Something that will turn everyone in this country against the committee. And with the recent execution of the *duc d'Orléans,* who was on their side, I have no doubt they are looking to bury what I damn well hold. A gentleman my mother used to know is holding a set of papers for me with instructions to print every last page and distribute it to the masses should I or any name I wish to save be executed. And you are on that list. These *moutons* hold no power over me or us. None. Believe it."

She gaped. "If they hold no power over us, then why do you insist on leaving?"

"Because you and I both know things can and will go wrong. It is best we leave. Do you understand?"

She was not saving herself and leaving her family to die. "What about my cousin or my family?"

"We can send for them later."

"No." Trying not to get emotional, knowing she was saying good-bye, she choked out, "I am asking you to leave without me, Gérard. It is best."

He grabbed her. "No! What are you— What about the babe? Or the future of us? What about us?!"

Squeezing her eyes shut long enough to regain her ability to remain calm, she re-opened her eyes. "There could never be a future at the expense of my family. As for me, I am told they do not execute pregnant women."

He stared. "Until after they give birth, damn you." After a pulsing moment, he pointed rigidly. "I am not done with you. You are coming with me whether you damn well want to or not. I will be back in two days. And if you see Naudet, if he *dares* show his face to you, tell that *bourgeoisie* son of a sodomite, he is dead for doing this to me. *Dead!*"

"Please do not speak of killing people. Or you are no different from these revolutionaries."

"It is either them or us. And it is not going to be us. Do you understand?"

Grabbing his face, she captured his lips, desperately wanting and needing to erase everything happening to them.

Dropping the clothing he held, he also grabbed her face and kissed her, molding his lips harder against hers. The searing heat of his tongue feverishly worked against hers as his fingers dug into the skin of her face. He kissed her, harder and harder.

She could feel his genuine passion and affection for her.

It pulsed from his hand and his lips. It was—

He broke away and dragged in several ragged breaths. "Wait to hear from me." He gathered his clothes, bundling them again then stalked to the door. "Pack whatever you need and make sure it fits into one sack and one sack only. No trunks. The less we carry, the more effective our movements will be. More importantly, do not stray from your regular routine until you hear from me."

Her heart pounded, realizing he wasn't accepting that she wasn't going.

Though she didn't want to believe in the dread scraping itself into her, a dread that whispered of horrible, horrible things to come, things that would happen to him if he tried to leave, she swung toward him and knew she had to say it. "Meeting you has changed my entire perspective on life and men. I have no regrets. None. I adore you."

He paused and jerked toward her, staring.

Blinking back tears she did not want to cry, she set her hands on her belly. "If it is a boy, what shall I name him? I will let you decide."

His features twisted. "Do not *dare* say good-bye to me. I will come back for you in two days. *Two.*"

No. He would not. She was not going. "What shall I name him?" she softly insisted. "Please. It will make me happy. And I need happy thoughts."

He was quiet for a moment. "Henri. After my mother's father. In English it is *Henry.*"

Henry. English. Someday she would learn to speak it. Someday. "And if it is a girl?"

"We will name her after my mother. Marguerite. In English it is Margaret."

Margaret. English. She did her best to smile for him. "Thank you. I genuinely needed that. Now where will I be able to find you? Should I need to speak to you one last time before you—"

"*No.*" He kept rigidly pointing. "You are not staying in this hell alone. *Especially* if you are pregnant with *my* child! You, I and the babe will be leaving Paris in two days. Two. I need time to gather money, weapons and call in more than a few favors from the people I do trust, which obviously is *not* Naudet.

That damn *sodomite*, I—" He jerked open the door and was about to step out, when he paused.

Capturing her gaze, he rumbled out, "Watching over you these past three months was the greatest honor of my life. Everything about you makes it difficult for me to let you go. Honor me by loving me, and I swear I will spend my life being everything you need me to be and more. Once we get to England, we will marry."

She swallowed, realizing he had proposed.

No longer meeting her gaze, he stepped out and slammed the door behind him.

A shaky breath escaped her. Why did a part of her want to take the risk and go with him and leave France for a chance to be with him? Was it possible she was already in love?

Mon Dieu. She was.

LESSON TEN

Trust, when broken, can shatter us into a million pieces. Gather those jagged pieces, one by one, and hold them firmly to your heart. For you will need every piece later when you attempt to rebuild what was so cruelly taken.

-The School of Gallantry

The Andelot estate – three minutes to ten that evening

Running down the massive, candlelit corridor which had long been empty of servants given he convinced his father to dismiss every last one in order to save them from the mounting chaos overtaking Paris, Gérard whipped aside the soiled clothing he still held and bounded up the vast spiraling stairs leading toward the upper floor.

"*Monseigneur!*" he shouted, jumping up onto the landing. "*Monseigneur!*" He darted toward his father's private quarters knowing the man had most likely retired.

The door at the end of the massive corridor swung open.

The duc veered out in a robe, a pistol in hand, and stared.

Gérard slid to a halt, and between seething breaths, choked out, "We have to leave France. We have two days to plan and only three days to do it."

Those blue eyes widened as the lines etched into that aged, regal face deepened. "What the devil is going on?"

There was too much to say. Too much to plan. Too much to do. His hands quaked. "*Sa Majesté* is going to trial." He tried not to heave knowing it. "There will be thirty-three charges set against him. *Thirty-bloody-three!* There is no saving him or his family. They will all die and we are next. I was informed not even an hour ago, that your name and mine, is next given we are so closely related to *Sa Majesté.* They are amassing charges as we speak."

The duc dragged in a long breath and let it out through his nostrils. After a long moment, he took Gérard's hand and placed the pistol into it, molding his fingers against the rosewood handle. "This is my country, and no one will ever run me out of it." That voice hardened. "Take whatever you can and leave. Go to London to the address you have been writing to since you were seven. Your mother's family will welcome you and get you through this, and whatever money you need, they most certainly have that and more."

Gérard's vision blurred. It was as if everyone around him had given up on wanting to live. "No. I am not leaving you."

"There is nothing more to be said. Now go. Ready yourself."

"Are you mad? You cannot stay. They will cleave your very head from your shoulders if you do!"

Setting a heavy hand on Gérard's shoulder, the duc grudgingly met his gaze. "You and I both know I am well beyond saving. The one and only person I ever believed in was your mother, and as you well know, these people took her from me. They— Honor her, me and our name by marrying into what we deserve. The Andelot title carries six generations of prestige no one will *ever* take from us. The moment you get to London, embrace a new life and only associate with people of worth. People of pedigree. The daughter of a viscount or higher in standing is who you must marry. Do this for me and our name. Swear to it. Swear to it so I may die in peace."

Gérard edged back, his heart pounding. "I..." Shite. There was no way around this. He had to say it. "I regret to inform you that it is too late for me to embrace what you want. Our name is going to who I deem best, and her name is Thérèse Angelique Clavette. She is the daughter of a butcher and now a renowned actress at *Théâtre Française*. I have taken her virginity and must therefore honor her by marrying her the moment she and I get to England. For it is the right thing to do. The only thing to do. Do you understand?"

Those features stilled. The duc said nothing. He stiffly turned and slowly walked back to his room. He closed the door.

Gérard felt the weight of the pistol tremble in his hand. He half-squatted and set it down onto the floor of the corridor with a clack. Quickly rising, he dragged in several breaths and shifting his jaw. He stalked toward the closed door, more than ready to take on his father in the name of what he wanted and what he saw in Thérèse's eyes when she told him he had changed her perspective on men. It held a promise of far more than love. It held a promise of forever. Something he thought he would never find.

Opening the door to the half-lit bedchamber, Gérard stepped in. Rolling up his linen sleeves, he announced, "Fist wager. If I win, you come with me and Thérèse to England. If you win, you can stay and die. I will give you that right."

The duc, who had seated himself on the edge of his bed, stared out vacantly at nothing in particular. He didn't even blink. After a long pulsing moment, he slowly rose and removed his robe, revealing his night shirt. He went over to the hearth and picked up an iron poker. Turning, he pointed its sharp tip straight at him. "You are no son of mine to take sides with the very people who murdered your mother. You are dead to me. All of my sons are dead. *Dead!*"

Gérard dropped his hands, feeling numb and..betrayed. For in his greatest hour of need, during a time when the woman he had endangered, a woman who might very well be carrying his babe, needed protection, his father had decided to lose the last of his mind.

"I harbor a great affection for her," Gérard confessed, "and have ever since I met her. She defies convention but retains a beautiful mind and a beautiful heart." To hell with pride and whatever lashing it would bring. This was about saving the woman he loved. And if it meant pleading and getting beaten, he would do that and more. "I need you to help me, *Monseigneur*. If there is ever a time I need you to be a father to me it is now. Help me to protect her, because I cannot do it on my own against an entire nation that wants me dead. Do you understand? Help me. Please. Help me protect her."

Those nostrils flared. "No. I am done swallowing the way these people take everything from us. They will not take our name." Walking up to him, the duc stared him down, fingering the poker with thick fingers. "She is not yours to save. Nor does her kind deserve to be saved. Denounce her and I will go with you to London this very night."

Gérard's eyes widened, knowing his father was asking him to murder Thérèse and leave her to die. Merely because she was not pedigree.

"Denounce her," his father bit out. "Denounce her and we will leave this very night. We will become the father and son we deserve to be. The sort your mother would have wanted us to be."

Gérard's throat tightened. This man was not his father. *This* was the mere skeleton of a hateful name that deserved to be buried right along with the revolution. He had known for some time that his father's mind was no longer his own, but it had taken this moment to finally accept it.

They were father and son no more. "I would sooner denounce you, *Monseigneur*, than let her die. To abandon her when she needs me most would be nothing short of murder. If you wish to stay here and die, so be it. Cling to your *filthy, rotting* name and see if it saves you. As for me? I am taking her to England and giving her the life she deserves. For despite what you think, my title is not what will make her a duchess. She is already that and more."

The duc's lips parted. "You are choosing her over your own father?"

"Yes. I am. *Adieu, Monseigneur.* May I never see you again." Glaring at his father, Gérard swung away and was about to leave, when a *crack* rattled inside his skull. Choking pain slashed its way straight to his teeth and every bone.

He swayed, one last breath leaving him before everything spilled into nothing but black.

✴✴✴✴

Théâtre Française

Forty-two minutes later

Gathering jars of cosmetics and perfume bottles from her lacquered, oak dressing table, Thérèse paused and then rolled her eyes, setting them all back down, one by one by one. She kept forgetting she had servants to do things for her.

It was a life she was still getting used to.

Tightening the large red bow around the waist of her blue and white gown with hands that still quaked knowing she was more or less waiting for Citoyen de Sade to report her, she swiped up her reticule and was about to blow out the remaining candles in the room when she heard a thundering boom and an echo from beyond the closed door of her dressing room.

Thérèse paused, brows coming together. It sounded like a pistol being fired. In the theatre?

Female screams and random male shouts of actors suddenly penetrated the silence.

Her pulse roared. What—

Swinging toward its direction, she gathered her skirts to keep them from tangling around her slippered feet and ran to the door, her breaths uneven. Jerking open the door, she peered out into the candle-lit corridor.

A few people, who had been gathering props, darted by. *"Grab a sword! Move! Move, move, move!"*

"There are none on hand! All swords taken off the set an hour ago! Someone needs to find a way out and fetch the bloody *gendarmerie nationale!"*

Her eyes widened. Oh, God. What was happening? She scrambled down and out of the corridor, to better see what was going on.

Another echoing crack of a pistol being fired pierced the air, causing her to almost fall against the nearest wall. She dragged in heavy breaths, scanning the red curtained area and walkways leading out to vast auditorium, stage and lobby beyond.

Screams and male shouts from the auditorium made her realize she needed to run toward the back of the theatre, not the front. But not before she had something to swing with.

Grabbing up a metal pole bearing the blue, white and red flag of the new Republic, she flipped it and wrapped the flag around the pole to get a better grip on it.

Another echoing crack of a pistol being fired pierced the air.

"*Thérèse!*"

She froze, gripping the pole hard and swung toward Jacques's voice. "Jacques!"

From across the stage, he sprinted toward her, whipping off his periwig. He skidded in, his dark eyes wide and his chest heaving. He grabbed her and swung them behind a prop against the wall. Leaning, he whispered, "Stay quiet. Stay. Quiet."

She tightened her hold on the metal pole in an effort to keep herself and her panicked mind steady. "What—"

"A man is looking for you," he rasped, shaking her. "*He shot Rémy in the head. He shot him for refusing to let him pass and just shot two others.*"

The metal pole clattered from her trembling hands in a blurring effort to make sense of what was happening. "*Rémyyyyyy!*" Blinded by the terror of knowing her cousin had been shot, she tried shoving past Jacques, only to be yanked back. "Release me!" she screamed, shoving at him again. "We cannot leave him to die! We cannot—"

Jacques grabbed her shoulders hard and violently shoved her into the wall back behind the prop, clamping a hand against her mouth. "*Thérèse,*" he hissed, hovering so close they were nose to nose. "Cease yelling or he will bloody find us. There is nothing you can do for Rémy. Now stay quiet. Do you hear me?"

She clung to Jacques, attempting to sob in silence. It only echoed around them.

Jacques's hands jumped to the sides of her face, his breaths as uneven as hers. "*For God's sake, stay quiet. I need you to stay quiet.*"

Another sob escaped her.

Pressing her harder against the wall, Jacques stared down at her, his chest rising and falling against hers and then captured her mouth with his, working his tongue hard against her own.

She choked and hit him, trying to tear away.

He broke away and glared. "I am trying to keep you quiet," he bit out in between breaths.

"You are being vile right now!" She shoved him, stumbling out from behind the prop.

A stocky figure in an evening robe that billowed around his swiftly moving frame stalked toward her from across the stage, making her eyes widen. He tossed the smoking pistol he held, sending it clattering and skidding across the wooden stage. He dug into the satchel draped around his shoulder, pulling out another pistol that was clearly already primed and pointed it straight at them.

"*Jacques!*" Thérèse shoved him toward the back of the theatre. "*Move!*"

"Do not move or by God I will murder you both in a single shot!" the older man boomed, stalking toward them, the pistol pointed straight at them. "Stay where you are!"

They both froze, knowing full well there was nowhere to go.

Jacques set his body against Thérèse and rammed her hard against the wall, using his entire body like a shield. He pressed his backside firmly against her, forcing her to remain against the wall. He widened his stance toward the man. "Leave her be. She has done nothing to earn this!"

An older gentleman with curling grey hair falling into piercing blue eyes came to a halt before them. His face tightened with visible rage as he continued to hold the pistol straight at them, his large hand trembling in an effort to keep it level. "Step aside lest your father weep."

"No," Jacques bit out. "Shoot me if you must but I am not letting you touch her."

Thérèse couldn't breathe between disbelieving gasps and knew that if she was going to die, she would do it saving the life of a boy who had yet to touch a dream. For she, at least, had touched so many of them with the tips of outstretched fingers.

"No! Do not harm him*! Please!*" She pulled herself away from the wall, from behind Jacques, and set herself between that pistol and Jacques, tears streaming down her face and her lips trembling. "Before I die," she choked out, unable to hold back her sobs, "at least..list me my sins. I beg of you!"

The man with the pistol paused and lowered the pistol, skimming her appearance in between ragged breaths. He fingered the trigger of the pistol and searched her face. "Are you Thérèse Angelique Clavette?" he tonelessly asked. "The butcher's daughter?"

A sob escaped her, knowing she was going to die. He knew her real name.

Setting trembling hands against her belly, she prayed unto God Himself she wasn't pregnant, if only to give her soul rest knowing the babe would not be murdered right along with her. "What have I done? What have I—"

The older man's expression stilled. "You cannot have him," he breathed out. "He does not belong to the Republic. He belongs to the Andelot name. A name your sort of people could *never* even *begin* to bring honor to."

Her lips parted in wavering disbelief. This man was Gérard's father. She staggered, refusing to believe this man had just..murdered Rémy. He had murdered her darling smiling, happy Rémy who had always foolishly said, 'You will be the death of me.'

The sobs rolling from her throat became too hysterical for her to control. Anger ripped apart any rational thoughts of her even trying to plead for herself. "Damn you into hell!" she roared. "My cousin was the kindest man humanity could have ever beheld and you...*you murdered him*!" she screamed. "*Over a name! How vile are you?!*"

The pistol slowly lifted.

No longer feeling a part of this world, she eerily envisioned Gérard with his mouth quirked and those blue eyes being playful. Eyes she would never see again.

An echoing crack of a pistol being fired thundered, making her jump as acrid soot filled her nostrils. She staggered forward. Then paused.

There was no pain. None.

The pistol the duc held clattered to floor and skid out of sight.

She trembled, almost unable to keep standing as her gaze fell in disbelief to the duc who had collapsed onto the floor, holding his bleeding thigh in between hoarse gasps.

Her eyes widened, realizing that standing behind the duc was—

Citoyen de Sade widened his stance and slowly blew at the barrel of the smoking pistol, wisping away grey tendrils of smoke into the air around him. Dark eyes met hers. "I would have aimed for his head, but I believe in giving every man his due suffering." Lowering the pistol, he strode toward her. "It will be all right. Breathe."

Everything frayed. She fainted, falling into an abyss that was now her life.

****

Early morning, July of 1793
The residence of Citoyen de Sade

The fact that the sun was shining on a day such as this was nothing short of a mockery. In Thérèse's opinion, a thunderstorm and torrents of rain laced with hail would have better reflected the torturous mood she was in.

As bright sunlight spilled through the latticed windows of the vast corridor, illuminating the black and white tiles of the floor beneath her booted feet, every fissure within the marble eerily appeared like tiny veins pushing up through the surface of skin.

She always noticed the cracks in the marble. She had walked through this very corridor with Sade many times, thinking every aspect of his home, right down to its cracked tiles, was a morbid illusion of imperfection that did not reflect the man.

Quietly entering his cluttered parlor, which was scattered with parchment, obscene books, nude sketches, canes, whips and shackles, she walked over to her usual chair, cradling her two-month-old son, Henri, and seated herself. She absently smoothed that small soft head that gave her so much joy. A joy that had allowed her to survive through the darkness that threatened to swallow her.

The silence was deafening.

She eyed the parlor entrance and continued to gently rock Henri.

Although she wasn't one to pray, except on Sunday at church whilst standing beside whispering women who refused to share her bench, Thérèse silently focused on the only words she could muster. *Please let him be pardoned, Lord. He has not earned death. He has so much to accomplish in life. Let him live. Please.*

She glanced again toward the open door, tears pressing against the lids of her eyes. A tear slipped down her cheek. She swiped it away with the hand that wasn't holding Henri.

Steps echoed from down the corridor, making her quickly rise.

"*Thérèse?*" Sade called in a strained tone.

"Yes?" she choked out, using her free hand to brush away more tears with the tips of trembling fingers. She had become ridiculously dependent on the man for any covert information. Information he graciously freely shared without asking for anything in return. She was certain the amount of pain he saw rolling out of her satisfied whatever morbid fantasies he sought to quell.

Citoyen de Sade veered into the small parlor and jerked to a halt, adjusting the black attire he only ever wore when attending a session at the Convention. His stern features assessed her before softening. "I have asked you to call upon me this morning because I finally have news. Are you ready to hear it?"

She pinched her lips hard in an effort to remain calm. "Yes."

He pointed at her. "No crying."

She nodded, her eyes and throat burning as she struggled to obey.

He lowered his hand. "As you already know, his father was guillotined for crimes against the Republic that included the murder of your cousin and two others. Apparently, Gérard was never informed of the charges or the murders seeing he was placed in a different prison. Although he already know his father is no longer with us, he does not know about the attempt made against your life. For the state of his mind, I insist we not tell him and suggest you protect him against what his father did. Gérard is not the same man. Given his high level of aggression toward the soldiers, who are barely capable of keeping him against the wall even with weapons in hand, this situation could escalate beyond your control."

She swallowed. Dearest God. What had been done to him? "Did they torture him?"

"Yes." His voice grew ragged. "They were trying to extract information pertaining to papers he was holding and only ever stopped long enough for him not to die, seeing if he did, those papers would be released to the public. The torture had been going on since they arrested him last year."

Oh, God. She pinched her eyes, her very soul trembling. "They cannot continue to hold him indefinitely like this." She opened her eyes. "What is his sentence? What is his crime? Has it been decided? Answer me!"

Widening his stance, Sade announced, "He would have been guillotined along with his father, but given these papers and that his family in London had the King of England himself write on his behalf, Robespierre decided Gérard would be temporarily released under the proviso that he stay in Paris until called upon to answer questions about certain papers he possesses. Whatever the hell those papers are, and whoever the hell is holding them, is keeping him alive. Robespierre is scared to the point of shitting to the thirteenth power. And that is saying something."

Relief flooded her trembling body as she repeatedly kissed Henri's sleeping head. "Henri, my darling, you are going to finally meet your papa. I knew justice would prevail. I knew it!" She sat in the chair again and nuzzled Henri's head.

That voice hardened. "I suggest you not celebrate Gérard's release quite yet. Especially given what I now know. Are you listening?"

She searched that face in dread. "Yes. I..I am listening. What?"

Sade held her gaze. "Robespierre wants those papers. The only reason he is releasing Gérard from prison is because he is hoping Gérard will lead him to whoever is holding those documents. Which means if those papers do not surface as quickly as Robespierre would like, Gérard will end up dead. No more trials, no more prison, no more torture sessions. He is dead."

The darkness of those words made her realize Gérard would never be safe. Ever. "We need to get him out of France. We need to urge him to take whatever money he can and leave."

Striding toward her, Sade seated himself in the chair beside her. "He has no money. Everything the Andelot name ever owned, including its fourteen estates and all of its millions, have been confiscated. He does not know it yet, but he has nothing. Even all of his clothes are being put up for auction in a few weeks."

Dearest God. How could a government strip a man of *everything* he had been born with merely because he was an aristocrat?

His father's sins were not his.

They had never been his.

She had to stay strong. She had to get Gérard through this. No more sniffling or crying or— Tears would not save him. Only the butcher girl with a cleaver could.

With her free hand, she took hold of Sade's large one, meeting those deeply set dark eyes. "Your kindness in overseeing this matter is much appreciated. Whatever money he needs in order to leave the country, I will oversee it. However much he requires, it is his. All that matters is we save him. We have to save him."

These past few months without Gérard had been nothing short of a numbing blur.

After his father's senseless rampage, the city of Paris had sensationalized the story to the point of mania, setting an even greater divide between the remaining aristocrats and the people. Pamphleteers waved absurd sketches and posters of her gripping the flag of the Republic with windblown hair while standing up against a crotchety duc of Andelot holding a pistol to her heart.

Despite her pregnancy, and no one knowing who the child really belonged to, her popularity as an actress exploded to the point where the new manager at the *Théâtre Française* paid her beyond what any actress had ever been paid in order to keep her on stage. The contracts she signed commanded she only be allowed to take two months off to give birth and recover. She was expected to return to the stage in two weeks.

And the men? By God and by Satan. It had only gotten worse. Flowers and gifts and letters and more gifts arrived on the hour, no matter how many times she turned them away.

Even Jacques had lost his mind given the near-death moment they had shared. Outside of the theatre, he had called on her flat late one night and refused to leave despite her protests. It resulted in her smacking him.

Not that it changed anything. He remained at her elbow.

And as of four months ago, which scared her to the point of confiding in Sade, Robespierre had sought to become her greatest admirer and called on her in a regular fashion, frequently inviting her to private gatherings and public events. While she had no doubt Gérard would snap her neck for it, Sade had assured her that if she could be strategic about her association with Robespierre, they could use it to their benefit. To help Gérard.

So she maintained the association.

"When will he be released?" she finally asked.

Sade squeezed her hand. "This afternoon."

Her lips trembled and she could no longer see past her tears. She hadn't seen him since the night he left the theatre. Before his father had lost his mind and gave all of Paris a reason to curse the Andelot name. Her only consolation was that Gérard had not been butchered in that slaughter. He had been locked in a leather trunk at the foot of his father's bed, bleeding from the head, barely conscious, when the *gendarmerie nationale* marched onto the Andelot estate in a hunt to find him and create a long list of charges that strangely kept getting changed.

Though she had repeatedly tried to see him during all sixteen of his trials that were reset, the locations of the courtrooms kept changing, as well as where he was being held. There were more than fifty-two prisons across all of Paris, all of them always full and all of them always changing names, making it impossible for her to find his name on any of the lists.

She couldn't imagine what he had lived through.

A part of her felt responsible. After all, she had played along with his game of going against the Republic. All in the name of money and fame, both of which she now had, but both of which meant nothing without Gérard.

More tears slipped down her cheek.

Releasing her hand, Sade reached up and swiped her tear, dragging it against her skin. He glanced at it and dabbed his tongue to its wetness. "Who knew pain had so much flavor."

She eyed him in exasperation. She had long ceased questioning Sade's savage oddities. The moment she thought she understood the man, she did not. He was as charming as he was Satanic. But he had more than proven to be endearing enough for her to embrace him for what he really was: a seeker of pleasure and pain. He took pride in it and she had come to respect that. "Gérard will not be pleased when he learns of our association."

He grudgingly stared her down. "Did I ever fuck you or whip you throughout any of this?"

She sniffed. "Cease with that language. You and I both know we are friends, but Gérard will never believe it. Or accept it. Especially given your last conversation with him and what you wanted of us."

Sade didn't meet her gaze. "This is how we must proceed if we are to save him. You will be given an hour to convince him to give me the papers, after which I will find someone I trust to get him out of Paris. I will wait until he is well out of reach before I get those papers into Robespierre's hands. By then, no one will be able to touch him. In doing so, your association with Gérard must end. For the safety of your child and your life, if you stay in France, you cannot maintain any further contact or let anyone know you and he were ever involved. You have to let him go. Do you understand?"

Her throat tightened, and she no longer felt herself breathing. She was being forced to say good-bye to a beautiful dream that had never been hers. "No. An hour will not be enough. Is there any way to—"

He gripped her knee. Hard. "It would be too risky, and he requires a full night of darkness to get him out of Paris and as close to the border as possible."

"What if I go with him? I want to go with him. I want to—"

"The more people who travel with him, the less likely he will make it. Do you want him to live or not?"

A sob escaped her knowing she would never see him again. All these months of being without him, without knowing what he was going through while their child had been growing within her, had brutalized her mind and soul to the point of mania. And now, with their child in her arms, she was being asked to stay in France and live through who knows how much longer without him.

She kept sobbing and sobbing and.. sobbing.

"Woman, you are agitating me. If you keep crying, I will lay you on my lap naked and give you something to cry about."

Swallowing back whatever tears she could choke back, she swiped at her eyes. "I will do anything to.. save him. Tell me, and I will do it. What happens next?"

"While I will do my best to convince him on my own, if I am unsuccessful, it will be up to you to get those papers into my hands. You have an hour to do it. I will fetch him from *La Force* upon his release this afternoon. We are incredibly blessed in that Robespierre has tasked me to watch over him and report his activities. Once Gérard has travelled outside of Paris all night, tomorrow at noon, I will deliver the papers to Robespierre and report his disappearance. At that point, I will not be able to protect him from whatever happens. Do you understand?"

A shaky breath escaped her as she kissed Henri's head with trembling lips in an effort to remind herself that she couldn't be selfish. She would always have Henri to remember him by. Always. A strange sense of regal calm overtook her knowing that the only way to save Gérard was to let him go. "I will ensure he gives you the papers."

"Good. I will deliver him tonight at your château shortly after darkness falls. Leave the door to the servants' quarters unlocked and dismiss all of your servants for the night using any means possible so no one sees you with him. Ensure he leaves no later than ten tonight. I will be waiting outside your château to take him to an unmarked coach that will carry him out of Paris to another unmarked coach that will take him to the border. Is that understood?"

She half-nodded, feeling numb. Her child would have no father. And she would have no husband. Ever. Not after Gérard. No eyes would ever be blue enough. No heart would ever be passionate enough. He had blinded her to all men. "Given I must let him go, I beseech you to prepare him for how things will end so what little time I have with him is not spent in argument. Can you do that?"

"Consider it done. Expect him shortly after nightfall. You will have an hour."

One hour to end what she knew *no* amount of hours would ever end.

Although she wasn't ready to say good-bye to her Gérard or what they had shared, she most certainly was ready to save his life and push him out into a world that needed him more than she did. He was only twenty-two. And his gallant nature and his gallant heart and all the good he would do for the world outside of France was only the beginning of what awaited the ever beautiful Gérard, the *Duc de Andelot.*

LESSON ELEVEN

Glory, glory be. But...for how long?

-**The School of Gallantry**

That afternoon

La Force, one of many crowded prisons throughout Paris

Although Gérard wanted to spit and curse and swing at the sky he could barely see beyond the rusting bars, he figured God needed a reprieve from his ever-growing long list of complaints. All that mattered was he was getting out.

The two dozen strangers crowded into his stone cell were the definition of the sort of panic every human went through when they realized death was near.

Women silently knelt with their ivory rosaries, their children huddled near, those faces covered with snot from hours of crying, while men, once they realized their shouts were of no use, eventually sat and carved their last messages into the walls with their own shoe buckles.

Gérard wished he could offer each and every one of them words of comfort, but what was the point of dangling any emotion for them or the world to see? It couldn't smash stone walls or end a revolution.

After everything he had endured and seen with his own two eyes, there was no more room for emotion in France. Many buildings throughout Paris, which he had been repeatedly forced to see from the open cart on his way to and from countless prisons, were always burning. The heat from the rising flames that cracked toward the open skies made the sooty air appear as if everything were melting from rippling intensity. It had penetrated his pulsing skin in the same way the blurring faces and shouts of the *bourgeois* and lowers classes had penetrated his mind.

And they thought he was the animal.

Going to and from trials and cart to cart and prison to prison for months at a time, witnessing death on the streets of Paris had become the norm. Barely a week earlier, his open, mud-spattered cart had clattered past the corpse of an old neighbor, Vicomte de Laroche, an elderly titled man with four grandchildren he always boasted to the world about. The elderly man always had a smile for his fellow French and was often seen tossing coins to impoverished children.

Vicomte de Laroche had lain mangled, the blood from his slit-open throat caked and sprayed across cobbled streets. Those open eyes had stared up to the heavens as flies crawled across his expressionless face and mouth.

Gérard had almost fallen out of the cart as he rolled by that unmoving elderly body. He had watched as several young men in red wool caps stripped Laroche of his expensive clothing and casually donned it as if they had just gone shopping in the finest district.

It was something Gérard would remember for the rest of his life.

He swore onto the memory of elderly Laroche, that the moment he left the walls of this prison, he would ensure everyone in Laroche's family made it out of France alive.

Well-exhausted from standing within the overly crowded holding chamber, where he awaited his release, Gérard seated himself back on the dirt-pounded floor beside a young girl of about fourteen. She arranged her mud-spattered gown around her slippered feet.

She had been shoved into the cell less than an hour earlier without anyone.

What a fourteen-year-old girl was doing in prison at all was beyond his understanding.

Surprisingly, she appeared to be taking it well. A bit *too* well. Earlier, she had been humming a ditty as if she were waiting for a friend at a coffeehouse.

Lowering his gaze, he dug his fingers into the frayed wool of his breeches in an effort to remain calm knowing there was nothing he could do to help her or anyone else in this prison.

Several roaches with dangling antennas crawled out from beneath the cracks of the stone wall beside him. They paused in stealth unison.

The girl beside him frantically removed her slipper from her right foot and turned, raising the slipper above her head, waiting for their approach. When the roaches ticked in a group in the opposite direction (for they must have known she was anything but receptive to a visit), she shoved her stockinged foot back into her mud-slathered satin shoe and leaned her head back against the hard stone wall.

Gérard shifted his jaw and wanted to point out to the girl that it was ridiculous to worry about roaches given what awaited her. But seeing it could very well be her last hours of her life, it didn't seem fair to say anything but, "Well done. I doubt they will ever come back."

She set her chin in pride and seated herself beside him. She then eyed him and said in broken French, "Do..they..." She scooped fingers toward her mouth to indicate what she was trying to say.

Christ. She didn't even speak French. This fucking war was being waged against everyone. He angled toward her, his brows coming together. He spoke slowly in French, "What...*language* do you..*speak?*"

She paused and eventually managed, "*Anglais.*"

Astounded, he sat up and quickly offered in English, "What are you doing in this prison?"

Her mouth opened and closed in astonishment. Her green eyes brightened. "Heavens, above! You speak English. And quite beautifully, might I add! How do you do?" She shook his hand, then hugged him and froze, her nose wrinkling. She released him and edged away. "The French certainly do stink."

He rolled his eyes.

"Are you in here for long?" she asked.

"No. Not much longer."

Her slim brows came together and flickered. "You cannot leave me! While this has been quite the adventure I plan to put into poetry, no one here speaks any English. And my French is not what it should be. You have to help me. They barely understand anything I say."

His chest tightened. "Where are your parents?"

She jabbed a finger toward the wall. "Back at the house too many streets away. We have not been able to leave France since the revolution broke out. We were visiting Mama's family at the time, and Papa decided it was best we all stay and chronicle what was happening. Only far more happened than he had ever bargained for. Mama slaps his arm about it every day given they closed the borders and..here we are. We get along rather well with everyone, seeing we have more than enough money to share with whoever needs it, but I was outside this morning and these..two soldiers with red caps were shooting their pistols at a dog and laughing about it. So I..threw a rock at them and..." She grudgingly huffed out a breath. "My French is not what it should be. But I do know one thing. I am set for trial." She paused. "I will get a lawyer, yes?"

Fuck. What the girl didn't know was the Revolutionary Tribunal had long done away with trials. He had actually been one of the last to have seen such 'justice'. The Tribunal was now sending everyone straight to the guillotine. No matter the charges. Less paperwork. "Do you know the address of your parents?"

She rubbed at her nose. "Nineteen Soubise." She hesitated. "You seem very kind." She smiled. "What is your name?"

What it would always be despite what the revolution sought to destroy. "Gérard. My father was guillotined a few months ago, which makes me the Duke of Andelot. Seventh generation now."

Her brows shot up. "*A duke?* I never thought I would be sitting next to a duke in prison. At a supper table, yes, but not in prison."

That was actually funny. But he still didn't have it in him to laugh.

"My papa is a marquess," she added. "A British one. My name is Lady Madelaine. I will be sixteen in ten months."

A British aristocratic girl of fifteen sitting in a French prison awaiting death for throwing a rock. France had lost the last of its fucking mind. He eyed those around him, ensuring there were no men who might take an interest in her. "Keep to yourself and stay close to other women. I will ensure the moment I leave this holding cell that I get into contact with your parents. Hopefully, we will be able to get you out by tonight. All right?"

A breath escaped her. "That would be lovely, thank you."

He tapped at her forehead. "Next time, keep those rocks to yourself."

"You French are so easily agitated."

"What gave it away? The guillotine or the men holding the rope?"

She set her chin on her knees and scooted closer. "Are you married?"

He puffed out a breath. Even at fifteen, they only had one agenda. "No."

She paused. "Are you looking to marry?"

He gave her a pointed look. "Damn right I am. I have an incredible girl waiting for me." Or he *hoped* she was waiting. The very thought of Thérèse not waiting after everything he had been through would only— "There may even be a babe. Though I have no idea. These *défenseurs officieux* refuse to tell me anything. No letters or visitors or a spit of information for eight whole months. Even now, I have no idea how much longer before I get out." Savages.

The hope of tomorrow was what had kept him from the hell of today.

She paused again. "Is she pretty?"

Bright azure eyes he missed beyond breath flashed in his mind. He swallowed. "Yes. Very."

Shouts of riled, faceless people beyond the prison walls echoed through the barred slits above his head and into the small stone chamber. He glanced up toward the narrow slits that revealed a bright blue sky.

He groaned and swiped at his unevenly shorn hair. It was taking foreveeeeer.

Even worse, he couldn't remember the last time food had touched his lips. It had been two or three days. He was beginning to feel his limbs wanting to float away from his body as a result of it. He wanted a massive roast smothered in gravy with the bone still wedged into it and he wanted..brandy. Especially brandy. He wanted it so much. So. Much.

But what he wanted even more than food and brandy or anything else was...*Thérèse*. She and only she and that laughter and that wit and those bright, playful eyes could strip away all of this festering, festering darkness that clung to his mind and his soul like oozing tar.

Bringing trembling hands to his lips, he folded them and attempted to believe God was still somewhere listening, even though within his heart he sensed He wasn't. How could He be? He was far too busy listening to countless screams throughout all of France.

Gérard could still smell the acrid stench of thick smoke clinging to his disheveled hair and clothing. Smoke that had leached into the prison from surrounding fires. Everything smelled of burnt dreams and fallen walls, but above all else, it reeked of senseless murder.

Aside from the strewn bodies and decapitated heads spiked across the city like ornaments meant to honor the coming of the devil, his father and his king had long joined them. He hadn't grieved for his father at all. But for his king and his godfather he had shed countless tears. He hadn't even had the chance to thank the man for gifting him with papers that ultimately saved his own life.

After all that he had seen, Gérard would never consider himself French again. British was what he was and would always be, like his mother. British, like his aunt who still lived in London. British.

Eyeing the narrow wooden door that remained closed, he leaned further back against the stone wall as the sobs of children and women echoed around them.

A loud clink of a key being turned in the rusty lock broke through the din, eerily echoing in the small space.

Everyone scrambled to their feet, waiting.

Including Gérard and his new British friend.

The door banged open.

An older gentleman dressed entirely in black with the Republic's tri-colored sash draped over his coat, strode into the room followed by three soldiers.

"I am *Citoyen* Durand," he announced.

The man announced it every time he entered as if they were all idiots incapable of remembering a name.

Durand eyed them all and then pointed at Gérard. "You. *Citoyen Andelot.* Come with me."

Citoyen? No. He was not putting up with any of that given he was on his way out. Gérard pointed back at the man. "I am not *Citoyen.* I am *Monseigneur de Andelot.* Allow me to repeat that, piss-taker. I am *Monseigneur de Andelot.*"

Durand lowered his chin. "Are you wishing to stay in prison, *Citoyen?* I would be more than happy to re-introduce you to the rack you were tied to barely a week ago."

Uh..no. Fortunately, he was on his way out and still had money. His lawyer had assured him the Republic was not interested in taking the estate. Yet. Which meant he had a lot of gold to bury and a list of people to get out of France. If they were still alive, that is.

Quickly turning to the girl beside him, he grabbed her face with both hands and forced her to look up at him. "If your parents do not come for you, my lady, I will," he rasped. "Keep to yourself and trust no one. Do you understand?"

She half-nodded against his hands.

He tweaked her freckled nose. "Be brave. Get those roaches."

She put up a hand.

Turning, he brushed off his trousers, knowing he would never have to sit on a floor ever again, and setting his shoulders, walked toward the open door.

He walked. No more of him being dragged. He was walking like a duke and a man.

The soldiers pointed their bayonets straight at his head.

So much for duke or man. Knowing the protocol, he grudgingly set his hands on his head and followed Monsieur Durand out into the dank stone corridor, the slap of Gérard's bare feet echoing. His pulse roared wondering if Thérèse would be waiting for him.

It was the one thing that kept him breathing through the shackles that held him and the studded whips that had gouged his back. Her. The hope of them.

A narrow door was unlocked, and with his hands still on his head, he was let out to a brightly lit brick courtyard outside the prison leading to a set of massive gates where countless soldiers directed a long line of carts with countless prisoners who had yet to be admitted.

He squinted against the bright, shimmering sunlight and dragged in a slow, deep breath of air that did not fester with the smell of feces or urine. He wanted to remember this moment. *Freedom.* And this time, while he was out in the world, he'd make damn sure his back wasn't facing the wrong people.

Durand held out a folded parchment. "Carry this with you at all times whilst in public. It will ensure you are not arrested until called upon by *Citoyen* Robespierre himself. You are not allowed to leave Paris or you will be arrested and found guilty of being an enemy of the Republic whose penalty is death without trial. You may remove your hands from your head and are free to leave."

Gérard lowered his hands and snatched the parchment. Robespierre could kiss his arse. He wagged the parchment at the man. "Tell Robespierre a full decanter of brandy laced with arsenic will be waiting for him over at my house. Have him come by any time. Any. Time."

Durand narrowed his gaze and gestured toward a black lacquered coach. "That be yours. Now off with you! Before I put you back in and have them lash off whatever is left of your skin." The man glared and swung away, yelling out to surrounding soldiers to open the gates.

Adjusting his frayed and well-stained linen shirt, Gérard eyed the coach that had an emblazoned letter of S with a sword going through it. He squinted at it but was unable to make a correlation. *S?* Who the hell was S?

He quickly made his way toward the coach as a pock-marked man in sailor clothing opened the door and unfolded the steps, revealing the black buckled shoes of a man wearing red, clocked stockings and black knee breeches.

His pulse roared, knowing it was not his lawyer or anyone he knew, based on the color of those stockings alone. Where the hell was Thérèse? Had she sent someone else to fetch him?

Crushing the parchment in his hand, he jogged toward it, and skipping over the unfolded stairs and onto the landing, he sat on the upholstered seat opposite the man, ready for whatever the hell this moment brought.

The door slammed shut.

It took Gérard a few astounded half-breaths to realize that the dark-eyed man with the side-curl periwig sitting across from him was none other than the man who had originally unraveled his entire life: *Citoyen de Sade.*

The blood from his head drained and for a moment the world swayed.

After everything he and his mind and his body had been through, he couldn't and wouldn't live knowing he hadn't been there to protect his Thérèse from this vile piece of—

Gnashing his teeth, Gérard jumped to his feet, letting the parchment flutter from his hand and rigidly snapped up a fist. *"You have three breaths to tell me where the fuck she is. Three!"*

Sade angled his gold-headed cane and unsheathed its length, revealing a thin sharp blade within it. He pointed it at Gérard and gently tapped at the sleeve of his raised arm with it. "Sit. You have no quarrels with me. None. I come on behalf of more than Robespierre. I come on behalf of Thérèse. She is waiting to see you."

The trembling in Gérard's arm and fisted hand gave way to a long breath he'd been holding. Relief cascaded through him as he lowered his hand. He fell back onto the upholstered seat. She was waiting. He almost couldn't believe it.

The carriage clattered forward, rocking him into feeling as if he might lose consciousness.

Sade swept the blade back into his cane and thudded it against the floor of the coach. "My nose is bleeding from the stench you give off. Christ. When was the last time you bathed?"

Hissing out a breath, Gérard admitted, "I have no idea. I had to damn well barter to even get chalk for my teeth, yet alone soap." He sat up. "I need you to take this carriage straight to Nineteen Soubise. There is a young girl being imprisoned for throwing a rock at soldiers who were shooting at a dog. Her parents need to know about it. You are part of the Convention. What should her parents do? I would hardly think you bastards would want to wage a war against all of England. The girl's father is a *marquis*."

"You seem to think I am here to take orders," Sade tossed back in agitation. Thumping the roof with his cane, he was quiet for a moment. Unlatching the window, he yelled out to the driver, *"Nineteen Soubise! Make haste!"* He glared at Gérard. "The only reason I am assisting you with this girl is because I am making up for sins I committed in my youth. Nothing more." He sighed. "Whilst there are no guarantees, have the *marquis* send a lawyer straight over to Fouquier-Tinville. Given she was only rescuing a dog, Fouquier will hardly hold her. The man is forever complaining about the amount of executions that keep him from going to dinner. He will wave it through for that alone."

These men were nothing more than maggots squirming into people's bodies. "He complains about the amount of executions keeping him from fucking dinner?" Gérard echoed.

"Robespierre keeps us very busy. We are merely trying to keep up with the all demands."

However long his freedom lasted, Gérard needed to settle the last of his rattled mind. "There is an elderly gentleman I once knew. I saw him dead on the street when I was coming back from deposition. He had a wife and four grandchildren and a widowed daughter. I need to know what happened to them. "

"How about we assume they are dead? Hm? It would make life so much easier for all of us." Sade grudgingly leaned over and was about to latch the window of the coach again, but instead, paused and nudged it back open. Wide open. "My eye sockets are burning. Your stench is worse than a cunt filled with cheese curds and chopped onion."

Gérard gave him a withering look. "Compared to some of the other men I met, I am wearing incredibly expensive cologne."

"Yes, and along with that *cologne*, you have a beard the size of woman's arse." He tsked. "Not at all attractive. Not. At. All. You most certainly will not be getting fucked tonight."

Gérard glanced down at himself, the gnarled tendrils of coarse, black facial hair covering the wide expanse of his chest in a manner he had long stopped paying attention to or caring about. Until now. He swallowed, refusing to imagine what he looked like or what Thérèse would think or say. While he knew he would never be the same man he was before going into prison, he still had his pride. And he'd be *damned* if he'd arrive looking like a broken man.

Pointing to Sade's cane with the blade hidden in it, Gérard wagged his fingers. "Hand it over. I need it."

Sade's brows went up. "Oh, now, now, there is no reason to kill yourself over the fact that she will not fuck you."

Gérard glared. "She and I *never* fucked. We made love. There is a difference." Leaning forward, he snatched the cane from the man's hand and unsheathed the blade using the gold head. Tossing its bottom onto the seat, he angled the blade toward himself and grabbing his beard hard, held it out and sheared it as close to his chin as he could.

Sade smirked. "Hopefully, there are no holes in the road or I foresee this ending badly."

Ignoring him, Gérard finished shearing his beard. He tossed it all to the floor.

A boot kicked out toward him. "I hardly want your hair all over my carriage."

Gérard swept the blade back into the casing of the cane and tossed it at him. "You should have told me before I started." He scrubbed his face, his fingers digging past all the hair he still needed to shave. "Christ, this all has to go."

Gérard heaved out a breath in complete exasperation. "After we make this stop over at this girl's house, take me to my estate. Because I am not seeing Thérèse like this. I need a bath, a fresh set of clothes and something to eat. A roast, at the very least. I am *also* not showing up empty handed when I see Thérèse. I may have been in prison, but I am delivering myself to that woman in style. Do you know that woman once made me buy her a waist-long necklace consisting of two hundred and thirty-nine pearls that cost me almost eight thousand? And that does not include the diamond necklace I got for her. I am about to put both to shame and buy her a ring with a garnet the size of my mouth. I am going to ask her to marry me. Today."

Sade fingered his cane and tilted his head, observing him. He casually sniffed and then smiled. "I would not bother with flowers or a ring or cleaning yourself up, for that matter. 'Tis a waste of your breath and time. I would focus more on.. *praying*."

Leaning forward so he could set his elbows on each knee, Gérard stared the man down for a pulsing moment. "Maybe you do nothing to impress your women – *or men* – but I need a bath. *Why?* Because I need to feel human again. *Why?* Because I doubt I will *ever* be human again. But I can fucking try. Is that difficult for you to understand, you tosspot? After I visit this poor girl's house, you will take me to my estate, after which I will tend to my appearance, buy a goddamn ring and go straight to Thérèse. In that exact order or I will give you what you clearly want and love most: *pain*. Lots of it."

Using the handle of the cane to scratch at his own chin, Sade's mouth quirked. "Allow me to return the favor of pain, *tosspot*. You have no estate. Not a single million. Not even a single *sol*. Everything you ever owned, right down to the buckles on your shoes, now belongs to the Republic so it can further grow this ever glorious nation dedicated to *liberté, égalité, et fraternité*. You are now a true *citoyen*, neither above or below the rest of us. Which means you cannot give orders or buy your woman a ring because you only own the beard on your face and the stench of your body. Rather depressing, is it not?"

Gérard's throat tightened.

The lawyers had lied. Much like they had about everything else. They had never been on his side, and now his entire life was gone. The estates. The house he grew up in. His horse. He froze, the portrait of his mother that had been hanging in the gallery of his home flashing within his mind. It was the only known portrait he had of his mother. "What about the portraits on the walls? What did they—"

"All of it is being sold in the next few weeks."

No. No, no— "They intend to sell my mother's likeness?" he rasped. "Surely that is worth nothing to the Republic. Surely—"

"The frames are worth several *livres* a piece. The portraits themselves will most likely be burned."

Everything swayed, and Gérard knew it had nothing to do with the carriage he was riding in. All that had once been his life no longer existed. And now the Republic was trying to erase far more than his mother and the father they had executed. They were trying to erase him.

Dragging in uneven breaths, he whispered, "Does Thérèse know?"

"Yes. I told her this morning."

Closing his eyes in disbelief, Gérard set his head back against the seat and for a flicker of a moment, considered putting a bullet through his own head. Not that he ever would, for in doing so, he would only let these fuck-tarts win; and win they most certainly would not.

Keeping his eyes closed, for he was too tired to even want to use his sight for anything, he quietly asked, "Am I a father?"

"Yes. You have a boy. She named him Henri Rémy Maitenon."

He set trembling hands against his head. He had a boy. And his darling Thérèse, had named him *Henri Rémy Maitenon*. After his mother's father, after her all too jolly cousin he genuinely admired, and.. her stage name.

What should have been the greatest moment of his life, knowing he was a father, was, in fact, nothing but a vile nightmare. Because he couldn't even provide his son or the woman he had been hoping to marry with the life a true Andelot deserved.

He was nothing. He was *worth* nothing. And his son would grow up knowing it. Without money, how was he going to provide for his family? He didn't have the means to.

Lowering his hands, he lifted his head and glanced toward the small glass window of the coach that displayed blurred, brick buildings with shattered windows and charred doors.

This was the world his son would be growing up in. This. "How has she been providing for herself and my son? Did she have to sell the jewelry I gave her?"

Citoyen de Sade tapped his knee with the cane. "No. The woman is worth almost forty thousand a year and is doing quite well for herself. She is not only the most sought after actress in all of Paris, but has become every man's cock-hard fantasy to whom they all masturbate to and openly revere. Even Robespierre has a twitching fancy for her. She is, after all, in his eyes, the very symbol of what a woman should be: the French flag in one hand and a dead aristocrat in the other. She fainted into a flag she had been earlier holding as a weapon against a certain aristo who got carried away. It made news."

Gérard dug his fingers into his thighs in an effort to remain calm. He was beginning to believe getting his skin lashed on the hour for not giving up those papers might have been far, far better than facing this. Evenly spacing his words so as not to betray his disbelief, he asked, "Are you saying Robespierre is calling on Thérèse?"

Sade was quiet for a moment. "Yes. They have been publicly associating for some time and have gotten to know each other rather well."

His eyes widened. "What the hell does he want from her? Is she in any danger?"

Sade hesitated. "No. She is not in any danger. Far from it. She is merely an ornament he uses to elevate his name. She attends every gathering he asks her to. Last week, the two attended a gathering commemorating an upcoming *ménagerie* of all the exotic animals that were seized and collected from Versailles and other estates across the land. There are plans to create a zoo for the *citoyens* of Paris so they might freely enjoy seeing creatures such as.. *zebras*. For some reason, she wanted me to mention zebras to you."

The darkness in his head now became the darkness in his heart. For it was a message from Thérèse herself. It was over. She had taken her zebra from another man, embraced the Republic, and her fame, and betrayed him.

That bright-eyed girl who had literally given him a slice of heaven in the silence of the forest had indeed been taken from him, as he had predicted. And now Robespierre, the same man who had taken *his* freedom, *his* money, *his* life, *his* mother's only known likeness, was set to take the last of what was his: *Thérèse*. And Thérèse, damn her soul, was letting the man do it.

Given she was not in any danger, it meant she was doing it to save *him*. All at the cost of her body, her mind and her soul.

Gérard could barely breathe. "Is she already bedding him?"

Sade eyed him. "No. Not yet."

Dragging in a breath, knowing he hadn't lost her soul yet, he slowly let it out. "I know what she is doing and I am not letting *him* touch her. Not in my name. Not to save me. I would sooner die than ever let that happen."

Sade lifted a brow. "You heroes tout death to be the ultimate form of sacrifice, yet you fail to recognize what we – the all-knowing wicked – take the most glee in. If you are ignorant enough to die for her, *tosspot*, that means Robespierre gets everything he wants, including the woman you *died* for." He tsked. "Not a very brilliant plan if you ask me."

Fuck.

The coach came to a halt as the driver called out, "Nineteen Soubise!"

Too many people to save and only one man willing to do it. *What the fuck?!* Throwing open the door, he jumped down and stalked his way with bare feet to the door of a small château whose windows had all been boarded up and nailed with thick pieces of wood to protect the glass. He pounded on the door.

Panicked, hushed voices from within made him pause. His pounding would hardly get anyone to open the door.

Setting a shoulder against the door, he yelled out in English, "Although the Republic refuses to acknowledge my title and right to it, I am the Duke of Andelot. I was just released from prison and came to tell you that your daughter, Lady Madeleine, is being held in *La Force*. If you do not open this door, she will most certainly die because the Revolutionary Tribunal is sending everyone in the holding cells straight to the guillotine. *Do you understand?*"

The scrambling of booted feet came to the door and the latch was hit.

Gérard stepped back as the door opened.

A dark-haired gentleman of about forty and a petite woman of the same age, both dressed in expensive clothing, scrambled toward him.

Angling closer, Gérard confessed, "I was beside your daughter in prison before I was released. She is alive but God only knows for how much longer."

The woman let out a wail, clamping a bare hand over her mouth.

The gentleman quickly ushered her back inside and stepped back out, closing the door behind himself. He intently searched Gérard's face. "Why are they holding my daughter? She was playing with friends and dolls earlier. How— What are the charges? They cannot— *She is only fifteen!*"

Gérard puffed out a breath. "Apparently, she threw a rock at soldiers who were shooting pistols at a dog."

The man grabbed his head. "The girl has grown a bit wild given everything she has been seeing on a regular basis. She is not herself."

"Believe me. I understand and am here to help. I was told if you send a lawyer straight over to Fouquier-Tinville, they would consider dropping the charges. But I suggest you do it now. Because they start lining people up for the next guillotine cart in an hour."

The man's eyes widened. "Dearest God." He swung away and flung open the door with trembling hands and was about to run inside, when he swung back, his chest heaving. "I am indebted to you, *Monseigneur*. Where can I find you? I wish to repay this favor in any manner you require."

He could use favors. Glancing back at the open door of the coach, he yelled out in French from over his shoulder, "*Sade*! Where the hell will I be staying? Do you know?"

Sade leaned forward in his seat and called back, "My house at Thirteen Place Dauphine! Courtesy of Robespierre until further notice!"

Oh, hell no. He rigidly pointed at the man and boomed in French, "*Go tell Robespierre to slice his prick off with a dagger!*" He swung toward the man, cleared his throat and politely said in English, "Thirteen Place Dauphine. Though I know not for how much longer."

The man grabbed his hand with both of his and shook it. "Thank you." He ran inside, yelling for the servants to ready a horse.

Gérard puffed out a breath, hoping to God the girl got out. Stalking his way back to the coach, he climbed inside, slammed the door behind himself and fell into the seat. He pointed at Sade's head. "I am not staying with you. Hell, I would feel safer going back to prison and being tortured. Because at least there were no attempts at sodomy."

Sade stared him down, those black eyes taking on an all too serious nature. "That is what they all say before they bend over." Sade patted the flap of his trousers. "Come sit on it."

"Why not call on Naudet and have him take care of it?"

"That one is dead. He shot himself in the head when you were arrested."

Gérard's startled gaze flew to Sade's. "What?"

"He was loyal to you. He was a good man. That is all you need know."

Gérard swallowed. Everyone around him was dying. "I need to see Thérèse," he choked out.

With the smack of already bored lips, Sade set his shoulders against the upholstered seat. "Unfortunately, you will not be able to see her until nightfall. Which is probably how long it will take to clean you up anyway. I strongly caution you against thinking you have any further claim to her. She no longer belongs to you but the Republic known as Robespierre. And Robespierre, as you well know, is still very much in charge of every guillotine and how fast that blade falls. Which is why you will only have one hour with her, after which you leave France for however long it takes for peace to return. One hour and you and she are done."

Gérard sat up, his pulse roaring. "No. I am *not* giving up the only person I have left in my life. I am not—"

"Listen to me." Sade glanced out of the window as the carriage started rolling forward again. "No one is going to touch her. She will be fine. I promise. You, on the other hand, will not be. The fact you are still breathing is a miracle you can only attribute to the papers your godfather blessed you with. Which is why I suggest you give me the papers, seize the hour you have with her and leave Paris. If you want, I will even give you money to buy a ring which you can give to her tonight."

Gérard swallowed the aching tightness ravaging his throat. "What will become of Thérèse and my son?"

"As you well know, she is her own woman, but if you want, I can provide her protection. It would be an honor."

Oh, fuck no. "*You?*" he echoed.

"Yes. Me. I plan to teach that woman how to crack the whip and scare all the men in Paris, including Robespierre. You can thank me for it later."

Gérard closed his eyes. How was he ever going to breathe again? How was he ever going rationalize what he was about to do? "Can I really trust you to take care of her?"

"You can trust me to never go against her will, if that is what you are asking. Because if she wants to act like the devil and lick whatever crop I hold, I am not about to stop her. Have you met her? The woman is the definition of sex. Asking her not to go near another man again is like asking Satan not to sin."

Opening his eyes, Gérard stared the man down. "She has only ever been owned by herself. That is what gives her strength and that is what allows me to do this. This revolution will not last forever. I will see her again, and she will be mine again."

Sade tsked. "Love is a whip of nails that gashes its way past all reason. Give it ten years, and I promise, you will not even remember her name."

Drawing in a shaky breath, Gérard slowly shook his head. "No. In ten years, her name will be carved on every tree I pass. In twenty, it will be carved into my skin. And in thirty, the entire world will know that I, the *Duc de Andelot*, will not rest until Thérèse is what she should be and will always be: *mine*."

LESSON TWELVE

You must kiss away every tear and every sorrow

in order to believe in the glory of tomorrow.

-The School of Gallantry

Evening - Château de Maitenon

Staring at the clock set on the marble mantle of the hearth, Thérèse watched and listened as that ornate gold face ticked loud enough to drown out the rhythm of her heart and her uneven breaths. Every minute was taking too long. Even a second was too long.

Removing her white lace fichu from her moonstone gown, she draped it on the green velvet chaise beside her. It soundlessly slipped to the floor. She blankly stared at it, wondering how much longer she would have to wait.

The sound of heavy booted feet echoing down the corridor, just outside her reading room, made her heart skid. She swung toward the open door and swallowed, praying it was him.

A tall, male figure dressed in a simple grey-wool coat, billowing linen shirt and frayed matching trousers that hung loosely on an overly lean frame, appeared in the doorway of the candlelit room. A shockingly lean face whose cheekbones were so visible they were deep slashes, along with unevenly shorn black hair that had been finger swept in an attempt to hide its wild state, made her unable to believe what she was looking at.

Those steel blue eyes were the only identifiable characteristic.

It was the ghost of what had once been. And not what was.

Tears blinded her. A sob shook her to the core.

His features tightened. "*Ma biche,*" he rasped, quickly moving toward her. "What the hell are you doing? No. None of that. You in tears is not what I want to remember. Now come here. Come to me. Show me something still remains between us."

How could she pretend otherwise?

Running toward him in tears, she flung herself into his arms and dug her fingers into his back, attempting to tell herself that this was real. That Gérard was finally in her arms. If even for an hour. The scent of leather and cheap soap clung to her breaths. He no longer smelled the same. The scent of expensive amberwood cologne which she had once known so achingly well was gone. And soon he would be, too.

She sobbed, unable to be strong.

His large hands, which were now shockingly scabbed and scarred, cupped her face and tilted it up toward him. He searched her face, a ragged breath escaping him. "Do not cry." He dug his fingers rigidly into her piled, gathered hair, still searching her face. "Christ. I did nothing but worry about you."

Her hand jumped up to his lips and covered it, her fingers trembling. "And I did nothing but worry about you."

His features and his eyes softened. "As you can see, I am fine. I survived."

"I want to go with you," she choked out. "I want to go with you, but—"

"No. You will stay here. You have a name and a stronghold. Use it. We will find each other again, I promise." He possessively gripped her hair tighter, keeping her from moving. "*Ma biche.* Look at me."

She stiffened, her blurred gaze flying up to his.

His unspeaking eyes prolonged the moment. "Whilst I am honored you think me worthy of saving, you are playing a very dangerous game if you think you can dictate any control over Robespierre. He cannot be trusted."

She swallowed. "I know that."

"I am not going to ask what you and he share. It does not matter. I trust you completely. All that matters is that you are safe. Are you safe?"

Her heart squeezed. "Yes. I am. Sade has been incredibly generous with his time and the theatre is my greatest haven. We all look out for each other."

A breath escaped him. "Good." Folding his arms around her, he set his lips against her forehead, lingering in between half-breaths, as if unable to do more.

She swallowed and leaned into his solid warmth, almost unable to stand.

He released her and took her right hand. "Come." His rough, calloused large fingers methodically wove into hers, one by one. He kissed her hand and then turned them and tugged. "I want to see my boy. My Henri. Where is he?"

Bless his darling heart. "This way." She hurried him out of the parlor, up the stairs and into the corridor. Opening a door, she revealed the candlelit nursery where Henri slept in an ornate cradle with his name carved into it.

Squeezing Gérard's large hand, she led him inside and up to the cradle.

Gérard released her hand. He paused and edging himself down, stared at the small, peaceful face whose tiny lips suckled in a dream-like state. "*Jésus,*" he breathed out. He leaned in and slowly slid both hands beneath Henri. Lifting him, he brought their son into his arms and against the crook of his arm. He stared down at Henri with flickering dark brows. "He does not even look real. How old is he?"

Thérèse swallowed, tears burning her eyes again. "He is two months now," she whispered. "He used to be much smaller."

"*Smaller?* Not possible." Gérard curved a finger against Henri's small cheek before dragging it to his head.

They both lingered in silence, as Gérard touched and admired their son's hands, face and feet. Henri eventually blinked his eyes open, staring sourly up at them for interrupting his sleep. A small hand jerked up toward them.

A gruff laugh escaped Gérard. "This one may give us trouble."

That lip quivered, and Henri let out a shrill cry.

Gérard's brows went up. He pushed Henri back into her arms. "Make him stop before I cry right along with him."

Thérèse rolled her eyes and taking Henri into her arms, nestled her son against herself as his small head nudged toward her, opening lips for what he needed to go back to sleep. She smiled, unfastened her bodice and pulled her breast from her corset, letting Henri latch on and suckle the milk he wanted.

Gérard stared, moving closer to watch. "You did not hire a wet nurse?"

She smiled. "No. I enjoy being close to him. This is our time together. He and I."

He said nothing.

She eyed Gérard, trying to stay calm. "He is almost done. Around this time of night, he actually sleeps a lot longer. Which means you and I will have some time."

He said nothing. Reaching out, he touched their son's head, resting his fingers against him.

To see Gérard's large hand tenderly touching Henri's smallness made her very soul squeeze.

When Henri had fallen back asleep, she handed him off to Gérard and tucked her breast away, fastening her bodice back into place.

Lingering with Henri for a while longer, Gérard kissed that small head several times, then turned and placed Henri back into the cradle. He stared down at their son, smoothing that small arm. "He is so amazing."

She smiled brokenly. "I know. Why would he not be? He is half of you and half of me." When Gérard had still been in prison, holding Henri reminded her that Gérard had been real. That he still existed.

He slowly turned to her. "Come." Taking her hand, he led them back out of the room.

Quietly closing the door, he finally said, "I gave Sade the papers."

Relief flooded her. She closed her eyes, a half-breath escaping her, knowing she would not have to spend their time convincing him of it.

He was quiet for a long moment. "I am leaving you in Sade's care."

Opening her eyes, she met his gaze. "I am fully capable of taking care of myself."

An undefined emotion pulsed from him. "I know that. It is the only reason why I am able to do this." Swiping his face as if to erase whatever he was thinking, he turned and stalked down the corridor. He walked faster.

Startled to think he was already leaving, she panicked and bustled after him. "Gérard? Where are you going? You are not leaving yet, are you?"

He jerked to a halt and then gritting his teeth, turned and smashed his fist into the wall, denting the plaster. A tremor shook the corridor.

She jumped, sensing his time in prison was about to crawl out. "Gérard. You have every right to be angry, but please do not waste what little time we have assaulting walls."

He dug his scarred fingers into his neck and half-nodded. "You are right. I..forgive me. I..." He swung back toward her, his chest now rising and falling unevenly. "If I disappear from your life, in ten years time will you forget me? Even if I am unable to knock on your door?"

Tears burned her eyes. "No. Never."

"What about twenty years?"

"I will always remember you."

"*Always?* Do you swear it?"

She fought against the tears that sought to overwhelm her. "We will see each other again once this revolution is done. I know we will."

He pointed at her. "Damn right we will. Because you are mine. You will *always* be mine, and I wish to ensure it." Stalking back toward her, he dug into his pocket and lowering himself to one knee, held up a small gold ring with a large garnet. "I have nothing to give you but this, and even this is borrowed. Wear it knowing I will come back for you. However long that may be. Will you wait for me?"

Tears blinded her and she choked out, "Yes. I will wait for you."

He quickly rose and taking her hand, pushed the ring onto her finger. He kissed it, pressing his lips against it. "When we see each other again, will you marry me?"

She sniffed, her hand trembling against his. "Yes."

"You have made me the happiest of men in the worst of times and for that, I thank you." He searched her face. "No more tears. Not during our last moments. Kiss me. Kiss me and—" Grabbing her face, he captured her mouth with his own, forcing her lips apart with his tongue.

They kissed ever so slowly, lingering the feel of each other.

Trying to go slow, however, was pointless. It didn't last.

He frantically worked his tongue against hers and she frantically worked her tongue against his, her heart pounding.

She scrambled to shove off his coat.

His hands jumped to her wrists hard, seizing them. He turned them and shoved her against the nearest wall, causing her to gasp against the aggression she sensed had nothing to do with passion. Her eyes snapped open, her pulse thundering.

Gérard stared down at her in between heavy breaths, holding her wrists high above her head against the wall. "You are not seeing me without my clothes. They stay on."

Gone was her beloved rake who had once openly pleasured himself and showed off his body. Dread scraped her. "Gérard," she whispered up at him. "Sade told me what they did. And regardless of what was done, I will embrace whatever lies beneath your clothes."

His features tightened. "I want you to remember what was. Not what is." He released her wrists and held up his scabbed and heavily scarred hands between them. "This is best part of my body right now. *This.*"

She swallowed and gently brought each hand to her lips, kissing the rough skin and the fingers that had been gashed but healing. She traced her fingers against them. "Talk to me. Do not keep it in. Whatever you have to say, I am here listening."

He watched her fingers against his own and tonelessly said, "It never ended. I was either whipped until I lost consciousness or forced to watch executions at the square by blade or fire. They would tie men and women naked and toss them into the river calling it a worthy marriage. They—" His voice cracked. "I preferred the whip."

She cradled his face with trembling hands and kissed his forehead repeatedly in an attempt to convey that she had cried as many tears as he had endured pain. Sade had been right to protect Gérard from ever knowing what his father had done to her and her cousin. It would only hurt him more. And there was no need to burden him. Not after everything he had been through.

He tugged away his hands. "All that matters is that you are mine. You are mine now."

"Yes. I am. I am yours now."

He nodded. Dragging in a deep breath that fully widened his chest, he gripped her bodice with both hands and ripped her bodice down to her waist with a violent tug.

She startled as he shoved down the gown and flipped her toward the wall, tugging and removing all of the strings on her corset with aggressive tugs that made her stagger as she tried to steady herself against the wall with both hands. Her heart pounded as he finished stripping her completely.

When she was fully naked, he turned her back to him and yanked her up and into his arms, heading down the corridor. "Where is your room?"

She tightened her hold on his shoulders and neck, astounded by the fact that he had stripped her in less than a minute. She could barely breathe, much less focus.

He glanced down at her, still walking. "Where is your room?"

"Next to Henri's. Over there." She floppily pointed.

He stalked them down the corridor, toward that direction and angled them into the room. Walking up to her bed, he set her onto it and grabbed her face with both hands, leaning toward her from over the side of the bed.

Fixedly holding her gaze, he said, "We are doing this as many times as our bodies will allow so you *never* forget feeling me. Are we understood in this?"

That fierce passion she remembered all too well had not changed. Her heart pounded. "Yes."

"Good." With the swing of his body, he used his knees to spread her legs wide.

Unbuttoning the flap on his trousers, he released the hard length of his cock with a hand and lowering himself to her naked body, rammed his cock into her.

She gasped, gladly taking in that fullness. A fullness she missed so, so much.

Rigidly holding onto the sides of her head, he held her gaze and worked his cock into her again and again, the tempo of his hips and his body thumping the bed and her body into a delirium they both felt.

With each thump of his cock that pushed deeper and deeper against her womb, she felt herself spiraling against core tightening sensations that rippled through her body until she cried out in complete disbelief as to how good it felt to know something other than angst and pain. She missed being with him and touching him and holding him.

He withdrew and between savage breaths, spilled seed onto her stomach. He gasped.

She panted, trying to regain breaths, knowing he was protecting her to the end. "Maybe we should try for more children?"

He shook his head. "No. It would be too much of a burden on you. Henri is all we need." He captured her lips, working his tongue against her mouth.

She melted against him and used her tongue to taste him and remember him, savoring every glorious moment of holding him despite all of his bundled clothing.

Releasing her mouth, his scarred hands skimmed her entire body, her thighs, her stomach which had been stretched from having the baby, and her breasts. He sucked on each of her breasts hard, holding her milk-hardened breasts, forcing both her breasts to lactate and spill.

She gasped and tried swatting him away. "Whatever are you doing? Leave them be."

His head popped up, and he stared her down. "I am ensuring that what you are feeding my child is worthy of him."

Despite his riled intensity, she burst into startled laughter and swatted at him again. "Do leave some for the poor boy, will you?"

He smirked and grabbed her, rolled her onto his chest. Kissing her throat, he sucked on her neck, his mouth pulsing against her skin.

She raked her fingers through the softness of his black hair, wanting and needing to remember everything about him. Surely, the man she had fallen in love with months ago was still in that mind and in that heart.

They continued to touch and kiss and kiss and touch.

He eventually spread her thighs open again and slid his hard length into her wetness, ready to start again. He rolled his hips into her and rasped, "Do you love me?"

Her throat tightened. She smoothed the sides of his overly lean, shaven face. "I think we both know our affection for each other will forever bind us."

He searched her face, still rigidly pushing in and out of her. "Say it."

"I am not about to give you a reason to stay."

He gritted his teeth and slammed his cock into her in reprimand. "*Say the words.*"

She gasped. "No."

He rammed into her again.

If she said it, it would give him a reason to stay. And she was not that selfish. "No."

He stilled against her. Leaning in until they were nose to nose, he savagely held her gaze and said in a raw tone, "Allow me to gift you with what I am feeling right now due to your inability to proclaim what I know you feel." He lowered his head and then bit into her shoulder hard.

She winced, feeling those teeth pinching far more than skin.

He clamped down even harder. And harder and harder still.

Tears now stung her eyes from the pain. She shoved him.

He released his hold on her shoulder, heavy breaths escaping him. "If you refuse to say the words," he rasped, resuming steady, hard strokes, "then you had better use the strength of your hand. Either way, you are telling me that you love me before I leave tonight."

She swallowed, the pleasuring sensations making it impossible for her to focus. She gasped, knowing she was about to climax.

His cock pushed harder into her. "Do you love me?"

"I am not about to—"

He rode her harder. "Say it, damn you. I need you to—"

She could barely breathe against his urgency and those strokes. Without thinking, she choked out, "I love you." She cried out in disbelief, her entire body trembling.

He trembled with her, hissing out a breath as his pleasure and seed filled her womb.

She clung to him, and he clung to her, their breaths jagged.

"Thérèse." He kissed her lips hard, his fingers tracing her face. "I knew you loved me," he whispered against her mouth. "I knew all along. The dream of us and how we first met kept me alive. Do you know that?"

She wanted to cry.

He lifted his disheveled head, glancing back at the clock on the side of the room. He paused and quickly withdrew. "I have to go." He kissed her lips hard one last time, lingering for a long moment as if to ensure they both remembered it, then rose, sliding his hand across her face, throat and breast. He watched his hand and searched her face. Averting his gaze, he dragged away his hand and rose, sliding off the bed with a thud.

He quietly buttoned his breeches. "I love you, too."

She scrambled to sit up, not at all ready to let him go. Still naked, she slid off the bed and rounded him, taking both of his hands into hers. She kissed the scars on them and lifted her eyes to his. "Gérard, we will be together again. I know it."

He didn't meet her gaze.

She kissed his hands again. "I will always belong to you. And if God wills it, we *will* be together. I love you. And by saying it, I pray you take the words and save yourself. Swear to me you will leave tonight and never look back."

He snapped his gaze to hers, the feral intensity in his expression overwhelming her. "I have to stay a bit longer. Just a few days. There is a family I have to help."

Panic gripped her. "No. You cannot stay. If you do not leave tonight, Sade told me tomorrow will never come."

"*Thérèse*. I will only stay long enough to help. I am bound by the promise I made to Larouche when I saw him dead on the street. He has a family. I have to—"

"Gérard. Sade will not be able to protect you beyond another night. You *have* to go."

"*Thérèse—*"

She shook him. "You have suffered enough! I am begging you to fight for yourself, damn you. Fight! Forget about what you owe to the world and remember what you owe to yourself."

He averted his gaze. "Fine. I will leave tonight."

A breath escaped her.

He grabbed her face and kissed her lips hard, his breaths uneven. "I should have married you. I should have married you the moment we arrived into Paris after our time in the forest."

She grabbed his face. "Gérard," she whispered. "Like you had said, marriage is nothing more than a piece of paper. It does not decide if two people end up together. Paper will burn, but what we share will remain strong. It will last forever."

He lingered and touched a finger to her bare shoulder, tracing the still sore bite mark he had left. He leaned in and kissed the bite mark. Twice. "Forgive me," he whispered. "I am not the same man. I..they murdered me."

"No. They did not. You are here with me. You are still the same man. Never forget it." She cradled his head against her shoulder.

The clock chimed ten times.

He removed her hands from his head. "Tell Henri when he is old enough to understand that the only reason his father is not in his life is because he was not as strong as his mother."

Smoothing away her tears with his thumbs, he searched her face. "Stay in Paris and never leave. I will find you. No matter where you are, I will find you.

In the meantime, Sade will look after you and protect you." Gérard released her face. Letting out a slow breath, he turned and quietly strode toward the door.

Glancing back at her one last time, he disappeared.

Frantically padding after him, almost too blind to see past her tears, she swung into the corridor in one last effort to see him before he disappeared from her life. To her astonishment, he re-entered Henri's room. In the deafening silence, and through the open door of Henri's room, she could hear him whispering to their son, "You were born of love. Remember that."

She clasped a quaking hand against her mouth to keep herself from screaming at the horror of knowing that this amazing, beautiful man, and whatever was left of him, was being forced out of her life and his country because of vile people in a corrupted government wanting nothing more than what the last government wanted: *power.*

When Gérard re-appeared into the corridor, she swung back into her room, knowing if she looked at him again, if even for another breath, she wouldn't be able to let him go. And she had to. She had to let him go. So he might live.

She heard Gérard's heavy footsteps go down the corridor and down the stairwell. Those steps paused as if he stopped near her reading room. More steps and thudding, no longer within the corridor below, made her realize he had gone into her reading room. He noisily rummaged for something, books thudding onto the floor.

She edged out into the corridor, heart pounding, wondering what he was looking for.

He kept rummaging.

The noise eventually stopped.

His heavy footsteps went through the rest of the house until they faded.

A door opened and closed, announcing he was gone.

Sliding down the frame of the doorway, naked, she numbly stayed there and stared at the garnet ring on her finger. She was never going to love another man again.

****

Tucking the leather bound book of Voltaire under his arm, which his beloved Thérèse had carried in her basket when they first met in the forest, Gérard glanced down and fingered the small knitted boot in his hand. The tiny knitted boot he had slipped from his son's foot to have something to remember him by. His pulse roared.

He couldn't breathe. He couldn't think. He would have to carry this disgusting anguish with him knowing he would not be there for Thérèse or for his son. They would be living life without him.

He crossed into the shadows of the narrow road covered by the fog.

Savagely pressing the knitted white boot that achingly smelled of powder and freshly starched linen which spoke of how much Thérèse tended to their child, he shoved it into his coat pocket and yanked open the door to the waiting coach. Hauling himself up and into it, he slammed the door and fell onto the upholstered seat across from Sade who quietly sat in the shadows opposite him. Gérard fingered the leather bound book before setting it beside him.

"There is a connecting coach waiting for you outside of Paris," Sade announced. "We will part ways from there."

Grabbing up the flask of brandy from the seat beside him, Gérard uncorked it. Taking a long swallow, he drowned himself in its all too familiar taste and flavor that he hadn't indulged in since well before prison. He swallowed as much as he could without breathing and then broke away from the rim of his flask with a hiss, letting the fiery heat of that smooth liquid coat his throat and stomach.

A strange sense of clarity overtook him. One that made him realize brandy really did not have the power over him he thought it did. The greater power belonged to the beat of his heart and doing what was right.

Despite the promise he made to Thérèse, he had people to save. He had made old Laroche a promise from that cart. He would give himself five days to find them and help them.

Leaning forward in his seat, Gérard took another quick swig and announced in between ragged, brandy-fired breaths, "I want those fucking papers back. Because I am *not* leaving until I know Laroche's entire family has been spared along with anyone else I know. You will tell Thérèse I left and darted across that border so she does not have to worry about me again. In the meantime, you and I are going to strike a few people from the guillotine list before I go. Do you understand?"

That tone hardened. "Your death is assured if you stay and try to help people."

"Not if I do it right." Gérard corked his brandy and set it aside. "Where are the papers?"

Sade muttered something and then grabbed the leather valise from beside him, tossing it at him. "Now what?"

Catching its weight, Gérard gripped the edges of the leather hard. "You tell Robespierre I hold thirty-two pages of documents collected by royal spies that will damn well turn all of France against him and this revolution. You tell him I will give him a single page for each person he lets me strike from the guillotine list. The names will be of my choosing, not his. He will then let me get those people out of the country before he can put them back on that list. Thirty-two pages equals thirty-two lives."

"Are you including *yourself* in any of those pages?"

"By the time half these pages are released to Robespierre, I will be long gone. Which is why I need your help. Negotiate this for me with Robespierre. Can you do that?"

Sade snorted. "You must seem to think I am God. And whilst I genuinely appreciate your newfound faith in me, I—"

"My godfather died in the name of this country. And with the papers he bestowed upon me, I intend to honor him by saving more than myself." Gérard slowly let out a breath. "I need money. Are you willing to lend me a few hundred more? So I can start gathering resources to shuffle people out?"

Sade sighed. Reaching into his coat pocket, he withdrew a massive wad of bound money that required a few tugs before it was able to make its way out.

"This was supposed to be allotted for your journey to London." Wagging it at him for a moment, he tossed it into his lap. "Try not to spend it all on rescuing others. You have to get yourself out, you know."

Gérard blinked, picking up the weighty assignats. He dragged in a breath and thumbed through it in the shadows that were barely lit by the street lamp fingering its way in through the glass window of the coach. "Christ. This is—"

"Five thousand. No need to count."

"Thank you, Sade."

"Do not thank me, *Monseigneur*. Every last *livre* came from Thérèse's own pocket. She wanted to give you more but I talked her out of it. Moving such large amounts of money from her accounts would have raised a few brows from the bankers who are closely connected with the Convention. Be aware that this money was supposed to get you out of the country, so I suggest you put away enough to enable that to still happen."

Gérard swallowed, knowing his woman was now taking care of him given he couldn't do it. It was as bitter as it was sweet. For while his pride hated it, his heart reveled in knowing she loved him enough to want to save him.

He brought the money to his lips, kissing its edges, wishing to God it was her. Wishing to God he could carry her in his pocket much like a wad of paper. "I am the luckiest bastard alive."

Sade was quiet for a moment. "If you do not want her knowing about you staying in Paris, I suggest we settle you into your own quarters separate from my own given she visits me often. I will inform the Committee of Public Safety of the move to ensure there are no misunderstandings and will hold a private meeting with Robespierre about striking people from the list. I cannot guarantee he will agree to it."

Stuffing the money into his inner coat pocket, Gérard tightened his hold on the valise. "I understand." He pointed. "You, Sade, have a friend in me to the last breath. If you ever need someone to swing a fist for you, call on me. I will do it without even asking you why."

The man's cane thumped the roof of the carriage, signaling them onward. "You and I both know people betray each other when it matters most."

"When your own father betrays you, trust is a relatively non-existent word."

"Then why trust me?"

"If Thérèse trusts you, there is a reason for it."

Sade swiped his face. "So you intend on staying?"

"Yes. I have to."

"I need you to leave tonight, *boudin*. I am asking you to leave tonight."

Gérard took another swig of brandy. "I will leave once the Laroche's family is safe."

"Even knowing you may die?"

"Especially knowing it. I will not be the coward my father was and seek to only save myself."

"Allow me to respond to your righteousness." Sade jumped up and whip-lashed the cane against Gérard's thigh so hard, Gérard felt as if the muscle in his leg had leeched out more than blood.

The flask clattered from Gérard's hand, spraying everywhere. Choking on blinding pain that reminded him all too well of endless days in prison, Gérard jumped up and grabbed that cane with every riled beat of his heart.

Unsheathing the blade from within it, Gérard used his leather boot to shove Sade down against the seat. Angling the tip of the blade into the man's chest just below his lace cravat, he bit out, "Do not think you can intimidate me. Unlike the rest of this godforsaken world, I will *always* do what is right."

Sade grabbed the blade with his bare hand and turned it, spurting blood as the man whirled the blade back into his own gashed hand. He shoved Gérard back onto the seat with the bash of a shoulder and used the tip of the blade to now hold Gérard in place. "What is right can sometimes be wrong," Sade bit out, blood leaching its way down his hand and sleeve. He leaned down and grabbed Gérard's face with rigid fingers. "Do you understand?"

Gérard cringed in between disbelieving, ragged breaths. He paused, realizing he could feel Sade's.. *erection* digging into his outer thigh. "I said friends. Not lovers."

Sade straightened and smacked him upside the head. "*That* is for making me gash my hand."

Sitting down with a mutter, he swept the blade back into the cane and tossed its blood-slathered handle. Grabbing up the flask of brandy, Sade poured it onto the open slit of his wound with a loud hiss, then gulped the rest of the brandy with the tilt of his head. He whipped the flask at him. "Next time you rile me like that, you will no longer be a virgin."

Gérard cleared his throat. "I will remember that."

Sade methodically yanked off his cravat and wrapped the white lace hard around the wound, securing it tightly into place. "Doing the right thing is not always the best thing. I should know." Shoving his hand into his pocket, he withdrew a lock of dark hair tied with a red ribbon. Wagging it at him, he kissed it and then shoved it back into his pocket. "A woman's heart can only be tested so many times before it ceases to beat for you."

Gérard shifted his jaw, slowly rubbing at the pinching, raw soreness of his thigh that still seared his skin from the blow Sade delivered. There was a measure of comfort in that pain. It meant he was still breathing. "Who was she?"

Sade averted his gaze to the night darkened window. "My wife."

Astounded, Gérard leaned toward him. "You were married?"

"Still am. I damn well preferred every last woman over her, and yet she haunts me the most." That voice became detached. "She lives in a convent and will not see me. Like you, I have loved greatly, but *love* does not fucking keep the world from burning. In fact, sometimes, it becomes the very reason *why* everything burns. Remember that."

Closing his eyes, Gérard eased out a breath knowing that although he was leaving his Thérèse behind, he would never let her go. Not until his soul and his body were dead.

LESSON THIRTEEN

The unfortunate queen of our beloved France

never once said, 'Let them eat cake!'

Those were my words, gentlemen.

And yes, I licked the crumbs off every plate.

-The School of Gallantry

Eleven days later – afternoon
Residence of Citoyen de Sade

"Cease panicking." Sade angled in. "Have more faith in me as a teacher and as your friend. I promise you will be in control of how this ends. Now set those books aside so I may begin."

Thérèse frantically pushed aside piles of obscene books from Sade's desk to make room for the small silver tray he was holding. She patted the open space.

Setting the tray before her, Sade nudged it into place with a bandaged hand that covered a wound that had been threaded shut from 'an accident' he did not care to explain.

She refused to ask. She had a feeling a quarrel with a lover was at fault.

Leaning in, Sade tapped at the silver edge of the tray that displayed a beautiful array of over eighteen cinnamon-sprinkled sweets piled like a pyramid. He peered toward her, his dark, deeply set eyes becoming ominous. "These, *mon coeur*, are from my days of youth. When I used to truly have fun at the expense of every whore around me. They will ensure you remain in control of whatever this evening with Robespierre brings given you two will be alone. They are called 'slumber cakes'. I am giving you a personal and full guarantee that with one cake, Robespierre will flop on the dock at whatever hour you clock. He will lose consciousness for at least three hours."

Thérèse blinked. "Can I give him the whole tray?"

A maniacal laugh escaped him. "Now, now, before you get overly excited, understand that with these cakes come a measure of responsibility. Lesson one: it takes about twenty minutes for its effects to set in. Lesson two: if you offer any wine or cognac to go with one, it will take about eight minutes, instead of twenty. And yes, my little flea, I have counted. So keep an eye on that clock if you wish to stay out of trouble. Once he falls into unconsciousness, you have anywhere from about three to five hours of no movement. Aside from maybe some twitching."

Nature certainly seemed to know women needed a bit of assistance when it came to dealing with men. Thérèse leaned in toward the tray and sniffed at the large, savory and honey-scented mounds, poking at what appeared to look like an ordinary sweet. "What is it made of? Is it any good?"

"It makes the soul melt. Which makes these...*incredibly* dangerous." He picked one up and shoved it entirely into his mouth, chewing it in between appreciative nods. "Some of the ingredients include: a ridiculous amount of poppy seeds that have to be well-measured lest it result in death, laudanum, a good dash of cantharide and aniseed. Together, it produces *delirium*."

Leaning back, she cringed and pointed at his mouth. "Should you be...eating that?"

He grinned, still chewing. "Whilst darling of you to worry, I have grown rather tolerant. It takes eight of these to render this son of a bitch unconscious." Still grinning, Sade yanked out a handkerchief with the snap of his wrist and dabbed at the corners of his mouth before tucking it away. "Lesson three and this is a rhyme easy to remember: serve one and he is done. Serve two or more and he will end up dead on the floor. So keep him away from eating more than one. Let me repeat that. *One and only one.* And ensure he eats the whole thing or you may end up with his cock between your thighs whether you want it or not."

Certainly not good. Certainly not an option. "One and done. Anything more and he is dead on the floor." She quirked a brow. "Do I get the recipe?"

Sade smirked. "*Why?* Do you plan on using it again?"

She set her chin. "Any man who dares come to my door will be served nothing but cake."

He pointed at her with the tilt of a finger. "You are the best student I have had yet. All I ask is that you not kill them all." He leaned in and pinched her cheek hard between fingers, making her wince. He pinched harder.

"*Ow!*" She smacked his hand hard to get him to stop. "Cease pinching me, you brute."

His brows went up. Angling toward her, he smacked at her hand hard in return. "Now you."

She paused, in between rubbing her stinging cheek and hand, realizing the man was getting overly excited. She pointed at him, missing his nose. "I am on to you."

Catching his tongue between teeth, he met her gaze. "Playing with crops does not require penetration or nudity. Penetration of the anus, however, *does* make the pain worthwhile. Are you interested in either?"

At this rate, she was going to need to open up her own bakery full of 'slumber cakes' and sell them to every woman in Paris in order to liberate the female population from men. She plucked up said sweet from the tray, sidled closer to Sade and shoved the entire sweet into his mouth with the tap of dainty fingers. "If you ever ask to penetrate me again, I will ensure you eat the whole tray. Do we understand each other, Sade dearest?"

He chewed and enthusiastically nodded. "Perfectly."

The chiming of the bell made them pause.

Swallowing the rest of the cake, he held up a wagging finger. "Allow me." Striding out of the small parlor to the door in the foyer, he yanked open the door. He paused, as if astounded by what he saw. "These female callers of mine keep getting...*younger.* How might I help you, little one?"

An overly young girl's voice struggled to convey a bit of French, "I am..*Mademoiselle* Madeleine. I am..looking...*Monseigneur de Andelot.*"

Thérèse's eyes widened. Dearest God. The girl was looking for Gérard. Why was she—

Gathering her skirts, Thérèse hurried to the door, her breaths uneven. She stumbled in from behind Sade and almost shoved the man out of the way.

A prim young girl of about thirteen or maybe even fourteen, wearing an expensive lilac gown with a large white sash around her corseted waist, peered up at her from beneath a bonnet with a matching colored sash that framed a freckled, pale face with eager green eyes.

Seeing people were glancing toward them from the street and that a coach waited with a man peering out of it, Thérèse grabbed the girl's arm, not caring for protocol and hurried her into the house. "Sade, close the door."

He obeyed with the heave of a breath, slamming the door shut.

Hurrying the girl into the parlor, she turned the girl toward herself by those slim shoulders and searched that youthful face. "You are looking for *Monseigneur de Andelot?*"

She nodded. "*Oui.* I..*anglais.* He keep me from...guillotine. I..thank him." Those green eyes brightened. "Are you..his? In prison..he said..you pretty. He..right."

Thérèse couldn't see past her tears anymore. A sob escaped her as she turned away, trying to compose herself. Whose life had he not touched? Whose life had he not tried to save? He was everywhere. There were times when she was on stage, whilst looking out onto the audience, she thought she saw his face. Only to look back, startled, and find the seat empty.

The girl bustled around her, lilac skirts rustling, and gaped up at her in horror. "Is..did he..*guillotine?!*"

Crossing herself, if only to acknowledge to God that she was genuinely blessed knowing Gérard had crossed the border weeks ago, Thérèse offered the girl a bright smile through her remaining tears and shook her head. "No. He lives. I am told he is past French borders and on his way to England to be with his family. He is safe."

The girl's lips parted into a wide *O*. She excitedly clapped her satin gloves together, letting the small reticule at her wrist, sway. "Papa will...we visit! We..leave to London..two days! We..permitted. The Convention approved it!" She paused, leaned in and whispered, "Is there..address for... *Monseigneur de Andelot?*"

Swallowing hard, Thérèse grabbed the girl's hands and squeezed them hard, trying to take joy in knowing they both could share in knowing Gérard was safe. "No. I wish there were. But from what I understand, his aunt lives in London. Other than that, I have no other information."

Those features sagged. A long breath escaped her. Pinching her lips, she turned and eyed the room and paused. Her eyes widened. "*Gâteuax!*" She bustled over to the table cluttered with obscene books and leaning over the silver tray of small cakes, daintily plucked one up and pointed at it and then her mouth. "*Oui?*" She pushed the entire thing into her mouth.

Thérèse gasped, her heart skidding. She sprinted at the girl. "No! *No, no oui!*" Grabbing at the girl's mouth hard, she frantically opened those puckered lips and using a finger, she scooped everything out without taking the time to explain.

Standing frozen, with her mouth still wide open, the girl gaped up at her.

Citoyen de Sade's laughter filled the room.

Thérèse ignored him. "Spit everything out and do not swallow a crumb of it." Grabbing Sade's tin ash pan, Thérèse set it beneath the girl's chin. "*Now spit!* Spit, spit, spit."

Grudgingly, the girl leaned forward and flapped her tongue out enough to let clumps of the remaining sweet fall against ashes. She spit several times, paused and then spit several more times. Eyeing Thérèse, while still holding out her tongue, she barely managed to say against her outstretched tongue, "Eeees eeet.. gaaawn?"

Heavens above, all she needed was a girl dying. "Stay still. There are still traces of it on your tongue." Taking the own sleeve of her own gown, Thérèse swiped at that pink tongue several times and then stepped back and let out a shaky breath.

She staggered over to a chair and sat, setting a trembling hand to her stomacher. Maybe this was a sign from God that she was playing a game that went beyond her acting skills. But what else was she to do? Give her body to Robespierre? Or any man, for that matter? How could she? She was an actress. Not a whore.

And despite what society thought, the two did not always go together.

The girl sidled over to her and seated herself in an upholstered chair beside Thérèse. She daintily arranged her gown and eyed her.

Thérèse eyed the girl, in turn.

Lady Madeleine smiled and smoothed her skirts.

The girl was clearly intent on staying. Huh. "Was there something you wanted?"

Those green eyes brightened as she eagerly nodded, her curls swaying. She leaned toward her and fingered Thérèse's coiffed hair. "You are.. *perfect.*"

Thérèse leaned toward the girl and gripped that hand, squeezing it. "I am far from perfect. But I thank you for the compliment."

Lady Madeleine pinched her lips together, her gaze falling to Thérèse's bosom. She glanced down at her own, brows coming together. "How do I..make big?"

An exasperated laugh escaped Thérèse. This girl's father was going to have his hands full. Thérèse removed her fichu from around her décolletage. "Sade, turn away, please. A beauty lesson is about to commence."

Sade rolled his eyes and gave them his back.

Thérèse stood and leaning toward the girl, gestured toward her décolletage. "Might I?"

Lady Madeleine quickly leaned toward her, nodding.

Pulling away the material of the girl's décolletage, Thérèse tucked the fichu into each side of that corset, strategically molding it around those small breasts until they were visibly a full size bigger within the corset. Adjusting the material back into place, Thérèse admired her handiwork and then seated herself beside the girl again. "My mother used to do it for me all the time before I grew into mine. Once yours are fully in, take pride in whatever size they may be. The Lord only gives us what our backs can carry. Be thankful for it."

Lady Madeleine's brows went up as she adjusted her new breasts. She grinned and pushed her chest further out. "*Big.*"

Who knew fake breasts could make a girl happy.

A knock came to the door.

The girl's eyes widened as she scrambled up from her seat. "Papa...waiting." Lady Madeleine scrambled to yank open her reticule. Digging into it, she withdrew a calling card and tapped at the address. "London...visit!"

Taking the card, Thérèse smiled. "I will." One day, when the madness of Paris had found a lull, she planned to surprise Gérard. He wouldn't be the one to find her. She would be the one to find him.

Lady Madeleine waved with both hands. "*Adieu!*"

Barely lifting a heavy hand to wave the girl off, Thérèse flopped it back onto the chair, still in disbelief that the girl had almost eaten Sade's slumber cake.

"Stay where you are, Thérèse," Sade called. "I will see the girl out."

"Thank you," she murmured.

Striding toward the door, Sade bent toward the young girl and started speaking to her in English, his tone friendly, smooth and conversational. As if he were not at all a man who enjoyed whipping the skin off the delicate thighs of his lovers.

The girl paused, and her voice became all the more animated and exuberant about whatever they were talking about. She even clapped. Twice.

The voice of another gentleman came in through the open door.

Sade lowered his voice, now sounding firm and secretive, and offered more words of English to both of them.

More words were exchanged.

Eventually, he closed the door.

Sade strode into the room, adjusting his coat around his frame and seated himself across from her with an amused smirk. "An overly excited little thing about sweets, was she not?"

Thérèse fanned her face with the calling card. "My heart about stopped."

He shrugged. "Ah, now, she simply would have been twitching for a few days. She was already doing that."

She gave him a withering look. "Your humor is not at all appropriate. She is just a girl." She eyed him. "I did not realize you spoke English. Did you have a tutor?"

He paused. "Ah, well, I..no. I learned a smidge of it while I was in one of the asylums next to some British sop for six years. Few know I speak it."

Squinting, she could tell something had rattled him. Which *never* happened. The man was up to something. "What did you tell her and her father?"

He cracked his knuckles. "I mentioned the weather."

She lowered her chin. "You never talk about the weather. You, *citoyen*, are lying."

He stared her down. "What are you going to do about it? Take a crop to my arse?" He rose and pointed to his backside, looking over his shoulder.

Life would have been so much easier without men in it.

Getting up, she tucked away the calling card into her décolletage and walked by his still pushed out rear. She smacked his bum hard. "A little thank you for your assistance. Now if you will excuse me, Sade dearest, I have to get back home and be ready to entertain Robespierre tonight. I only pray to whatever God there is I have no use for that cake."

"Thérèse?"

She paused, sensing the urgency in his tone, and turned. "Yes? What is it?"

Sade blinked rapidly but didn't meet her gaze. He cracked his knuckles, staring down at his large hands while doing it. "There is a reason I am giving you those cakes. Robespierre is on to us."

She froze, her pulse roaring. "What do you mean?"

"Being a person of character will never work in your favor when fighting against a man who has a warped sense of morality." He widened his stance, still staring down at his hands. "Make the world your stage. It will turn you into the woman you need to be if you plan to survive on your own with a child out of wedlock. I am introducing you to what your life is about to look like for the rest of your life. Remember that."

She edged toward him, her hands now giving way to the shakes. "Sade. What are you saying? What do you know? I care nothing for myself in this moment, but my son—"

"You need not worry. Robespierre will not make a martyr out of you. You are too popular for that. But popularity is not going to protect you forever. This revolution will pass and with it, a new society will arise where you will be scorned for the independence you seek to take. You will therefore have to learn how to survive being the object of everyone's desire and hate. And no one understands the pain of becoming both more than I."

He strode toward her, his voice issuing a challenge. "Pain equals strength, Thérèse. And the greater the pain you are willing to endure, the greater the strength. I adore you, and this is my way of gifting you with something your own father never could have. This is only the beginning of what I will teach you about men and life." He grabbed her hand and yanking it toward his mouth, he bit into it. Hard.

She gasped and shoved him away.

He averted his gaze. "Have faith that after tonight, you can and will survive anything. I have to go. Grab a slumber cake for your *tête-à-tête* and tell Robespierre that his latest speech to the people was done in poor taste. He is no God, and I fucking hate him." With that, he stalked out.

She staggered and swung toward where he had gone. "*Sade?*" She tried to keep the panic and fear out of her voice. "Will he hurt me?"

He leaned back in from the corridor. "No. But he will demean everything you are to get what he wants. It is what Robespierre does best. When the time is right, feed him cake." He pointed at her. "You only ever become a whore when others make you feel like one. Remember that." He hesitated. "I have to go." He disappeared.

She closed her eyes and threw back her head. Oh, God.

****

Château de Maitenon, 10:23 p.m.

Given the time they had spent together over the past few months between ceremonies and gatherings and countless dinner parties, Thérèse was not at all surprised why so many women always gathered around Robespierre, be it during his passionate speeches in the galleries or whilst out on the streets of Paris. Aside from a few pockmarks on his face, he was charming, always impeccably well-dressed, right down to the gleaming shine of his buckled boot, and was very well-spoken. He was never one to brag about his level of power.

He didn't have to.

When it came to women, he elicited more than the quaking of their thighs. He elicited the dripping that happened between them. It was what made him the political stronghold and weapon he was. For in being able to win over every woman he met with his regal presence, he exercised the power over every woman's household and the brothers and the uncles and the husbands and lovers they associated with.

The unprecedented granting of divorce rights to women made him *incredibly* popular.

In the galleries, she had watched in complete and genuine awe, how at the end of a half-hour speech where he spoke of 'maternal love' and 'France' as if his very heart were breaking and he were speaking of his own mother, women used perfumed handkerchief to dab the corners of their eyes in half-fainting reverence and then waited with those same handkerchiefs until he was close enough for them to tuck it into his pocket.

He never took offense to anything these women did. Even those who tried to run up and smack him for sending someone they knew to the guillotine.

He merely swerved away from whatever aggressive advances met him, while soldiers did the rest, and with the gallant bow of his wigged head, always offered, "I am touched by your devotion and am administering an equal amount of devotion to the glory of France."

Whilst his political rivals, openly fussed, "*Robespierre is nothing but a damn priest!*" others, who knew Robespierre best, merrily countered, "*What a man Robespierre is with all his women. He is a priest who wishes to be God.*"

Indeed, Parisian women not only worshipped him and his guillotining ways, but wore necklaces containing his silhouetted likeness around their delicate throats to pay homage to his greatness. Thérèse had never bothered to impress him with such antics and instead, always wore Gérard's pearls. It made her feel protected, and above all.. loved.

Despite her fear and disdain for the man, she *was* mildly impressed that ever since their first introduction months earlier he had never once tried to kiss more than her hand. She was even *more* impressed knowing that despite them now being alone in her *château* for what had been close to two hours (in which she had to excuse herself and feed Henri once before returning him to the nanny), the man had not indicated anything was wrong.

She didn't know what to make of it after Sade's baleful warning.

Robespierre appeared no different.

Either way, the butcher girl from Giverny was ready for it and him.

"Your play," she announced, trying to exude her casual self.

Still holding all of his playing cards between large ungloved fingers, Robespierre squinted at his cards before glancing at her from across the table. Brown eyes captured hers. "I do believe I am about to lose this hand. And I never lose. Not even when I want to."

God, how she hated him.

She glanced at her own cards and laid out her best card onto the lacquered oak table. "Oh, come now, *citoyen.* Everyone must admit defeat at least once in their lifetime. Even someone as powerful as you cannot control an honest game of cards and its outcome."

He eyed the card she had laid out and grudgingly tossed his cards onto the table with the flick of a wrist. "Remind me to never wager France against you."

"I doubt France would ever forgive you if you did that. Now pay up. You owe me a hundred *sols.*" She tossed her own cards and leaned across the table to gather everything into a neat pile with the tap of fingers.

Robespierre opened his coat and withdrew a leather purse. He tossed it onto the table, the coins within chinking as he leaned back against his chair. "I admit defeat. Fifty *livres,* along with my humble admiration. Keep the entire purse and buy yourself a pretty trinket."

"How very kind and generous of you." Fifty *livres,* her arse. Her darling Gérard gave her a full thousand without barely knowing her.

Setting aside the cards, she dragged his leather purse toward herself and nudged it toward the edge of the table. "Any new gossip worth entertaining me with?" He usually shared *something.* He enjoyed his profession too damn much. "Did anything exciting happen this week?"

"No. Not really."

She paused. He usually shared something. Which meant...caution. "Your most recent speech was well done," she conversationally offered. "Am I to understand you intend to instate voting rights to women?"

He snorted. "God, no. We already gave freedom to black slaves and let Jews do whatever they do in their temples. How much more can we, as a Republic, do?"

She refrained from narrowing her gaze. "Women deserve the same rights as blacks and Jews and free white men. I hardly see any differences. We all breathe the same air."

His voice became noticeably agitated. "I suggest you cease pushing schemes. We all know how passionate you are about...*being a woman.*"

Something was definitely amiss. He was less of a gentleman. Her fingernails clicked one by one against the card table in an effort to remain calm. "Why would I not be passionate about the rights of a woman? I am one."

"Oh, believe me, I know that. And you do what all women do best." Holding her gaze with penetrating intent that now spoke of anything but trust, he leaned toward the card table and asked in a low menacing tone, "Have you ever had any direct association with a certain young gentleman named Andelot?"

The serpent had slithered out of its lair. As Sade predicted.

She offered up her best quizzical face, more than ready to take him on given everything he put her beloved Gérard through. "I have, yes. The man's father murdered my cousin and almost put a bullet through my own head."

He stared as if he knew *everything.* "No more games. You and I are going to talk. And I expect you to cooperate."

Fortunately, Sade prepared her for this. "Last I knew, we were in my home and not in a courtroom. Are you accusing me of something?"

He tsked. "You need not worry about your neck. You are far too popular for me to harm or dispose of. People would turn against me, and I have no time for that. But it does not mean I cannot get you to do what I want you to do, for in the end, Andelot is the only pawn I wish to take from this game."

No longer intimidated given her Gérard was far from reach, she stared him down, in turn. "I have no doubt the very thought of him must irk you after he escaped you and Paris."

He lowered his chin. "I am rather surprised you know so little. Did your aristo lover forget to inform you about the fact that he decided to stay?"

She paused. "Pardon?"

He shoved the cards off the table, scattering them across the floor. "There was a reason I released Andelot from prison. Sade said you would be able to get Andelot to give up the papers."

She stared, her heart pounding. Sade was..?

Robespierre eyed her. "Sade has been in alliance with me from the beginning. Unfortunately, that demented bastard has a tendency to get attached to his victims. Which is why this ends tonight. There was a reason why I allowed for our association. With trust comes power, and I needed power over you in order to get power over Andelot."

She clasped a trembling hand over the ring Gérard had given her in an effort to draw strength from it. Sade had been a lie. Much like most men were. But at least Sade was able to remain human enough to warn her.

"Are you surprised?" Robespierre prodded.

She set her chin. "No. Not at all. Sade has proven to be the master of pain." With only enough mercy to provide the salve one needed to survive the pain. "So what happens next?"

Robespierre examined his nails. "Andelot will be arrested and executed for insubordination."

Blinking rapidly in an effort to understand what was happening, Thérèse leaned into the table, almost falling into it. "But he escaped Paris. He is not here. He is not—"

"Only four men have ever escaped me and the Committee of Public Safety. And those men, I assure you, are all dead, and your Andelot is next. Maybe I ought to ensure you are at the square with all the women who knit when that blade comes down. How loud and how long will you scream? Because the moment you do, all of Paris will know you are a traitor. And *that* is when your popularity will bleed into nothing and allow me to send you to the blade next if you do not cooperate."

She stared wordlessly, her heart pounding. Ten. Thousand. Curses. Gérard never left. He took her heart and her tears and her pleas to rescue himself and..stayed. It was as if his life no longer mattered to him.

Robespierre eyed her, his overly wide features tightening. "I am somewhat astounded by the devotion you feel toward a man whose father murdered your cousin."

How could Gérard do this to her?

Tears pricked her eyes. "Can we not talk about what happened to my cousin? Gérard is not his father. His sins only include that he always tries to do the right thing."

He held her gaze. "I am an incredibly busy man, madame. These next upcoming weeks will demand my attention regarding new laws and ensuring Austria does not overrun what is finally ours. Which means I have very little time for you, this or Andelot."

He stood. Picking up his chair, he set its back toward her with a thud, then sat, straddling the chair so his legs were positioned more openly. He draped his elbows on the back of the chair and casually leaned his chest into the chair. He searched her face. "This ends tonight. Because I want those papers and intend to return to my regular way of life. Do you understand?"

It was obvious he wanted far more than she and her little slumber cake were ready for. She regally set her chin in an effort to remain calm. "I am more than willing to negotiate."

"I bet you are." He lowered his chin, his eyes darkening. "Remove the blade attached to your thigh." He tapped the card table. "Set it here or I will go to the window and signal my guards outside to do it for me."

A breath escaped her. She should have known her blade was not going to last. Grudgingly hitching up her skirt, she unlatched the leather sheath strapped to her thigh and tossed it with a clatter onto the table. She yanked down her skirt.

He assessed her. "If I were to ask you to dance with me right now, despite there being no music, would you do it in the name of what remains of this game?"

Sade had been right about one thing. If she survived this, she would be able to survive anything. "Dancing when the music has died is what I do best." Rising from her chair, she gathered her vermillion skirts and sashayed past his chair, determined to show him she held no fear.

He skimmed her appearance, following her sashay, and slowly stripped his wig from his head, revealing the dark brown hair beneath it. He set it onto the card table and rose from the chair he straddled. He walked toward her and rounding her, held out a bare hand. "Madame."

Setting her own hand in his, she icily offered, "*Citoyen.*"

Robespierre yanked her close and with his other hand pressed her body, inch by inch against his own, his fingers digging into the fabric of her gown in a smooth, exploratory manner.

The sharp scent of ink and licorice pierced her breath.

"Are you ready to negotiate?" he asked.

She chanted to herself to remain calm. "More than ready."

"Good." Robespierre swayed with her from side to side, using his body to guide her in the direction he wanted to go. "You will get those papers for me by tomorrow morning."

"And in return?"

"We go back to our regular way of life. It will be as if nothing happened."

"And Andelot?"

"He will be locked away with a relative of his until the Committee of Public Safety has had a chance to review those documents. Because as it stands, eight-year-old Louis Charles of France *and* your *duc* are the two remaining heirs to the throne."

She fought her own panic by evening each labored breath. "You mean to kill an eight-year-old boy and a man who has already suffered well beyond what is human? Is this a democracy or tyranny?"

"Madame, madame. I only provide and owe protection to peaceable citizens."

"I am asking for leniency."

"Then ask."

"What can I do to negotiate for their lives? Both of them?"

"The boy is not part of this negotiation. But..Andelot is." He searched her face. "I am not as heartless as I appear. I want those papers far more than I want him dead. As long as he stays out of the country, he is no threat to me."

She met his gaze, trying to decipher if he was playing yet another game.

"Get those papers to me by tomorrow morning and I will give him three days to leave France. Consider it a gallant gesture from one of your greatest admirers."

She dragged in an astounded breath. "Three days will not be enough. It takes closer to four days to get to the border."

"That is his problem. Not mine."

She hesitated. "Would he be given travelling papers? To make it past the border?"

"His travelling papers are already in order and in my pocket." His brown eyes held her gaze as his rough fingers rounded to the front of her bodice. "Now show me how grateful you are."

Oh, this one was well-trained.

As he unhooked the top of her bodice, she gripped his fingers. "My body is not part of this negotiation."

He brought them to a rigid halt, still holding her in place against himself. He returned his fingers to her bodice. "Do you want those travelling papers for him or not? It is a one-time offer with a bit of inconvenience for you."

Rape was an 'inconvenience'? The bastard. She swallowed, trying to remain calm. "Let me see the papers first."

He sighed, released her and opening his coat, withdrew a folded parchment. He held it out. "He has three days to make it to the border. After which, he is dead."

Taking it, she frantically unfolded the stiff parchment and was astounded to find the travelling papers were, in fact, real. She paused. Based on the date scribed above Robespierre's signature, if Gérard left tonight, he could make it.

She met Robespierre's gaze. If there was one thing she knew about Robespierre was that when he gave his word, no matter what it was, he retained it. She called it his 'demented' sense of honor. "You will never touch me again if I permit this."

He stared her down. "You and I both know I get easily bored. I have a country to run." He snatched back the travelling papers and tucked it back into his coat pocket. "'Tis quite simple. Tomorrow morning, after you deliver those papers into my hands, you get a chance to save his life."

A sense of calm overtook her. *Strength is pain. And pain gives strength.*

She turned and walked to the doorway, her skirts rustling in the silence of the parlor. She turned and met Robespierre's gaze in the only way an actress could. "I prefer we do this in my boudoir, *citoyen*. Not here in the parlor."

"Of course." He removed his coat and whipped it toward the chair. The chair wobbled and clattered to the floor from the weight of his coat.

It was all too symbolic. Little did the bastard know he was about to become that chair.

Unraveling his lace cravat, he tossed that onto the toppled chair as well, while also removing his waistcoat. He yanked off his linen shirt, revealing a surprisingly well-defined muscled chest whose bulk shifted.

She lowered her chin, trying not to admit the enemy was well-equipped.

He flexed his chest muscles. "I thought I would give you something to admire."

Every man was a rooster looking for a hen to..how did Sade say it? *Fuck.*

Little did these roosters know she was no hen.

He strode toward her. "You had better move."

She planned on it. Gathering her skirts, she bustled her way up the stairs, moving as fast as she could without ripping her gown.

"Faster," he tauntingly called up after her.

She now sprinted down the corridor, toward her bedchamber whose door was already open. She paused long enough for him to see her enter into it.

Scrambling around her four-poster bed, she skidded over to the side table with the silver tray strategically set with a glass of cognac and a single slumber cake. She kissed Gérard's ring to give herself strength, then angled herself toward the tray in rehearsed measure, her fingers daintily set against her own lips.

Sade, if you betray me in this, I will cleave every limb off your torso.

She eyed the open door of her bedchamber, waiting.

Robespierre draped a long, muscled arm against the frame of the doorway.

On cue, she let her hand fall away from her lips and pretended to chew on cake, tapping a prim hand to her chest as if she were attempting to swallow.

He pushed away from the doorway. Slamming the door behind him, he rounded the bed and sidled up to her. He grabbed the back of her neck, his hands tracing her body.

In between half-breaths, she relented to that aggressive touch, knowing any form of resistance would work against her plan.

Robespierre leaned in and sucked on the side of her throat extra hard, startling her.

She plucked up the glass of cognac and jerked toward him, breaking his advance with an elbow. Taking several long sips of cognac, she met his gaze over the rim of the glass, mentally playing the come-hither game of trust. After all, if he saw her drinking and eating, he wouldn't suspect a breath of what was about to happen next.

He swiped the cognac from her hand and tossed it back, setting down the glass with a chink on the tray. He grabbed her face and tongued her, sucking her tongue deep into his own mouth.

She struggled not to gag, permitting him to do it, and eventually broke away.

He leaned past her, grabbed up the small cake and pushed the whole thing into his mouth. He chewed. "Try to enjoy this, will you?"

She staggered in relief knowing he had shoved the entire slumber cake into his own mouth without her having to do it for him. She only prayed it worked.

Eight minutes.

He chewed, watching her. Kicking off his buckled shoes, he unbuttoned his breeches and shoved them down along with his undergarments and silk stockings. He fell onto the bed naked, rolling onto his back. Setting both hands behind his head, he said in between chews, "Undress, find a sheath and straddle me."

These men seriously needed to learn more about bedside manners. Rape aside, did fathers not teach their sons the basics? "I will undress and straddle you in due time," she offered. "We have all night."

Seven minutes.

The moment this was over, she was getting into her carriage and strangling Sade *and* Gérard with more than her hands.

Robespierre veered a wagging finger toward her clothing.

Unbelievable. Removing her pearls, which Gérard had given her, she tucked them into the drawer of the side table to keep them from seeing what was about to happen.

Turning back, she slipped off her shoes with unhurried ease and shifted her hips from side to side in an effort to give him something to look at. Slowly, slowly, slowly she undid the hooks on her gown so he could watch.

One by one by one by one.

Six minutes. She was putting her faith in Sade now. Which was a very scary thought.

Robespierre swallowed what remained of the cake and shifted his muscled, naked body toward her to watch, propping his dark head on his hand. "A little faster."

This was about to get challenging. "Of course."

Quickly finishing with all the hooks and pins, she edged open her bodice to reveal her corset beneath. Holding his gaze, she presented one shoulder and slipped the sleeve entirely off. She then presented the other shoulder and slipped that sleeve entirely off.

Stripping while some mass murderer watched was actually relatively easy to do. Undressing and dressing at the theatre with as many as three dozen people always watching, depending how many people were in the room tending to her wardrobe, she had long set aside the notion that her body was her own. It belonged to the people.

She edged the gown down past her hips and shimmied out of it.

Robespierre gathered all the pillows from behind himself, his movements growing uneven. He blinked rapidly and set the two pillows behind his head with trembling hands, staggering to set himself against them. "Damn but that cognac was strong." He puffed out several more breaths, blinking against its effects while looking more and more flushed.

Miffed though she was with Sade, it appeared his slumber cake was, in fact, legitimate. It had only been three minutes and the leader of France was already waddling like a duck without its head.

Robespierre spit into his hand twice and drunkenly attempted to hold up his rigid cock. He masturbated himself with a wad of his own saliva, puffing out breaths. "Do you have a sheath?"

The man sought to rape her using a sheath he didn't even bother to bring or buy. How typical of a man. "No. I never use them," she said in the hopes of scaring him. "Men complain about its effectiveness, so why bother?"

He paused. "Are you...clean?"

Oh, this was too good to be true. Of course the man would worry about his level of exposure to disease given he thought she was a whore. What was wretched but not too wretched lest it not be believable? "Unfortunately, I have been unable to rid myself of.. *papillion d'amour*." Pubic lice. "Is that a problem?"

He hissed out a breath. "Yes, it is a problem. Damn you for—" He stared at her corset, masturbating himself again. "Undress. I will finish while watching you."

This she could manage.

She sat on the edge of the bed and lifting one leg onto it, gave him the illusion he was in complete control. Swallowing hard, she purposefully exposed her breasts knowing the sooner he spent, the sooner she was out of any danger.

Robespierre stared at her well-displayed breasts, now masturbating to the point of choking. He jerked his rigid cock, his chest heaving.

What was so disgusting about men was that most were so focused on their cocks, they didn't even notice when a woman was or was not participating.

Setting her chin, she undid the pink bow of her satin garter above the knee of her silk stocking and with the flick of her wrist, tossed the garter at him, letting it land near the cock his hand kept frantically masturbating.

Staring at her now exposed leg and thigh, he jerked faster and faster, his body trembling.

Four minutes.

Regally setting her other leg up onto the bed, she purposefully hitched up her chemise almost to her buttocks. She skimmed the tips of her fingers toward her inner thighs, letting him watch. She dipped her fingers closer and closer to her—

He gasped. Seed spurted as his hips thrust upward.

She cringed and almost scrambled off the bed.

His hand, which had been stroking his rigid cock, slowly released its hold. In between well-sated breaths, he continued to stare at her hand between her thighs as if that had been his undoing. His eyes rapidly blinked and grew heavy.

Three minutes.

His hand dropped limply to his side and his stiff cock deflated and flopped over on its side, his seed slathered against his open hand. He stared at her vacantly, his breaths becoming soft. He eventually closed his eyes.

She swallowed, knowing the effects of the slumber cake were taking their last hold. She tucked away each exposed breast back into her corset, trying to remain calm. She kept telling herself to breathe. To breathe. She had survived.

His eyes remained closed. A tremor of a twitch overtook his limbs.

Two minutes.

In the pulsing silence, she waited, her eyes and her throat burning at the sight of having to look at this bastard as he lay naked. A part of her had always known their association would end in her playing the part of a whore to keep Gérard safe. Unlike any role on stage, however, this part had become all too real.

The last remaining minute seemed to take forever.

She glanced at the clock and called out in a choked tone, "*Robespierre?*"

He didn't move and his lids no longer fluttered. His limbs remained still.

"Are you awake?" she rasped.

He slept.

She stared at him in complete disgust and loathing, wishing he were dead.

Rolling down her ungartered stocking with trembling hands, she pushed it off her ankle and toes. Dragging in uneven breaths, she gritted her teeth and snapped out the stocking toward his shaven face as hard as she could.

He didn't move or flinch. He was officially unconscious.

She let out a sob in disbelief, allowing herself to be Thérèse as opposed to *Nina.*

Raising her quaking arm, she whiplashed the silk stocking down at his face and chest again and again and again, trying to let out her anger, her hate, her despair, and the horror of knowing what she had to resort to in order to protect Gérard's life.

She wrapped the stocking taut between both hands and was about to wrap it around Robespierre's neck so she could choke him until he was dead, but froze.

His death would result in her own.

Her arm fell to her side. The stocking slipped from her fingers.

Leaning closer toward Robespierre over the side of the bed, she hatefully choked out, "You will not win this game. I will. And I will do it without risking my life and that of my son's."

He didn't move.

Numbly pushing herself away from the bed, she sobbed and kicked away her silk gown that was still on the floor. There was no such thing as real liberty for a woman. Such things did not exist in even in the most hailed of democratic societies. And this was proof of it. She had an unconscious, naked man she hated laying in her bed, because telling a man of power 'no' was no different than a death sentence.

Long live the revolution. May she continue to justify robbing men of their vile, sexual glory from here on out. She would feed every last one of these bastards cake.

A shaky breath escaped her. She would survive this.

She would get Gérard out of Paris and to the border well before those three days expired and she would do it using any means possible. She had forgiven him for breaking the first rule she set of not wanting children. But *this* she would never forgive. He had officially broken her second rule of their agreement: that he would never lie.

"*Thérèse!*" Sprinting booted feet thudded closer. "*Thérèse!*"

Her eyes widened, her heart pounding in disbelief. Gérard.

She scrambled toward the bedchamber door.

LESSON FOURTEEN

Never wage a war against your own beating heart.

-The School of Gallantry

The haze of brandy had long worn off given how quickly Gérard had left the one-room, roach-infested flat he was hiding in with the Laroche's family. Sade's urgency, sending him to Thérèse's *château*, insisting she was in danger, had sent him into a panic that barely got him into clothes.

The darkness of the night whispered of things Gérard dared not think about as he charged into Thérèse's château through the verandah door he knew the servants left open.

Stalking through the empty corridor, and listening for any sounds, he headed through the overly quiet house. Gérard jerked to a halt outside the ornate parlor, his gaze snapping to the middle of the room. His pulse roared at the astounded realization that a man's periwig and Thérèse's blade, which was usually attached to her thigh, were on the card table. A knocked over chair by the card table had been piled with a male coat, cravat, waistcoat and linen shirt.

He couldn't breathe. *Thérèse!*

Setting a trembling hand on the handle of the pistol attached to his leather belt, Gérard swung toward the stairwell and sprinted, his heart pounding. Taking the stairs three at a time, he came onto the landing and thudded straight for her bedchamber door. The same bedchamber where he and she had spent their last breathing hour in each other's arms.

He prayed that the mass of male clothing he saw did not mean she was being—

"Thérèse!" he yelled, thudding faster and faster toward her door. *"Thérèse!"*

To his astonishment, the door swung wide open, and Thérèse darted out into him.

She screeched as he grabbed her by the arms hard, his heart pounding.

Her disheveled, unpinned blond hair and thin chemise and corset that revealed far more than curves made him suck in a breath he wasn't prepared to take. Just beyond the open door of her bedchamber was none other than Robespierre, soundly asleep and naked, her silk stocking and satin garter draped over his bare, muscled chest.

Gérard staggered.

Capturing her gaze in a daze he could barely wade through, he noted the flush of her face and the well-bruised mark of sucked skin on her neck.

He was too dazed to even let it mean anything. *Jésus Christ.*

He grabbed her shoulders hard, barely breathing. *"Are you— Did he—"*

"I have no words for you right now. None." She narrowed her gaze as if *he* were Robespierre. "May I never—" She jumped forward and shoved him hard. *"How could you do this to me?!"* She shoved him again and again. "You were supposed to leave! Not—"

He choked and stumbled back. His throat tightened in disbelief, realizing Robespierre was not only naked but wasn't waking up. "I am trying to understand what I am seeing," Gérard rasped, edging back. "Did he—"

She shoved him again. Only harder. "I need you to get those papers to me now! *Do you understand?"*

God keep him from— Shifting his jaw, he removed his leather belt, setting it onto the floor with trembling hands to ensure he did not enter her bedchamber and use his pistol to slaughter Robespierre and send them all to the guillotine.

Rising to his full height, he angled toward Thérèse, his breath ragged. "Sade told me you were in danger. What the hell is going on?"

She slammed the door of the bedchamber shut and faced him. "Sade has been in alliance with Robespierre from the beginning."

He sucked in a breath. "No. That is not possible. He helped me. Us. He—"

"It was an illusion, Gérard. He works for the Republic. But when it mattered most, he did his best to help. And this is him helping. Right now, Robespierre is under the effects of Sade's slumber cake and will be for the next three to five hours. Which means you have a half hour to get those papers into my hands and three days to get to the border."

Unable to focus, he scrubbed his face. "I have six other people who are depending on me right now. The moment I give up those papers, I have no further stronghold. None."

"I am your stronghold, damn you!" She marched up to him and grabbed him by the lapels of his coat hard. "Get those papers into my hands and you will have the travelling documents you need to get across the border. I ensured it."

He stiffened. "You ensured it? By..?"

She leaned in closer and then froze. She tightened her hold on his coat. "Using my five thousand for brandy, I see. I can smell it on you." She glared and smacked him, stinging his cheek and released him. "You clearly made a choice of putting your sense of justice before the promise you made me. You will now live with it. Because this is me claiming my independence from you and men once and for all." She frantically grabbed at the ring on her finger, tugging it loose. She shoved it into his hands. "We are done. For as I had once told you, regrets come only after promises are broken. And you have broken every last one."

His pulse roared. "*Thérèse*, you cannot mean it. Put it back on. Now!" He grabbed her hand and attempted to shove the ring on her finger.

She smacked away his hands, sending the ring tinkering across the floor. "It will never go on my finger. Consider this my way of saving you."

He jumped toward her and grabbed her face hard, digging his fingers into those flushed cheeks in an attempt to look into her soul. If she had one. "You told me forever," he breathed out, "but last I knew, *ma biche*, it has only been eleven days. *Eleven fucking days!* What are you doing?"

She shoved his hands away from her face and glared up at him, her eyes and her tear-streaked features so hardened they did not belong to the woman he thought he knew. "If you do not get to the border in three days, you are dead. So I suggest you deliver those papers to me and get the hell out of my house and out of this country, because this is *not* a game. How *dare* you put your life in danger like this, you-you..*blaireau!* You are putting *everyone's* life before your own! *Everyone's!* Are you not worth more than what your father made you believe?" She shoved him, her voice hysterical. "Move on and live! Because *this* is not living!"

He swallowed against the tightness choking his throat. "For God's sake, talk to me. Why are you half naked and why is he naked?! Why are you—"

She grabbed his face and squeezed it tight, digging her nails into his cheeks. "If you require proof of the fact that he pleasured me, all you need do is touch a finger between my thighs."

The corridor blurred. "Did he rape you?"

She released him and stared him down. "No. I raped him. Now give me the papers and get out of my life."

Something whispered to him that she had purposefully done this. She had purposefully given her body to Robespierre to ensure that he, Gérard Antoine Tolbert, the last remaining heir to the great duché of Andelot, do exactly what she wanted him to do: leave Paris forever.

He would have preferred being dead.

He caught himself against the nearest wall, chanting to himself that he wouldn't hurt her for hurting him beyond what he could endure. His breaths became too uneven for him to control. His gaze veered toward the garnet ring near his boot. Gritting his teeth, he swiped it up and shoved it into his pocket knowing it wasn't even his to throw away. "I need to hold my son."

Her gaze snapped to his. Her features stilled. "There is no time. You have to leave."

He would have preferred being repeatedly stabbed in the chest. This hell was— He stalked down the corridor, straight toward Henri's room. Grabbing the knob, he banged open the door.

Thérèse scrambled after him and seized him by the waist hard. "You have to leave, damn you! You have to—"

He shoved her away from himself, refusing to leave until he held their son.

A startled wail made his heart drop. He jogged up to Henri's cradle and lifted him out with trembling hands. He held his son against his face, wanting to remember that softness, that warmth he would never get to know. He wanted to walk out the door with Henri in his arms. He wanted to do it and never look back.

Thérèse pushed away from the wall and scrambled toward him with an anguished sob. "Gérard, I beg of you. You are assuring your death every minute you stay. *I am begging you!*" She sobbed. "*Do you mean to slaughter yourself?* Get me those papers so you can leave. You have to leave tonight or you will never make it to the border on time!"

Henri's quivering wail and outstretched hands that brushed at his chest and face made Gérard realize he had lost the last of his rational mind thinking he could tear his son away from Thérèse merely because she had slept with another man in an effort to save him.

Whilst he would never forgive her for butchering the last of his heart in an effort to save his meaningless and worthless life, he knew he couldn't put his own son at risk.

Tears streamed from his eyes as he kissed those soft, small cheeks and pressed his lips hard against that head that shifted against him.

He numbly passed his son to Thérèse.

Refusing to look at her, he tonelessly said, "Sade will bring you the papers."

He left.

****

Twenty minutes later
Citoyen de Sade's residence

"If you had left when I told you to," Sade said in a toneless, cool voice from beside him, "none of this would have ever happened. Fortunately, you now have travelling papers."

Sitting on the staircase steps facing the bolted foyer door, Gérard dragged the leather valise with the remaining papers the Republic wanted closer to himself.

While a part of him wanted to open the valise and flick the papers out one by one without caring as to what would happen next, he still had the Laroche's elderly wife, her widowed daughter and four of the woman's children to get out of France.

Gérard squeezed his eyes shut and rasped, "I would have left days ago, but no one was willing to take the Laroche family out of Paris. No one would take my money. Not even when I asked them to save the children."

Sade remained quiet for a long moment. He swiped his face. "Given most of the people I associate with are part of the Convention, no one I know will help them. And if word gets back to Robespierre that I am assisting other aristocrats, my head will be in a basket right along with yours." A breath escaped Sade. "Lady Madeleine's father informed me he can leave Paris anytime. He can take you tonight, if need be. The sooner you leave, the more likely you will make it before the papers expire."

Half-nodding, he whispered, "What about the Laroche family?"

"Thérèse knows a lot of men at the theatre who might be able to help get them out."

Gérard almost ripped the valise he held apart. "No. I have no need for her help."

Sade smacked him upside the head. "Your pain has no fucking place in this." He rose to his feet and snatched the leather valise out of his hands. "I will get this to her myself to ensure Robespierre no longer harasses her. She has endured enough on your behalf. Now get ready to leave."

Gérard swallowed, his eyes still burning from seeing Robespierre naked on her bed. "You should have let me die," he whispered. A sob escaped him. "What happened to her was. . I will forever blame myself for it."

Sade fingered the valise. "You are young. And so is she. You will both survive this and learn that life is not meant to be lived like a fairytale."

"She loved me," Gérard choked out. "I know she did."

"Yes, and you betrayed her by trying to be a fucking hero to everyone but her and yourself."

Jumping up, Gérard gritted his teeth and swung at Sade, his breaths becoming more and more riled. "How could you have let that fucking bastard—"

Sade grabbed Gérard's throat hard and shoved him into the wall, thudding him hard into it. Meeting his gaze, Sade bit out, "Begging your pardon, Gérard, but if you are dead, the glory of your love hardly matters, does it? I negotiated to get those travelling papers for you. I saved your goddamn life. And I did not have to. So be thankful. If you dare swing at me again, I will take you to Robespierre myself the moment he wakes up. I have no qualms doing it."

Gérard was too numb to respond.

Sade released him with a shove. "Get Laroche's family ready to leave within the hour. You will leave shortly after they do with Lady Madeleine's family." His voice darkened. "One day, when you are old enough to see past the pain, you will be thankful."

Gérard rose to his feet and whispered, "I will never see past the pain. *Ever*. My godfather is dead, my father is dead, and now this?"

No. He wasn't ready to— Gérard flexed his hands and stalked to the door, banging it open.

Shoving his trembling hands into his pockets, he jerked to a halt, his fingers grazing the garnet ring Thérèse had returned. He dug the stone into his skin, chanting to himself that she would forgive him. She would forgive him for putting his righteousness before her safety.

Walking out into the night, he dragged in uneven breaths, trying to focus.

If she truly loved him, she would forgive him. Because that is what people who truly loved each other did. They forgave each other.

He only prayed her love was strong enough to save them both.

LESSON FIFTEEN

Once upon a time, I had a dream.

But I let it die so it might resurrect into something new.

-The School of Gallantry

An hour later

In the corridor of an abandoned window-shattered building

Setting down the lantern onto the warped floors at their feet, Thérèse shoved the large basket she was holding into Jacques's hands. "Tell Andelot there is plenty of food and money for him and the Laroche family. His travelling papers are in the basket, as well. Give it to him. I will wait outside in the carriage. I have to get back to the house before Robespierre wakes up."

Jacques angled in. "Are you saying this Andelot is the father of your child?" he demanded. "That godforsaken *aristo* impregnated you and then left you to suffer scandal as if—"

She gave him a withering look. "Whilst I am thankful for your assistance, Jacques, let us not complicate an already complicated night. You are here to assist the Laroche family out of Paris. You are not here to rescue me or my reputation."

He grabbed her shoulders hard. "Knowing he was the one who put you through having a child out of wedlock is..." He stared her down. "I will avenge you and your honor."

She yanked herself out of his grip and glared. "There is no honor to avenge. Leave him be. He has suffered enough. And despite him and I parting ways, I love him. I will always love him."

"What about me?" He angled toward her. "I at least have proven myself. Was I not the one to place myself before you when that bastard's father—"

"*Jacques.*" She swallowed, knowing he was still twisting that night into meaning more. "I hardly want to return to that night. How dare you speak of it?"

He averted his gaze. "My only regret is that you cannot see past him."

"My only regret is that you continue to think we are more than friends."

He was quiet for a long moment. "I am still your servant. You know that."

"And I thank you for that, Jacques. These people are depending on you. Now please. Deliver the basket." She edged back. "I will leave the lantern here in the corridor for you." Gathering her veil, she drew it over her head.

Watching him disappear through one of the farthest doors leading into a small flat, she let out a shaky breath and hurried down the darkened corridor past half-open doors leading into abandoned, empty rooms that had once belonged to the *haute ton.*

A dark figure loomed before her from one of the open rooms.

She froze, realizing it was Gérard.

His features were anguished. The faint light of the lantern in the corridor barely illuminated his blue eyes.

She swallowed, knowing he had heard her entire conversation with Jacques. "I wish you a safe journey. May you cross the border before those papers expire."

Gérard's riled intensity thrummed in the narrow corridor as he lowered himself onto one knee. He said nothing. He only kept kneeling, never once breaking their gaze.

Her pulse roared, knowing he was asking her to leave with him. She quickly angled around him to pass.

"*No!*" Gérard grabbed her arm hard, his bare fingers digging into her skin. Jumping to his feet, he yanked her into one of the abandoned, darkened rooms. Shoving her against the nearest wall, he then quietly shut the door with a soft click, drowning out all light.

That strategic, overly soft closing of that door whispered of the storm he was holding within.

It scared her.

Plastered against the wall in complete darkness, her heart pounded knowing he planned on having the last word. Her vision was smeared with black.

Although she could see nothing, she felt him draw near.

He set a large hand on each side of her and leaned in close enough for her to smell the sting of brandy. "I am begging you to forgive me," he rasped. "Forgive me for forcing you to do what you did."

"Forgiveness will not save you. You and I both know that. You need to let me go."

He was quiet for a moment. "Thérèse." His voice cracked. "I love you."

"In time, you will come to love someone else."

He set his head against hers. "Never. Tell me I can come back for you. Tell me we are not done and I will come back and—"

"No," she choked out. She didn't trust that he would leave. Or that he would wait long enough. "When I said we were done, I meant it."

He lifted his head. "Then you do not love me. You never loved me."

"If you think that, then you most certainly deserve what I am doing."

His voice darkened. "You have one of two choices. You either turn around and face the wall and let me hurt you in the way you are hurting me right now or you can kiss me and we forgive each other before we take this too far. You decide."

Her throat tightened. Why was it Robespierre did not terrify her half as much as Gérard did in this moment? Maybe because she knew of the flame that really burned within him. Kissing him and breaking both of their already broken hearts was not an option.

If this was his way of letting her go, she loved him enough to let him do it.

Wordlessly, she turned, her skirts rustling against his trouser-clad legs and faced the wall. She set her hands against his large ones, which still draped each side of her against the wall. "Do what you will," she managed, her voice amplified given she was so near the wall. If she didn't hurt him, he wouldn't leave. And he had to leave. "I will never again be yours. You are a drunk and a liar."

His breaths became ragged in the silence as he continued to linger behind her, unmoving. He finally leaned in. "So you would rather endure the pain of living without me than forgiving me?"

She closed her eyes, willing herself not to love him anymore if only to give him the chance at living a new life. One he did not want to take. "Pain is strength," she whispered.

He stilled. "Then I am about to test yours. In thirty years, I will make you cry. In thirty years, you will remember this fucking day and wish to God you would have chosen otherwise."

Removing his hands from beside her, the leather belt around his waist, the one holding his pistols, creaked as he unfastened it. "Are you ready to know real pain? The sort that will bring you to your knees?"

She squeezed her eyes tighter, her limbs trembling as she leaned into the wall, readying herself for that belt to whip her.

He set his belt and weapons at his feet with a loud clatter. Rounding her, he opened the door with a bang and left, his heavy steps disappearing down the corridor.

In between uneven, astounded breaths, she opened her eyes and waited. She waited and waited in the darkness of the room that was barely illuminated by the lantern still sitting in the corridor.

Realizing, he wasn't coming back, she slid down the wall and let out an anguished sob. He knew. He knew that the greatest pain was not one delivered to the skin but one delivered to the soul. He was officially sentencing her to a life of living in pain without him.

In thirty years, I will make you cry. In thirty years, you will remember this fucking day and wish to God you would have chosen otherwise.

May those thirty years never come.

PART TWO

EVERY FALL HAS A RISE

LESSON SIXTEEN

Pain? What pain?

-The School of Gallantry

London, England – 1830
The quaint little townhouse of Madame de Maitenon

Life was so beautifully strange. It kept introducing her to so many mis-adventures she did not expect. Of course, it took a brilliant woman such as herself to keep up with all the drama knowing that her darling, bright-eyed granddaughter, Maybelle de Maitenon, was a far greater misfit than she had ever been at her age.

Some things were inherited. Sadly.

Thérèse waved away her overly stuffy, British butler and said in fluent, though heavily accented English, "We thank you for the cognac, Clive. You may leave us."

The butler inclined his balding head and stiffly walked out of the crimson parlor.

Thérèse tapped the tray with a finger, intent on keeping her granddaughter from leaving the country. "Drink. And when you are done, I will hope your lips are loosened enough for us to discuss what it is you are doing with your life.

Because your father, Henri, heaven rest his poor soul, was as stubborn as I and would have hardly wanted you to prance out into the world on your own or he would have never left you in my care. You know full well he and I only ever argued about my way of life but that in the end, we still loved each other."

Maybelle eyed the full glass of cognac, which had been set onto the gleaming surface of the walnut table before her, and heaved out an exasperated sigh as she sank into a chair, the curls of her gathered blonde hair quivering from the movement. "I take it there is no tea in the cupboards?"

Thérèse rolled her eyes. Tea was not going to get them through this day. "Och. Tea. The English are overly obsessed with it." They both needed something stronger given the state of their finances the poor girl did not know about.

Rising from the settee she was draped against, Thérèse offered with theatrical flair, "We have every right to toast to all of our upcoming adventures. After all, you will finally get to visit your beloved Egypt, while I, I will finally have my School of Gallantry." There. She said it.

Maybelle paused. "Your School of Gallantry?"

"Ah." Thérèse bustled over toward the small writing bureau set in the corner of the parlor and snatched up a piece of parchment from atop a pile of correspondences. Turning, she bustled back again, her verdant skirts rustling. With a smile, she held out the sizable cream-colored parchment.

Her granddaughter mutely stared at the parchment dangling before her.

Still smiling, Thérèse grandly envisioned the words she herself had written a few months earlier when the idea first came to her. She needed money, after all, and British men were more than willing to give it when offered the right service.

Madame Thérése's School of Gallantry
All gentlemen welcome.
Learn from the most celebrated demimondaine of France
Everything there is to know about love and seduction.
Only a limited amount of

Applications are being accepted
at 11 Berwick Street.
Discretion is guaranteed and advised.

Maybelle gaped at the parchment with wide blue eyes but still said nothing.

"Well?" Thérèse prodded, still holding out the advertisement. "What do you think?"

Her granddaughter rose from her parlor chair and snatched hold of the parchment. "Our reputation is already limp. Why on earth do you feel the need to flog it to death? You promised Papa you'd never return to being a demimondaine. You promised."

There were some things one could not change, including one's reputation that went back too many years to count. Whilst yes, she had entertained a long list of men in her lifetime given she had always wanted to believe there was a man worth loving out in that world, her name as a courtesan had always been far more exaggerated. Though.. not by much.

Whilst being scandalous was advantageous in keeping most of the world away, it became incredibly annoying when it drove away the very people one wanted to stay. Sadly, her own granddaughter had a tendency to think her love for sex equated to her love for money. And whilst she loved sex, yes, one did not need sex to survive. Money, on the hand, one *needed* to survive.

Thérèse arched a silver brow. "This is not a return. I am merely selling techniques."

"*Techniques?*" Maybelle smacked the parchment with the back of her hand. "It's ludicrous. What man would ever admit to needing lessons in seduction? You of all people should know that it comes natural to men."

What little this girl knew. "Does it? How odd. I suppose the thirty men who have already enlisted are merely looking for entertainment." Thérèse plucked the advertisement back and smoothed the edges of it.

"Are we having trouble with our finances?" Maybelle prodded. "Is that it?"

Oh, dear. She couldn't let the girl know their finances had been a mess long before she arrived into England. Spoiling a grandchild for nine years was a terrible, terrible thing that resulted in far more than bankruptcy. "*Non.* Our finances are exceptionally good."

The last thing she wanted or needed was having the girl selling off all the countless items sitting up in the garret. Items she had acquired when she was barely twenty and still in love with...a duke. A duke whose face she only ever saw in her dreams and in the attic. An attic that was filled with countless paintings, trinkets, clothing and furniture she had purchased from the Andelot estate when France set all of his items on sale. She had outbid everyone for every last item.

It had cost her everything she had been worth, sending her into bankruptcy.

Love made one stupid for life.

Not wanting to get emotional about a past that no longer mattered, Thérèse set her chin and nonchalantly added, "Although I did have some assistance from the lovely widow, Lady Chartwell. The woman fondly shares my vision of educating men."

Those blue eyes widened.

Thérèse knew her granddaughter well enough to say, "You are not pleased, I see."

Not good. The girl would end up going to Egypt using money they did not have and she would be left alone with nothing more than a garret full of items she refused to sell and a bunch of British men who knew nothing about life or women. No and no.

Thérèse wandered back toward the bureau, setting the advertisement onto it. She tilted her head to one side and centered the parchment before her as if she were straightening a painting. "London has always been so boring compared to Paris. I am used to more excitement. More passion. As you know, I have long sworn off my occupation and sadly, have no great- grandchildren to occupy my time. What is worse, you and I have completely different interests. A pile of old rocks set upon endless hot sand is nothing short of torture. I am too delicate for such things." She hoped the pity-me routine would make the girl stay. Money aside, she would miss her.

"No one forced you to stay in London," Maybelle argued in exasperation. "You *chose* to stay here. Furthermore, I won't have you calling the pyramids a pile of old rocks. They are amazing historic monuments worthy of genuine fascination. I've already postponed my trip four times because of you and every time I was forced to pay my designated traveling companion ten pounds despite the fact I never traveled anywhere." Maybelle grudgingly crossed her arms over her chest, crinkling the bodice of her morning gown. "So what is it that you want this time? Aside from great-grandchildren."

The girl knew her all too well. "*Want?* What would make you think that I want anything?" The only thing she wanted was enough money to ensure her granddaughter could *eventually* go to Egypt in style. She knew the dear had her heart set on it and going to Egypt with barely a few measly pounds in one's pockets would be no different than sentencing the girl to months of licking the sand she was so excited about seeing.

Maybelle narrowed her gaze. "You know exactly how I feel about these things, which is why you are trying to leverage this against me. Otherwise, you would have never told me. You would have waited until I left England and *then* opened the school."

Not true. "I am not trying to leverage anything. The advertisements have long been sent and the townhouse rented. It is done, *ma chére.* Classes begin next week. And in the end, I confess that the most difficult aspect was having to choose only four out of the thirty who originally enlisted."

Maybelle paused. "You are renting out an *entire* townhouse to host only *four* men?"

If Thérèse could stop being so soft-hearted and actually take the money she needed from these desperate men, yes. The problem was she actually wanted to help these poor aristocratic bastards knowing they were needy enough to turn to a woman for advice.

It made her pity them. Some of them even reminded her of Andelot. Pieces of him. One had scarred hands like Andelot. Another wore a queue like her Andelot had, despite it long being out of style. Each and every one of these men made her realize she could do some good given all the bad her reputation had brought.

"*Oui*, but it is only temporary," Thérèse finally offered. "Until I regulate the schedule and coordinate the lesson plans. As time goes on, I will add more men. Which of course will mean more work. It will require more teachers. More hosts. More toys." This was just the beginning of a lucrative new career that would not require sex or relationships from her. Merely talk of sex and relationships. It was genius.

Thérèse eyed her granddaughter, hoping she could recruit the girl for a few months until their finances were what they needed to be. "You would not consider staying and becoming a hostess for a few months, would you?" She bit back a knowing smile and playfully chided, "Though we should qualify you more by dispensing of your virginity."

Maybelle gasped. "I believe you are the only grandmother in the history of England to ever say such a thing to her granddaughter. That aside, do you even realize what you'll be promoting by opening such a school? Do you?"

Thérèse let a full smile appear and continued to tease, "I will proudly be promoting the pleasure of all my fellow women who are fortunate enough to come across my *étudiants*."

Maybelle lowered her chin but did not break their gaze. "No. You will proudly be promoting the idea that women are poodles and should be petted at will."

Thérèse tsked, puckering her lips. "*Ma chére*. If a man knows nothing about seduction, the courtship becomes merely *poom-poom*. Animal copulation. And it is the woman who suffers, for a man can always find pleasure. But a woman? Not so. We cannot keep men from the conquests they seek, but we can educate the lust-ridden fools and in turn benefit, *oui*?"

A withering look appeared. "All right. Name your price."

Thérèse paused. "Price? You mean for the school?" It varied depending on what these men could or could not afford but... "I agreed on one hundred pounds per week."

Another gasp escaped her granddaughter. *"One hundred pounds per week?"* she squeaked. "For mere advice? Are they mad?"

No. They were desperate. Like her. "It is a very respectable price. Understand that an experienced *demimondaine* such as myself could actually demand much more."

Maybelle sighed. *"Grand-mére,* please. I will gladly bargain with you, if need be, but for heaven's sake, you must close the school before you become an even bigger celebrity of the wrong sort."

Why did no one share in her vision of educating men when it came to relationships? They all needed it. They all seemed to think their money and good looks would save them. Not that her granddaughter understood. The girl avoided men at every turn and sometimes Thérèse blamed herself for it. She had spent too many years educating the girl about life, sex and men and apparently had *over-educated* her.

Her own past aside, she wanted great-grandchildren. At least ten of them. Was that too much to ask for, given her days of ever having a bigger family were at an end? Her own family back in France, rot them all, right down to her ten brothers, had abandoned her when her finances ran out, joining the rest of the world in accusing her of immoral ways.

It was her and Maybelle now.

"I will not bargain for the school *but--"* Thérèse paused, then turned toward her. "I will bargain for the money you wish to travel with. Since I still hold all the purse strings." Purse strings that had long frayed and let the purse hit the floor. She had been spoiling her granddaughter and buying the girl everything and anything she wanted since she first met the glorious little, rambunctious thing.

Finances aside, Thérèse had only ever been truly broken twice. When she was forced to let Gérard go to save him and when her own son, Henri, had hied off to England at fifteen, unable to accept what it was she had to do to enable them to survive. Her ability to save those she loved seemed only possible when she let them go. And when her beloved Henri had succumbed to illness and died, leaving behind a daughter after he had married so incredibly young, she sought to do everything right by ensuring she protected the girl. Maybelle was all she had left and yet even that would soon be gone given the girl was clearly intent on travelling as opposed to giving her great-grandchildren.

There were good men out there. Her Gérard had been one of them.

Maybe it was time to insist. Before she ended up completely alone. "Once, *ma chére*. It is all I ask."

Maybelle lifted both brows. "Once what?"

The subject of the girl's abstinence needed to be touched upon. "I have taught you everything I know, and yet here you are at one and twenty, and have only kissed one man. Why?"

"I did *not* kiss that man," Maybelle sternly corrected, holding up a rigid finger and shaking it. "He kissed me."

This was definitely a problem. That disinterest seemed to only grow.

Thérèse sighed. "I do not understand. You have no intentions of ever marrying, and yet you hold onto your virginity as if it were worth a dowry. A woman's innocence is only valued by men. The moment you dispense of it, you take your first step toward freedom. Your first step toward ensuring you do not belong to anyone but yourself."

"Yes. I am well aware of that."

"Then what is the problem?" Maybe the girl was..? "Do you prefer women? Hm?"

Maybelle's cheeks flushed. "I want it to be memorable, is all. I want to look upon a man and say to myself, *oh, yes, I'll bed that one please.* Besides. You know the *ton*. They keep all the titled, good-looking men to themselves and give us their horrid remnants no one else wants."

Pausing before her, Thérèse shook her head almost pitifully. "You think the *ton* is keeping the good men away? Pffff. The *ton* has no power over us. We are our own government which no man rules. *We* define ourselves. And that is why I am asking *you* to define yourself. Without the *ton's* ridiculous restrictions. I say, storm the Season. Claim the man of your choosing and enjoy life. Perhaps then you would not be so horribly tense."

Maybelle glared. "Horribly tense? Need I remind you, we cannot even attend social gatherings unless they're being hosted at a brothel."

Everyone was a pundit these days. "You, Maybelle, are my granddaughter. As such, you have the ability to place every man at your feet. Make a name for yourself, and the sort of men you want will come by the dozen."

"*Grand-mère*, I am not interested in becoming a *demimondaine*. Life is difficult enough with you being one."

Thérèse tried not to whine. "But you have the makings of greatness."

"Greatness indeed. I learned from Papa long ago never to overextend myself to anyone as it leads to very bad things. Surely, you remember how obsessed he was with Mama. And she'd been dead for twelve years."

"Henri was born a romantic." Like his father. "What can I say." Thérèse sighed, reached out and took hold of Maybelle's hands, squeezing them tightly. "Have I returned to being a *demimondaine* after becoming your guardian? *Non.* Yet why is it men continue to roll at my feet, begging to be patted at any cost? Because I cannot escape the name I have created. Nor do I want to. I enjoy sex." And passion. She had a great teacher.

Maybelle released her hands, shook her head and stepped back. "I will not watch you destroy whatever integrity London has left by teaching all the men how to take advantage of women. It is not right."

Thérèse lowered her voice. "I will tell you what is not right, Maybelle. Because of who I wish to be, because of who I have always been, I have not only sent my son to an early grave, but am now forcing his child to flee from me in the same manner he did. I know what will happen once you leave today. You will not return. You will disappear from my life. As Henri did." As his father had. Of course, she had wanted it that way. For him.

Maybelle's pretty features softened. She took hold of Thérèse's shoulders and squeezed them gently, assuredly. "I would never abandon you. Ever. Seeing the pyramids is a dream of mine. You know that. And the way that Ferlini man is going about destroying them, there may very well be nothing left for me to see. You've read the papers. He is damn well smashing tops off pyramids and plundering tombs wherever he goes."

How was she going to tell the girl they couldn't afford the trip? Thérèse pinched her lips together, her eyes now burning with tears. Tears she hadn't cried since she threw herself at her son's bedside while he lay dying.

Blinking back tears that threatened to fall, Thérèse pulled away and sniffed. She fingered the emerald bracelets she had on, bracelets given to her by Lady Madeleine who had gone on to marry a Persian prince, but knew they wouldn't fetch enough. She would have to sell the diamonds and pearls Gérard had given her when she was the girl's age. It would allow her Maybelle to travel to her heart's content and be abroad for however long she wanted to be.

Which could be a long time. Maybe she would meet a man and never come back.

Waving a hand, Thérèse eventually muttered, "Go. Follow your heart, your love. I will pay for everything and manage the school on my own. You will see."

There was a moment of silence.

After a moment, Maybelle announced, "I will stay for two months. But only two months."

Bless you for loving me. Two months would allow her to gather enough funds without selling the diamonds or pearls. Oh, how she loved the girl! This girl had shown her the one thing she had failed to learn in her lifetime. That mercy and forgiveness equaled real love.

Turning back toward her, Thérèse half-clapped, unable to contain her joy. "Two months will be *magnifique!* You will join me at the school on opening day, *oui?* Aside from all the men you will meet, I have countless rooms filled with all sorts of treasures and adventures."

Maybelle pointed. "Let us not get carried away. I am not interested in school-boys learning how to please a woman. I know more than the basics thanks to you. Understand, *Grand-mère,* that the trouble with most men, even the experienced ones, is that they are forever seeking out attachments and are for the most part quite possessive. Albeit in different forms, but it all ends the same. If it isn't a wife they require, it is a mistress, and if it isn't a mistress, it is some other form of convention they ultimately define in their own terms. Which is why I see absolutely no point in pursuing a single one of them."

Thérèse had certainly over-educated the girl. She had tried to keep her from getting hurt by over-sexed blighters only to— *Merde.* Her granddaughter apparently wanted the sex without the commitment. Too much like a man. But in a man's world..she supposed it was a good thing.

Maybelle took in a deep, calming breath and let it out. "Now. I propose that over the next two months we point all of our efforts in the direction of your school and then in the direction of my travels. Then we will both be happy. And that is what we want, yes? To be happy?"

Maybe the girl needed an introduction to what she loved most but thought was unattainable: titled men. And she knew just the man to offer the girl a ballroom full of them.

Thérèse held up a finger into the air, causing all of her bracelets to fall down the length of her wrist. "I have an idea."

Her granddaughter stepped back.

Thérèse ignored that poor humor. "Lord Hughes owes me a favor. A considerable one, I admit." She had finally let the poor man kiss her after dealing with well over a year of pleading. It wasn't bad. It didn't make her toes curl, but at her age, nothing ever did anymore. She liked him.

Thérèse winked with great exaggeration, trying to remain playful. "I shall therefore see to it that he invites us to several of his soirées. He does not care what the *ton* thinks." She smiled and folded her hands before her. "I promise to find you a man incapable of demanding any attachments."

Maybelle's blonde eyebrows rose.

"And when we find him," Thérèse went on, "it will then be entirely up to you to make the best of it."

Maybe the girl would even find a man right here in London and..stay.

****

Three weeks later at the house of Lord Hughes, evening

As elegantly dressed men and women whisked in and out of sight, adorned in perfectly tailored and expensive satiny hues of onyx, periwinkle, and alabaster, Thérèse kept her granddaughter tucked near the oak paneled wall to ensure they had the best view of every man in the house.

A young mustached gentleman, a mere baron grinned and nodded his pleasantries toward Thérèse as he passed by.

No chance, Monsieur Baron. Keep walking. I only have sex with grown men, not boys. She did, however, politely return his nod, given she had no intention on being rude to potential candidates for her school.

Maybelle leaned in from behind and peered past the double bouffant sleeves of Thérèse's low-cut, plum evening gown.

A tall, dark-haired gentleman clad in expensive black evening attire strode past making her granddaughter pause.

It made Thérèse also pause. She glanced back at her granddaughter.

Those big, eager blue eyes followed the gentleman, her lips parting.

Oho. And there it was. Lust at first sight.

A breath escaped Thérèse. Oh, to be young again. She missed the excitement of seeing a man that made her skin tingle and her stomach flip.

Maybelle gathered her cream satin skirts and bustled out from behind Thérèse to place herself on better display. She pertly waited.

Thérèse bit back a smile. Youth was so adorably stupid.

Maybelle released her satin skirts and silently watched as the gentleman rounded the dance floor and disappeared through the French doors leading out onto the darkened terrace.

Well, well. Her granddaughter had taken an interest in a real challenge. And in a duke, no less. Dukes, when done right, were certainly hard to resist. She should know. "You have very good taste. That, *ma chére*, is none other than the Duke of Rutherford. Better known to London as the man tragically ruined by his father's lust."

Oh, yes. She had every finger on the pulse of London's throat. It had enabled her to survive its prudish, overly regulated ways.

Maybelle's eyes widened. "Ruined by his father's lust? You don't mean his father actually--"

"Och, *mais non!*" The dirty, dirty thing. "Where is your mind tonight?"

Thérèse glanced around, snapped open her ostrich fan and leaned toward her. She hid the bottom half of their faces behind the confines of her fan and lowered her voice. "You see, a little over six years ago, his father died in the arms of a courtesan. Laudanum overdose. Dreadful, dreadful scandal. But then the *réel* rumors commenced. That the woman was not a courtesan at all, but a lady of high, respectable society. Well. That made it even more *difficile* for the *ton* to accept and ever since, the duke's poor mama has desperately tried to marry him off to whoever will have him. Despite his dire circumstances, the man refuses to compromise his lineage and will not marry below him. And so there you have it. Ruined by his own father's lust."

Maybelle eyed her. "What if I wanted him? For a night, that is. What would you suggest?"

Who knew getting great-grandchildren was going to be this easy. She only hoped the girl didn't get into *too* much trouble. Thérèse leaned away and snapped her fan closed, letting it dangle by its velvet string attached to her gloved wrist. "Seeing you want only one night, I suggest you keep it simple."

"How simple?" Maybelle prodded.

Thérèse lifted her other hand, pulled out a small, tin box from the wrist of her glove, opened it and held it out for her. "Here. Have a mint. I will make an introduction for you before the end of the hour."

Maybelle lowered her voice a touch more. "Why an introduction? Is it because of his rank?"

Thérèse laughed. "Of course not. It is because of *my* rank. You want him, *oui?*" She shook the box at her, rattling the candies within. "Do take one, *ma chére*. Men adore the smell of mint. It seduces their senses."

Maybelle wrinkled her nose, plucked up the mint between two fingers and tucked it into her own glove. She turned and watched the doors leading to the balcony. "So how does one even go about seducing a man of such status? Surely it complicates matters."

Whilst, yes, everyone in London might consider her to be a bad grandmother for pushing her granddaughter toward pursuing lust, she knew the girl only wanted an experience, not a commitment. Lust was tamable and eventually fled. Whilst commitment? That was complicated.

Besides, at one and twenty, how much longer did society expect such a passionate, pretty girl to wait? "A title is but a barrier, not a complication." Thérèse plucked up a mint, placed it onto the tip of her tongue and slid the tin back into the unbuttoned space at the wrist of her glove. "Perhaps you should consider visiting the school and sitting in on a few lessons. We discuss social barriers all the time." Or rather, she did. The men were a touch shy.

"No. No, thank you. I shall manage. Without stepping onto your pirate ship." Maybelle eyed the balcony again. "I wish to approach him out in the garden. Might I?"

And she thought she was brash when she was younger. Thérèse sighed. "I will not argue." She paused. "But. Before you go. Be certain that I do not notice you are abandoning me or I shall come across as a very bad chaperone." She would go out and check on the girl in exactly twenty minutes to ensure it did not get *too* out of hand given they were in public.

Maybelle took to busily arranging her skirts. As she did so, she snuck one dainty step to the left. Toward the direction of the balcony. Then another. And another.

Thérèse did her best not to laugh. Instead, she lifted her chin and continued to stare out before her, appearing genuinely occupied with listening to the orchestra and watching all of the couples whirl and dance. *Twenty minutes will allow for conversation that I will then...interrupt.*

Her granddaughter, being well outside of chaperone scope, sashayed her way toward the French doors leading outside and casually disappeared out into the night.

A breath escaped Thérèse. She missed being naughty.

Someone sidled up next to her. A gent whose ivory waistcoat could not hide a touch of a belly protruding forth from his evening jacket, leaned in. Mischievous brown eyes brightened as they searched her face. "You look glorious, as always. I am ever so pleased you came. How are you, my dear?"

She fully turned toward her good friend of several years, Lord Hughes. She smiled. "I am incredibly well, *merci*. More so than usual. For tonight is a very glorious night. My granddaughter is officially interested in men, which means I may still have a chance at great-grandchildren. How is *your* evening?"

"Complicated." He puffed out a breath and leaned in. "My nephew is in a devilishly awkward position. He needs a bit female perspective. I was hoping you could talk to him. Do you have time for him this week?"

She eyed him, now curious. She had met Hugh's nephew, Lord Caldwell, once before. Dashing, blond and playful. Or so he liked others to believe. "Of course. Is he having problems with women?"

"Yes and no. I will put it into writing given there is too much to say. Simply know that he will be calling on you soon."

Her life was never droll. "I will talk to him."

"Thank you. I appreciate that. The boy means a lot to me."

Her voice softened. "Yes, I know." She rather admired how Hughes wielded a crop toward the world but when it came to his nephew, the man fell to his knee with a tear in his eye.

Setting his gloved hands behind his back, Hughes cleared his throat, scanning the dance floor. He lowered his voice. "That kiss we shared not too long ago was amazing. It gave me hope."

Using her fan, she tapped at his arm. "It has taken some time, but I will admit you have grown on me."

He rolled his eyes. "You make me sound like a damn wart."

She laughed. "My days of finding passion are long over, Hughes. If you want me, you have to accept the fact you will be nothing more than an accessory I shove into my reticule. I have more use for rouge than I do for men at this point."

He paused and leaned in closer. "I swore I would never commit to a woman again, but I am not getting younger and you make me feel..young. I need that. Will you marry me? I hear you need money, and whilst my finances aren't as glorious as I would like them to be, I do have enough to help you and your granddaughter along. What do you say?"

Poor Hughes. The man had no idea that asking a woman to marry him at a gathering as if offering pork pie was anything but a compliment. Fortunately for him, she rather liked pork pie. It was food meant for comfort. Which is all she needed anymore. He made her laugh and was well beyond dependable. Not having to worry about money would also be nice. What was marriage anyway? A piece of paper. "Consider us engaged."

He searched her face, his lips parting. "Do you mean it?"

She smirked. "We have known each other for a long time. I know what to expect from you, and you know what to expect from me. We call on each other practically every day. Why not save us both a carriage ride?"

"God love you." He grabbed her face, despite the crowd of the ballroom surrounding them, and soundly kissed her on the lips. Releasing her, he grinned. "You have given me a reason not to grow old."

She pointed her fan at him. "Do not put such a burden on me, Hughes. Or you will go bald."

He grinned. "So when do we set the date for the church? Next month?"

A breath escaped her. He was moving far too quick. "No. Next year."

His brows came together. "Next year?" he echoed. "Why so damn—"

"Hughes, my granddaughter comes first and she plans to go to Egypt. We have to wait until she comes back. She would be upset if I married without her being there."

"Oh." He lowered his voice. "Can I call on you at your house later tonight? After these festivities are over? So we could..?"

She adjusted the collar of his coat. "No. Not tonight."

"Tomorrow night?"

"No."

He glared. "When?"

"One does not plan these things, Hughes. One simply lets it happen."

He puffed out a breath. "The trouble is you never let it happen. Even our kiss did not last quite as long as I would have wanted it to. You ended it well before I was done."

"What did you expect? We will always be friends first."

"Then why marry me?"

"Because at my age, I prefer a friend in my home as opposed to a man I have to train."

He eyed her. "That goddamn school of yours is going to your head. You had better watch your derriere. Do you realize what London is saying?"

She groaned. "It is no different than what France was saying when I left it. A school of this caliber is serving a far greater purpose beyond my need for money." She set her chin with renewed pride. "These men need me. They require proper guidance and assurance. I am the mother they wished they had."

He snorted. "And why do you think it is your responsibility to guide men half your age?"

She was quiet for a moment, knowing true passion had to be guided whilst one was young. "Maybe some of these men will get to live the sort of life that should have been mine. Not every relationship has to end up in shambles." She tried to keep the angst from her voice, but it remained. She had often wondered what life would have been like had she told Gérard that night she refused to let him go.

Hughes lowered his shaven chin, his brown eyes hardening. "I know that look and that tone. You are thinking about that bastard right now. That French duke of yours. Admit it."

A sentimental breath escaped her. "I always think about Andelot. If I have a thought, he is usually in it. It is something you will have to accept."

He was quiet for a moment. "Are you devoted to me?"

"Would I have agreed to marry you if I was not?"

"I want to hear you say it. Are you devoted to me?"

Och. Men. Even the less needier ones were still needy. "I am devoted to you. Yes."

"Good." He stared her down. "Because your Andelot is in London, you know."

Her heart skidded. She swung fully to Hughes, eyes widening. "You lie."

Swiping his face, he shifted from boot to boot. "I am not one to keep anything from you and you know it. This is me setting aside my jealousy and being a friend." He puffed out a breath. "There is a gentleman by the name of *duc de Andelot* who started frequenting Mrs. Berkley's whipping club a few weeks ago. Apparently, he is well known in Russia for unusual rope binding techniques. Mrs. Berkley is insisting he try on all the girls so they can learn how to do it. According to gossip, they line up every single fucking night to try it."

She gasped. Rope binding techniques? Out of Russia? He—

She'd been upset with Gérard for some time given he had not even made an attempt to contact her. Not once. Of course, she *had* told him they were done and *had* left France many, many years ago in order to be with Henri here in England.

A shaky breath escaped her. Gérard went to Russia. Which meant he hadn't forgotten what they shared, after all. Why else would he have gone to Russia? It was the one place she had always wanted to go.

She was quiet for a moment. "Do you know if he has been asking about me?"

Hughes glared. "What happened to your devotion?"

Of all times to agree to an engagement. "Hughes. Whilst you and I are very good friends and I adore you, you know what Andelot means to me. No man will ever go near it."

He leaned in close. "He does not deserve you given how long he waited. Let it go."

A breath escaped her. "I should at least see him."

"Think twice before you ask for the devil to appear." From behind a gloved hand, he offered, "Apparently, he wears an array of masks in public. Even in private. No one has ever seen him without it. Something happened to his face."

Dread scraped her. "What do you mean?"

He shrugged. "Hell if I know. Mrs. Berkley only tells me so much."

There was only one reason as to why Gérard would have come back into her life after all these years and still not have announced himself. He was out to finish what he had started thirty years ago. Delivering her pain. Rope binding was just the beginning.

She grabbed Hughes arm, shaking it. "Do you know where he is staying?"

He snorted. "Even if I did, dearest, I would never tell you. The man binds up women like little roasts about to go on a spit. Hardly something you want to get involved with."

She rolled her eyes. "His ropes hardly scare me."

"Are you insinuating you wish to—"

"If he wishes it, why would I not? I have been waiting for him. I knew it was only a matter of time before he would come back."

Hughes pulled in his chin, his face flushing. "I will bloody smack him with a duel."

She glared. "*Non.* Are you a friend to me or not?"

He glared back. "We are engaged, madame. Or did you already forget?"

She adjusted her pearls. The ones Gérard had given her. How fitting that she was wearing them right now. "I will marry you next year if he does not appear to me."

Rolling his tongue against the inside of his cheek, Hughes eyed her breasts and pearls. "And what if he appears *after* we marry? What happens then?"

She snapped her fan out at him, hitting his arm. "*Ça suffit.* You are whining now. Whatever will be, will be. You hardly own me nor will you ever. I know all about the women you continue to bed and crop despite the kiss we shared. You are a scoundrel, like the rest."

He cleared his throat. "I have needs you refuse to meet."

"I am retired from my profession. What more do you want?"

He muttered something.

She tapped her fan against his shoulder again. "Be the dear friend I know you to be and tell me more about Andelot. Is he married? Does he have a mistress or a lover I can talk to or visit? Do you know?"

He sighed. "I know nothing more except what Mrs. Berkley tells me. She calls him the Messiah and appears intent on turning him into a lover."

Thérèse almost gritted her teeth. She hated Mrs. Berkley. Hated, hated, hated that woman. That British red-haired vixen was always trying to outdo her and every courtesan and prostitute in London with her crops and whips and shackles and torture devices. Thérèse herself had long tried it all back in France. It was nothing new. Sade was well ahead of his time.

She paused. Ropes. Why ropes? What did Gérard get out of it? Pleasure? A sense of control over a woman? A need to be malicious? All three? It sounded nothing like him. Surely it was nothing but gossip. Surely he had not become the very thing the Revolution had wanted him to be: sordid.

Hughes leaned sideways and squinted toward the French doors leading to the balcony of the garden. "Uh..there appears to be a small crowd gathering. Where is your granddaughter?"

Thérèse froze. *Maybelle!* Her heart pounded. She had *completely* forgotten about the poor girl.

Gathering her skirts, she darted past men and women, shoving her way by the gathering crowd. Pushing through, she stumbled out onto the terrace and jerked to a halt at seeing the Duke of Rutherford on the stairs, his black hair well-mussed as his tall frame lingered before Maybelle who was busily swiping at the front of her skirts, glancing down in the process. Those dainty gloved hands stilled against the cream satin of her gown. Dirt marks and grass stains spattered the entire front of her bosom as well as the length of her knees.

Oh, dear. In only twenty minutes these two started more than a relationship.

Thérèse swept toward them. *"Ma chére?"*

Maybelle paused, turned and met her gaze, her porcelain skin well-flushed.

Smiling in an effort to assure the girl that everything would be all right, Thérèse quickly held out a gloved hand. "It is best we leave. People are beginning to gather."

Maybelle eyed the lighted balcony of people surrounding them.

The duke stepped toward them from behind, adjusting his evening coat. "I am to blame for this," he offered in a low, sincere tone. "Entirely. Allow me to settle this matter in private."

An offer? *Already?* Now here was a gentleman worthy of consideration. Aside from a title, he was wealthy enough to provide for her granddaughter and good-looking enough to give her those rosy-cheeked great-grandchildren.

Maybelle turned to the duke, startled by the offer.

Commitment was the girl's nightmare. Och. They would come back to this later. "No need, Your Grace. *Bonne nuit.*" Thérèse gently took Maybelle's arm, turned her away from the duke, and led them back toward the stairs leading to the balcony.

Toward the gathering crowd.

Leaning closer to Maybelle, Thérèse whispered, "There is no other way to depart except through the ballroom. Walk slowly, with dignity, and pretend all is well."

They walked up the remaining stairs of the balcony.

The men on that balcony, both young and old alike, openly gaped at them with unwavering fascination as they passed, while several women leaned in toward each other, whispering behind their elaborate, hand painted fans.

They marched on in a slow procession, past all the endless faces of the *ton*. It felt like days of old. Not at all what she missed. The stage is the only thing she missed.

The orchestra's minuet soon faded and they eventually left the ballroom.

Their steady steps on the marble floor echoed all around them as they headed toward the front entrance. "So," Thérèse whispered, tightening her hold on her granddaughter's arm. "Was he worth the parade?"

Maybelle eyed her and whispered back, "I promise to tell you everything later."

Oho and no. "Later, later. You will have me wait that long? Absolutely not. I—" Thérèse paused, realizing there was a figure standing in the shadows by the stairwell behind them.

A tall, broad-shouldered and well-muscled man with silvery-steel hair, dressed in expensive evening attire and leather riding boots leaned against the farthest wall. A cigar dangled from a black leather glove as he lifted it to his full lips, drawing attention to the fact that he wore a well-fitted, black velvet mask that hid half his face. He glanced at her in agitation, revealing only half of his masked face and ice-blue eyes, then pushed away from the wall, smoke wafting around him in the shadows as if he emerged out of hell. He stalked in the opposite direction, disappearing from sight.

Thérèse's grasp slipped. Dearest God. He really was back. And he was doing what he did best. Watching her from a distance.

Maybelle paused and turned toward her. "*Grand-mére?*"

Thérèse took in several deep, ragged breaths and shakily placed her gloved hand to her heaving bosom, unable to breathe. She felt like she was being shoved into a trunk with no way out. And the worst of it? She wanted him to turn the key.

"*Grand-mére?*" Maybelle's panicked voice echoed all around them in the now empty corridor. "What is it?"

"I feel..." Thérèse staggered back, trying to reach out for Maybelle with gloved hands to balance herself, then collapsed, allowing herself to career into the spiraling darkness she had no doubt Gérard wanted her to fall into.

LESSON SEVENTEEN

What if all the things you have come to believe

about yourself is nothing more than a lie?

-The School of Gallantry

Months later - August 28th, 1830
32 Belgrave Square - evening

At least there were still people in this godforsaken world a man could depend on.

Meaning, the Russians.

Grabbing hold of the brass handles leading into his study, Gérard flung the doors open, sending them slamming into the oak paneled walls that shook the large portraits and mirrors hanging throughout the room. The lit candles flickered, sending disfigured shadows across the high, crown molded ceilings.

Shadows were his domain now. And he was fucking proud of it. He loved it.

He glanced toward the walnut encased burgundy sofa, where a young unshaven Russian lingered. Black hair was scattered beneath a low-slung cap that shadowed the color of his eyes. A pinstripe waistcoat had been unevenly buttoned beneath a wool coat of respectable means. As always, Konstantin Alexander Levine wore no cravat around that neck and his linen shirt was left wide open for all the women to see.

Despite the young man's inability to properly dress himself and the fact Konstantin was a former guard for criminals, the Russian's demeanor had always been incredibly polite and noble.

Gérard adored the boy like a son and owed him his life.

Konstantin had taken a bullet to the shoulder for him back in Saint Petersburg when a bunch of anti-aristocratic idiots thought Gérard was a threat to their 'organization' given the peasants liked him for not only donating thousands of rubles to the poor every year, but also stripping down to a linen shirt and trousers, with his mask in place, while he went out into the fields with a scythe to muddy his own boots alongside his laborers. Everyone always seemed to have a problem accepting that aristocrats were capable of compassion and generosity and hard work. Fucking idiots.

"We meet again, my Russian friend," Gérard rumbled out in English. His Russian wasn't very good. "How is your shoulder?"

Konstantin thudded his left shoulder. "It healed well."

"I am infinitely pleased to hear it, and I am infinitely pleased you came. Although it took you long enough." Gérard smirked. "Did the boat sink and leave you to swim?"

Konstantin inclined his dark head. "It might as well have. Russia is not exactly next door, Your Grace. I stayed in Saint Petersburg a bit longer than I planned."

Gérard entered the room, striding toward him. "Might I offer you a drink, Levin? Sherry? Cognac? Or are you hungry? Shall I have the chef prepare something for you? Is there anything you wanted? Name it, and it is yours."

"No, thank you. I ate at an inn before coming into London. But I would like to take this moment to thank you for inviting me into a city I have always wanted to see. I only wish I had not arrived at night. I could hardly see anything."

Like there was anything to see. London held nothing but crowded buildings and a dirty river. Gérard preferred Russia. "There will be plenty of time for that. But I should probably warn you London is a bit quiet this time of year. The Season is long over and most homes are vacated by now. I personally prefer it. A man cannot think with crowds of people around him. So tell me. How was your journey?"

"I spent most of my time hanging over the railing of the boat, releasing my innards through my nose and my mouth. Other than that..it was pleasant." Konstantin hesitated and cleared his throat. "I also wish to thank you, Your Grace. I really do. I am still a bit overwhelmed and still do not believe I deserve it. I am asking that you reduce the amount. I hardly think—"

Gérard snapped up a hand. "There is no need for us to discuss this. It is done. The money will be in your hands by the end of this week, and all I ask is that you not let others know where the money came from. We are merely good comrades and nothing more."

"But the amount is—"

"The amount is respectable." A hundred thousand was nothing. "Are you telling me my life is worth less?"

Konstantin blinked. "No, I—"

"I am a generous man, Levin. Let us leave it at that. I have endured a lot and never give any less than what I believe a man deserves." He paused before Konstantin and lingered, staring him down through the slits of his mask. He gestured rigidly toward Konstantin's exposed throat. "What is this? Where is your cravat? You did this last time."

Konstantin's hand jumped to his bare throat. "I never wear cravats. Unless I am required to."

Gérard glared. The boy was going to make him look bad. "You cannot step out into public looking like you have lived in a cave all your life. 'Tis an insult to those who are forced to look upon you. Tomorrow, you are going straight to my tailor to conduct measurements for the sort of clothing a man like you should be wearing. Because if it looks cheap, it is cheap. And no one bows to cheap."

Gérard leaned in and adjusted the lapel of Konstantin's coat. He sighed. "I regret not giving you money sooner. When you awake tomorrow, my valet will properly shave you. With the amount of money going into your pocket, Levin, 'tis your duty to represent yourself well. Or no one will take you seriously."

Konstantin swiped his hand across his unshaven jaw. "Forgive me. I get lazy sometimes."

"I can see that." Gérard glanced toward the clock on the mantelpiece and paused, realizing it was almost time for his ten o'clock evening visit. The one he always made every Friday night in passing since coming to London months earlier. "I do not wish to be rude, but I have an appointment to keep. Are you tired? Or are you up for joining me?"

Those brows shot up. "I would not be imposing?"

"No." He sure as hell had nothing to hide. Gérard turned and strode toward one of the bookshelves. He ran a hand across the bindings of all the leather books before stopping and yanking one out. The usual fare. *Candide: or The Optimist* by Voltaire.

Gérard carried over the warped leather binding and held it out. "Take this for me."

Konstantin took the book, eyeing it. "This has certainly seen a lot of use."

"Good books usually do." And he could say the same about the woman to whom it had once belonged. Gérard strode by trying not to get too agitated with the thought of seeing her still surrounded by countless men. It wasn't as if he had refrained from women. Far from it. Between the two of them, they probably fucked half the world. "Come. And bring Voltaire with you."

"Where are we going?"

Gérard paused, not looking at anything in particular. He didn't know how much longer he could hold out staying away from her. His marred face aside, he genuinely feared being turned away and didn't know what he'd do if she did.

Knowing the Russian was waiting for an answer, he offered, "I usually go alone, but I trust you. And truth be told, I would rather not be alone tonight." He was tired of pretending that he could fill the void.

He never could. Not even after thirty years.

****

When his coach paused in the shadows before a very respectable-looking townhome, outside the light of surrounding gaslights, Gérard gestured toward the book with his cane. A cane Sade had gifted to him the night half his face disappeared. "Read."

Konstantin shifted against the leather upholstered seat of the carriage and swiped up the book beside him. He hesitated. "Uh.. is there a reason you want me to—"

"Start at part two on page one hundred and three." Gérard pointed at him. "And above all, handle it with care. That is an original English printing." It was also all he had left of Thérèse.

Konstantin paged through the book, eventually finding the page. He cleared his throat. "*Part Two. Chapter One. How Candide quitted his companions and what happened to him. We soon became tired of everything in life; riches fatigue the possessor; ambition when satisfied, leaves only remorse behind it; the joys of love are but transient joys; and Candide, made to experience all the vicissitudes of fortune was soon disgusted with cultivating his garden.*"

Gérard unlatched the window of the carriage and leaned out, staring up at the window where Thérèse could always be found when he needed her most. A silver-haired beautiful, beautiful woman draped in an ivory robe sat beside the window reading by a brightly lit lamp that illuminated her pale face. She adjusted her silver braid over her shoulder.

Gérard continued to watch her, wondering what she was reading. Age might have changed the color of her hair and dabbed wrinkles around her eyes, but she was still so fucking gorgeous. She would always be. His only regret was knowing his marred face dictated his inability to call on her.

Konstantin leaned in and eyed the window. "Should we be doing this?"

Gérard tapped his lips with a finger, trying to focus, and gestured toward the book again, without looking away from Thérèse. "Read."

Konstantin shut the book, slid over to the window and leaned toward him. "Let me give you some advice. I have no idea how the English conduct themselves here, but in Russia, men are arrested for such things."

Gérard continued to watch Thérèse as she tilted her head, clearly thinking about something. Maybe him? He had wanted her to see him that one night. If only to see what would happen. Her in a faint said it all. "Since when is love a crime, Levin?" he asked in the darkness of the carriage.

Konstantin glanced back up to the window. "Who is she?"

In an effort to contain his angst, Gérard gripped his cane tighter, his black leather glove creaking. "A whisper of everything I could have had but never will."

"Did she marry someone else?"

That would have been a blessing. She would have been to bed with only one man, instead of the countless she had embraced over the years. He sometimes wished he hadn't hired investigators to tell him about her life. Not that he had been a saint. Far from it. "She married every damn man in sight."

There was a pause. "I am very sorry to hear it."

Fuck. Blaming her in front of a man who did not know her was not what he wanted. She deserved better than that.

Gérard hit the end of the cane on the floor of the carriage. "I used to blame her for the path she took. But I have long since come to recognize it is I who destroyed her by not making an honorable woman of her. I was the one to drape her with her first set of diamonds." And pearls. How she loved her pearls.

Yes, he had bought her for his schemes, but had paid for her with his soul.

Gérard glanced back toward her window again and paused, his cane stilling. The window was now dark, reflecting the emptiness she had left within him.

An exasperated breath escaped him. Re-latching the carriage window with an agitated swipe of his gloved hand, he settled back against the seat and muttered, "She has retired for the night." Lifting his cane, he hit the roof of the carriage, commanding the driver to leave.

The driver snapped the reins and the carriage rolled forward, causing them to sway forward and back.

Gérard lowered his eyes to the gold head of his cane and rigidly tapped the palm of his gloved hand against it. He only got in a few minutes of looking at her. "Next time, I come alone. You talk too much."

Konstantin quirked a brow. "Do you mean to tell me, since coming into London, you have been doing this every night?"

"I would never admit to such a thing."

"Which means you have been."

Gérard shifted his jaw. He used to come to her window every night when he first arrived in London. Glimpsing her was like drinking brandy. He couldn't get enough of it. He had eventually dwindled his nightly visits down to mere Friday nights. For the sake of what remained of his sanity. "What of it?"

"Is she the reason why you came to London?"

There was no sense in lying to a Russian. "Yes." And it took him too many years to find her.

"Have you called on her?"

Fuck that thought. "I would never."

"Why?"

Lifting his cane up toward his face, Gérard edged the gold handle across the left side of his tied mask, causing it to shift. "This." He lowered the cane from his mask. His marred face only bothered him when it came to Thérèse. The last thing he wanted was to see pity in her eyes.

His face aside, and the early financial struggles he had endured, which his mother's family in England had kindly helped him through, he had actually led a good life.

After leaving France, everything had miraculously turned to gold. Quite literally. It was as if he had merely been living in the wrong country with the wrong people all his life. Everything became whatever he wanted it to be. Except for the one thing he had always wanted most: Thérèse.

Konstantin gripped the book. "Forgive me for prying, but what actually happened between you and her?"

"Too much." His words of what had come to pass between them were blurred. Some things he remembered all too well, others he did not. Not because age had erased the past but because he and his soul wanted to erase the past. He wanted to replace it with something new.

He averted his gaze to the dark night beyond the glass window at his shoulder. "I had to let them go." And the worst of it? He had never even gotten a chance to see his son again. A babe in a cradle is all the boy would be to him. Both in his mind and in his heart.

He seethed out a breath, and verbally related more to Konstantin, half of which meant nothing to him. Because it didn't matter anymore. It changed nothing.

Gérard rolled his eyes. "I have heard she associates with an array of men because of some *school* where she gives men advice on-on.. *private matters.*" He shook his head, not at all surprised. "She was always outrageous. She lived for it." His fisted hand hit the seat hard, reverberating through the carriage. "I need brandy," he breathed out.

It was a pathetic way of letting himself whine given he hadn't touched brandy or any liqueur after the woman called him a drunk and a liar the night they parted. Those words had burned the brandy right out of him. He had refused to even listen to the doctor when he was told to drink a good bottle of any spirit to quell the pain that marred the left section of his face not even two hours after she had left him.

In some way, he knew he had earned it.

Whilst on the ship with half his face bandaged and suffering in agonizing pain, a bright-eyed Japanese stowaway had taken pity on him, shared his opium, and despite their little language barrier, introduced him to the art of knotting *Asanawa* ropes to keep his hands and his mind occupied through the pain. It turned into a passion of perfecting an elaborate array of knots that represented who he was and how he felt.

Konstantin squinted. "So you have been in London these past few months and still have not called on her or your granddaughter?"

Gérard tossed his cane from one hand to the other, back and forth, knowing full well what the boy was getting at. "My face aside, I genuinely doubt Thérèse would permit me to have an association with Maybelle. She and I did not part on the best of terms."

There was a moment of silence. "How do you know what she will or will not allow if you have not called on her?"

He didn't know. Gérard glanced toward the window and the night beyond. He knew he was wasting what little was left of their time. If he called on her, at least he would finally know what was or wasn't possible. He also wanted to meet his granddaughter. Usually, the girl sat with Thérèse at the window, but for some reason, she hadn't been at the window in weeks. It bothered him.

"Call on her." Konstantin leaned closer. "After everything you survived, including a whole revolution, there is no shame in what you endured or why you wear a mask. Call on her."

Gently tapping the cane against the floor of the carriage, Gérard fixed his sight at nothing in particular. "Will you go with me if I call on them?"

"It would be an honor. When do you want to go? Shall we go tomorrow?"

Gérard's gaze snapped toward him, his throat tightening at the thought. "Are you mad? No. The day after." He hardly looked decent. "I need time to trim my hair. As do you."

Konstantin bit back a smile. "The trimming of our hair should only take a half hour."

Lowering his chin, Gérard drawled, "Whilst I appreciate your intentions, I ask that you refrain from any further comments."

Konstantin held up a hand and then set it against his mouth.

If only women were just as cooperative and understanding.

****

Two days later

Grand-mére,

Edmund and I are not in Cairo quite yet. We have yet another month before we arrive at our destination. Shortly before boarding our connecting ship, I

wanted to write a quick missive and thank you for the marvelous sense of hu-
mor you clearly do not lack. Edmund found the leather dildo you packed in our
trunks in honor of our new marriage. He and I decided to leave it on the seat of
a hackney we hired and hope it will find better use at the hands of whoever
finds it. Leather dildo aside, I miss you very much and wish to assure you my
marriage is everything I imagined it would be. Edmund and I intend to travel
for some time. I promise to write again the moment we arrive in Cairo. I am
breathlessly awaiting that first glimpse of the pyramids.

Sending you all of my love,
Maybelle

Gently folding the letter, Thérèse kissed it and then tucked it into the drawer of her writing desk. She sighed. There was no word of a pregnancy yet.

A knock came to the door, making her pause and glance toward it. *"Oui?"*

Clive cleared his throat from the other side. "There are two gentlemen here to see you, Madame. The Duke of Andelot and a Mr. Levin. Both are in the parlor waiting. Are you at home? Or shall I take their cards?"

Her heart popped. Dearest God. He was— *"Oui!* I will be right down!"

Scrambling up from the writing desk, the chair she was sitting in toppled over with a *bang* and clattered against the fullness of her skirts. She winced, not bothering with it, and bustled over to her dressing table.

Thérèse jerked to a halt before the mirror and gaped at herself. Her gathered hair, which had fully silvered by the time she was forty, had actually become her trademark. One she was proud of. It accented her eyes and whispered of all the adventures she had embraced.

While she had repeatedly sought out Andelot's whereabouts and had even knocked on Mrs. Berkley's door to do it, no one seemed interested in helping her. Mrs. Berkley, the evil thing that she was, took pride in ensuring she did not find him.

Thank goodness she was wearing a decent outfit.

Grabbing up her pearls from her jewelry box, which she knew he would recognize given the amount of money they cost him back in the day, she frantically draped them over her throat and arranged them.

Dabbing some rouge on her lips and some perfume on her wrists, she arranged her lace gown and drew in a shaky breath. It was like being eighteen again. Feeling like she mattered to him was beautiful, and no matter what happened, she would cherish this moment which she thought she would never see.

She took hold of the cane, which the doctor insisted she use. The man still believed her fainting spell had been due to apoplexy, despite her protests that it had merely been shock. She now decided having something to occupy her hand was a good thing.

Canes exuded power. One swing and—

Gathering her skirts, with the cane in hand, she darted toward the bedchamber door and flung it open. She set her chin, hitting the cane to the ground with one hand and tried to regally walk down the corridor, but her mind and her silly heart would not have it. She swung up the cane and broke out into a run, gathering her skirts again and did her best to run down the stairs without tripping over her own feet and gown.

Once she neared the foyer, her heels clicked frantically against the wood floors in a half-run as she drew closer to the parlor. Slowing her steps, she dragged in a calming breath, lowering the cane to the ground again and swept into the doorway with sashay worthy of more than a courtesan.

Gérard casually sat in one of the chairs. Upon seeing her, he uncrossed his leather riding boots, but otherwise did not rise.

Their eyes collided across the distance, making her throat tighten as the unnerving tingling in her stomach melted away all the years of angst she thought would never go away.

She barely managed half-breaths.

It was like returning to their days in the forest.

His face was, as last time, hidden beneath a well-fitted black velvet mask. Only those piercing blue eyes and the lower portion of his mouth and shaven jaw peered through. The visible marring of puckered skin on the left side of that jaw below the tied mask hinted at the damage hidden.

They stared wordlessly at each other in the pulsing silence.

Her hand gripped the cane hard in an attempt to even her breathing.

Gérard shifted his jaw beneath the mask and rose to his imposing height, clothed in all black, right down to his leather boots. That over-muscled physique appeared even more impressive than she had remembered. It hinted he had spent countless hours perfecting every muscle he had. That silvery-steel hair, which had been swept back from his forehead made him look all the more debonair.

Adjusting his black leather gloves in the manner of a duelist, he strode toward her, his booted steps steady and determined. He paused directly before her.

The scent of leather and expensive cologne wafted the air between them. She swallowed, fighting the tremor of her body. All the years of carefully cultivated poise evaporated. Every moment that she had laughed when she felt like crying, sighed when she felt like screaming, or climaxed with another man's name on her lips was gone.

She was a courtesan no more.

In his presence, as it had been then, she was nothing but a woman who wanted to belong to only one man. Him. Only him.

Widening his muscled stance, Gérard gruffly announced in English, "We will speak in English for the duration of this conversation. Because all things French are dead to me since I left Paris."

It was no surpise. Fortunately, her English was now as good as his.

She inclined her head toward him, her eyes never once leaving his masked face or the edges of that marred skin that peered out from beneath the velvet. Her chest tightened.

What had been done to him? Had it happened before he left Paris? Or after?

Gérard squared his jaw. "I am here because I wish to see my granddaughter. I wish to have the sort of relationship with her that you never allowed me to have with my son. I know I am asking for a lot, given how we parted, but I believe I have long since grown as a man and am worthy of that honor."

His words were surprisingly gentlemanly and kind. More than she would have ever hoped for. Unable to contain her joy of knowing they were in each other's lives again, she announced breathily, "I never thought I would see you again." She searched his masked face, wishing she could remove it. "You look well for yourself."

Gérard snorted and leaned in. "Oh, come, my dear. You need not lie. In answer to the question you have not asked, beneath this mask, half my face is gone."

She stilled, sensing the marring of his face bothered him more than he wished to admit. Why else would he wear a mask? What he didn't realize was that he would always be the dashing man who swept her into his life and onto the stage she had never quite left.

Gérard cleared his throat and tugged on his coat. "Can I meet my granddaughter? Is that at all a possibility?"

She brought her hands together, touched by the fact that he wanted to get to know Maybelle, and softly said, "Maybelle has left London with her husband."

His full lips parted below the mask. "She is married?"

"Yes. She married quite recently."

"And is she happy with the union?"

This was so strange. To be talking to him like this. About their granddaughter. "Yes. Very."

"Ah." He half-nodded, no longer meeting her gaze. "I am glad to hear it." He hesitated. "Who did she marry?"

She wanted to grab for him and embrace him and thank him for being so darling and downright charming given how they last parted. "His Grace, the Duke of Rutherford. They are currently on tour and will be visiting every city in Europe before travelling into Egypt. They are not expected to return for another eight months. When she does arrive back into London, you may call on her. I have no doubt she would want to meet her *grand-pére*. As such, I will..I will gladly notify you the moment she returns into town."

A breath escaped him. "I would appreciate that."

She nodded, hoping this meant he would be staying in London. "Where shall I send the missive when she arrives, Gérard? So she might call on you in person?" *She* wanted an address.

He lowered his chin. "I am living at Thirty-two Belgrave Square. I ask, however, that you do not address me by my birth name. It would give me too much hope."

A warming glow cheered her as her breath hitched. He wanted hope. Maybe there was a possibility for them to begin again. Maybe she only needed to give him the invitation he required.

Gérard set his shoulders and after a few pulsing moments offered, "I thank you for your time, madame. It was an honor to see you."

"And you." She lingered, hoping he would ask to see her again. She held his gaze.

He inclined his head. "I wish you a good-day." He rigidly rounded her, still holding her gaze in turn, and purposefully brushed past close enough for his entire frame to drag against hers. His hand grazed her skirts.

She almost staggered and sensed it was his way of silently prodding her into action. As if he were waiting for her to make the next move.

Tears stung her eyes. She prayed none of this was a game.

Disappearing out into the corridor, he called out, "Levin, in case you have not noticed, I am leaving." Swinging open the entrance door, Gérard walked out, leaving the door wide open.

The afternoon summer air and wind blew in.

Thérèse glanced toward the gentleman he had come with, tears blurring her sight. She pursed her lips in a noble attempt not to cry.

In an accent that hinted he was from one of the Slavic countries, Mr. Levin offered in English, "He needed to see you. He was sitting in a carriage outside your window every night for weeks."

Weeks? No. She knew it had been months given how long it had been since she had glimpsed him. That night that punched the breath out of her. It was obvious he was still struggling with whatever had happened to his face. It might have been the reason why he had stayed away despite being in London.

She set a trembling hand to her face and blindly attempted to use the cane to walk to a chair knowing he had been suffering and lingering outside her window all along. A sob escaped her.

Mr. Levin darted toward her and grabbed her hand and her corseted waist. He turned her and gently eased her into the nearest chair.

Heavens above. That gesture made her feel old. Eck. She was anything but.

She swiped at her tears with one hand, her manicured fingers trembling. She grabbed that arm, searching that youthful, rugged face. She needed to know the truth and this man, who was with Gérard, would know. "Where did the scarring come from? The ones hidden beneath the mask? What happened to him?"

"He never told me. But he mentioned it happened whilst trying to escape France. After you arranged transportation for him."

Her hand jumped to her mouth. Dearest God, she had failed him. She should have never left him that night. She closed her eyes, letting another tear slip down her cheek and said through her quaking hand, "Leave me."

Mr. Levin seated himself in a chair beside her. "I will leave once I am assured you are less distressed."

"Whilst kind, that will take more time than you have."

"I have time, madame," he gently offered. "Do you require anything? Shall I call for one of your servants?"

The whipping club and Mrs. Berkley aside, it gave her comfort knowing Gérard had surrounded himself with what appeared to be good people. "No. Thank you." She lowered her hand and sniffed softly. "Might I ask who you are to him?"

He inclined his head. "I am Mr. Levin. I am a friend."

"How long have you known him?"

"A few months. Though most of it was never in his presence."

"You have a heavy accent." Her eyes cut to his. "Are you from Russia?"

"Yes."

Oh, how she wanted to go. If only to see all the places Gérard had been to.

"I wish to assure you that in my country, Andelot is well-known for being everything a man should be. He is a legend in Moscow and is a patron to the poor and all things good. He is incredibly generous. Overly generous. To me and to everyone."

Her Gérard, in many ways, had remained the same. He was still a good man. Which was more than she could have ever hoped for. She reached out and delicately touched the man's arm. "Care for him, Mr. Levin. He needs a true friend. The sort he has never had due to his status and upbringing. Promise me you will be a good friend to him."

He hesitated. "I will ensure he stays out of trouble."

"*Merci.*" She removed her hand. She hesitated, having no doubt Gérard had probably heard about her entanglement with Hughes. Hughes was intent on proving to her he was worthy of her hand. And in some way, he was. He had been an incredibly good friend to her.

"Please tell him I am engaged to be married to Lord Hughes. He needs to know." Whilst she planned to end her association with Hughes knowing Gérard wanted to rekindle what had once been theirs, that did not excuse her from having to say it aloud. For she was still engaged.

Mr. Levin eyed her. "Pardon my asking, but is there any hope for him?"

She needed to end the engagement first. "I am not ready to answer that. Thank you for staying, Mr. Levin. It was very kind of you. I am quite well now."

"Of course." He rose. "Should you require anything, please send a missive to me at thirty-two Belgrave Square and address it to my name. I should be there for at least another two weeks until I find a place of my own. When I move, I will forward the new address."

"I appreciate your generosity." She swiped away the last of her tears. "*Au revoir*, Mr. Levin."

He hesitated, nodded and left.

When the door in the foyer closed, she frantically got up and hurried over to the window. Ensuring the curtain remained in place, she peered through a sliver of the fabric to see if she could glimpse Gérard.

She could see nothing. He was gone.

If she left it up to him, another thirty years would pass.

She sighed. It was time to start again.

LESSON EIGHTEEN

Let us begin again. Shall we?

-The School of Gallantry

Late morning

So much for not touching brandy ever again. Jesus Christ. The blur of last night was still fogging his brain. Let her marry. Why the fuck did he care?

Gérard shifted his jaw. He did care. A lot. And no amount of time would ever change it.

Knowing full well Konstantin was out serenading Lady Stone next door, Gérard didn't bother putting on his mask. Instead, he staggered out of his bedchamber, raking back his still damp hair with an agitated hand given it continued to fall into his eyes.

After soaking most of the morning in a hot bath, and despite being fully dressed and ready for the day, he was beginning to wonder if he should simply go back to bed. Of course, he would probably just lie there like the pathetic sop he was and think of Thérèse and the granddaughter who was as far out of reach as his son had been.

Trudging down the corridor and down the stairs, he veered into his study to write a missive to Mrs. Berkley about the invitation she had sent a few days earlier. He knew what the woman wanted, and despite her being attractive, he wasn't interested in complicating his life by involving himself with an overly ambitious young woman who wanted his money and seemed to think she could introduce him to something he'd never seen. Ha.

The calling bell rang, making him pause before his writing desk. He puffed out a breath, not at all up to trudging back upstairs to retrieve his mask.

Seeing his butler walk past the open door of the study, he called out, "No visitors."

The butler paused long enough to reply, "Yes, Your Grace."

Easing himself into the leather chair before his desk, he swiped over Mrs. Berkley's letter and angled it off to the side. He opened the top drawer, needing parchment and paused. The tiny knitted boot he slipped from his son's foot many, many years ago greeted him.

He stared at it, unable to breathe. He had not even been at the boy's wedding *or* funeral. It was as if the boy had never existed. Tears burned his eyes. Gérard fingered the softness of that boot before releasing it. He slammed the drawer shut.

Thérèse didn't even know the truth about what happened the night after she had left.

In one night, he lost everything. Including the right to his face.

Jumping to his booted feet, he swept everything off his desk, sending it crashing to the wooden floor. *Why marry now, Thérèse? After all these fucking years, why—* Grabbing his chair, he swung it up high over his head and gritting his teeth, he muscled it against the bookshelf behind him, slamming it against the shelves of books. Everything crashed down.

In between heaving breaths, he tried to calm himself but couldn't. He opened a drawer full of crystal ink wells and still needing to throw something, picked them all up and smashed them against the wall, one by one, spraying shards of glass everywhere.

There. Now he felt better.

"*Gérard?*" a familiar female accented voice echoed in English from the open doorway of his study behind him. "Whatever are you doing?"

He froze. Sweet merciful heaven. He had summoned her.

Knowing his mask wasn't on, he rigidly kept his back to her in between uneven, astounded breaths that were no longer attributed to the objects he had been throwing. He swallowed, the tension in his body coiling. "I am not decent. Go wait in the parlor until I am ready to see you."

Her gown rustled toward him. "No. I am not letting you hide from me."

Realizing she was approaching, he muttered, "Hell," and quickly removed his morning coat. He draped it over his head, burying himself in the heavy wool and satin material. He didn't care what she thought about him hiding. He simply wasn't ready to show his face.

Her full, saffron colored skirts appeared at his feet, coming into view below the coat. This was not how he envisioned taking her on. With a coat over his head. "What do you want?"

She lingered for a moment. "I am no longer engaged to Lord Hughes. I terminated the engagement this morning and wanted you to know it."

Well, well. This just got interesting. "Really? And why would you do that?"

She sighed. "I know why you came to London, Gérard. And I am here to welcome it."

Was she? "Welcome what?"

"A relationship."

He knew it. "Who says I want one?"

"Cease grouching." A hand smoothed its way across the fabric of his coat, pressing into the marred side of his face. "Remove this coat. Please do not hide from me."

He closed his eyes, knowing he wasn't ready to show her that half his face was gone. "Why are you here? What do you want?"

Her hand drifted away. "To apologize for that night and hurting you. I was angry and in my mind it was the only way to save you."

He had always known that and had long forgiven her for hurting him. He had loved her too much for that. "You need not worry. All is forgiven." He widened his stance, trying to be casual despite the coat on his head. "Was there anything else you wanted?"

A soft breath escaped her. "If all is forgiven, why this distance? Has everything changed?"

He paused. Was it really going to be this easy? They agreed and then kissed and would live happily ever after? Really? "Maybe I need time to adjust to having you back in my life. We hardly know each other anymore."

"I am well aware of that."

"Good. I am glad you do. Because last night, I drank a full decanter of brandy for the first time since leaving France. And I only drank it because I was tired of caring about the fact you once called me a drunk and a liar."

She was quiet for a long moment. "I regret those words," she said softly. "They were only spoken to ensure you left France, but if they also kept you from drinking, then I suppose I am genuinely proud of them. I am also proud of you. I did not realize it was possible for you to give up brandy."

He kept his eyes closed, that sultry voice luring him into a past he wanted to make his present and his future. Even after all these years. "I have proven to be much stronger than I thought myself capable of." He opened his eyes and in an effort to lighten the mood, offered, "By the by, the uh..the Russians do not chew glass. They chew on everything *but* glass. I thought you might want to know."

A laugh escaped her. "I thank you for clarifying that for me."

By God. Even that laugh was still the same. Melodious and mischievous.

They lingered.

She sighed. "Are you interested in joining me for an outing? Come. The weather is glorious so I rode out in my barouche. I will take you out for some ices and a paddle boat. I will pay for it."

He snorted. "*Ices and a paddle boat?* Christ, Thérèse, do be serious. Sixteen-year-olds do that sort of thing."

"And that is why they all have big smiles, Gérard. Because they are all on a paddle boat sucking on ices that makes them and life feel grand."

She hadn't changed a goddamn bit. She always had an answer for every-thing.

Opening his eyes, he grudgingly stared down at her skirts which were now brushing up against his trousers and boots. He edged back, agitated with her for trying to sprinkle mere sugar over all the open wounds he'd carried since she had announced they were done. "An outing insinuates you want to take our association public. What makes you think I want that?"

Her voice hardened. "Gérard, enough. How old are you?"

"Much older than I want to be."

"Exactly. You are wasting your time *and* mine. Did you honestly come all the way from Russia merely to grouch to me from beneath a coat? If you wish to pursue me, then do so. We are no longer children with a revolution breath-ing down our throats. We are now adults who know better than to argue, gripe and be irrational. Am I wrong in that?"

He eased out a breath. "No. I completely agree."

"Good. Now that we agree, how do you wish to proceed? I will respect whatever you decide. Regardless, given you wish to know our granddaughter and share in her life, we have to get along. Otherwise, what is the point of hav-ing you in our lives at all? We hardly need the drama. Society provides us plen-ty of that given who I am."

He dragged in a breath, tightening his hold on the coat. It was obvious their time apart had cleared most obstacles and matured them both. He had hoped for as much, but she hadn't seen his face yet. "My face is going to take some time for you to get used to. I myself am still not accustomed to it and I have had to plen-ty of time to look at it. As such, we should.. remain friends."

"Why? Because of your face?"

Making love to her in a mask would get awkward. "Yes. Understand that I am not ready to show my face. It may be a while."

"I see. So you and I will remain friends."

"Yes."

"Indefinitely?"

"Maybe."

"Is that what you want?"

Fuck. "No. Not really."

"Then why insist on something you do not want?"

He puffed out a breath, the bundled wool around him making it almost too warm for him to breathe. "Do you have any other ideas as to how we could lead a normal life together without you ever looking at me?"

She delicately snorted. "Gérard, nothing about my life is normal." She sighed. "I am still trying to piece together who you have become. Lord Hughes told me you enjoy ropes. Is that true?"

The wrong sort of news certainly travelled fast in London. He puffed out a breath. "No. I used to when I was younger. But I—"

"Apparently Mrs. Berkley had you show her girls how to do it. You surprise me." Her tone hardened. "Some of those girls are not even eighteen."

He winced. "I never went anywhere near her girls. Christ, the British are— My tastes are a little more respectable than that. Mrs. Berkley has a tendency to want things she is never going to get. She *wants* a demonstration. She came across an old box of my *nawa* ropes and started asking all too personal questions. I can assure you, I have not roped a woman in well over fifteen years."

Thérèse was quiet for a long moment. "How did you get into ropes?"

How the hell did they get on this topic? He sighed. "A Japanese stowaway was on my ship. He was part of some law enforcement specializing in the art of restraint and would sit there all day with a bunch of *nawa* and do nothing but knot ropes. He sidled over to me one morning, shoved some *nawa* into my hands and insisted I learn. The knots were elaborate and..kept me from thinking about my face." He hesitated and then admitted, "I was trying to fill voids. I was always trying to do things that did not remind me of you. Or us. If that makes any sense."

"I am ever so glad to hear ropes do not bring me to mind," she chided.

He smirked. "I am ever so glad to hear you still have a sense of humor. I appreciate that."

"My sense of humor is the only thing that kept me alive."

"Amen to that, madame. Amen to that."

Her skirts edged in closer. "Are you interested in taking off that coat and kissing me?"

He paused, momentarily wishing he had the coat off his head just so he could see her face. "Well, I..." He cleared his throat. "You really want me to kiss you?"

"Yes."

"As in right now?"

"Not through the coat, mind you." She leaned in.

Her nearness, which he could feel through the damn wool, made his chest tighten. He wasn't ready to let her see him, but he also wasn't ready to let this moment go. "What if I want everything else first and kisses last? Would you agree to that?"

She tsked. "You never were one to take things slow."

"In that, I have not changed, *ma biche*. You either dance with the devil or get out."

Her voice became sultry. "Surely you know the devil and I are good friends. I survived the revolution. As did the devil standing before me."

He shifted his jaw, tightening his hold on the coat. "I dare you to unbutton my trousers."

Edging in close, her hands casually undid the buttons on his trousers. "Anything else?"

An ache he had carried with him since he left France overtook his ability to breathe. All he wanted was to touch her. If only to make himself believe this was real. "We are going to have to get creative, because I am not going upstairs to get my mask. Can you turn around?"

She dragged her hands down his chest through the coat. "Remove your coat."

"No. I am not ready to—"

She pushed down the flap of his trousers and pushed down his undergarments, her soft fingers grazing the skin above his cock.

Christ. His cock grew hard. "Are you really wanting to do this right now?"

"I can always come back tomorrow."

"No." He grabbed her wrists, then turned her away with the jerk of his arms, letting his coat fall from his head. Before she could glance back, his one hand jumped to her eyes and the other to her throat, to keep her from moving or seeing anything. Her soft bundled hair grazed his chin, that sultry scent of jasmine and mint tingeing the air.

He paused, realizing white ribbons were tied into her hair.

His pulse roared. It was like feeling his heart beat again. He molded her possessively to his frame and chest, pressing his erection against her backside. "Are the white ribbons your way of saying you missed me?"

"My, you always were clever."

By God, how he had missed her. "My heart has not changed," he murmured. "Not by a beat."

Her chest rose and fell visibly before him, those breasts taunting him. "Neither has mine, Gérard. My heart is still yours. It was always yours."

His throat tightened. He buried his face into the softness of her jasmine scented hair. "How much do you remember?"

"Everything." She quieted her voice. "How much do you remember?"

"More than everything. Including what should have been."

A shaky breath escaped her. "Make love to me. Erase the years."

He kissed the soft skin on her neck. "Are you certain you want to do this right now?"

"Did I not wear enough white ribbons?"

He bit back a smile and gently guided her forward and toward his writing desk. "Keep your eyes closed and do not look back at me."

Her voice softened. "*Gérard*," she said in French, her full lips moving beneath the hand he held against her eyes. "Your face is not what I fell in love with. Let me see you."

He tightened his hold on her, the shock of hearing her speak French coupled with those words made him bury his face into her hair and breathe in deep. "*Thérèse*," he replied in French. "By not showing you my face, I am protecting you from a past you have yet to understand. Let us embrace that we are back together first and return to my face last. At another time when we are both ready. Can you do that for me? For us?"

She nodded against the hand that still covered her eyes. "*Oui.* Yes."

He kissed her throat. "Good," he murmured. "Stay where you are." He released her and unraveled his cravat, sliding it loose from around his throat and linen shirt. Snapping the silk tight, he lifted it over her head and wrapped it around her eyes twice, to ensure her sight was taken. He tied it firmly in place at the back of her head, pushing away her hair.

He gently traced her shoulder with a finger, dragging it down toward the front of her breast. He circled her nipple through the fabric of her gown. "Do you think we should try to make our way upstairs?"

Her lips parted in between breaths. "A desk is as good as any bed."

It certainly was. He turned her toward himself and dragging her into his arms, lowered his gaze to her lips and kissed her. Slow, at first, to match the beat of his heart. Her hands jumped to the expanse of his back and tightened their hold, her mouth sensually working against his.

She still kissed the same.

He staggered and frantically molded his hands against her curves. He tongued her harder, trying not to doubt any of this was real.

Her hand slid between them and grasped his rigid cock, stroking its length.

He gasped against her mouth, knowing he had to slow them down. Breaking their kiss, in between ragged breaths, he set her onto the lacquered desk, letting her slippered feet dangle and gripped her hands hard. "No more stroking or this man will not be able to deliver."

She puckered her full lips beneath the mask. "Has it been that long for you?"

He leaned in close, tracing his tongue across her lips and breathed out, "Yes. It has."

She paused, unable to see past the blindfold. "Did you leave the door open?"

"Did you need it closed?"

"That would be boring."

"My thoughts exactly." Jerking up her skirts, he exposed her completely to himself. He paused, perusing her pale shapely legs. "Very nice. How old are you again?"

A knowing smile touched her lips. "I walk three miles every day, regardless of whether I need an umbrella or not, drink my red wine and no longer touch meat. Meat ages a woman. This butcher girl should know."

Gérard shifted his jaw and quickly leaned down and kissed one thigh and the other. The scent of powder made him drag the tip of his tongue across her skin. "I do not remember you ever powdering your legs," he murmured. "When did that start?"

Her slippered feet and stockinged legs primly came together. "Legs need just as much attention as the face does."

God. If only he had been able to find her sooner. If only— "You were supposed to stay in France, damn you. Do you know how long it took and how much fucking money I spent trying to find you? Do you?"

She said nothing.

A breath escaped him. "We should have been together sooner. We should have—"

"No more regrets, Gérard. We have too many of those."

True. But it didn't hurt any less.

Kneeling, he dragged his hands down her thighs and dragged his lower teeth against the softness of that powdered skin. He closed his eyes, reveling in the feel of her and tried to remember that day in the forest when his horse came to skidding halt and he first saw her standing there in bare feet, her long, unraveling blond braid draped over her shoulder and a wicker basket in her hand. When her playful blue eyes had met his and she smiled—

He'd almost fallen off his damn horse.

Now, it was about to start all over again.

Opening his eyes, he continued to skim his hands across her bare skin. "Touching you is an honor. As it has always been. Do I have permission to make to love you, madame?"

Her voice smiled. "*Oui, Monseigneur.* I have been waiting a long time."

Rising, he slid his hands down her smooth pale thighs and slid his entire hand between the wetness of her slit.

She swayed in between breaths and grabbed his shoulders hard.

He shoved down his undergarment that was already exposed due to her earlier advance and readied his body and mind for what he was about to do. Gripping her open thighs, he laid her back against the desk, kissing her and slowly slid deep into her, chanting to himself to go slow.

She rolled her hips up into him.

He gasped. "*Thérèse.* I am trying to go slow."

"Why?" She rolled into his cock again. "Will this be the last time we are doing this?"

He hissed out an exasperated breath, realizing she always had the last say when it came to his mind and his heart. "No." He moved in and out of her faster, claiming her. He stroked harder and harder, eliciting gasps out of both of them.

Sliding his hands all over her body, he shoved away her gown which had bundled between them and pushed his cock deeper into her wetness, increasing his pace.

She moaned, pushing up into him.

"This is me taking back your body." He thrust. "You are mine again."

"And you are mine."

"Tell me you thought of me every time you fucked another," he rasped. He thrust.

"I did," she gasped. "No eyes were ever blue enough. No hands ever strong enough. No pleasure was ever.. great enough."

Those words made him realize they had both been living their lives wanting nothing but each other. It was too much. "Every woman I ever touched was you. *You.*"

She panted and trembled beneath him, her hands gripping his hair hard.

His pleasure overtook his ability to breathe. His rhythm became uncontrolled and frantic. His limbs trembled refusing to stop until he spilled.

She cried out.

Feeling her body tremor beneath his own, Gérard unraveled. He spilled seed into her as pleasure rippled through his entire body. He gasped, spilling more seed, working his cock faster in an effort to enjoy every pulsing coil of sensation that seemed to stop his heart. He stilled, trying to catch his breath and swallowed hard.

Dearest God. They were together again. Just like that.

It was the most glorious moment of his life.

Smoothing his hands across her face several times, he pulled out. He kissed her lips softly, then slid off the desk, tucking his cock away and buttoning his trousers back into place. He dragged her skirts back down in exasperation, covering her and puffed out a breath. "We went a bit fast."

She remained against his desk. "We can go slow next time." Her flushed face now turned toward him. Her cheek remained pressed against the lacquered desk, her eyes still blindfolded. "Kiss me again," she whispered up at him.

His chest tightened. He slowly draped himself beside her on the desk again, resting his marred face against the cool wood of the desk and touched her full lips with his thumb. "*Ma biche,*" he whispered, taking them back to a time when they were both young. He dragged her arm over his shoulder, while ensuring her blindfold didn't slip, gently set his mouth against hers.

Tears burned his eyes knowing they were finally claiming what had once been theirs.

Their mouths made love.

The hardness of the desk and their awkward positioning made him enjoy the luxury of the velvet heat of her working tongue even more. How he missed being hers.

He molded his mouth harder against hers, edging her head up off the desk enough to be able to deepen his kiss. If he didn't stop he would only end up ripping the clothing off her body and tying her into a submissive position so he could touch her all morning and all night.

He broke away, smoothing her hair. "Nothing has changed between us, has it?"

A breath escaped her. "No. Nothing."

290 | DELILAH MARVELLE

"What happens now?"

Her lips curved into a smile. "We live happily ever after."

He pressed his lips against her forehead.

She grinned. "Are you still up for an outing?"

He sighed, then slid her hand off his shoulder and sat up. "Are you certain you want to be seen with me in public? People stare."

She shifted against the desk, toward him. "Given the name I have made for myself, people stare at me, too. So you will be in good company."

God love her. God. Love. Her. He cradled her waist and gently lifted her off the desk and guided her body toward himself, tucking her against his chest. "Are you certain you want me back in your life, *ma biche?*"

She set her head against his chest and leaned into him. "I wanted you back the moment you left. You and I both know I only let you go to save you."

He closed his eyes at the unexpected reply and tightened his hold around her, savoring the feel of that softness. A softness he thought he would never feel again. "I missed you. So much." He lingered.

Seeing the chair he had earlier tossed and the books and everything from his desk strewn on the floor, he eventually asked her the one thing he had wanted and needed to know most. The thing that had haunted him the most. "What was our son like?"

She trailed a hand across his chest. "Henri had your eyes," she whispered.

"Did he?"

"Yes. I have a portrait of him back at the house that you can have. He was so dashing and charming. Very much like you. There was not a girl who did not adore him. He loved to read and was a gifted swordsman. He started competing when he was seven."

His lips parted. "A swordsmen? My son?"

She nodded against him. "He collected antique swords and would always ask me if his passion was something you would have approved of."

He squeezed his eyes shut. "What did you tell him?"

"That you were proud. And that one day, you would come back and see him fight."

He squeezed his eyes shut harder, tears overwhelming him. "Was he happy? Prior to his illness?"

She was quiet for a moment. And then sobbed against him, her shoulders trembling. "Yes. But he..he was always overly serious in nature. Over the years, I think he pieced together the story of what happened to you and me. I think he wanted to ensure he never lost out the way we did. He lived life too fast, too desperate not to miss a single beat. He left me and France too early." Her voice cracked. "Nothing I said or did would have stopped him. He had a path and he wanted to carve it out. He even..he blamed me for being the reason as to why you never came back. He said it was because I was a courtesan."

He swallowed, opened his eyes and smoothed her hair. "Remove that burden from yourself, Thérèse. I did not stay away to punish you. My face kept me from— It took me too many years to accept what had happened to me. And when I finally did try to find you, you had already left France and no one was able to tell me where you had gone. So I went back to Russia and stayed there thinking maybe..." A breath escaped him.

She nudged up her chin as if trying to see past the blindfold.

He knew she couldn't see anything.

"What happened to your face?" she whispered. "What—"

"I will tell you. But not now." The last thing he wanted was for her to blame herself. "No more crying for either of us. We are done with that. Come with me upstairs."

Angling toward her, he swept her legs and back into his arms, startling her as he tossed her into the air high enough to fully straighten himself. He paused. She felt lighter than what he remembered. But then again, he was physically stronger than he had ever been. Rolling her toward himself, he swung around and carried her out of his study and up the stairs.

One of her hands patted his arm, smoothing her hand against it. "You have more muscle than what I remember."

He almost bit her. "I worked with scythes in Russia for almost fifteen years. Every spring, summer and fall I was in the fields with my laborers. I own a lot of land in Russia. Prior to that, I invested and sailed merchant ships to the West

Indies. Despite owning well over ten ships, I was moving crates and barrels like any other man."

She hesitated. "Were you at all happy? Despite us being apart?"

What a question. "I would be lying if I told you my life had been glorious without you. It took a few years to define what happy meant, but once I found it, yes, I was happy. I had my mother's family and they helped me through a lot. I got to travel the world and grow my own fortune. I was happy. As happy as a man can be without the love of his life." He glanced down at her, noting that her head was wistfully leaning against his shoulder. "What about you? Were you happy?"

She sighed. "As happy as a woman can be without the love of her life. I managed."

He savagely tightened his hold and carried her down the corridor, eventually veering into his bedchamber. He slammed the door shut with his booted foot. Striding her over to the bed, he laid her on it, tucking her head against the pillows to ensure she was comfortable. "Let me get decent."

She hesitated. "And then what?"

"We go out for those ices and sit in a paddle boat like you wanted. We have 'fun'."

"And after that?"

"We come back here, make love, eat and lounge."

A breath escaped her. "Are you wanting me to stay the night?"

He leaned in close, his nose touching hers. "I am wanting more than that. Move in with me. My house is five times the size of that thing you call a townhouse. With Maybelle now married, it means when she returns from her travels, we will be hosting events and having great-grandchildren running about. They will all need room." He kissed her lips, straightened and stepped back.

She sat up, her pearls rustling, as she blindly tilted herself toward his voice. "Are we getting married?"

He bit back a smile, trudged toward his dressing mirror and side table. "Do you want us to?"

"Are you wanting to?"

He grinned, knowing this could go on all day. "Are you?"

"I almost married Hughes," she whined.

"I know." He sighed. "We should probably wait for our granddaughter to come back before we marry. What do you think?"

She perked. "So we will marry?"

"Was there any doubt, my dear? Why the hell do you think I came back?"

She flopped back onto the bed and grinned, despite the blindfold. "We had better both live to a hundred and fifty. Otherwise, I will feel cheated." Her grin faded. She was quiet for a long moment. "When do I get to see your face?"

"Eventually. Soon. Maybe tonight." He snatched up one of several velvet masks and strategically tied it over the puckered skin that disfigured his forehead almost down to his jaw. The garnet ring he had carried with him since Paris, gleamed up at him from the sideboard.

Although he had thought about purchasing a different ring, it was fitting that they not try to erase everything that had been. He glanced toward her, knowing she couldn't see anything yet, and shoved it into his waistcoat pocket.

Clearing his throat, he swept back his hair with tonic and leaned over toward the wardrobe, flinging it open. He fingered his way through several morning coats and dragged one off the hooks. He shrugged it on and walked over to her, leaning over the bed.

She tilted toward him.

He smirked. "I need my cravat back, *ma biche*." He reached around her, his fingers working around the knots, and paused, realizing her full lips had parted and that her breaths were uneven. He slowly continued to unknot the silk. "Are you wanting to go with me to Russia for a small while? While we wait for Maybelle to come back?"

She grabbed his arms. "Might we?"

He grinned. "I will take that to be a yes." He dragged down the loosened cravat and searched those stunning blue eyes. They appeared so much brighter than what he remembered.

Leaning away, he rose from the bed and went back to the mirror. He kissed the cravat that was now scented with jasmine and wrapped it around his neck.

He didn't care that it was wrinkled. He wanted it around his neck knowing it had been around her eyes. He tied it tightly into place and tucked it into his waistcoat.

Grabbing up a towel, he sipped it into a porcelain basin, dashing soap against it and walked over to her and wagged his fingers. "We should clean you up."

She rolled her eyes, leaned over and snatched the towel. "I will do it myself, thank you."

He grinned and seated himself on the edge of the bed, watching her gather her skirts and tilt her head as she rubbed the towel down her thighs, between them and around them.

Still grinning, he casually leaned back, to get a better view between her thighs.

The towel smacked his face. He rumbled out a laugh and jumped to his feet, whipping the towel across the room. He turned toward her and snapped out a hand. "I will pay for those ices and the paddle boat, madame. From what Mrs. Berkley tells me, your little school was not as financially successful as you were hoping it would be."

She puckered her lips. Slipping her hand into his, she eased off the bed, her skirts falling back down to her ankles and set her chin. "Unlike Mrs. Berkley, I have always tried to use my profession to help people. Not just myself."

He pressed his lips against her hand. "In my opinion, Mrs. Berkley is your evil twin."

She tilted her head tauntingly. "I will not argue with you in that. She most certainly is evil."

He laughed.

****

The Boating Lake at Regent's Park
Late afternoon

With her lace parasol tucked against her shoulder, which shaded her from the fading sun, she dreamily watched from her seat on the bow of the small paddleboat as Gérard leaned back, pulling the wooden oars with him. His muscled arms bulked through his morning coat as he continued to drop the oars up and out of the water, moving them across the water.

A wool cap had been pulled forward onto his head, shading his blue eyes and the mask he wore. A warm breeze fluttered her skirts against his outstretched leather boots.

The silence around them was only interrupted on occasion by chirping birds and other boats rowing across the lake.

It had been a glorious day. The sort of day they should have had *every day* in their youth.

She twirled her parasol. "Gérard?"

He captured her gaze, still rowing. "Yes, *ma biche?*"

She let out a breathy, disbelieving sigh. "Thank you for coming back into my life."

He paused from his rowing, letting the gliding boat slow to the middle of the lake. He quickly set the oars upward, to keep them from falling into the water and leaned toward her. "Thank you for letting me come back into your life," he rumbled out.

She excitedly twirled her parasol again. "The sun will be fading soon."

"I know."

"How about we row our way back to shore?"

"No. Not yet."

"But I was hoping to show you something up in my garret."

He lowered his chin. "Your garret?"

She nodded. "Yes."

"And what is up in your garret?" he drawled. "Aside from rafters?"

She bit back a smile. "If I tell you that, it would ruin the surprise. Might we please row our way back to shore? Because I really think you ought to see it. You will never be the same."

"In that case..I ought to hurry up." He puffed out a breath and yanked off one glove, setting it onto the seat beside him, then the other. He cracked his knuckles and eyed her. He cracked his knuckles again. "Give me two breaths."

She blinked. "Two breaths for what?"

He adjusted his cravat and then dug into his waistcoat. Leaning in as close as the boat would allow without tipping them over, he held her gaze and turned his wrist upward to reveal a garnet ring that gleamed in the sunlight between his fingers. "Will you marry me and become the duchess you have always been?"

She dragged in an astounded breath and leaned toward the ring, realizing it was the same ring he had given her the night he had originally proposed. He had held onto it. Tears stung her eyes as she set the parasol beside her. She jumped toward him and grabbed his face, kissing him.

The boat swayed violently beneath them, making them both freeze as water sprayed.

Gérard quickly leaned far backward, his boots thudding into the sides of the wooden boat in an attempt to use his weight to balance the boat.

A bubble of a laugh escaped her as the boat continued to rock. "If we fall in, we deserve it."

The boat eventually stilled.

He puffed out a breath, sitting back up again and held up the ring. "No more kissing until we leave the boat." He wagged his other hand at her. "Your hand, if you please."

She bit back a smile, removed her glove and regally held it out.

He slid the garnet ring onto her finger and then kissed it, his lips grazing the ring and knuckle. "I pronounce us husband and wife. The church can do the rest once our granddaughter gets back."

She held up the ring, letting it glint in the sun. "Gérard?"

He set his forearms on his knees. "Yes, *ma biche?*"

She tapped at the garnet. "Pretty though it is, its existence has always plagued me. You had no money at the time you gave this to me. Where did this ring come from?"

He adjusted his cap twice and winced. "Sade. He lent me money to buy it."

She choked and eyed it. "Do we really want Sade, the *marquis* of pain, sitting on my finger representing our love? Given everything we have been through?"

He blinked rapidly. "No."

She breezed her hand back to him.

He sighed, yanked off the ring and tossed it over his shoulder. A *plunk* resounded within the water.

"We begin again," she announced, setting her chin. "Without a revolution. Without Sade."

"And without brandy," he drawled, pointing at her.

"Amen." She plucked up her parasol and set it back on her shoulder. "Happiness hardly needs a ring. Besides, this butcher girl already has her pearls and her diamonds."

He smirked. "Shall we wander toward your garret, butcher girl?"

"Yes. We should, *Monsieur Highwayman*. Please honor me and row."

Gérard grinned and grabbed up the oars, taking them back to shore.

LESSON NINETEEN

Love defines us.

Let it define you.

-The School of Gallantry

"**O**ffer me a hint."

"No."

"A mere one."

Thérèse tsked. "We are almost there. Be patient."

"Patience is for people who did not have to wait thirty fucking years to be happy."

"Cease with that language. I think you can survive thirty seconds."

He rolled his eyes. "I *suppose.*"

Following Thérèse up the narrow stairwell leading up into the garret, Gérard held up the lantern to ensure they had enough light. She unlatched the small wooden door at the top of the stairwell and ducked into the space beyond it.

He quickly followed, also ducking.

Thérèse gestured toward their surroundings. "The fortune I made as an actress all went to this. I never quite recovered financially after it. It is yours."

"Mine? How so?"

Straightening in the large space of the sloped wooden rafters that was tightly packed with countless trunks, furniture, mirrors, vases, crystal chandeliers and—

He held up the lantern and paused, his eyes widening. He dragged in an astounded breath as light fell upon a row of neatly stacked paintings set against an ornate dresser that had once belonged to his mother. He slowly approached a painting he thought he would never see again.

Tears burned his eyes as he knelt and set the lantern before it.

The regal, shadowed face of a smiling, demure young woman with black hair and blue eyes greeted him. It was his mother. The one who had taught him that altruism and generosity was an art form. It was a likeness he thought he had lost the right to along with everything else.

Unable to see past his tears, his hand jumped to her kind, painted face. A face he missed so much. He grazed his finger across the face he had been unable to make real and see in his mind because of all the years that had passed.

In between uneven breaths, he glanced back at Thérèse in disbelief. "How did you..?"

She lingered, her head slightly tilted. "Sade informed me the Republic was selling everything that had ever belonged to you and your family. I outbid everyone for everything about a month after you left France. The only thing I could not save was your land and your homes."

He swallowed and slowly stood, the silence of the garret amplifying the beat of his heart. The dream of her that kept his soul and his heart alive all these years was *nothing* compared to the reality of her.

Drifting toward her, he whispered, "I am in awe of everything you are. Thank you for..." He paused before her and gently cupped her face, tilting it up toward him. "May I spend the rest of my days proving my worth to you."

She brokenly smiled up at him.

Kissing her lips, he released her, a breath escaping him.

He was done hiding. They had survived too much for him to belittle what they shared.

Stripping his wool cap, he tossed it. Lifting his hands to the back of his head, he untied the velvet strings that held his mask in place and let the mask fall. It cascaded in a rustle to his booted feet.

Her blue eyes captured his. Searching the side of his marred face with widened eyes, a hand jumped to her mouth, her fingernails digging into her own cheek.

He set his chin in an attempt to remain calm. "It used to be far worse. Time has faded most of the scarring to white."

Tears rolled down her face and dripped over her hand. "What was done to you?" she choked past her fingers.

He shifted his jaw and glanced off to the side, knowing he couldn't protect her from the truth forever. "Your beloved Jacques avenged you. He sought to ensure you no longer had an interest in me given you had no interest in him."

Her hand fell away. "*Jacques?*" she echoed. "I..from the theatre? He..?"

"Yes." He nodded. "Shortly after the Laroche family had departed in a coach heading for the border, Jacques returned with ten other men from the theatre. Despite bloodying up some of them good, I was outnumbered. While four held me down in the corridor, one by one, they proceeded to ensure I never wanted to come back. A few broken bones and a quick touch of a torch to the side of my face and it was done. In the course of one night, I lost everything. You, our son and my face."

A sob escaped her. "Forgive me for ever trusting that bastard. I— Forgive me for—" She jumped toward him and reaching up, grabbed his face with trembling hands.

He held her gaze and smiled, the weight of all the years lifting from his mind and soul. "You are holding me and loving me, *ma biche*. Despite my face. That is all that matters. It is all I ever wanted."

Her pale tear-streaked face twisted. Her lips trembled. "I love you. And I wish to assure you, you are as beautiful as ever."

He swallowed, the heat of her hands on his skin pulsing its way to the beat of his heart. Tears stung his eyes knowing she didn't care what his face looked like. She was holding him and still wanting him and loving him.

Her trembling hands smoothed his face as she searched his eyes. "No more masks, *Monsieur Highwayman.* There is no need for it."

A breath escaped him.

Grabbing her face hard, he seized those beautiful soft lips, molding her mouth against his in an attempt to demonstrate that their lives had never been complete without each other. As he slowly made love to her mouth, he undid the pins in her hair, letting them ping to the floor one by one, until her hair tumbled around them both in a silken curtain. He brushed it away from their faces.

He broke away from their kiss and searched her flushed face, refusing to believe any of this was real. He grazed his fingers through her silver strands that made her face shockingly perfect. "You aged beautifully. Do you know that?"

She rolled her eyes and smoothed her hands against his chest. "I went completely silver at forty."

He smirked. "Are you bragging?"

She nudged him.

He dragged his hands from her hair down to her bodice, toward the string of pearls he had given her once upon a spell when he had been falling in love with everything she was. He had recognized them that night he had sent her into a faint. "You still have them."

She grabbed his hands, tangling the pearls between them. "I wore them almost every single day. I had them re-strung twice." She kissed his hands and gushed, "I cannot wait for Maybelle to meet you."

He smiled. "Does she even know about me?"

She smiled and nodded. "Oh, yes. She does. She knows all about the man who introduced me to real passion."

He bit back a smile. "Christ. Now I am genuinely worried. What did you tell her?"

"Only enough to ensure she knew it was real."

He laughed and dragged his hands into her hair again. *"Ma biche?"*

She grinned and searched his face. *"Oui?"*

"Did you know my mother had an emerald ring that I hid behind the panel of the dresser her painting is resting against over there? I was always worried my father would sell it."

She paused. "Do you think it is still there?"

"There is only one way to find out." He grabbed her hand and quickly guided her back to the ornate dresser. Releasing her hand, he gently lifted his mother's painting and set it aside. Angling toward the dresser, he pulled out one of the empty drawers and set it aside. Lowering himself to better see into the slot he had made, he squinted and reached back into it. His fingers hit the fake panel that had been installed. He creaked it open, wedging the section loose. Letting it fall aside, he leaned in closer and felt his way around the small space. His finger grazed a small box. His heart skidded. It was still there.

Dragging it, he gripped it and pulled his arm back out. He turned back to Thérèse and tapped at the box. "It remained right where I left it." Striding toward her, he opened the ring box, revealing a massive emerald and gold ring.

She gasped. "That cannot be real."

He quirked a brow. "It is. The emerald came out of India." Pulling it out of the box, he shoved the box into his coat pocket and took her hand. "May I?"

A bubble of a laugh escaped her as she pertly held her hand up higher to him. "You most certainly may."

He kissed the heavy ring, silently thanking his mother for saving it for something this momentous, and slid the emerald onto Thérèse's finger. "It was my mother's favorite ring."

She blinked down at it, angling the emerald left and right in admiration. "Now, it is *my* favorite ring."

"If you bought everything from the estate, there could be more."

Her lips parted. She glanced toward the trunks and furniture. "Och, we will be here all night." She bustled back toward the dresser and started taking out more drawers, peering in.

He burst into laughter. His butcher girl was back. Diamonds and pearls were just the beginning. "*Thérèse.*"

She paused and glanced back at him.

"How about we do this later? Yes?"

She smirked, straightened and adjusted her emerald ring. "I suppose."

He let out a playful growl and ran at her, determined to kiss the smirk off that gorgeous face.

EPILOGUE

The past may define us,

but the future is what ultimately inspires us.

-The School of Gallantry

The Andelot estate
Saint Petersburg, Russia – six years later

Thérèse set an exasperated hand against her bosom.

This reunion was getting out of hand.

"*Hawksford*! Why the hell are you on the table?" Caldwell yelled from across the room. He gestured at all the children gathered around gaping up at him. "Is this the example you wish to set for our children? Russia is already full of idiots. There is no need to add to it."

Konstantin grabbed up a napkin, bundled it and whipped it at Caldwell's head. "The only idiot I see is the one insulting us Russians!"

Leona and Caroline burst into laughter and tried to usher the children away from the chaos.

Maybelle and Clementine tsked in unison, adjusting their expensive furs from their earlier walk in the snow.

"Now, now, hear me out." Hawksford held up a glass of wine high into the air and started pacing on the table from where he towered. "Now that I can see everyone," he drawled, "I wish to make a toast to the Duchess of Andelot who ensured each and every one of us enrolled in life's greatest lesson. And that is: Women *always* get the last word."

Thérèse rolled her eyes and tightened her hold on Gérard's arm.

Gérard leaned in and said into her ear, "Remind me to never invite any of these people over again."

Thérèse nudged him. "We only get to see them every two years. We will survive. We always do."

Hawksford's wife, Charlotte heaved out an exasperated breath, bustling over to the table. "Given I get the last word, the least you can do is get off the table."

Brayton casually walked up to the table and jumped onto it with a thud. He wagged his hands over to the group of children gathering with giggles. "Three at a time. No more than that. And *no* running. Or the tablecloth will outwit you."

Running up to the table, Banfield hoisted up one of the girls and set her onto the table.

Gérard puffed out a breath and held up a quick hand, stepping forward. "That table is two hundred years old. Might we show it some respect and..refrain?"

Everyone paused.

Hawksford quickly finished his wine and jumped off the table. He pointed up at Brayton. "You are setting a *very* bad example for these children."

Maybelle sidled in next to Thérèse. "*Grand-mére?*"

"*Oui?*" Thérèse asked.

Maybelle leaned in closer and asked from behind a hand, "Have you seen Edmund?"

Thérèse paused. She glanced around the crowded dining hall, realizing she had not seen the Duke of Rutherford in some time. "*Non.* Where did he go?"

Maybelle sighed. "I have no idea. There are too many people in this house."

Gérard veered back toward them. "Rutherford is still in the library reading to four children who are not even his own and have not let the poor man get past the first page due to all the questions."

Maybelle burst into laughter. "I will go save him. He is not very good at controlling children. He has a tendency to give into everything they want. Pardon me." She gathered her gown and hurried out of sight.

Taking her hand, Gérard gestured toward the corridor outside the dining hall. "Might we?"

"*Mais oui.*"

They stepped out into the candlelit corridor, hand in hand and strode toward the long row of glass windows facing out into snowy night.

Pausing before the glass, Gérard leaned toward it and used the heat of his breath to cloud the glass. He glanced at her and with a finger, he wrote, *No more students.*

She burst into laughter and shoved him.

He grinned and then kissed her, their hands smearing the words off the glass.

CPSIA information can be obtained at www.ICGtesting.com
Printed in the USA
LVOW10s1621080816

499499LV00005B/1230/P